Tsubasa: RESERVoir CHRoNiCLE by CLAMP

Sakura and Syaoran return! But they're not the people you know. Sakura is the princess of Clow—and possessor of a mysterious, misunderstood power that promises to change the world. Syaoran is her childhood friend, and leader of the archaeological dig that took his father's life. They reside in an alternate reality . . . where whatever you least expect can happen—and does. When Sakura ventures to the dig site to declare her love for Syaoran, a puzzling symbol is uncovered—which triggers

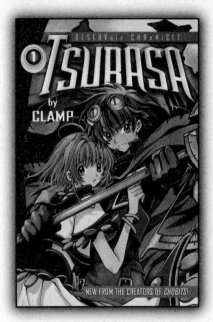

a remarkable quest. Now Syaoran embarks upon a desperate journey through the worlds of *X*, *Chobits*, *Magic Knight Rayearth*, *xxxHOLiC* and many more classic CLAMP series. All in the name of Syaoran's single goal: saving Sakura.

Volume 1: On sale May 2004 • Volume 2: On sale September 2004
Volume 3: On sale December 2004

 For more information and to sign up for Del Rey's manga e-newsletter, visit www.delreymanga.com

MOBILE SUIT GUNDAM SEED

Masatsugu Iwase

CREATED BY
Hajime Yatate AND Yoshiyuki Tomino

TRANSLATED AND ADAPTED BY
Jason DeAngelis

LETTERED BY
Studio Cutie

BALLANTINE BOOKS · NEW YORK

A Del Rey® Book
Published by The Random House Publishing Group

First published in Japan in 2003 by Kodansha Ltd., Tokyo.
This publication rights arranged through Kodansha Ltd.

 Published in the United States by The Random House Publishing Group, a division of Random House, Inc., New York, and simultaneously in Canada by Random House of Canada Limited, Toronto. First published in serialization and subsequently published in book form by Kodansha, Ltd., Tokyo in 2003.

www.delreymanga.com

A Library of Congress Control Number can be obtained from the publisher upon request.

ISBN 0-345-47045-1

Translator and adaptor—Jason DeAngelis
Lettering—Studio Cutie
Cover design—David Stevenson

Manufactured in the United States of America

First Edition: May 2004

1 2 3 4 5 6 7 8 9 10

Contents

Honorifics Explained

Throughout the Del Rey Manga books, you will find Japanese honorifics left intact in the translations. For those not familiar with how the Japanese use honorifics, and, more importantly, how they differ from American honorifics, we present this brief overview.

Politeness has always been a critical facet of Japanese culture. Ever since the feudal era, when Japan was a highly stratified society, use of honorifics—which can be defined as polite speech that indicates relationship or status—has played an essential role in the Japanese language. When addressing someone in Japanese, an honorific usually takes the form of a suffix attached to one's name (e.g. "Asuna-san"), as a title at the end of one's name, or in place of the name itself (e.g. "Negi-sensei" or simply "Sensei").

Honorifics can be expressions of respect or endearment. In the context of manga and anime, honorifics give insight into the nature of the relationship between characters. Many translations into English leave out these important honorifics, and therefore distort the feel of the original Japanese. Because Japanese honorifics contain nuances that English honorifics lack, it is our policy at Del Rey not to translate them. Here, instead, is a guide to some of the honorifics you may encounter in Del Rey Manga.

-*san*: This is the most common honorific and is equivalent to Mr., Miss, Ms., and Mrs. It is the all-purpose honorific and can be used in any situation where politeness is required.

-*sama*: This is one level higher than -*san*. It is used to confer great respect.

-*dono*: This comes from the word *tono*, which means *lord*. It is an even higher level than -*sama* and confers utmost respect.

-*kun*: This suffix is used at the end of boys' names to express familiarity or endearment. It is also sometimes used by men among friends, or when addressing someone younger or of a lower station.

-chan: This is used to express endearment, mostly toward girls. It is also used for little boys, pets, and between lovers. It gives a sense of childish cuteness.

Sempai: This title suggests that the addressee is one's senior in a group or organization. It is most often used in a school setting, where underclassmen refer to their upperclassmen as *sempai.* It can also be used in the workplace, such as when a newer employee addresses an employee who has seniority in the company.

Kohai: This is the opposite of *-sempai,* and is used toward underclassmen in school or newcomers in the workplace. It connotes that the addressee is of lower station.

Sensei: This title is used for teachers, doctors, or masters of any profession or art. Its literal meaning is, "one who has come before."

-[blank]: This is usually forgotten on these lists, but it's perhaps the most significant difference between Japanese and English. The lack of honorific means that the speaker has permission to address the person in a very intimate way. Usually, only family, spouses, or very close friends have this kind of license. Known as *yobisute,* it can be gratifying when someone who has earned the intimacy starts to call one by one's name without an honorific. But when that intimacy hasn't been earned, it can also be insulting.

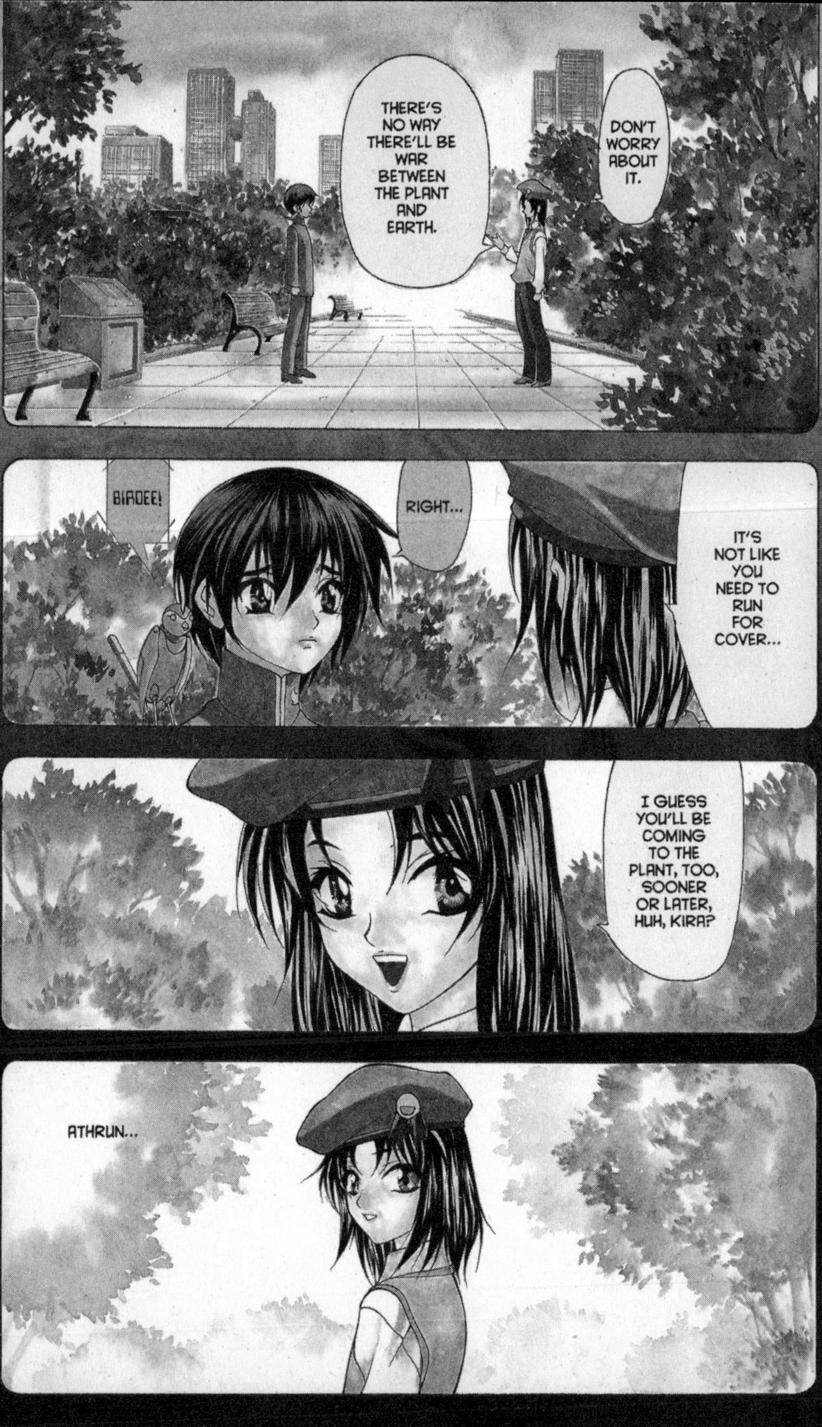
DON'T WORRY ABOUT IT.
THERE'S NO WAY THERE'LL BE WAR BETWEEN THE PLANT AND EARTH.
IT'S NOT LIKE YOU NEED TO RUN FOR COVER...
RIGHT...
BIRDEE!
I GUESS YOU'LL BE COMING TO THE PLANT, TOO, SOONER OR LATER, HUH, KIRA?
ATHRUN...

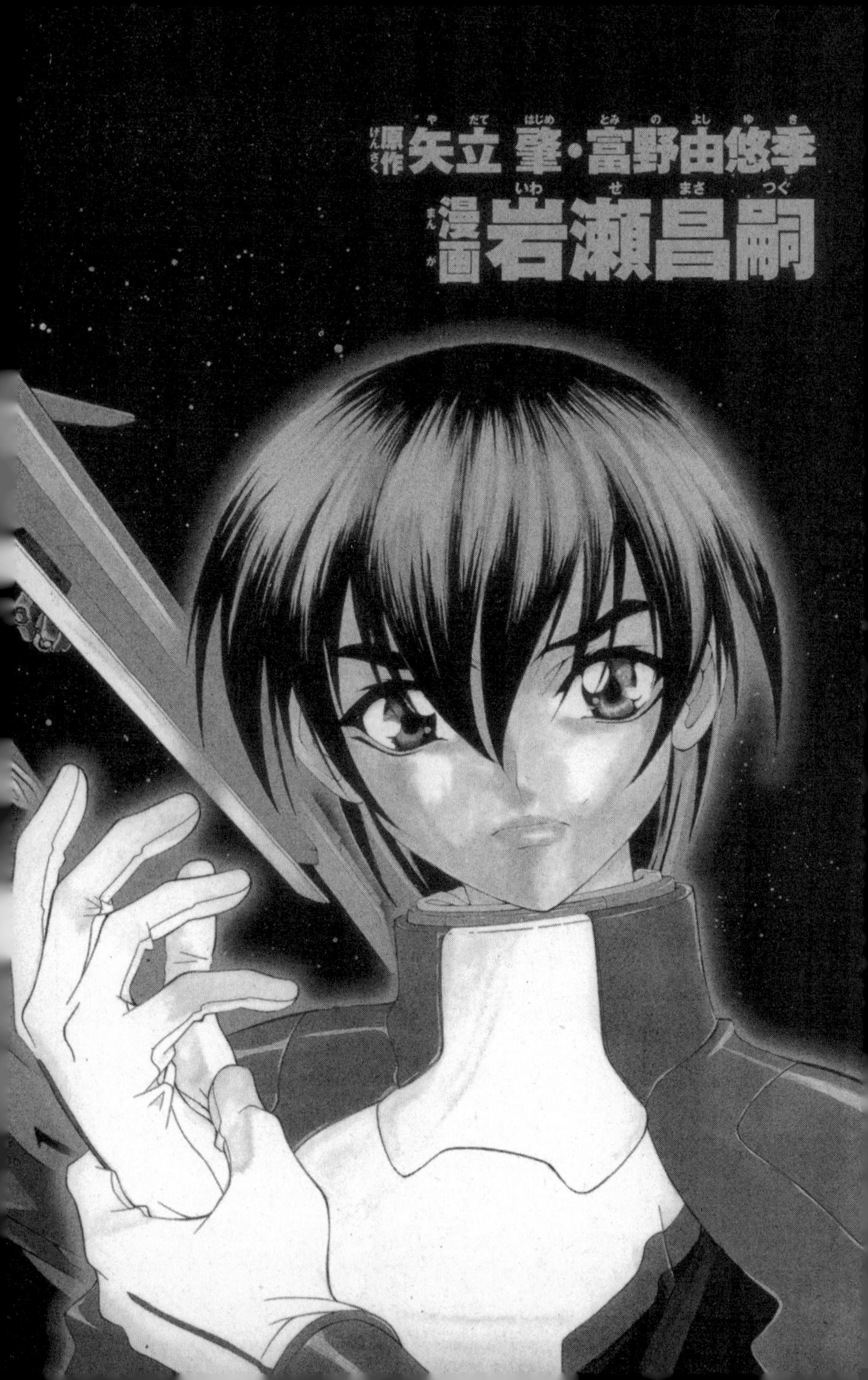
原作 矢立 肇・富野由悠季
漫画 岩瀬昌嗣

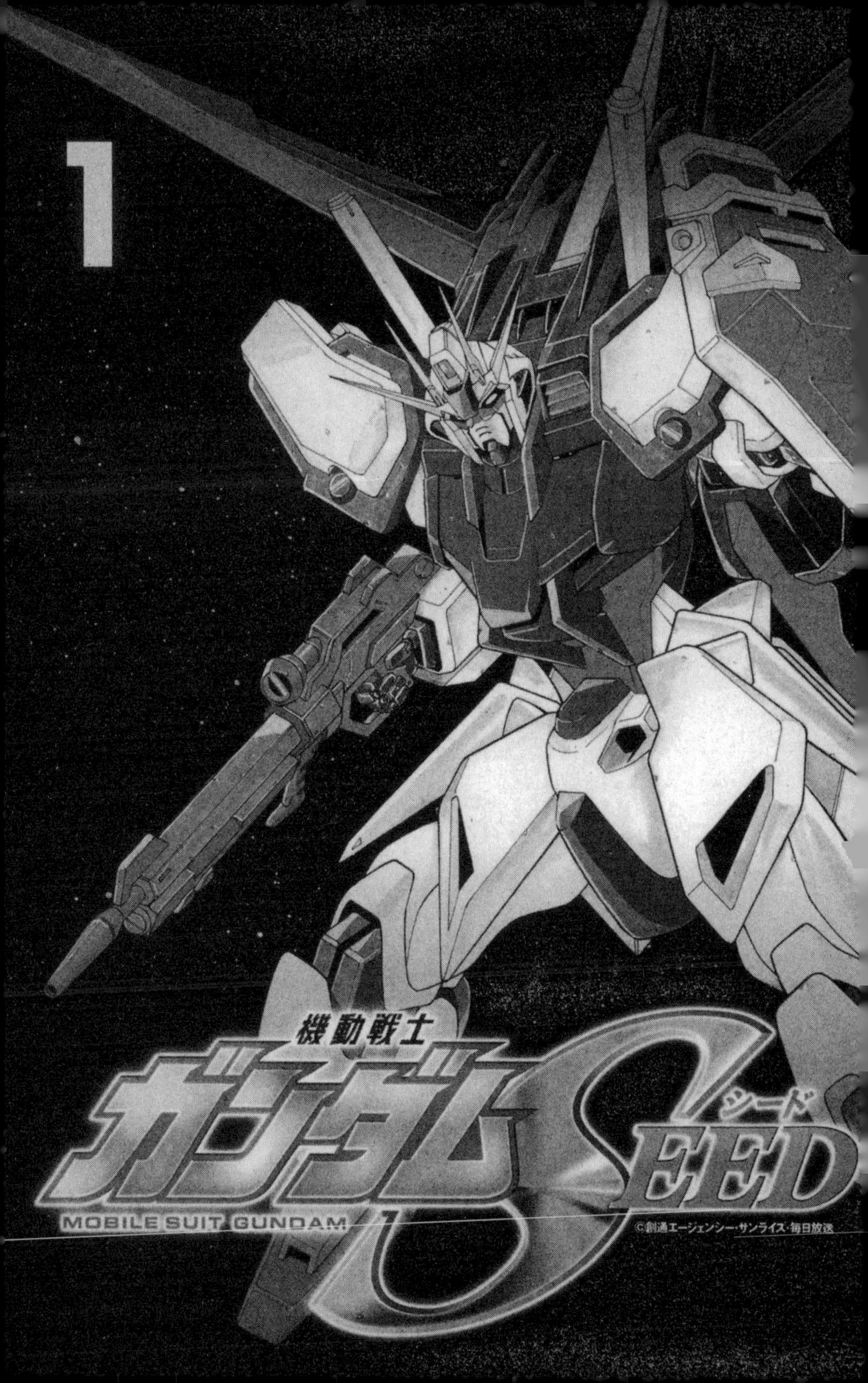

1
機動戦士
ガンダム
シード
SEED
MOBILE SUIT GUNDAM
©創通エージェンシー・サンライズ・毎日放送

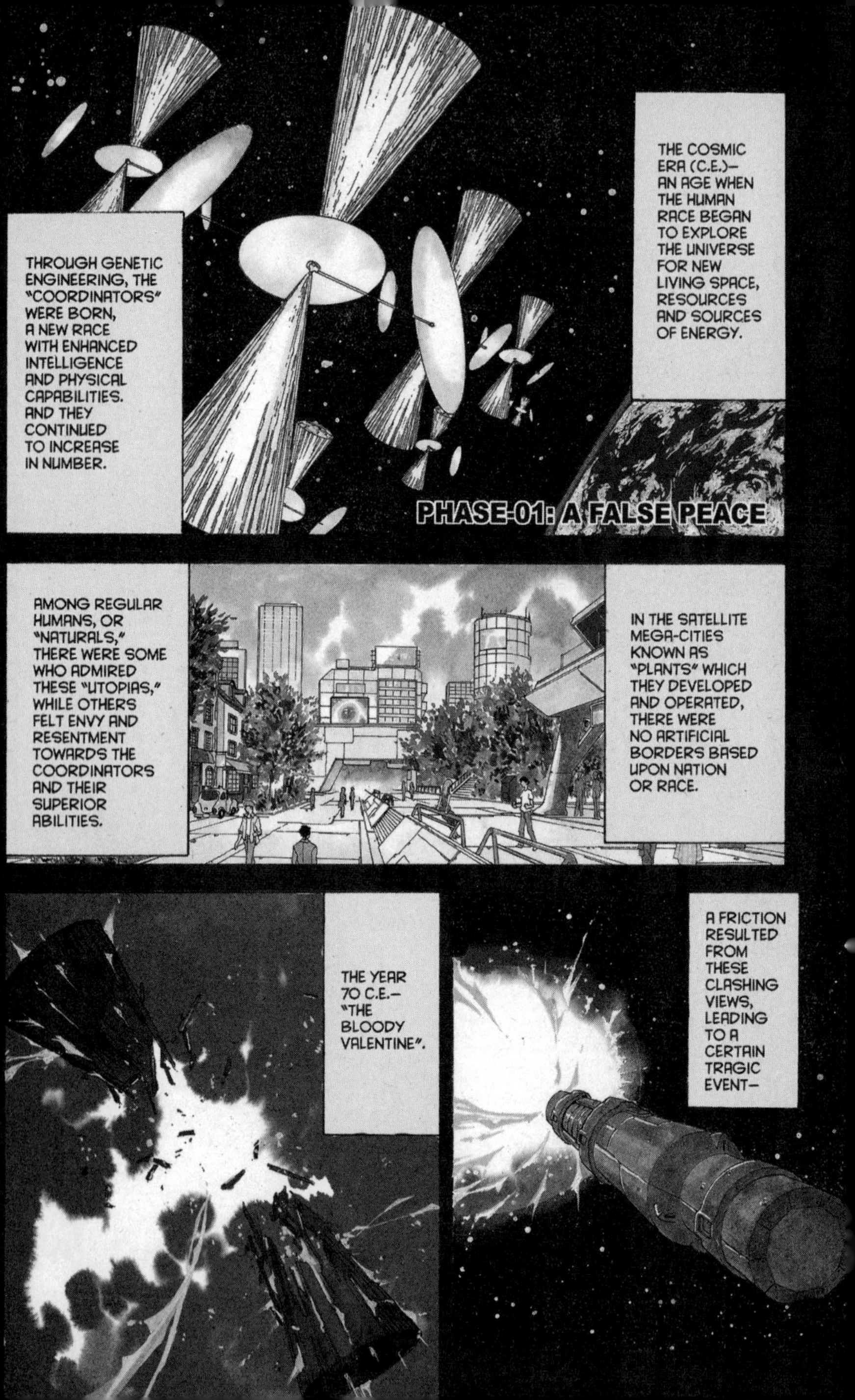
THE COSMIC ERA (C.E.)— AN AGE WHEN THE HUMAN RACE BEGAN TO EXPLORE THE UNIVERSE FOR NEW LIVING SPACE, RESOURCES AND SOURCES OF ENERGY.
THROUGH GENETIC ENGINEERING, THE "COORDINATORS" WERE BORN, A NEW RACE WITH ENHANCED INTELLIGENCE AND PHYSICAL CAPABILITIES. AND THEY CONTINUED TO INCREASE IN NUMBER.
PHASE-01: A FALSE PEACE
IN THE SATELLITE MEGA-CITIES KNOWN AS "PLANTS" WHICH THEY DEVELOPED AND OPERATED, THERE WERE NO ARTIFICIAL BORDERS BASED UPON NATION OR RACE.
AMONG REGULAR HUMANS, OR "NATURALS," THERE WERE SOME WHO ADMIRED THESE "UTOPIAS," WHILE OTHERS FELT ENVY AND RESENTMENT TOWARDS THE COORDINATORS AND THEIR SUPERIOR ABILITIES.
A FRICTION RESULTED FROM THESE CLASHING VIEWS, LEADING TO A CERTAIN TRAGIC EVENT—
THE YEAR 70 C.E.— "THE BLOODY VALENTINE".

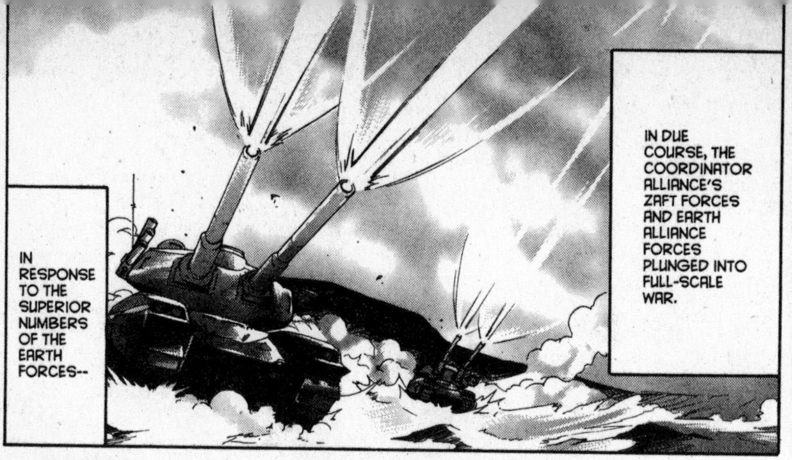
IN DUE COURSE, THE COORDINATOR ALLIANCE'S ZAFT FORCES AND EARTH ALLIANCE FORCES PLUNGED INTO FULL-SCALE WAR.
IN RESPONSE TO THE SUPERIOR NUMBERS OF THE EARTH FORCES--
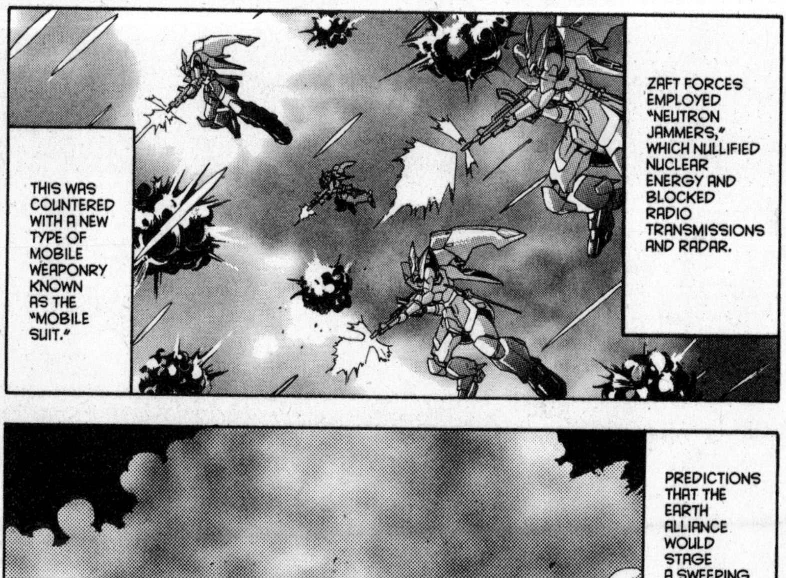
ZAFT FORCES EMPLOYED "NEUTRON JAMMERS," WHICH NULLIFIED NUCLEAR ENERGY AND BLOCKED RADIO TRANSMISSIONS AND RADAR.
THIS WAS COUNTERED WITH A NEW TYPE OF MOBILE WEAPONRY KNOWN AS THE "MOBILE SUIT."
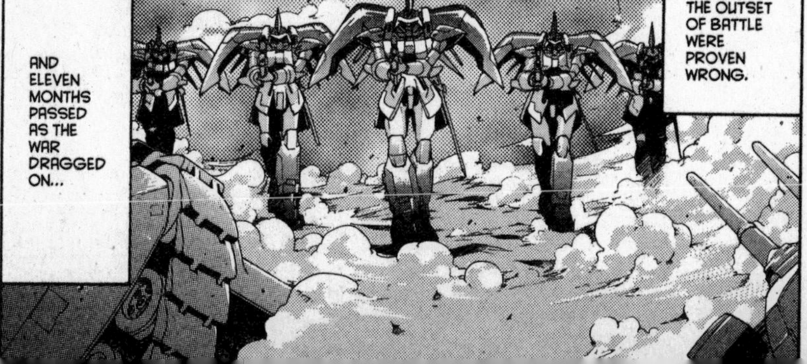
PREDICTIONS THAT THE EARTH ALLIANCE WOULD STAGE A SWEEPING VICTORY AT THE OUTSET OF BATTLE WERE PROVEN WRONG.
AND ELEVEN MONTHS PASSED AS THE WAR DRAGGED ON...

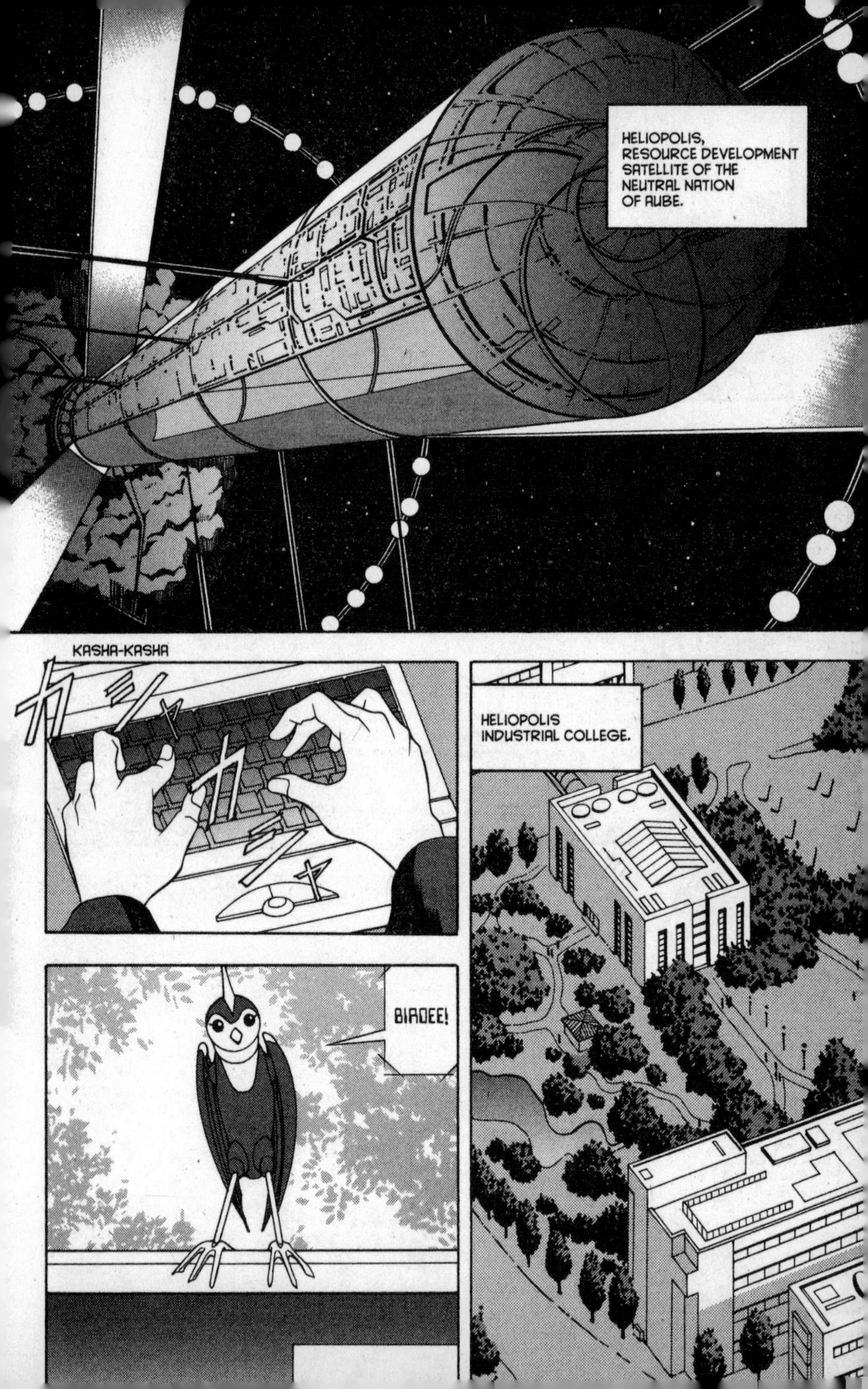
HELIOPOLIS, RESOURCE DEVELOPMENT SATELLITE OF THE NEUTRAL NATION OF AUBE.
HELIOPOLIS INDUSTRIAL COLLEGE.
KASHA-KASHA
BIRDEE!

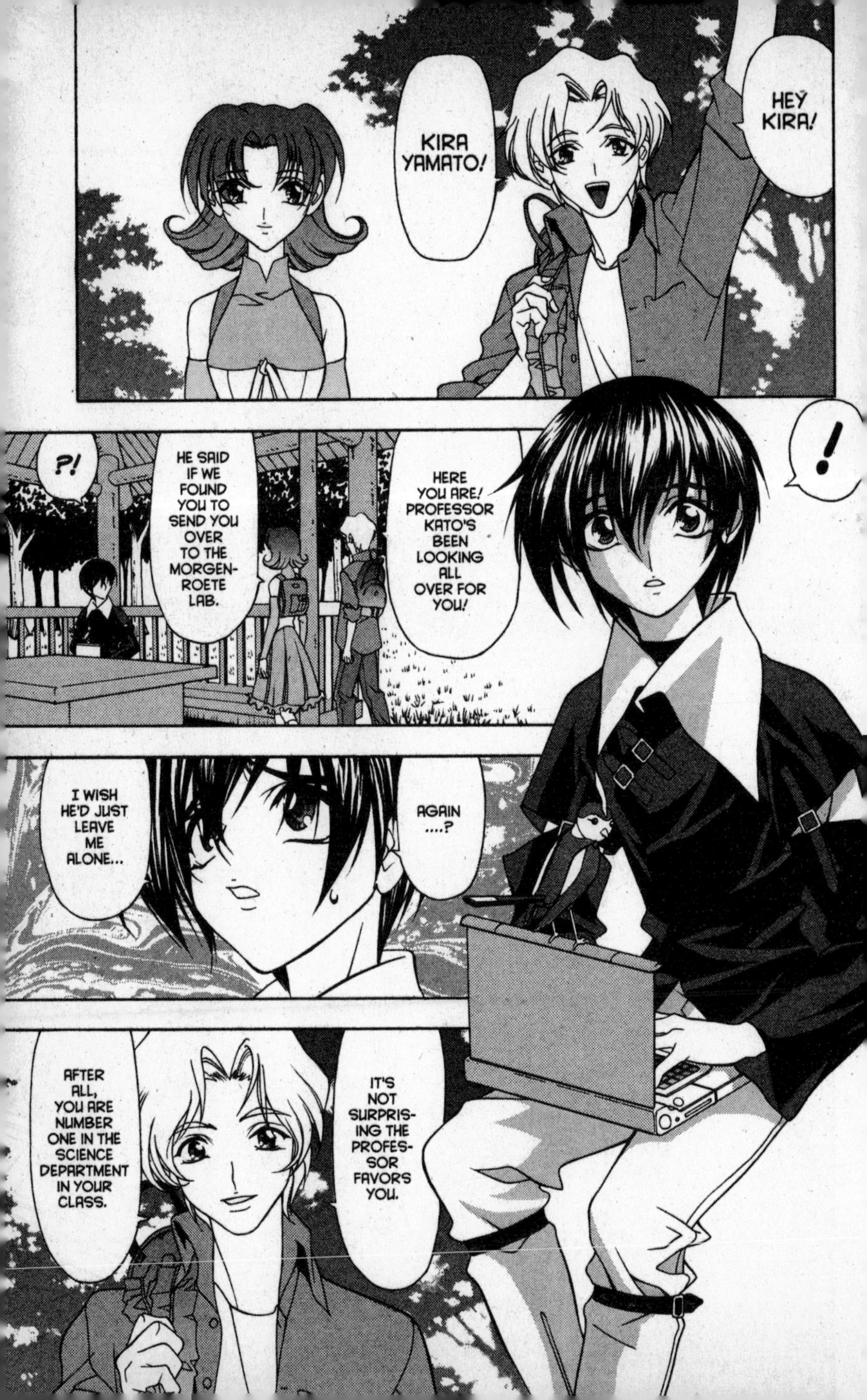
HEY KIRA!
KIRA YAMATO!
!
HERE YOU ARE! PROFESSOR KATO'S BEEN LOOKING ALL OVER FOR YOU!
HE SAID IF WE FOUND YOU TO SEND YOU OVER TO THE MORGEN-ROETE LAB.
?!
AGAIN ....?
I WISH HE'D JUST LEAVE ME ALONE...
IT'S NOT SURPRIS-ING THE PROFES-SOR FAVORS YOU.
AFTER ALL, YOU ARE NUMBER ONE IN THE SCIENCE DEPARTMENT IN YOUR CLASS.

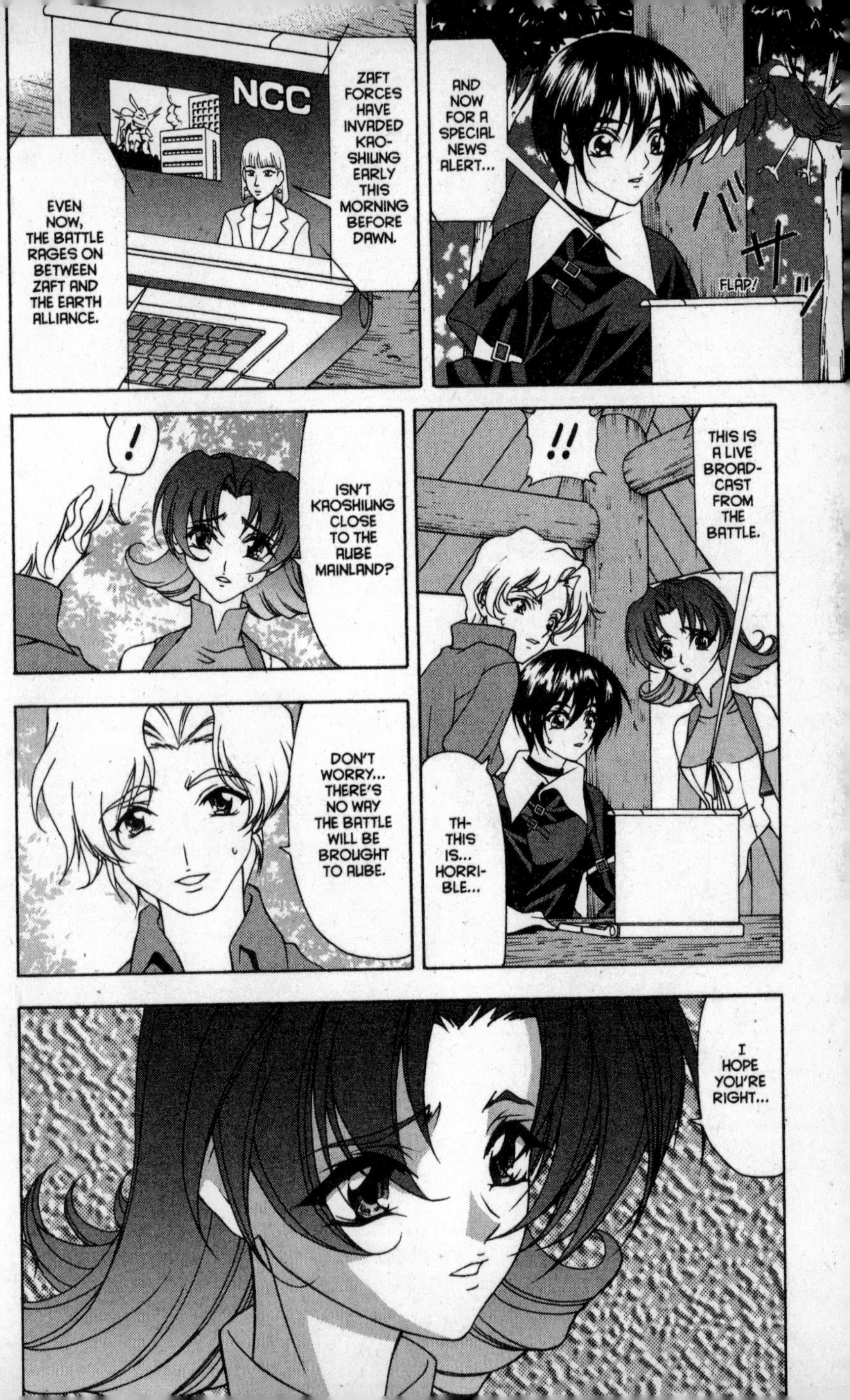
AND NOW FOR A SPECIAL NEWS ALERT...
FLAP!
NCC
ZAFT FORCES HAVE INVADED KAO-SHIUNG EARLY THIS MORNING BEFORE DAWN.
EVEN NOW, THE BATTLE RAGES ON BETWEEN ZAFT AND THE EARTH ALLIANCE.
!!
THIS IS A LIVE BROAD-CAST FROM THE BATTLE.
TH-THIS IS... HORRI-BLE...
!
ISN'T KAOSHIUNG CLOSE TO THE AUBE MAINLAND?
DON'T WORRY... THERE'S NO WAY THE BATTLE WILL BE BROUGHT TO AUBE.
I HOPE YOU'RE RIGHT...

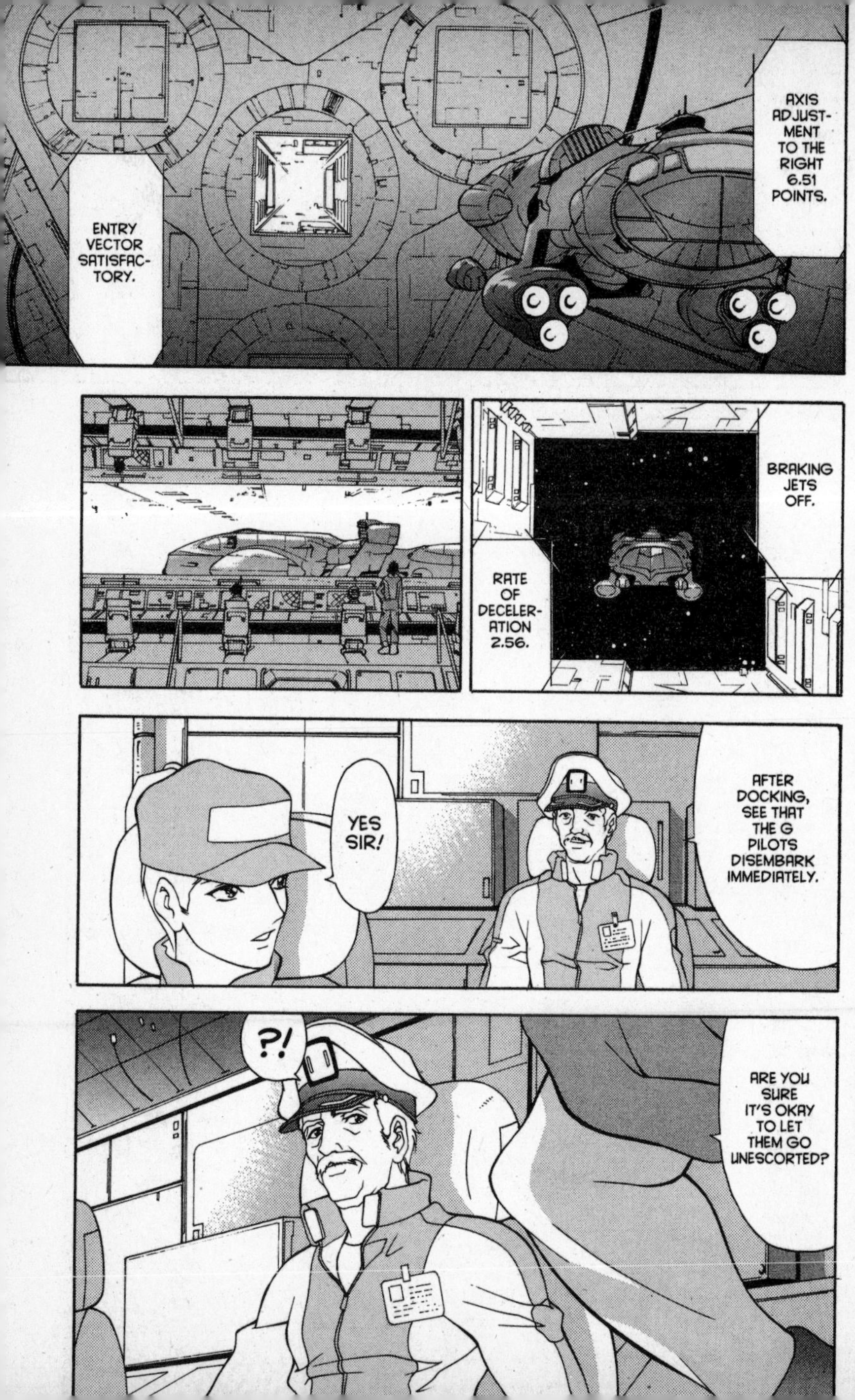
AXIS ADJUSTMENT TO THE RIGHT 6.51 POINTS.
ENTRY VECTOR SATISFACTORY.
BRAKING JETS OFF.
RATE OF DECELERATION 2.56.
AFTER DOCKING, SEE THAT THE G PILOTS DISEMBARK IMMEDIATELY.
YES SIR!
ARE YOU SURE IT'S OKAY TO LET THEM GO UNESCORTED?
?!

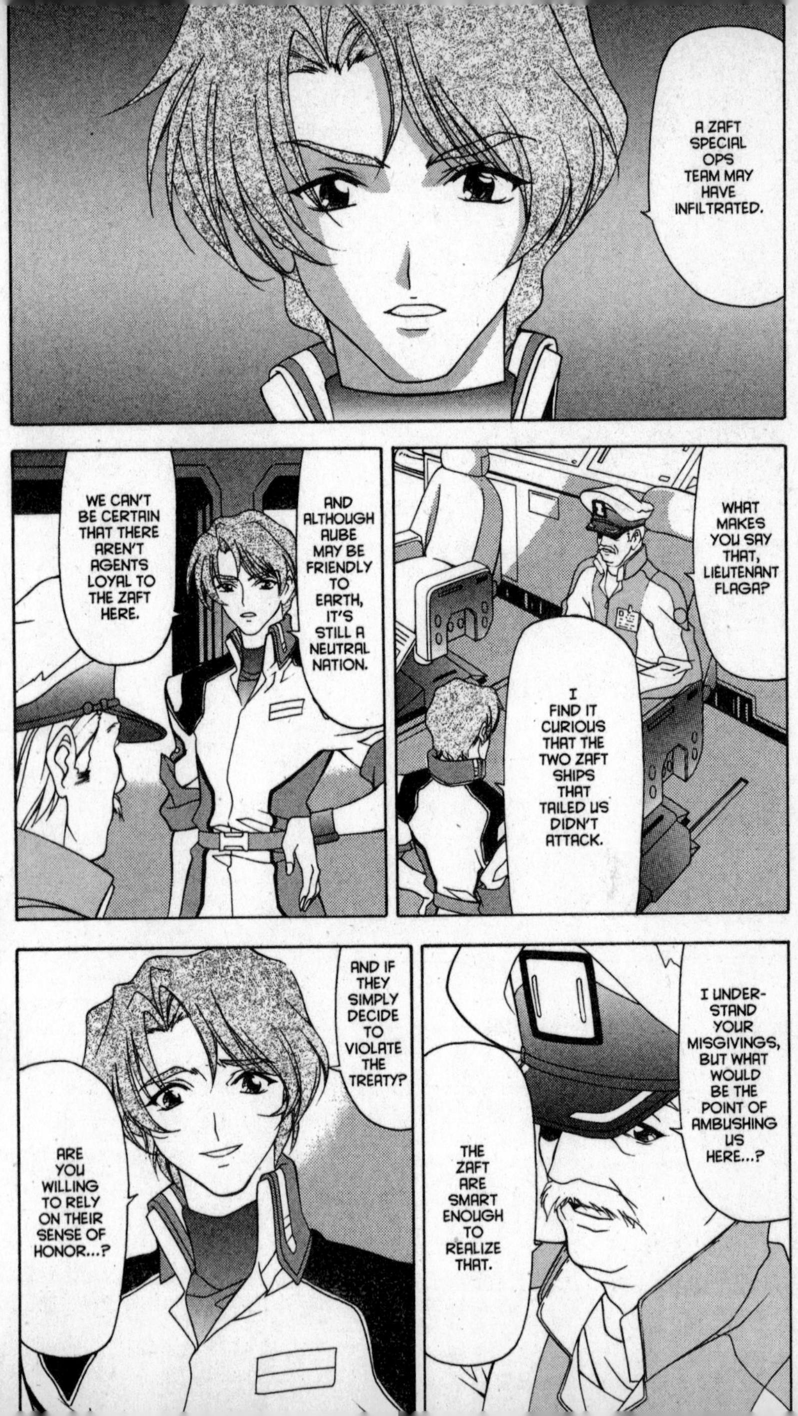
A ZAFT SPECIAL OPS TEAM MAY HAVE INFILTRATED.
WHAT MAKES YOU SAY THAT, LIEUTENANT FLAGA?
I FIND IT CURIOUS THAT THE TWO ZAFT SHIPS THAT TAILED US DIDN'T ATTACK.
AND ALTHOUGH AUBE MAY BE FRIENDLY TO EARTH, IT'S STILL A NEUTRAL NATION.
WE CAN'T BE CERTAIN THAT THERE AREN'T AGENTS LOYAL TO THE ZAFT HERE.
I UNDER-STAND YOUR MISGIVINGS, BUT WHAT WOULD BE THE POINT OF AMBUSHING US HERE...?
THE ZAFT ARE SMART ENOUGH TO REALIZE THAT.
AND IF THEY SIMPLY DECIDE TO VIOLATE THE TREATY?
ARE YOU WILLING TO RELY ON THEIR SENSE OF HONOR...?

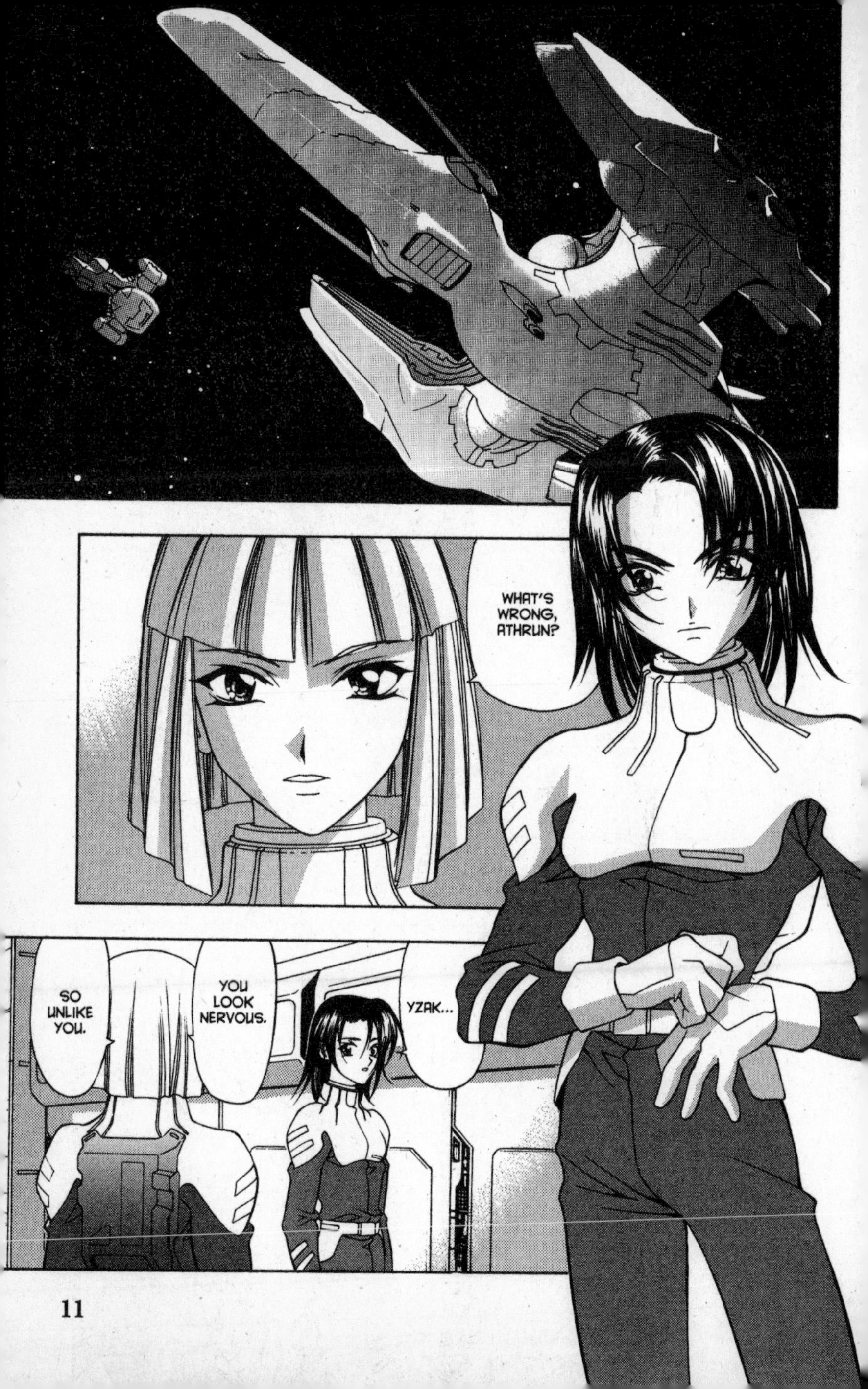
WHAT'S WRONG, ATHRUN?
YZAK...
YOU LOOK NERVOUS.
SO UNLIKE YOU.

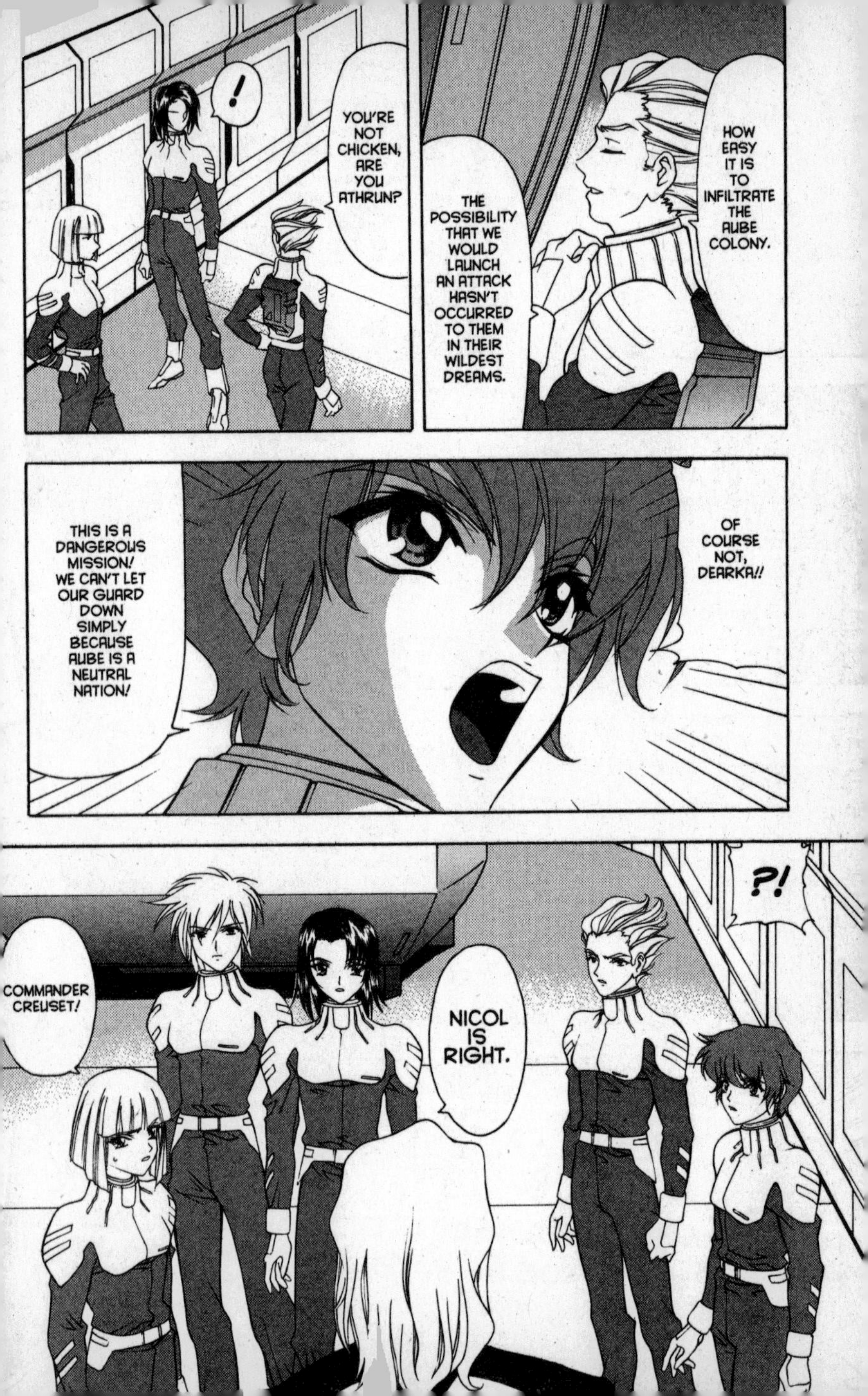
HOW EASY IT IS TO INFILTRATE THE AUBE COLONY.
THE POSSIBILITY THAT WE WOULD LAUNCH AN ATTACK HASN'T OCCURRED TO THEM IN THEIR WILDEST DREAMS.
YOU'RE NOT CHICKEN, ARE YOU ATHRUN?
!
OF COURSE NOT, DEARKA!!
THIS IS A DANGEROUS MISSION! WE CAN'T LET OUR GUARD DOWN SIMPLY BECAUSE AUBE IS A NEUTRAL NATION!
?!
NICOL IS RIGHT.
COMMANDER CREUSET!

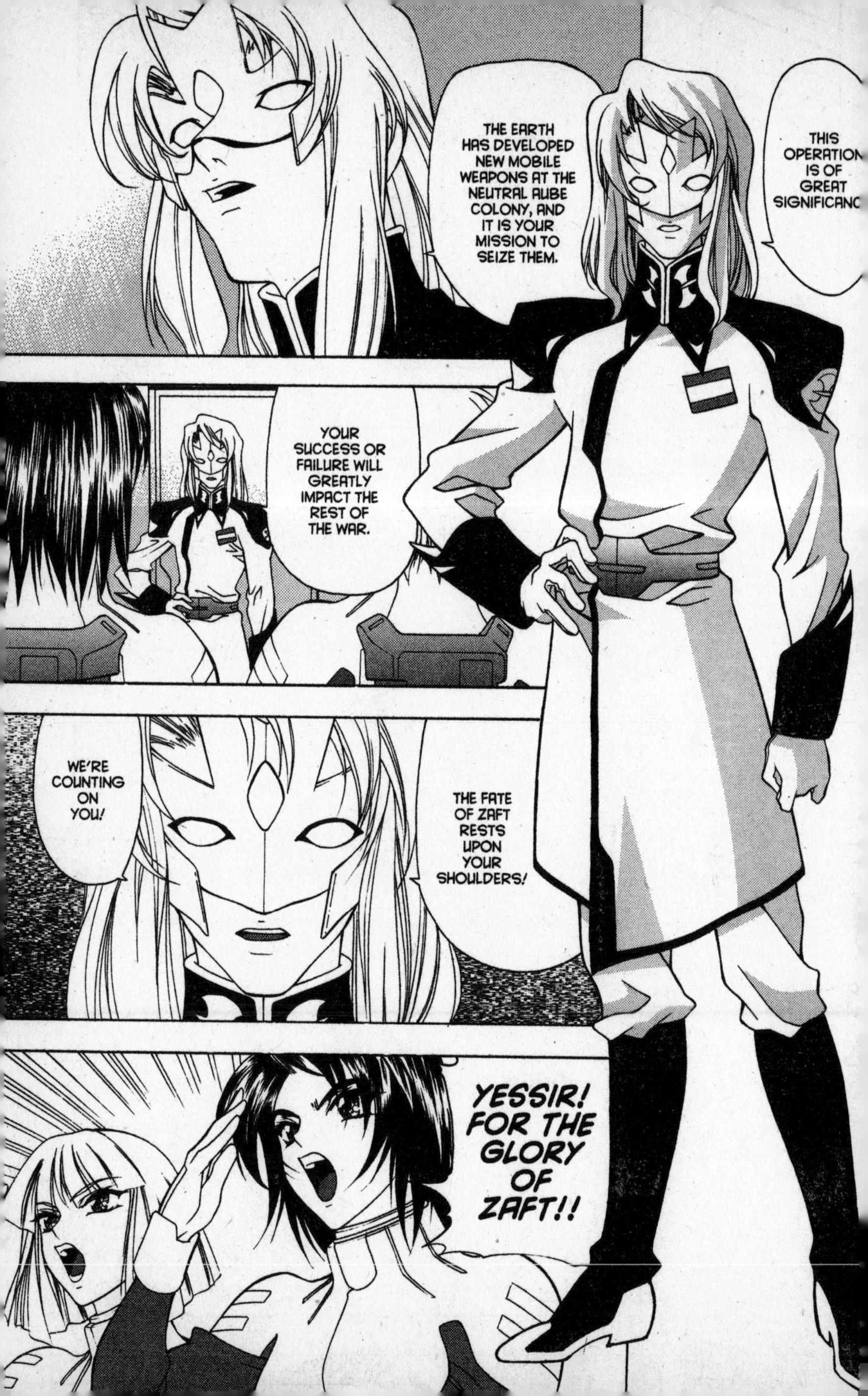

THIS OPERATION IS OF GREAT SIGNIFICANC
THE EARTH HAS DEVELOPED NEW MOBILE WEAPONS AT THE NEUTRAL AUBE COLONY, AND IT IS YOUR MISSION TO SEIZE THEM.
YOUR SUCCESS OR FAILURE WILL GREATLY IMPACT THE REST OF THE WAR.
THE FATE OF ZAFT RESTS UPON YOUR SHOULDERS!
WE'RE COUNTING ON YOU!
YESSIR! FOR THE GLORY OF ZAFT!!

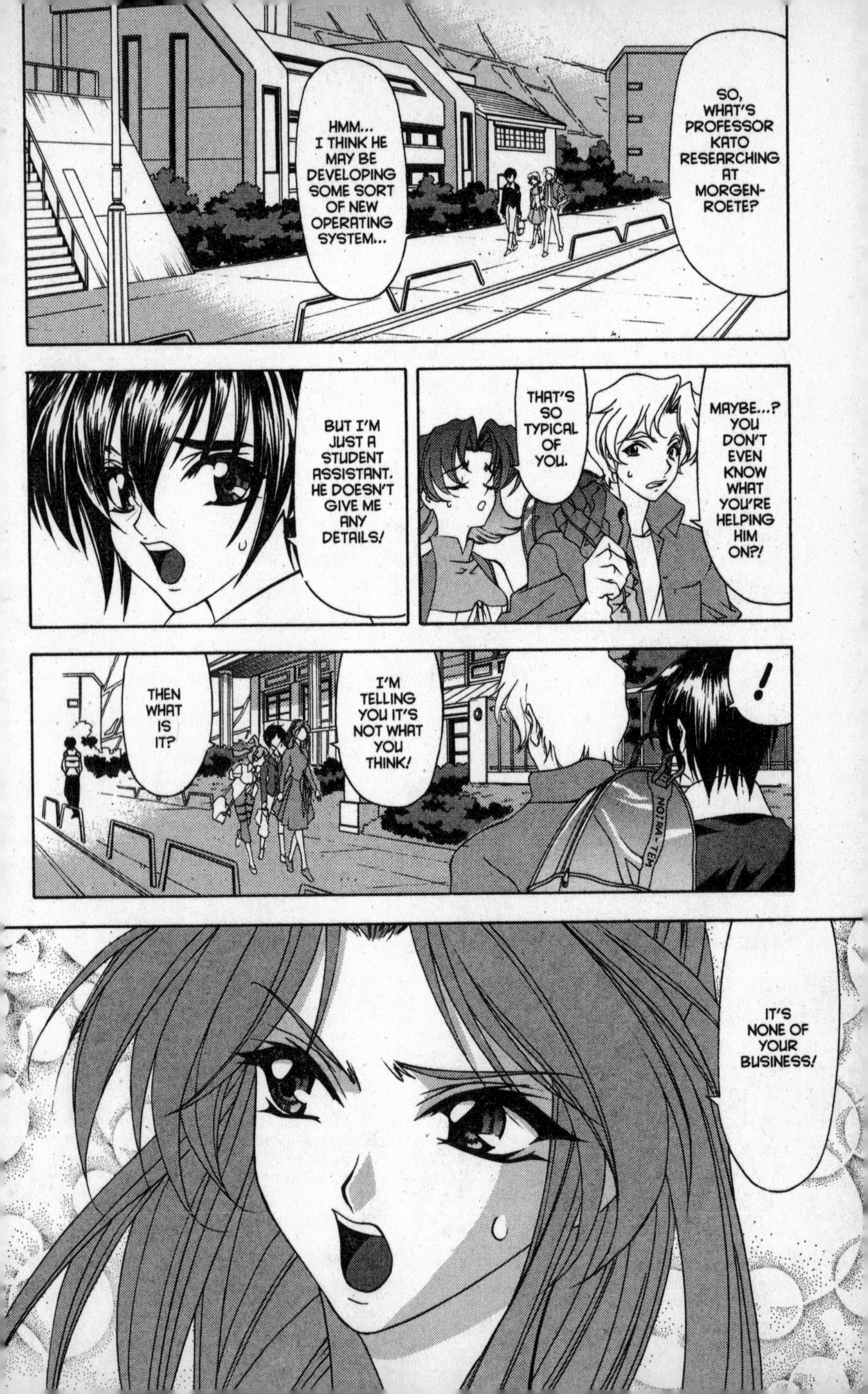
SO, WHAT'S PROFESSOR KATO RESEARCHING AT MORGEN-ROETE?
HMM... I THINK HE MAY BE DEVELOPING SOME SORT OF NEW OPERATING SYSTEM...
MAYBE...? YOU DON'T EVEN KNOW WHAT YOU'RE HELPING HIM ON?!
THAT'S SO TYPICAL OF YOU.
BUT I'M JUST A STUDENT ASSISTANT. HE DOESN'T GIVE ME ANY DETAILS!
!
I'M TELLING YOU IT'S NOT WHAT YOU THINK!
THEN WHAT IS IT?
IT'S NONE OF YOUR BUSINESS!

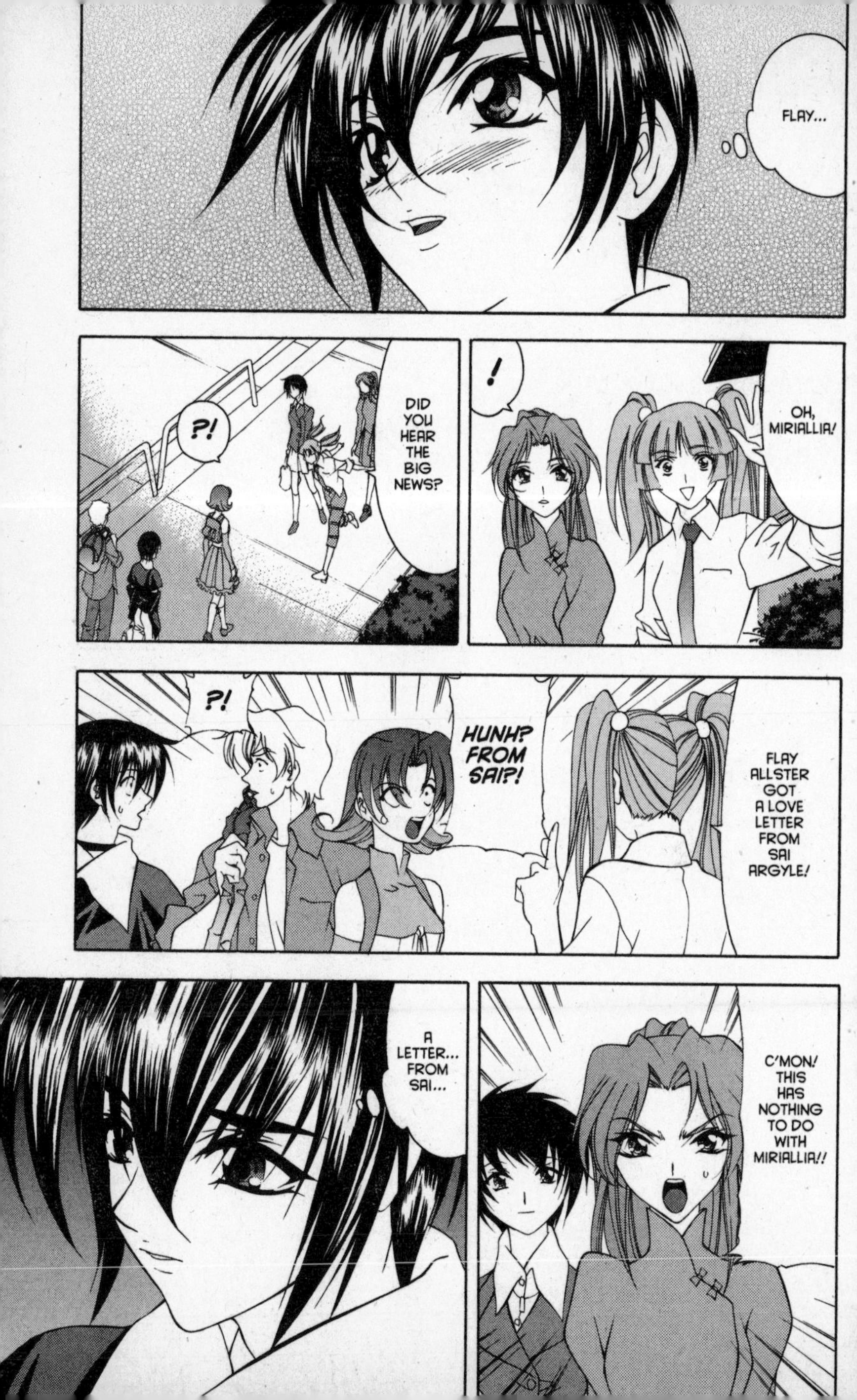
FLAY...
OH, MIRIALLIA!
!
DID YOU HEAR THE BIG NEWS?
?!
FLAY ALLSTER GOT A LOVE LETTER FROM SAI ARGYLE!
HUNH? FROM SAI?!
?!
C'MON! THIS HAS NOTHING TO DO WITH MIRIALLIA!!
A LETTER... FROM SAI...

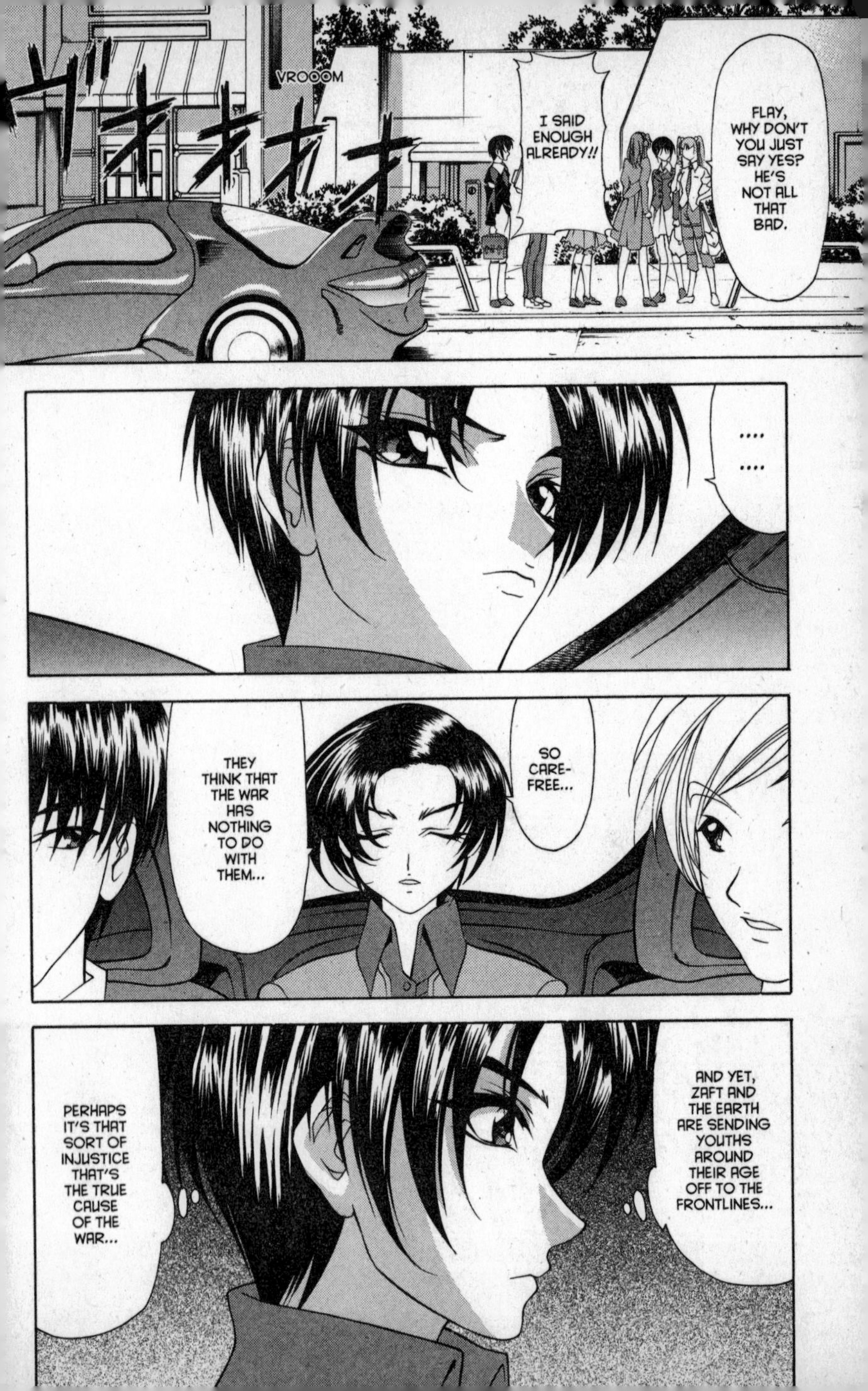
FLAY, WHY DON'T YOU JUST SAY YES? HE'S NOT ALL THAT BAD.
I SAID ENOUGH ALREADY!!
VROOOM
....
....
SO CARE-FREE...
THEY THINK THAT THE WAR HAS NOTHING TO DO WITH THEM...
AND YET, ZAFT AND THE EARTH ARE SENDING YOUTHS AROUND THEIR AGE OFF TO THE FRONTLINES...
PERHAPS IT'S THAT SORT OF INJUSTICE THAT'S THE TRUE CAUSE OF THE WAR...

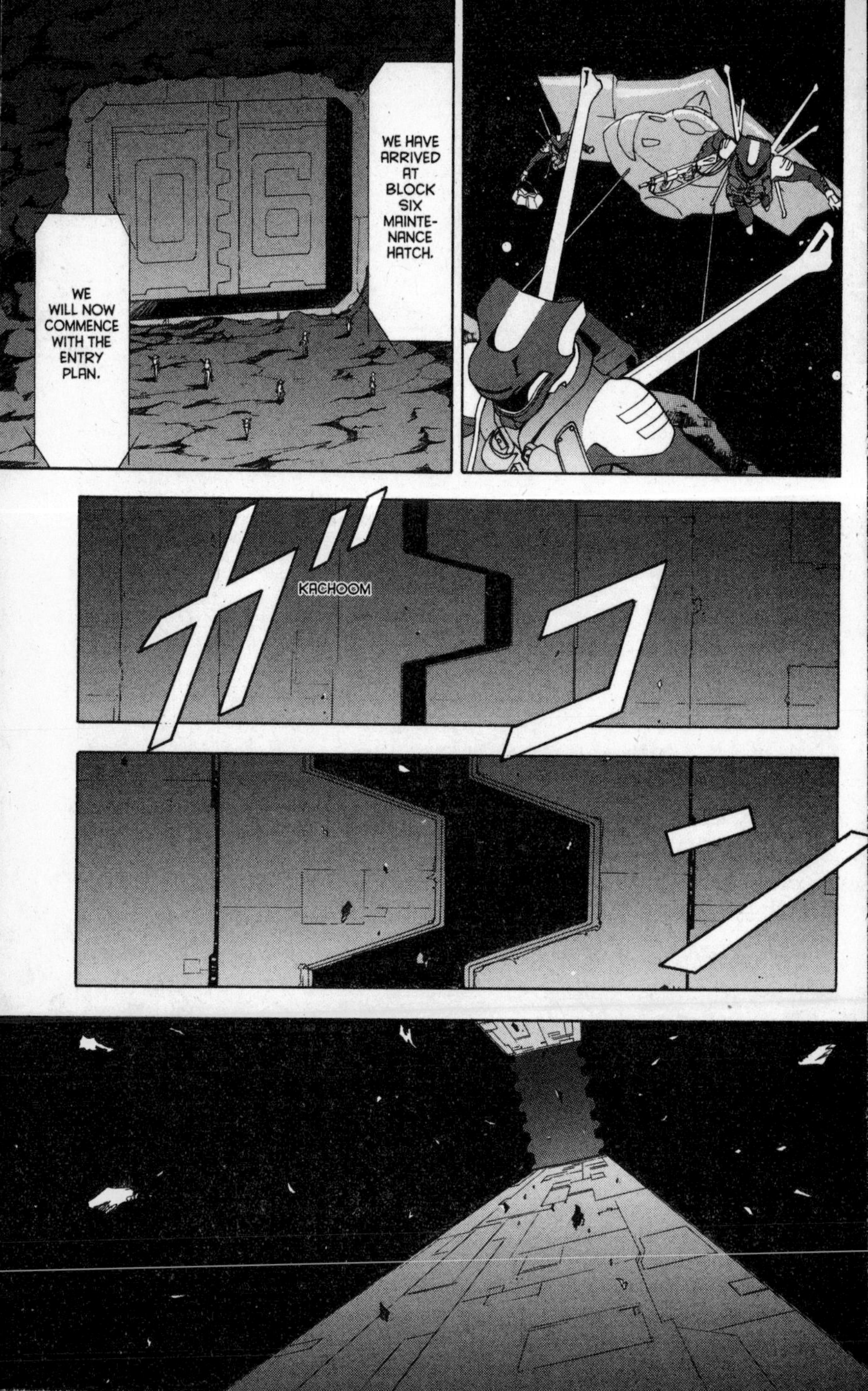

WE HAVE ARRIVED AT BLOCK SIX MAINTENANCE HATCH.
WE WILL NOW COMMENCE WITH THE ENTRY PLAN.
ガコーン
KACHOOM

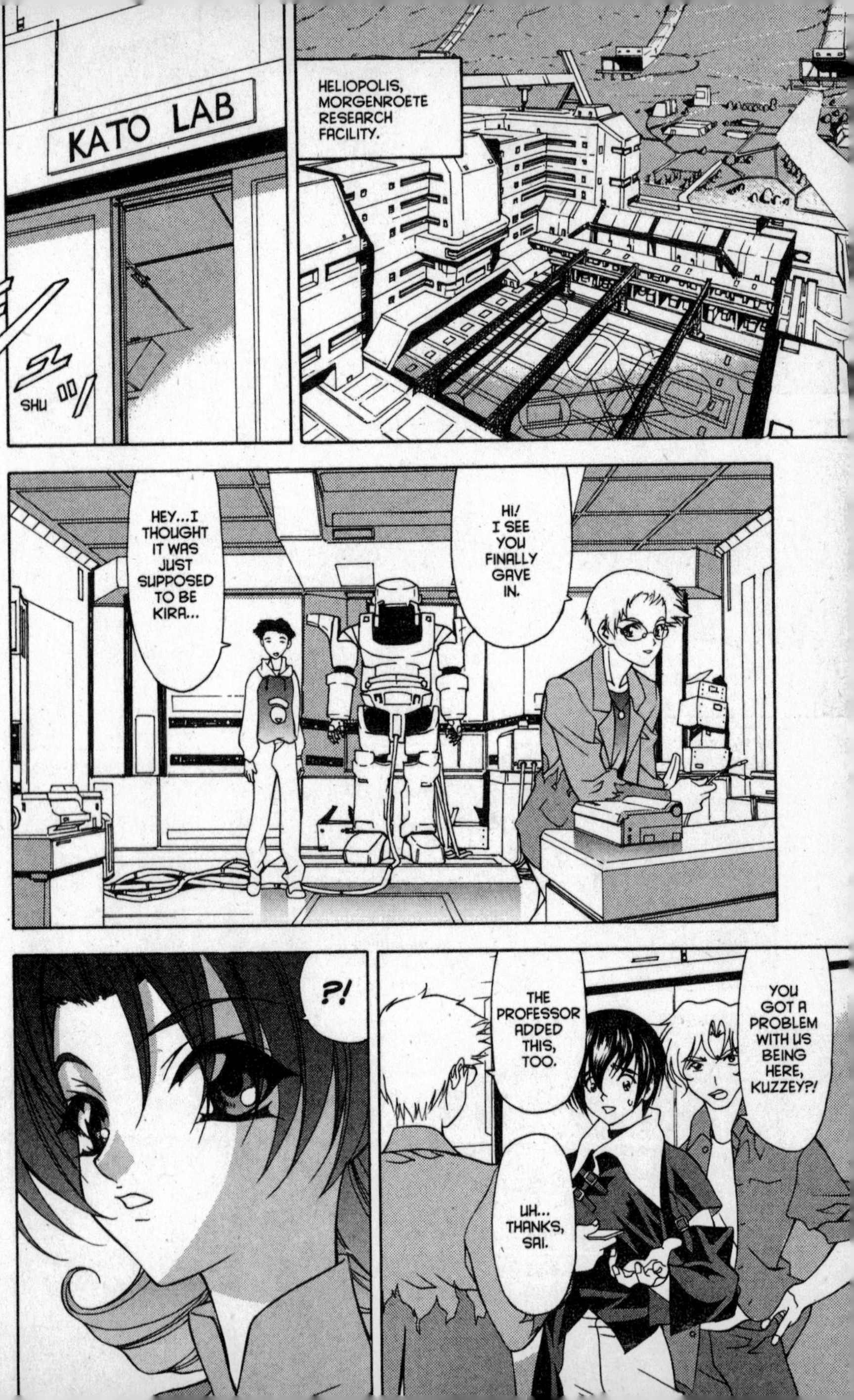
HELIOPOLIS, MORGENROETE RESEARCH FACILITY.
KATO LAB
SHU
HI! I SEE YOU FINALLY GAVE IN.
HEY...I THOUGHT IT WAS JUST SUPPOSED TO BE KIRA...
YOU GOT A PROBLEM WITH US BEING HERE, KUZZEY?!
THE PROFESSOR ADDED THIS, TOO.
UH... THANKS, SAI.
?!

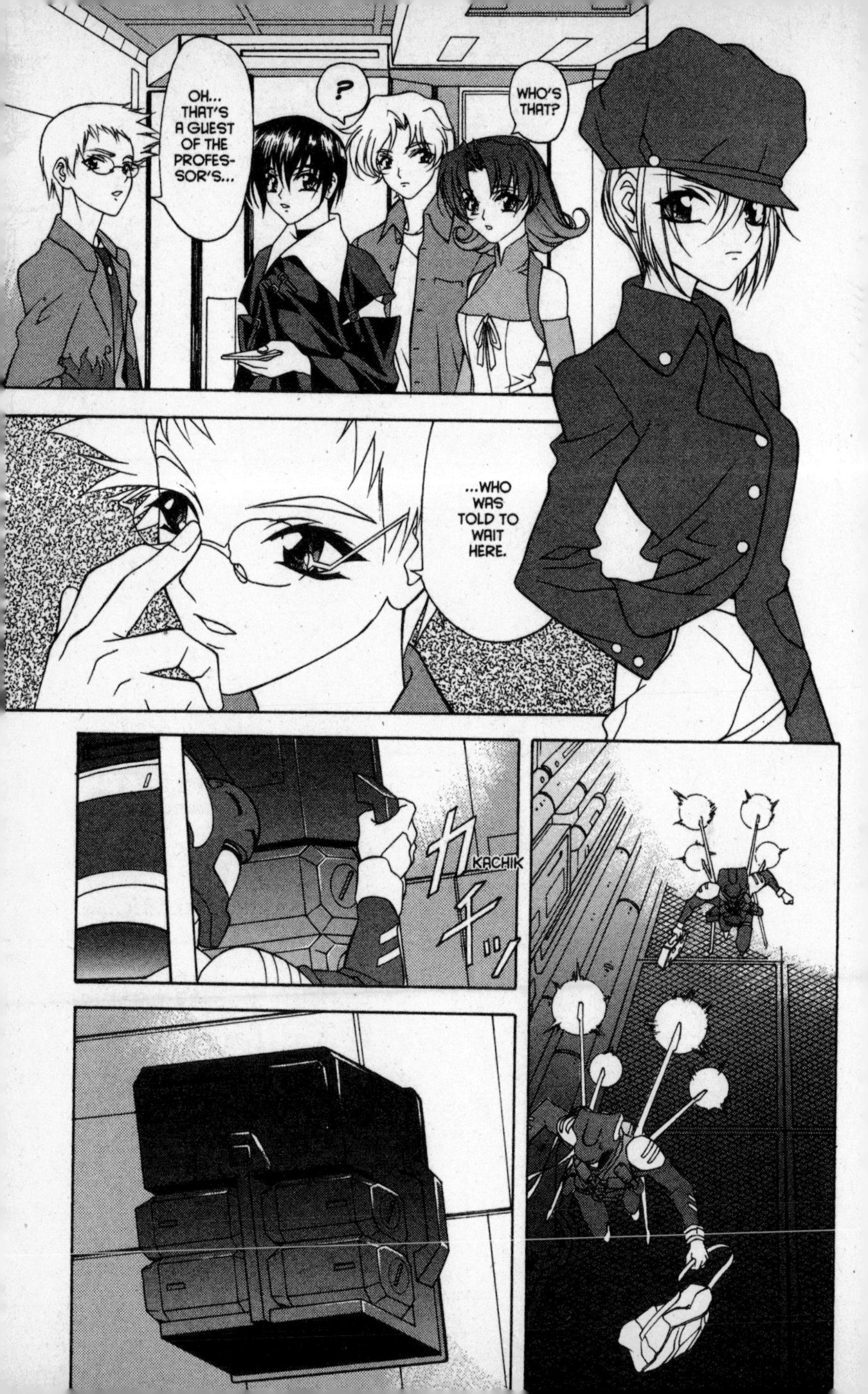
WHO'S THAT?
?
OH... THAT'S A GUEST OF THE PROFES-SOR'S...
...WHO WAS TOLD TO WAIT HERE.
KACHIK

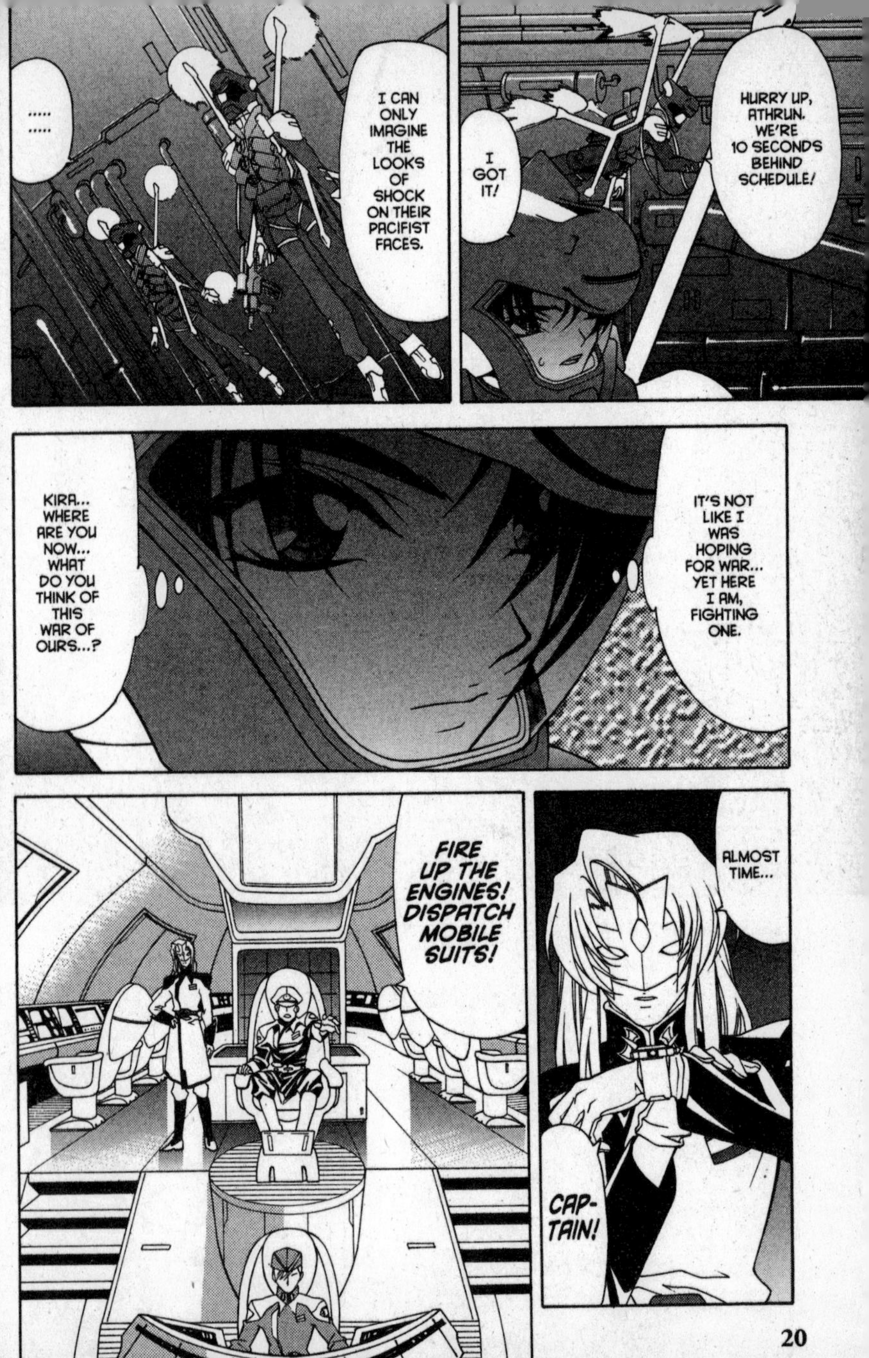
HURRY UP, ATHRUN. WE'RE 10 SECONDS BEHIND SCHEDULE!
I GOT IT!
I CAN ONLY IMAGINE THE LOOKS OF SHOCK ON THEIR PACIFIST FACES.
......
......
IT'S NOT LIKE I WAS HOPING FOR WAR... YET HERE I AM, FIGHTING ONE.
KIRA... WHERE ARE YOU NOW... WHAT DO YOU THINK OF THIS WAR OF OURS...?
ALMOST TIME...
CAP-TAIN!
FIRE UP THE ENGINES! DISPATCH MOBILE SUITS!

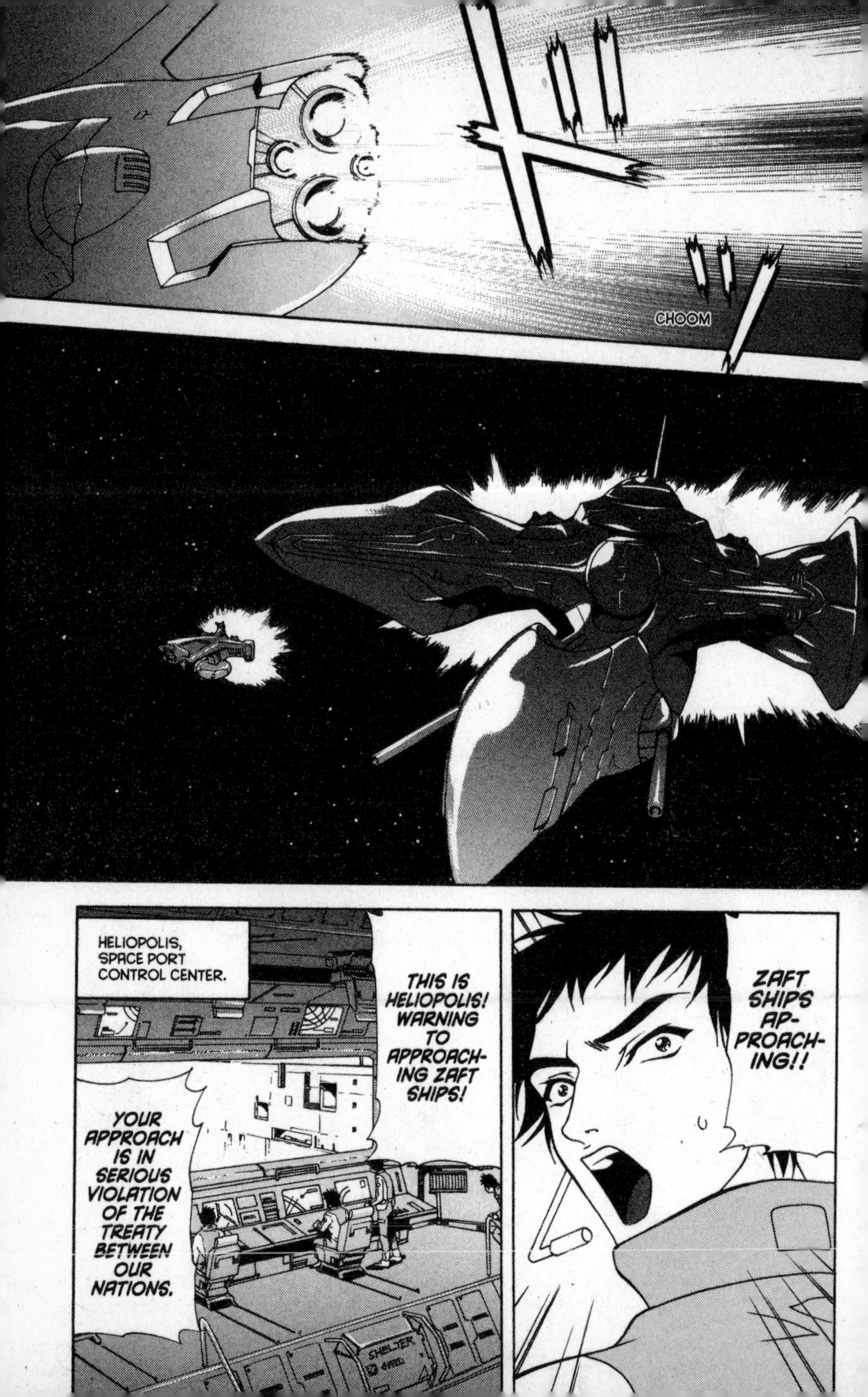
CHOOM
ZAFT SHIPS AP-PROACH-ING!!
HELIOPOLIS, SPACE PORT CONTROL CENTER.
THIS IS HELIOPOLIS! WARNING TO APPROACH-ING ZAFT SHIPS!
YOUR APPROACH IS IN SERIOUS VIOLATION OF THE TREATY BETWEEN OUR NATIONS.

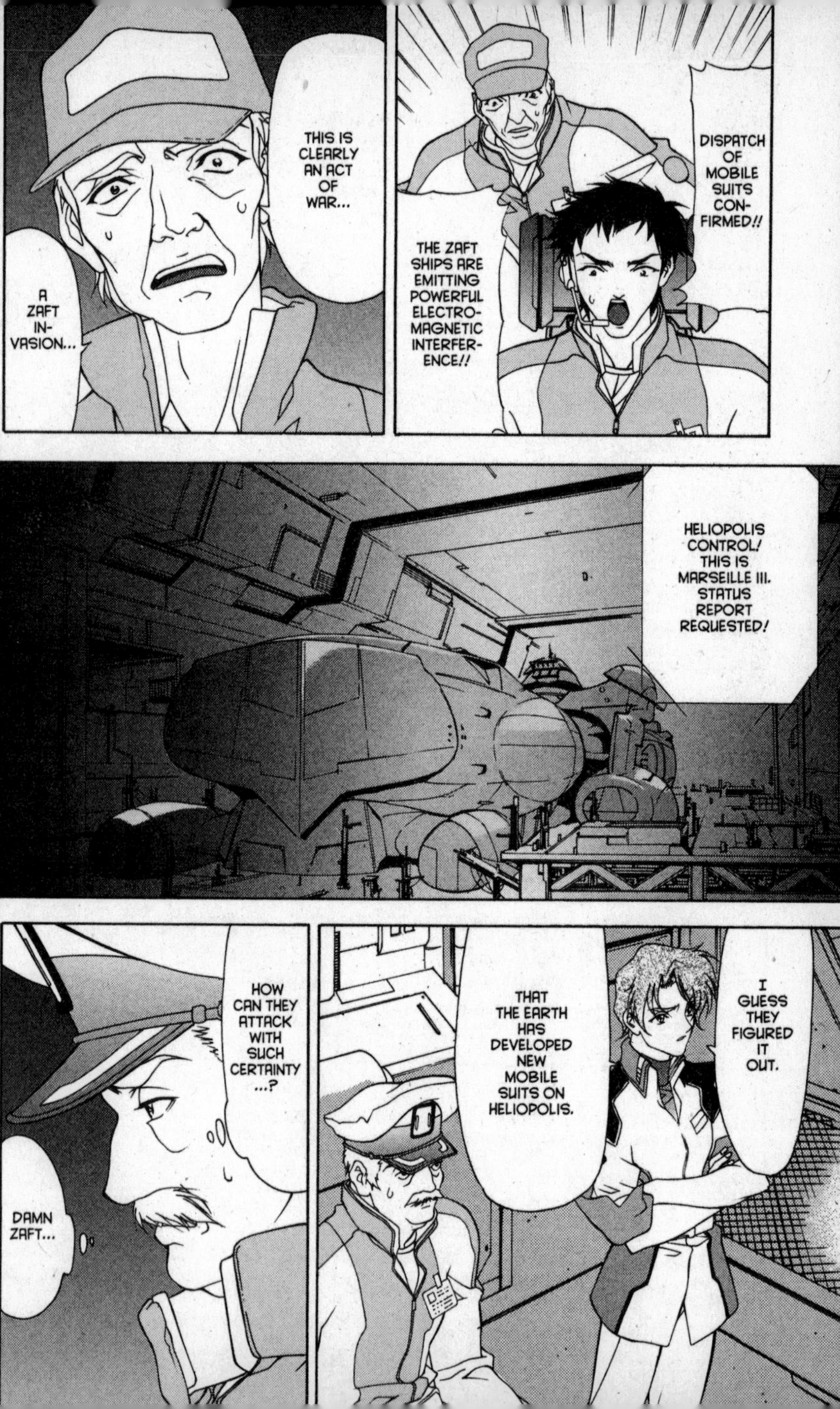
DISPATCH OF MOBILE SUITS CON-FIRMED!!
THE ZAFT SHIPS ARE EMITTING POWERFUL ELECTRO-MAGNETIC INTERFER-ENCE!!
THIS IS CLEARLY AN ACT OF WAR...
A ZAFT IN-VASION...
HELIOPOLIS CONTROL! THIS IS MARSEILLE III. STATUS REPORT REQUESTED!
I GUESS THEY FIGURED IT OUT.
THAT THE EARTH HAS DEVELOPED NEW MOBILE SUITS ON HELIOPOLIS.
HOW CAN THEY ATTACK WITH SUCH CERTAINTY ...?
DAMN ZAFT...

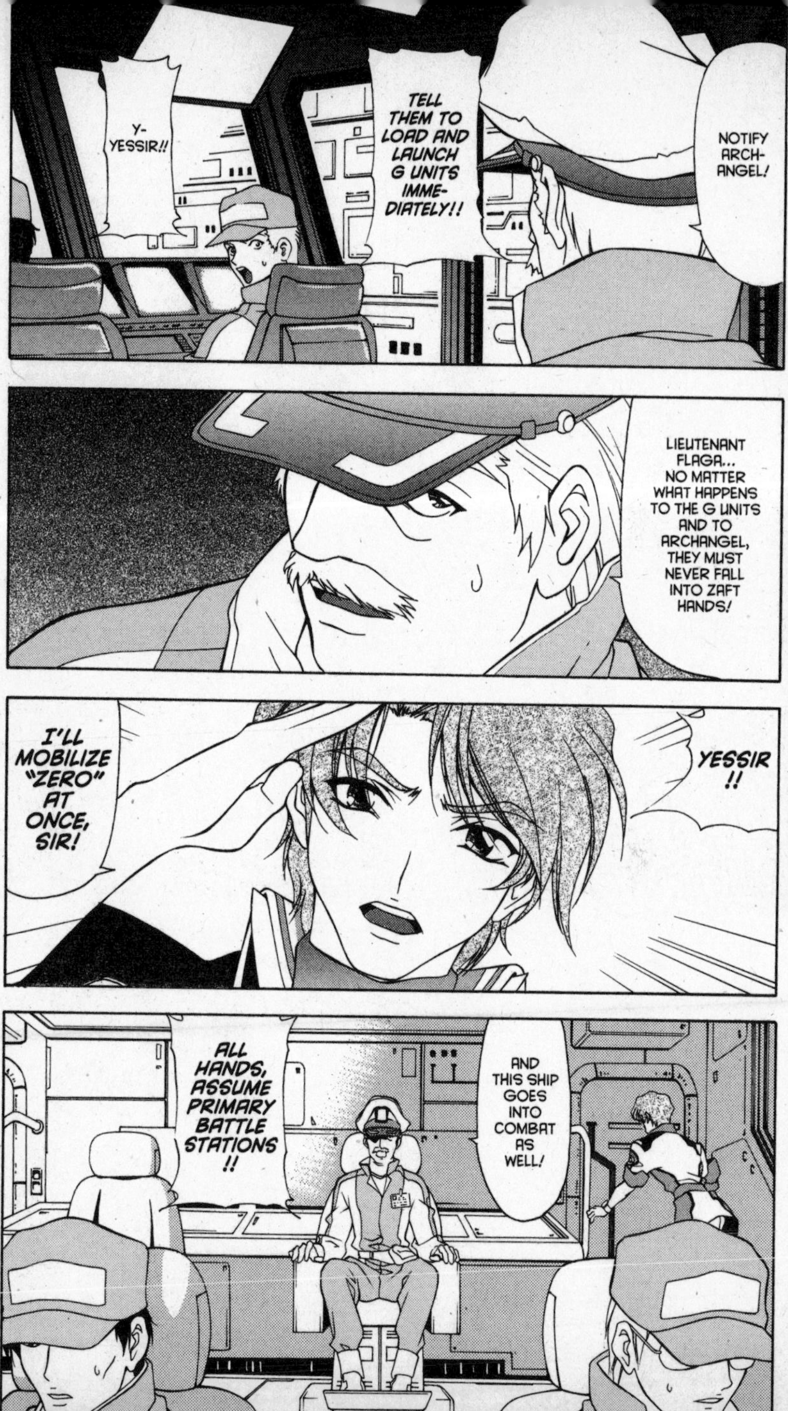

NOTIFY ARCH-ANGEL!
TELL THEM TO LOAD AND LAUNCH G UNITS IMME-DIATELY!!
Y-YESSIR!!
LIEUTENANT FLAGA... NO MATTER WHAT HAPPENS TO THE G UNITS AND TO ARCHANGEL, THEY MUST NEVER FALL INTO ZAFT HANDS!
YESSIR!!
I'LL MOBILIZE "ZERO" AT ONCE, SIR!
AND THIS SHIP GOES INTO COMBAT AS WELL!
ALL HANDS, ASSUME PRIMARY BATTLE STATIONS!!

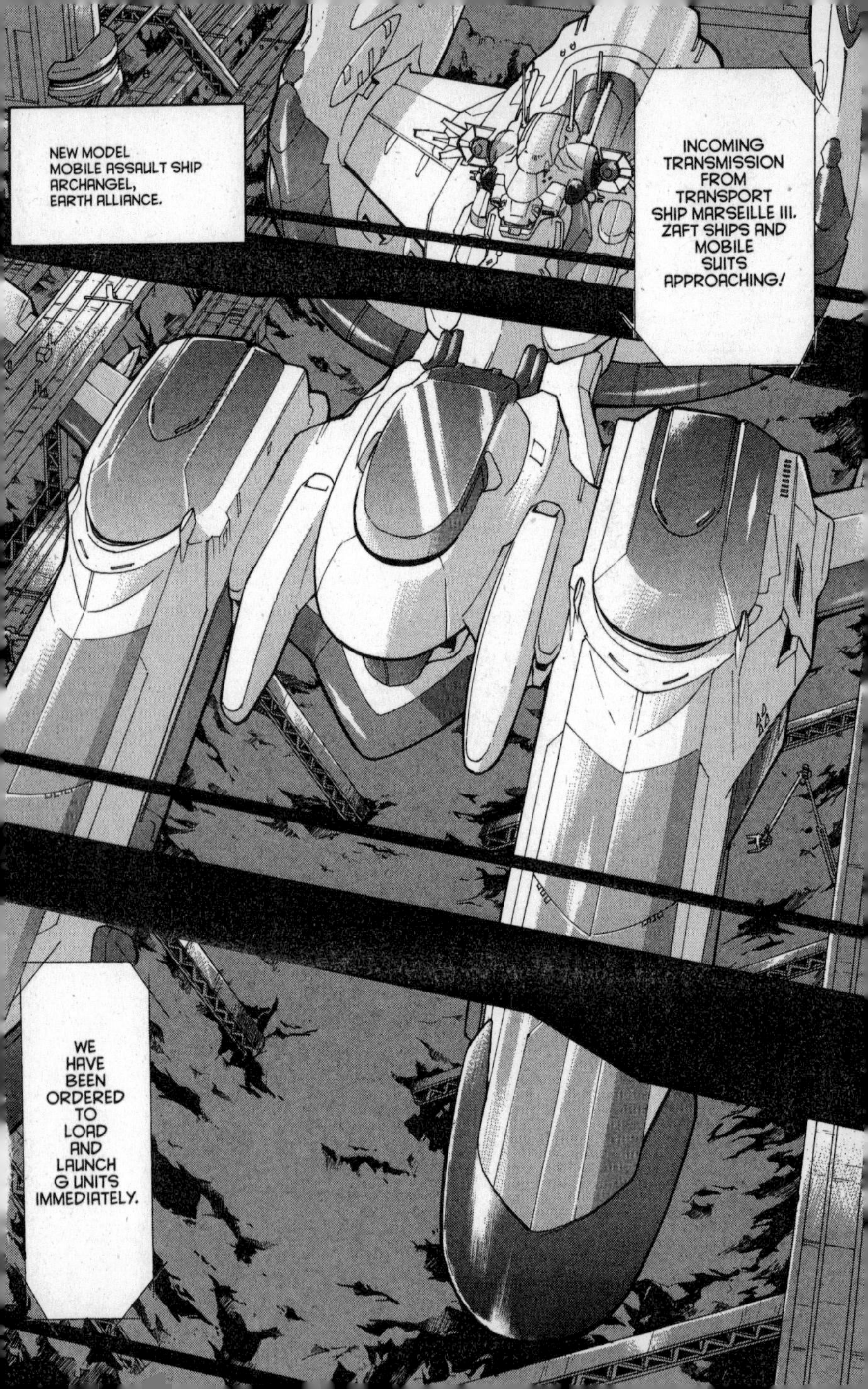
INCOMING TRANSMISSION FROM TRANSPORT SHIP MARSEILLE III. ZAFT SHIPS AND MOBILE SUITS APPROACHING!
NEW MODEL MOBILE ASSAULT SHIP ARCHANGEL, EARTH ALLIANCE.
WE HAVE BEEN ORDERED TO LOAD AND LAUNCH G UNITS IMMEDIATELY.

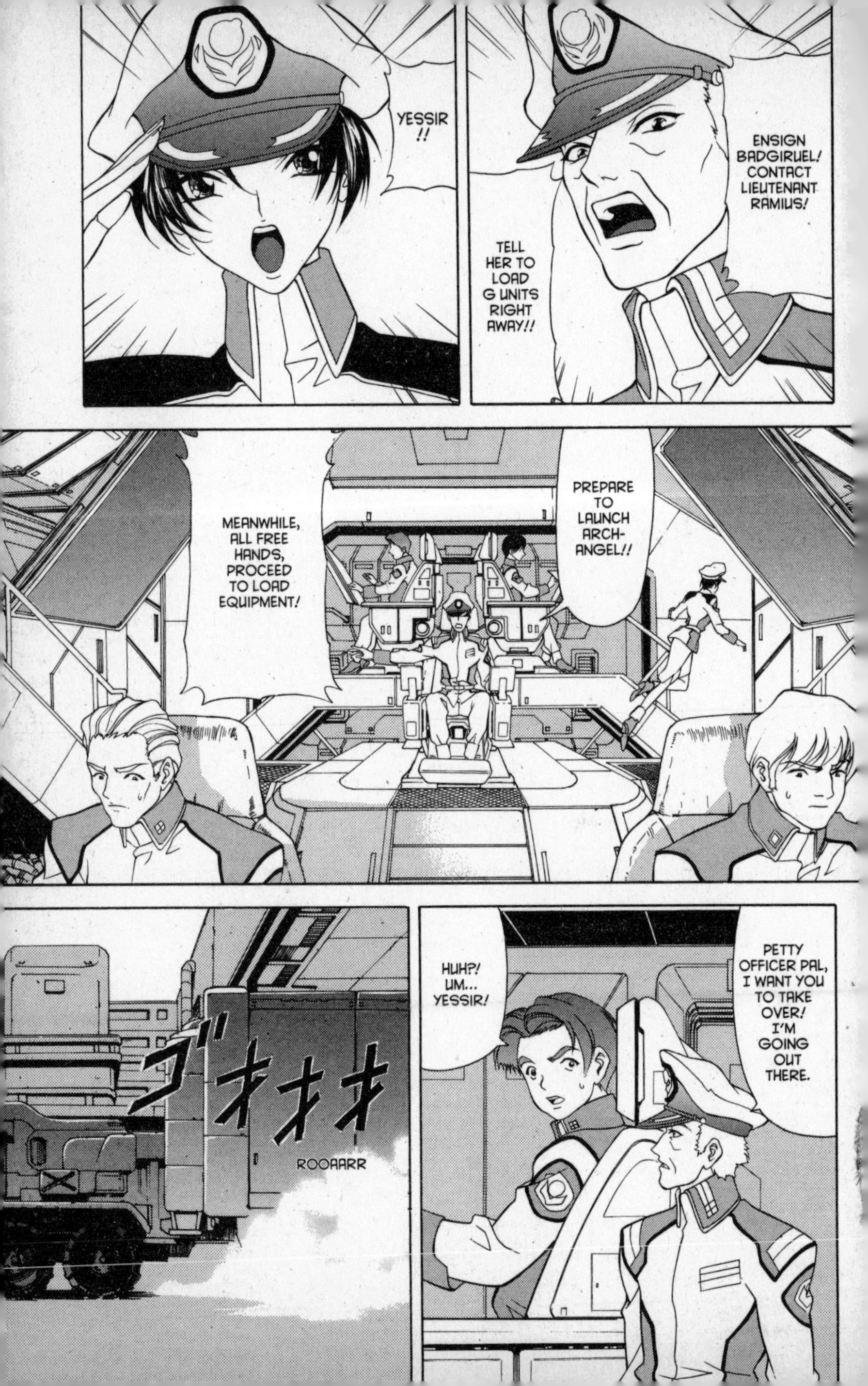
ENSIGN BADGIRUEL! CONTACT LIEUTENANT RAMIUS!
TELL HER TO LOAD G UNITS RIGHT AWAY!!
YESSIR!!
PREPARE TO LAUNCH ARCH-ANGEL!!
MEANWHILE, ALL FREE HANDS, PROCEED TO LOAD EQUIPMENT!
PETTY OFFICER PAL, I WANT YOU TO TAKE OVER! I'M GOING OUT THERE.
HUH?! UM... YESSIR!
ゴオオオ
ROOAARR

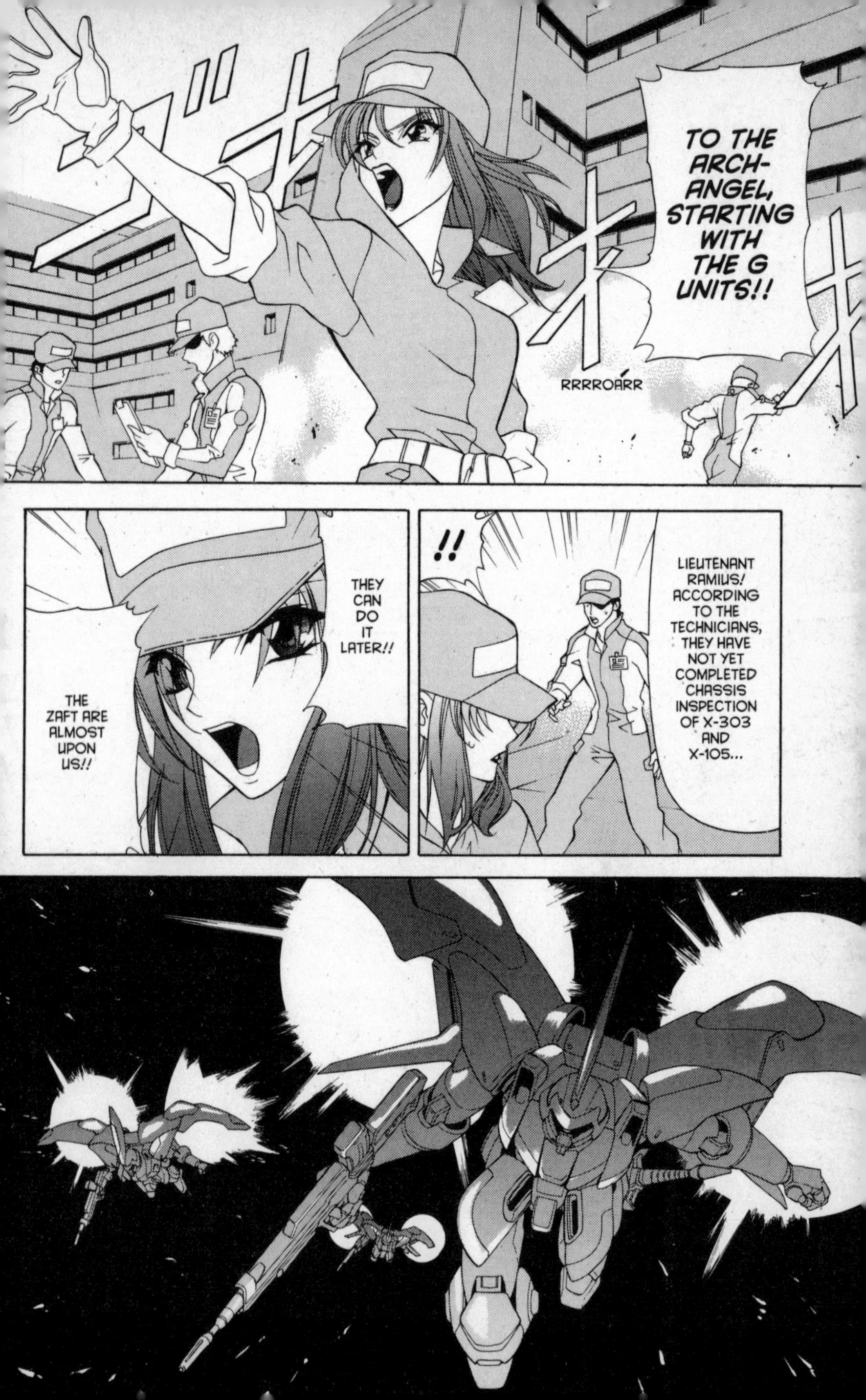
TO THE ARCH-ANGEL, STARTING WITH THE G UNITS!!
RRRROARR
!!
LIEUTENANT RAMIUS! ACCORDING TO THE TECHNICIANS, THEY HAVE NOT YET COMPLETED CHASSIS INSPECTION OF X-303 AND X-105...
THEY CAN DO IT LATER!!
THE ZAFT ARE ALMOST UPON US!!

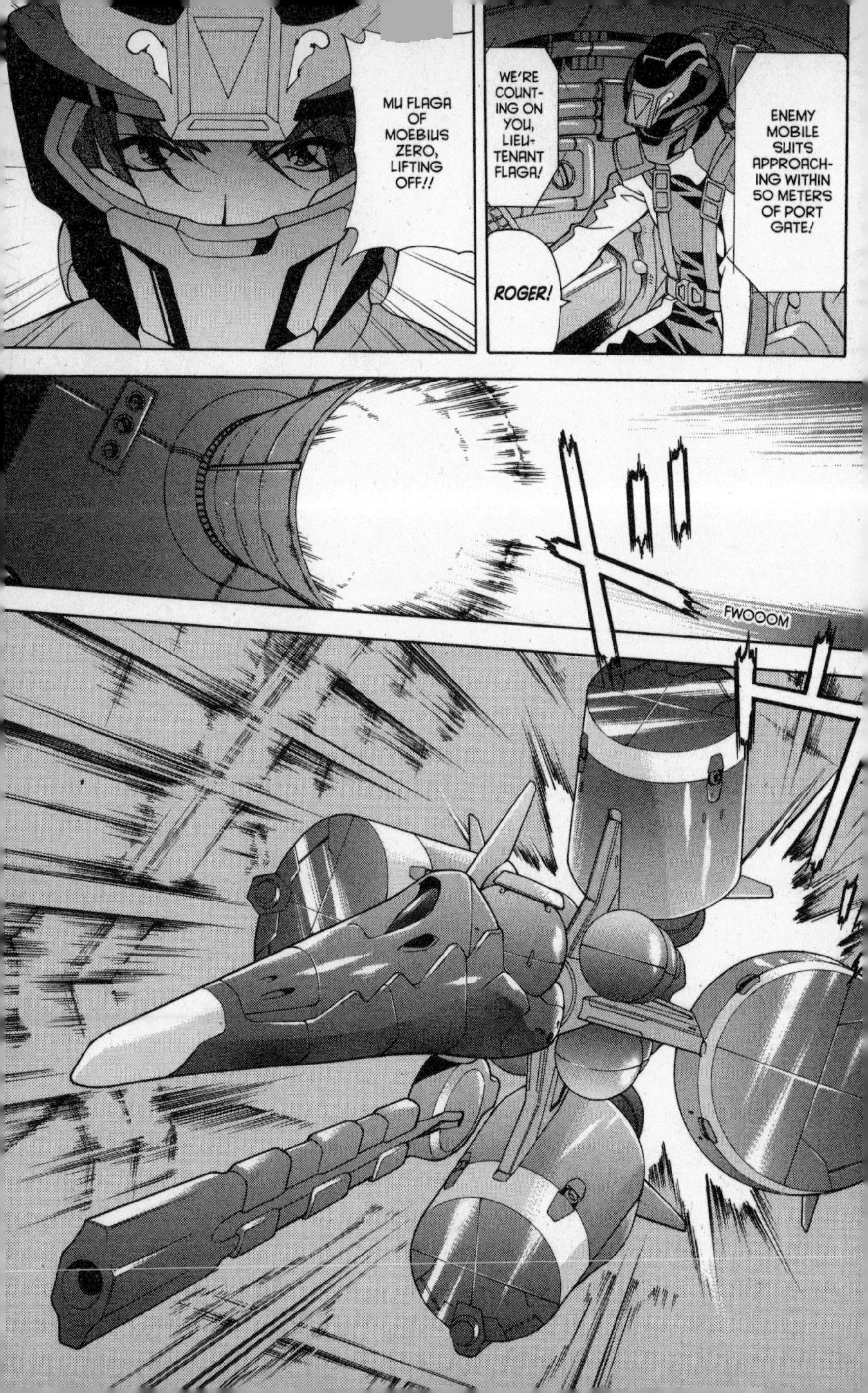
ENEMY MOBILE SUITS APPROACHING WITHIN 50 METERS OF PORT GATE!
WE'RE COUNTING ON YOU, LIEUTENANT FLAGA!
ROGER!
MU FLAGA OF MOEBIUS ZERO, LIFTING OFF!!
FWOOOM

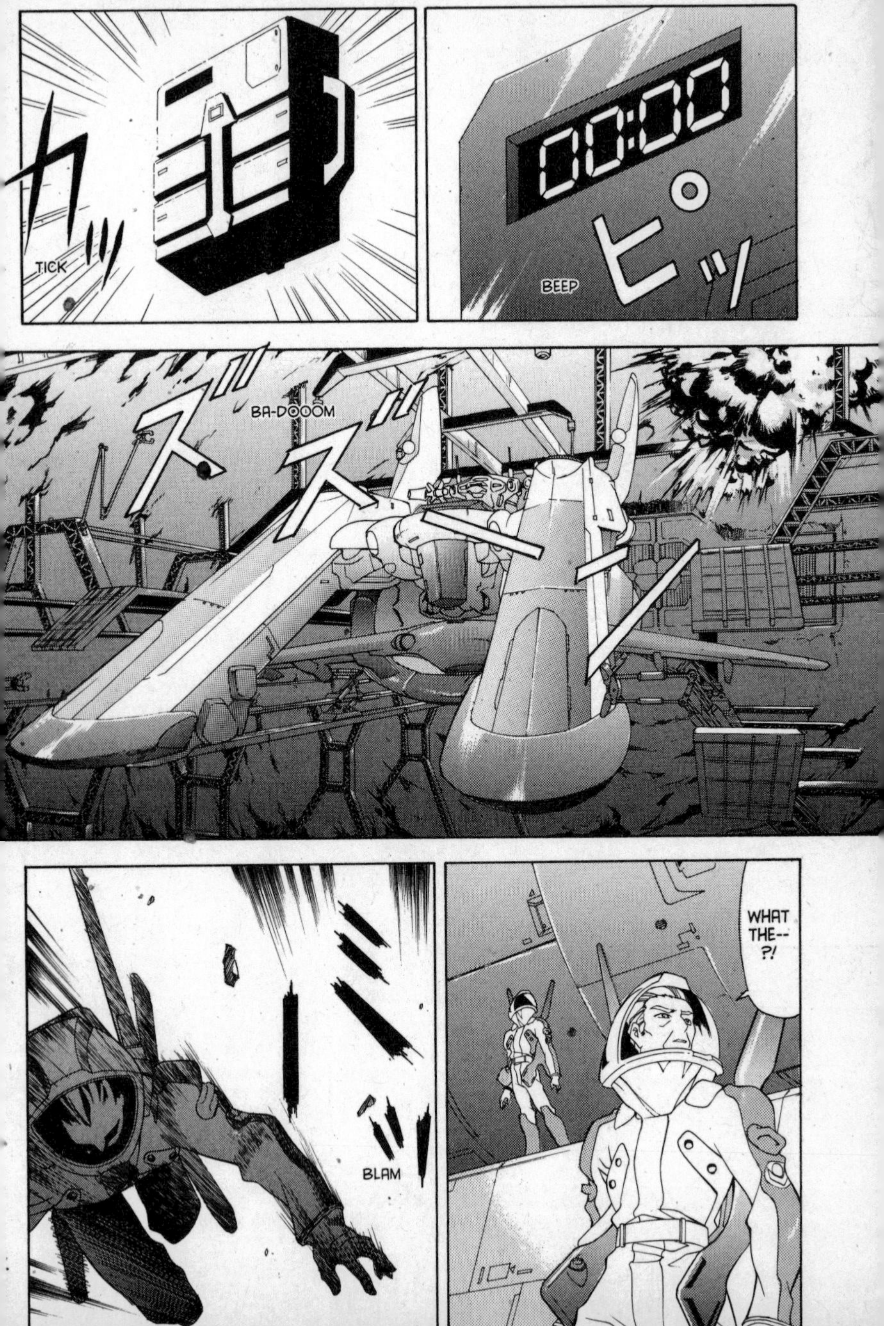
00:00
ピッ
BEEP
カッ
TICK
BA-DOOOM
WHAT THE-- ?!
BLAM

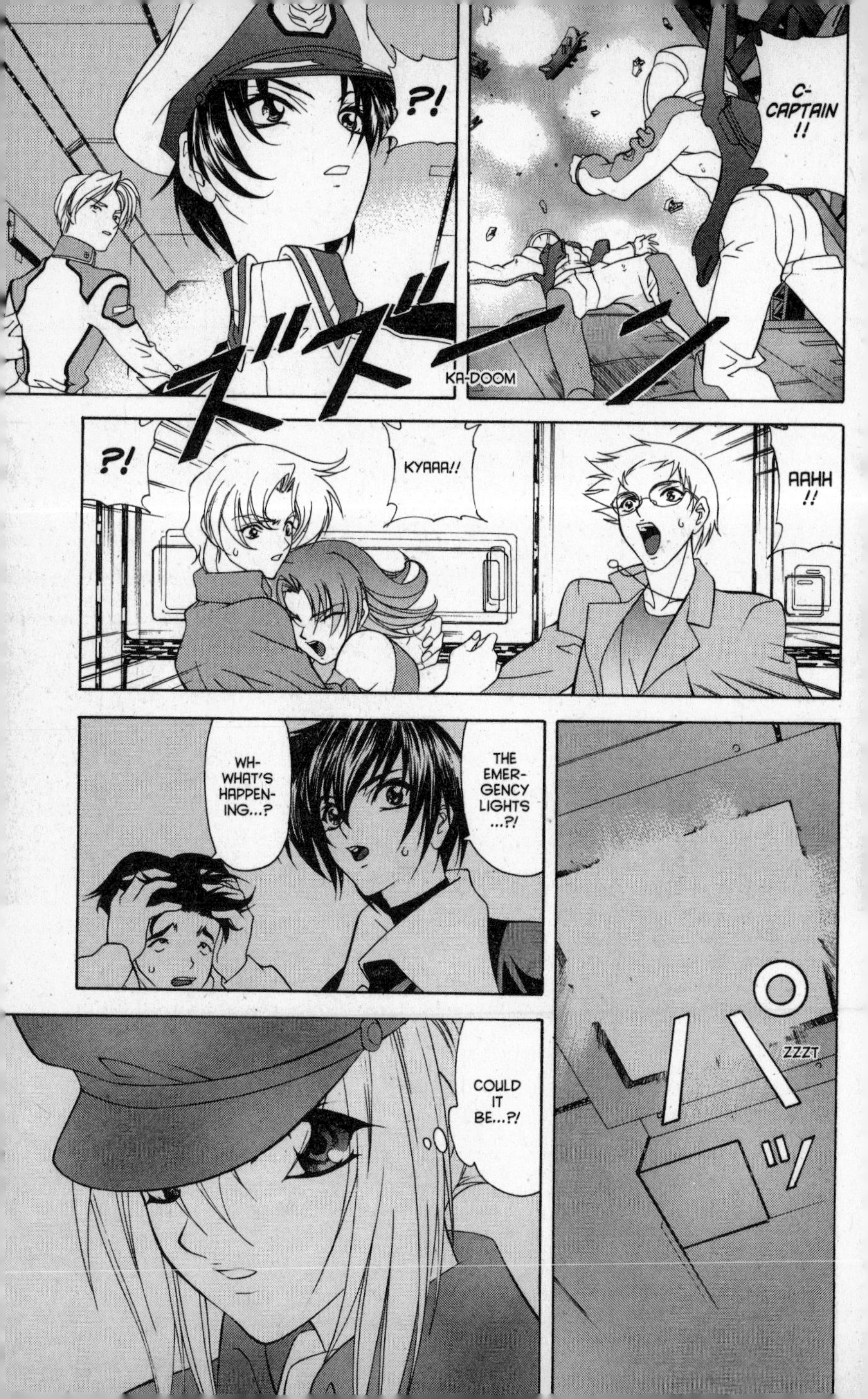
C-CAPTAIN!!
KA-DOOM
?!
AAHH!!
KYAAA!!
?!
ZZZT
THE EMERGENCY LIGHTS...?!
WH-WHAT'S HAPPENING...?
COULD IT BE...?!

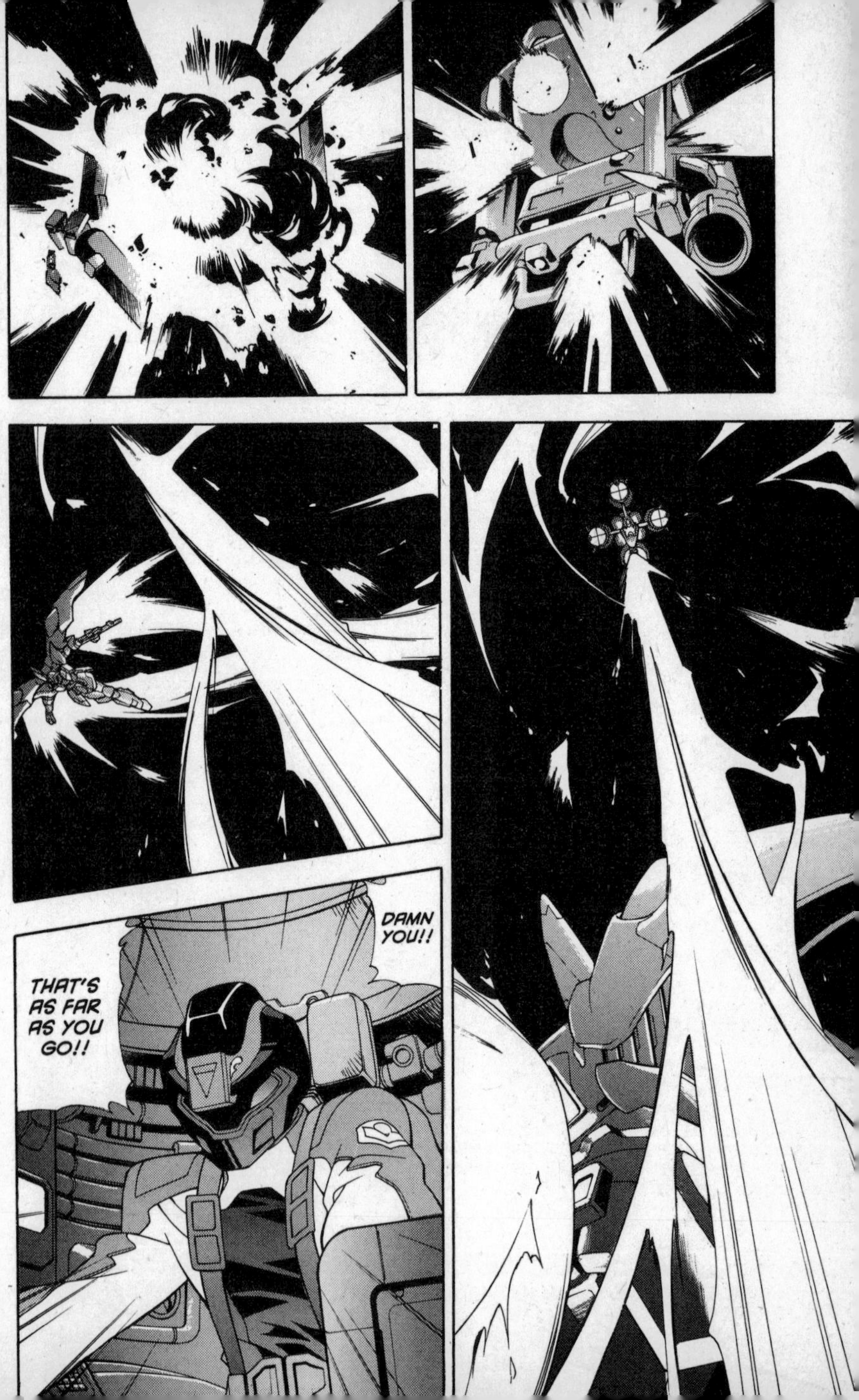
DAMN YOU!!
THAT'S AS FAR AS YOU GO!!

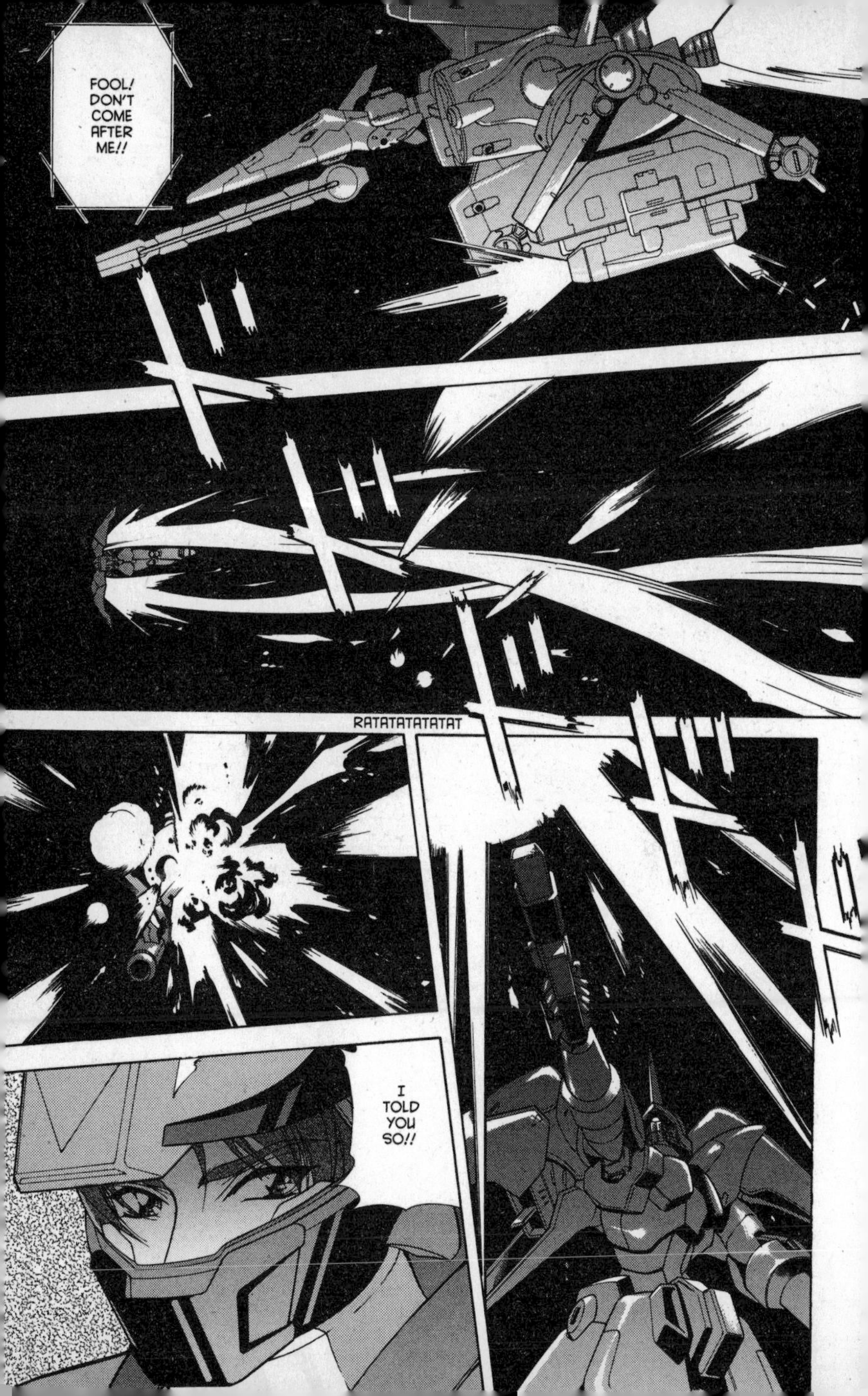
FOOL! DON'T COME AFTER ME!!
RATATATATATAT
I TOLD YOU SO!!

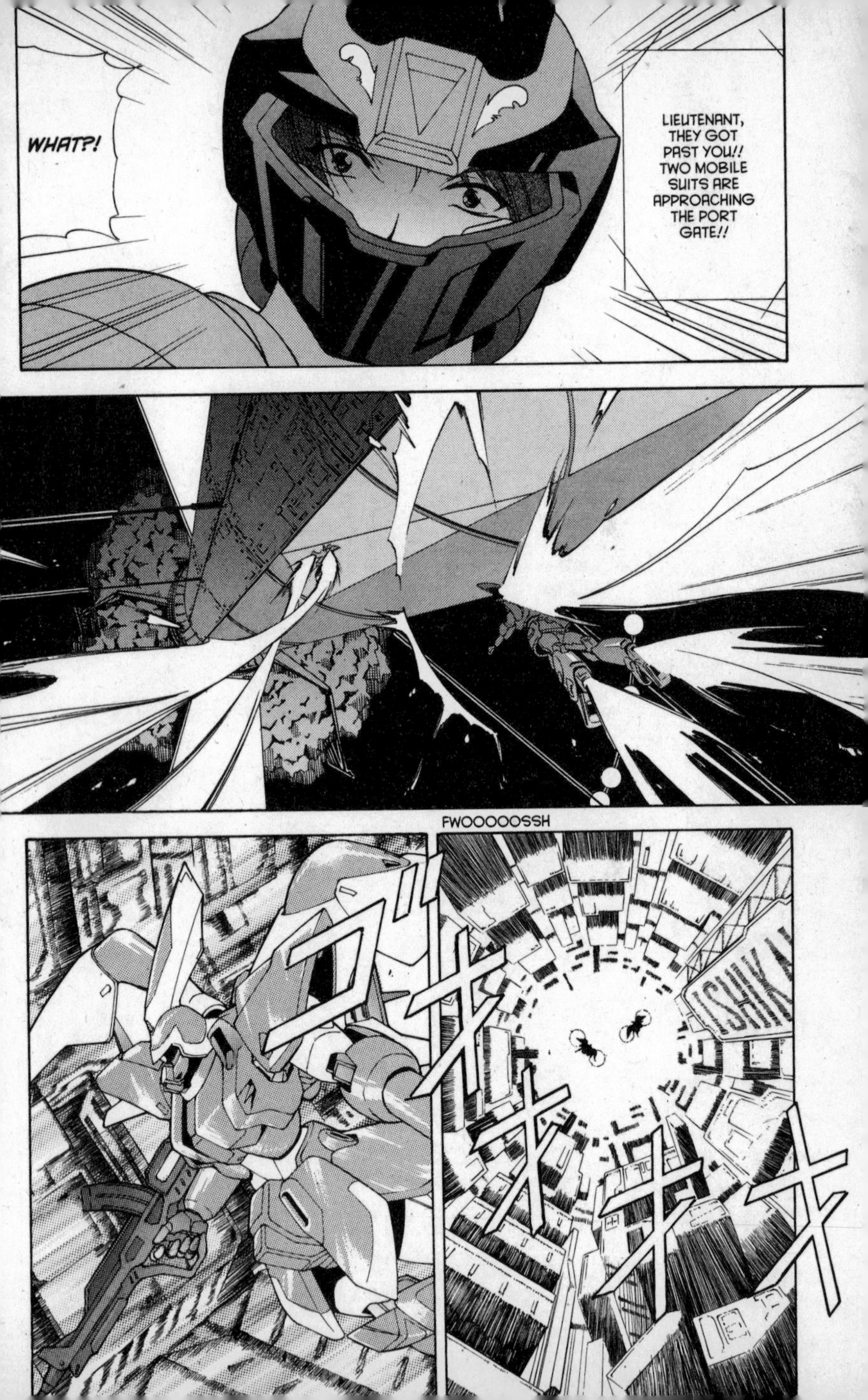
LIEUTENANT, THEY GOT PAST YOU!! TWO MOBILE SUITS ARE APPROACHING THE PORT GATE!!
WHAT?!
FWOOOOOSSH
ゴォォォォ

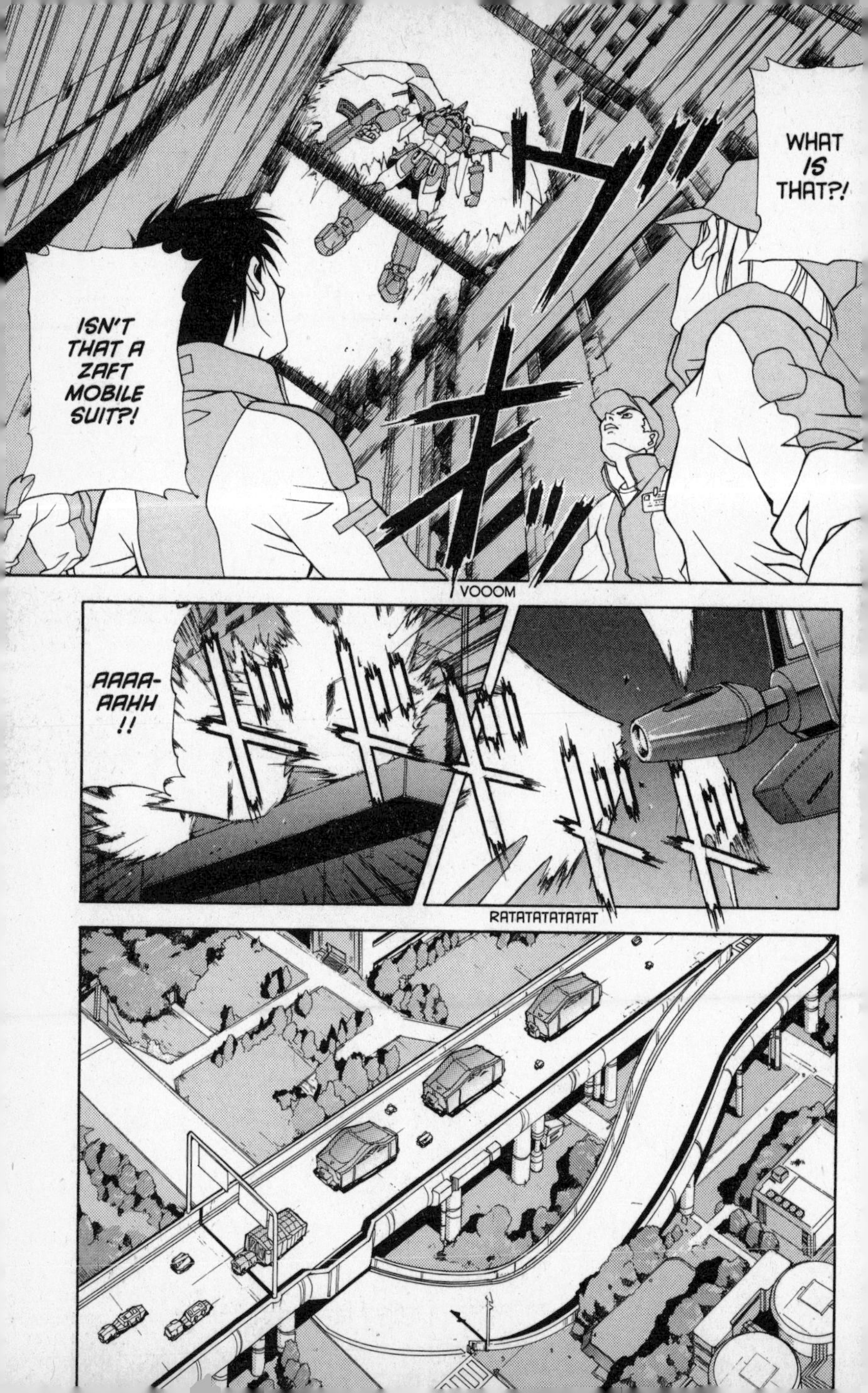
WHAT IS THAT?!
ISN'T THAT A ZAFT MOBILE SUIT?!
VOOOM
AAAA-AAHH !!
RATATATATATAT

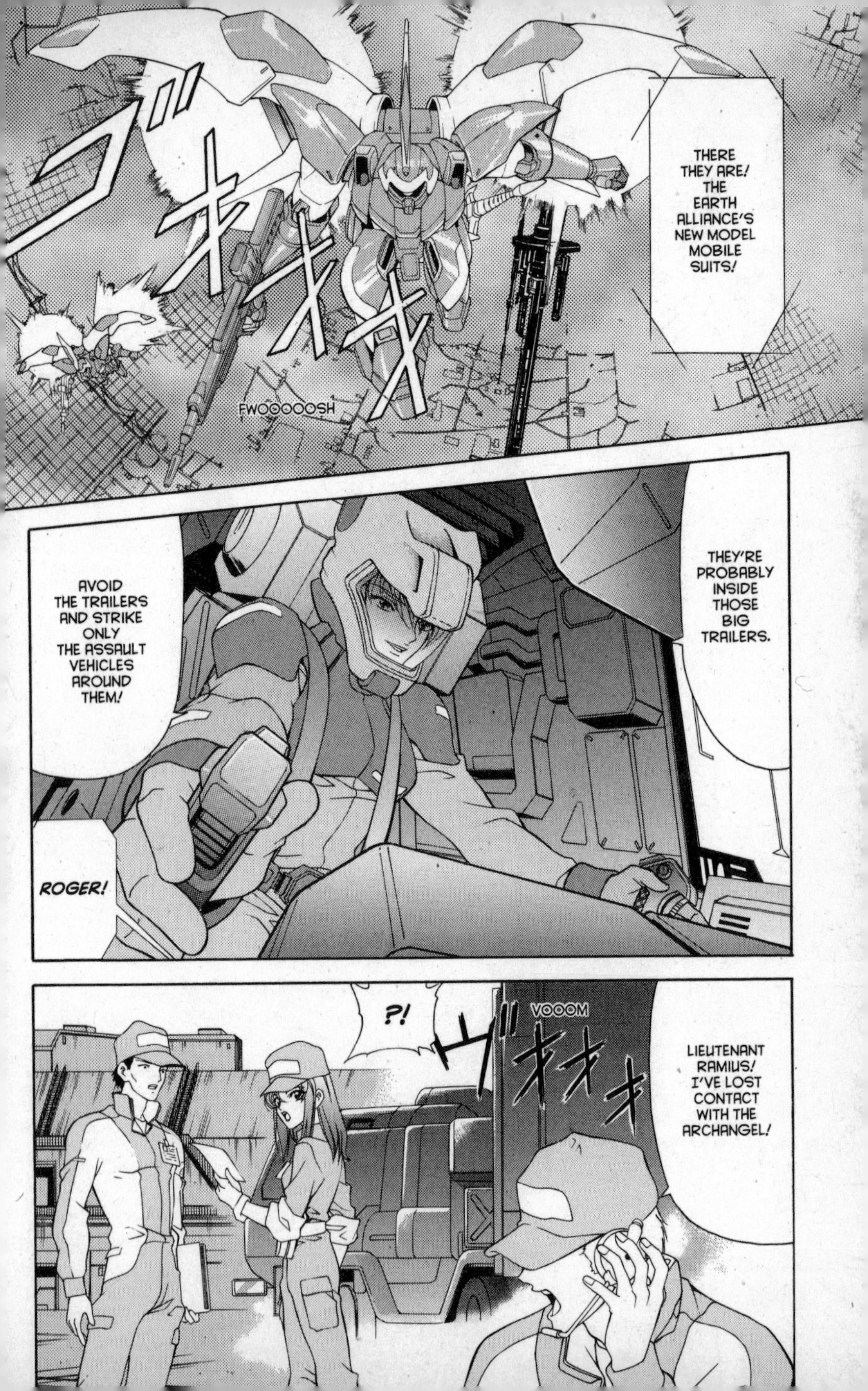
THERE THEY ARE! THE EARTH ALLIANCE'S NEW MODEL MOBILE SUITS!
FWOOOOOSH
THEY'RE PROBABLY INSIDE THOSE BIG TRAILERS.
AVOID THE TRAILERS AND STRIKE ONLY THE ASSAULT VEHICLES AROUND THEM!
ROGER!
VOOOM
LIEUTENANT RAMIUS! I'VE LOST CONTACT WITH THE ARCHANGEL!
?!

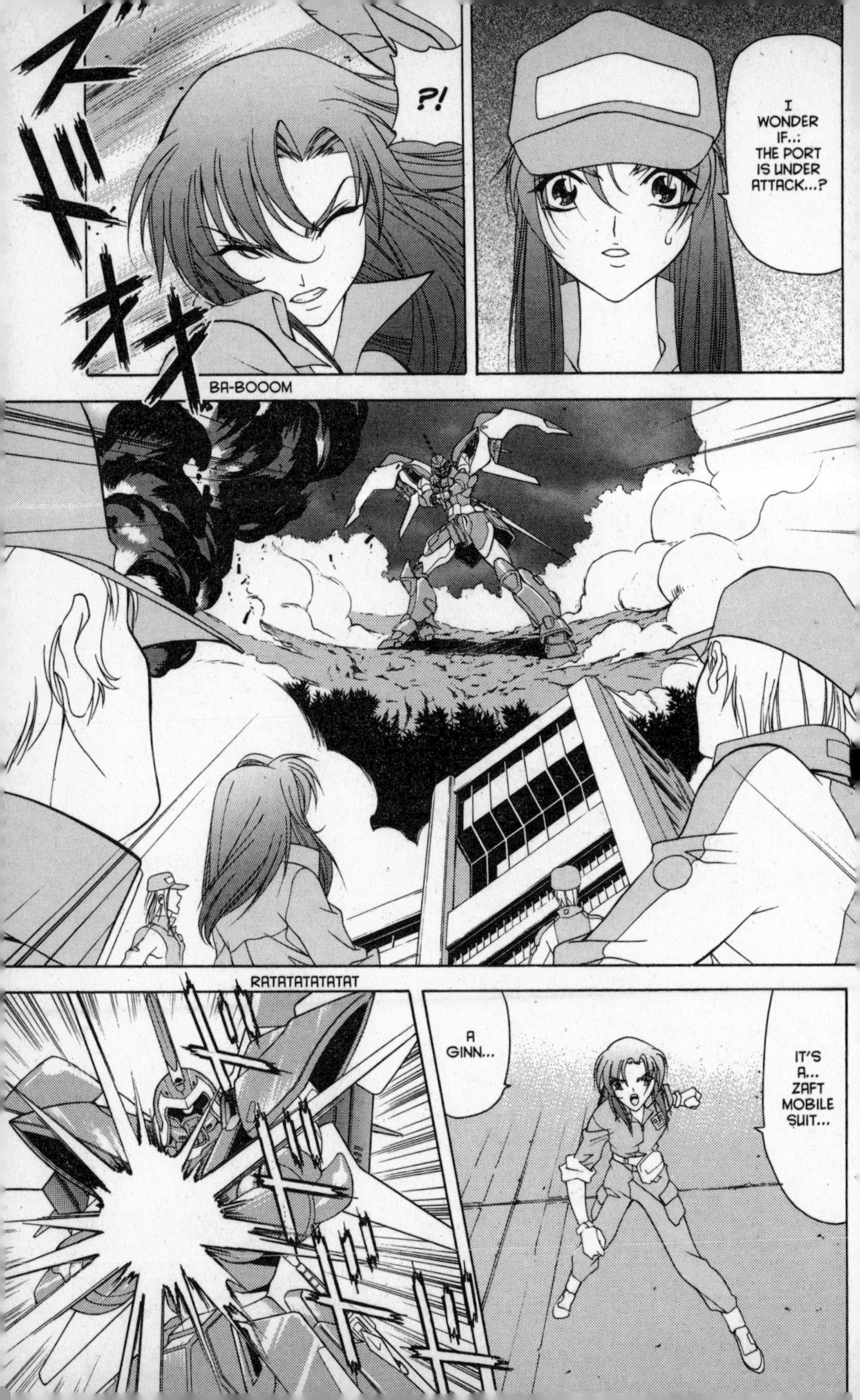
I WONDER IF...: THE PORT IS UNDER ATTACK...?
?!
BA-BOOOM
IT'S A... ZAFT MOBILE SUIT...
A GINN...
RATATATATATAT

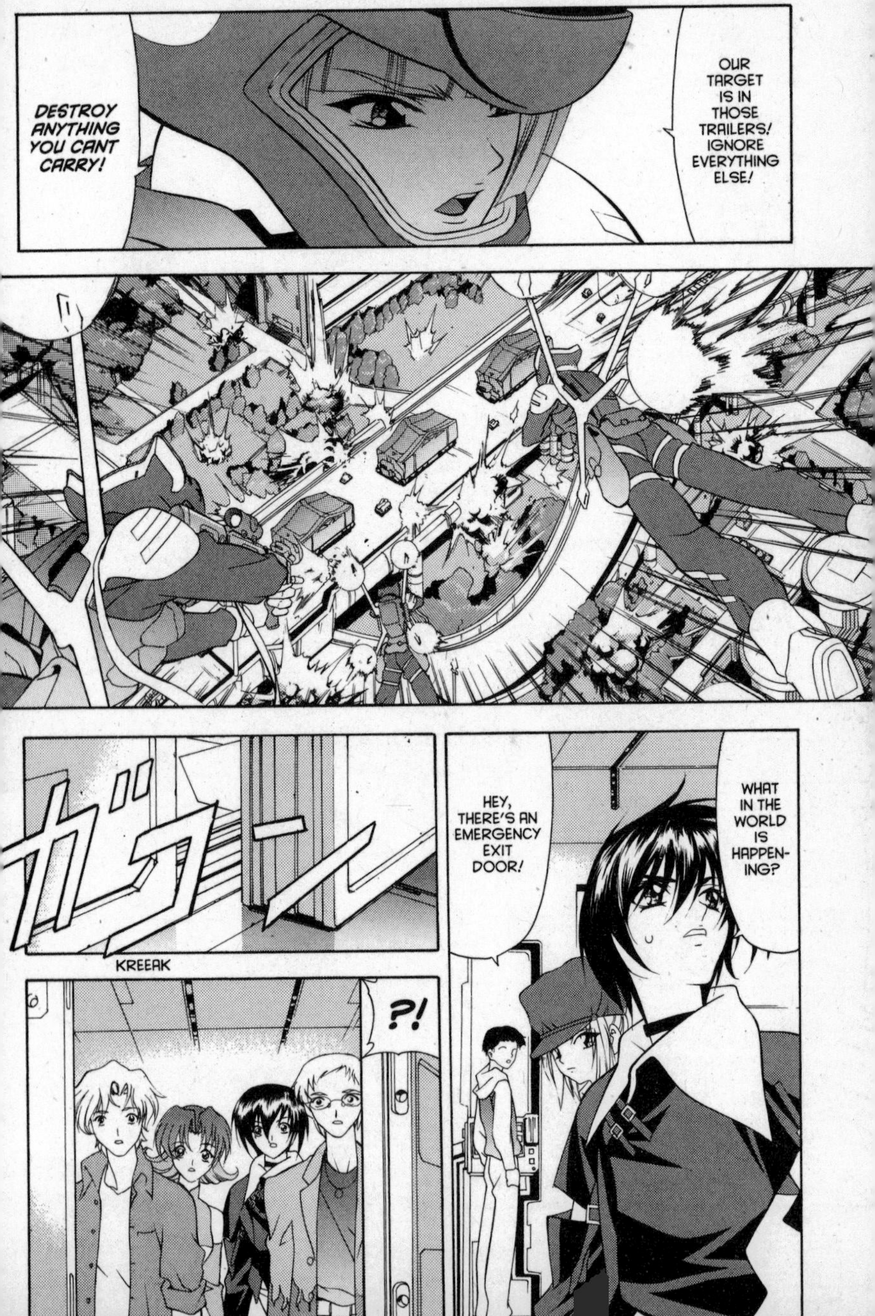
OUR TARGET IS IN THOSE TRAILERS! IGNORE EVERYTHING ELSE!
DESTROY ANYTHING YOU CANT CARRY!
!
WHAT IN THE WORLD IS HAPPEN-ING?
HEY, THERE'S AN EMERGENCY EXIT DOOR!
KREEAK
?!

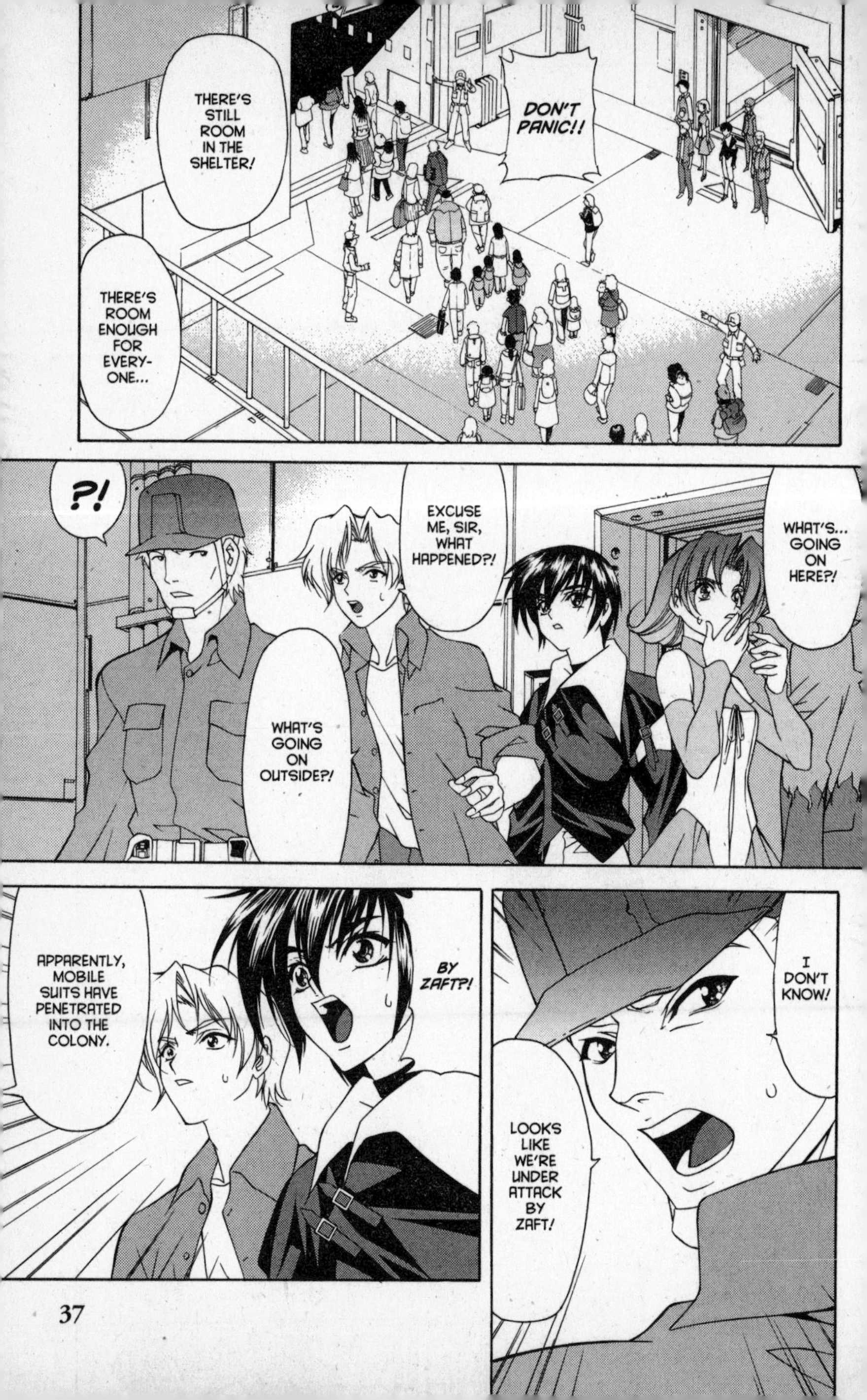
DON'T PANIC!!
THERE'S STILL ROOM IN THE SHELTER!
THERE'S ROOM ENOUGH FOR EVERY-ONE...
WHAT'S... GOING ON HERE?!
EXCUSE ME, SIR, WHAT HAPPENED?!
WHAT'S GOING ON OUTSIDE?!
?!
I DON'T KNOW!
LOOKS LIKE WE'RE UNDER ATTACK BY ZAFT!
BY ZAFT?!
APPARENTLY, MOBILE SUITS HAVE PENETRATED INTO THE COLONY.

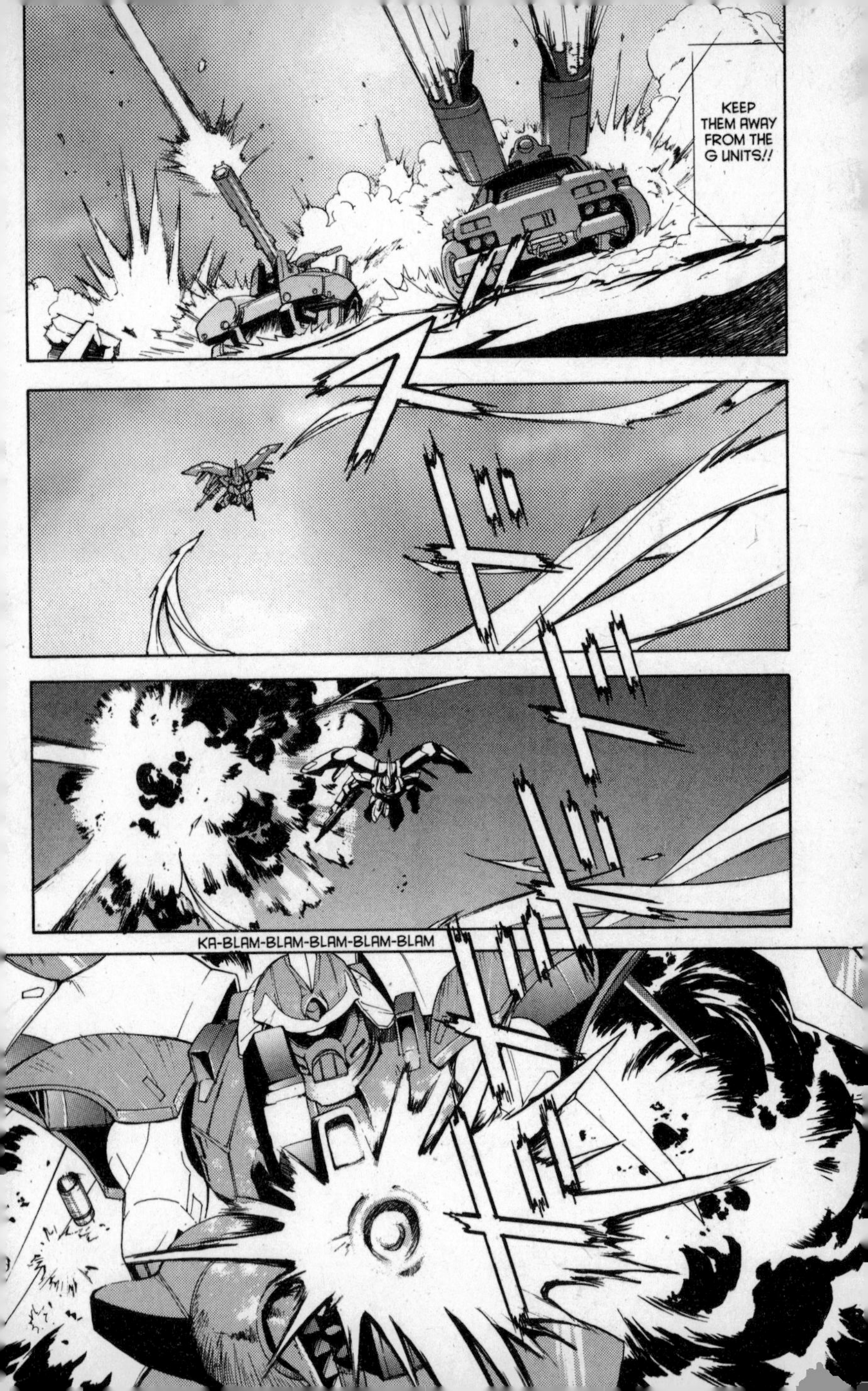
KEEP THEM AWAY FROM THE G UNITS!!
KA-BLAM-BLAM-BLAM-BLAM-BLAM

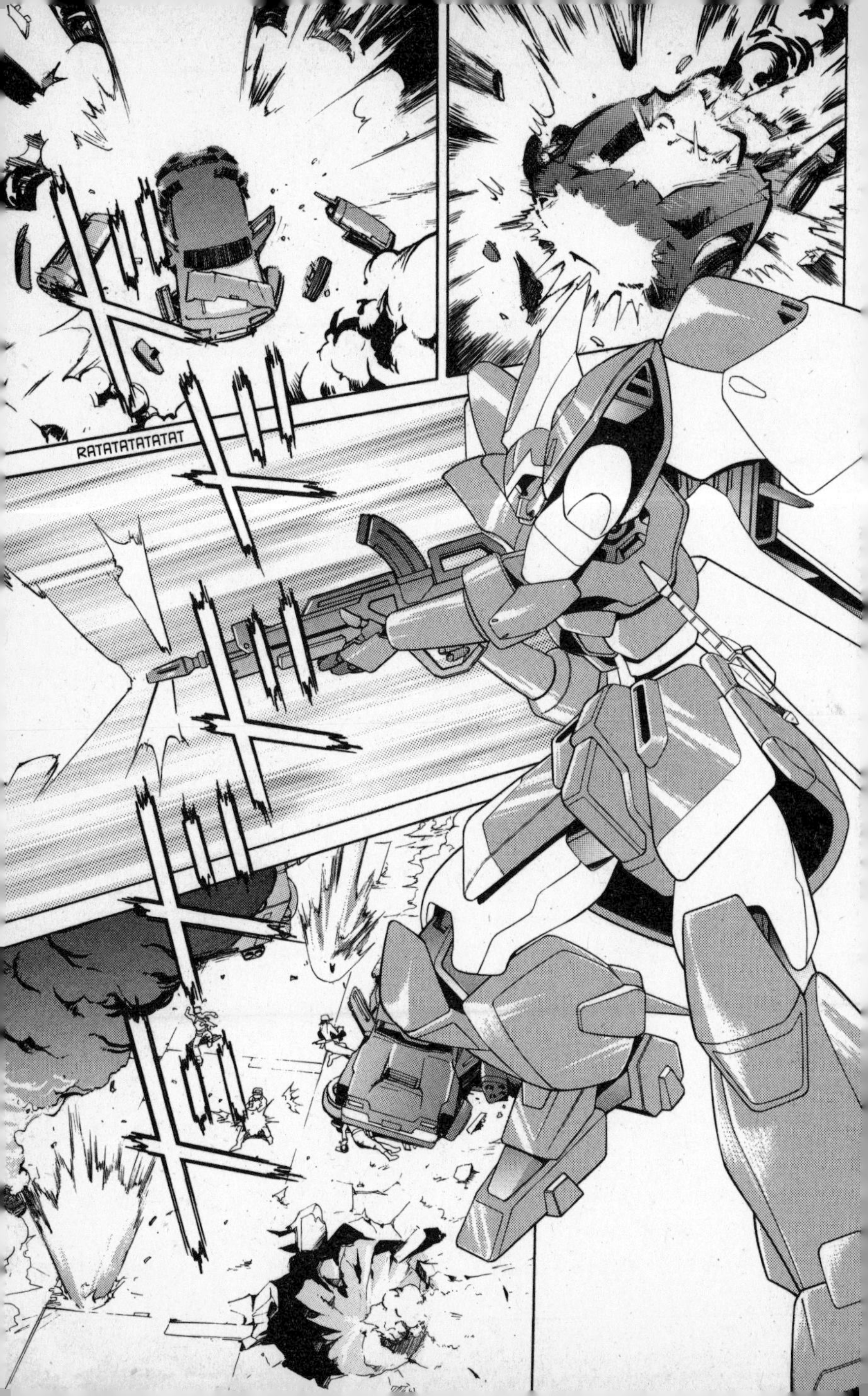
RATATATATATAT

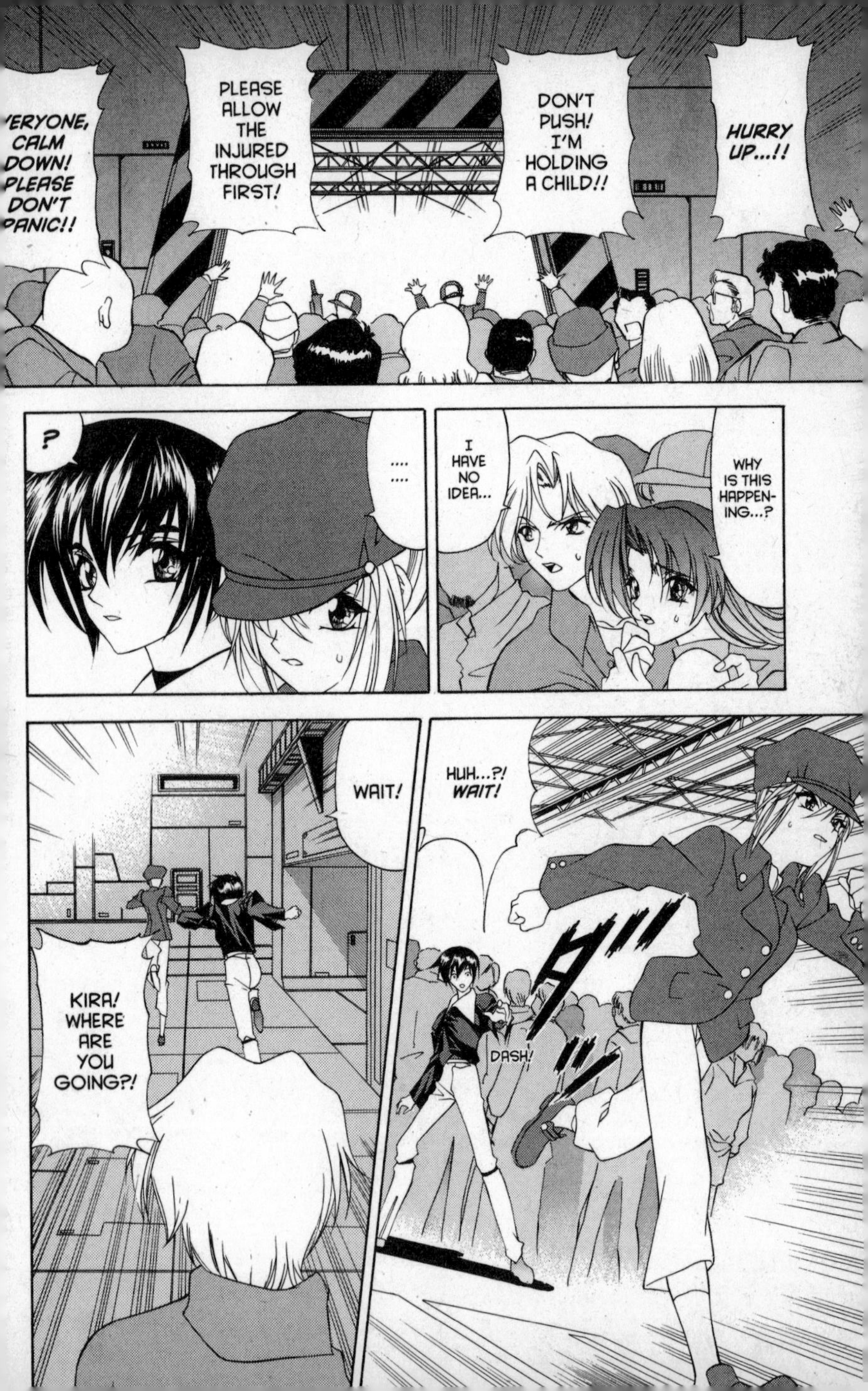
HURRY UP...!!
DON'T PUSH! I'M HOLDING A CHILD!!
PLEASE ALLOW THE INJURED THROUGH FIRST!
ERYONE, CALM DOWN! PLEASE DON'T PANIC!!
WHY IS THIS HAPPENING...?
I HAVE NO IDEA...
....
....
?
HUH...?! WAIT!
DASH!
WAIT!
KIRA! WHERE ARE YOU GOING?!

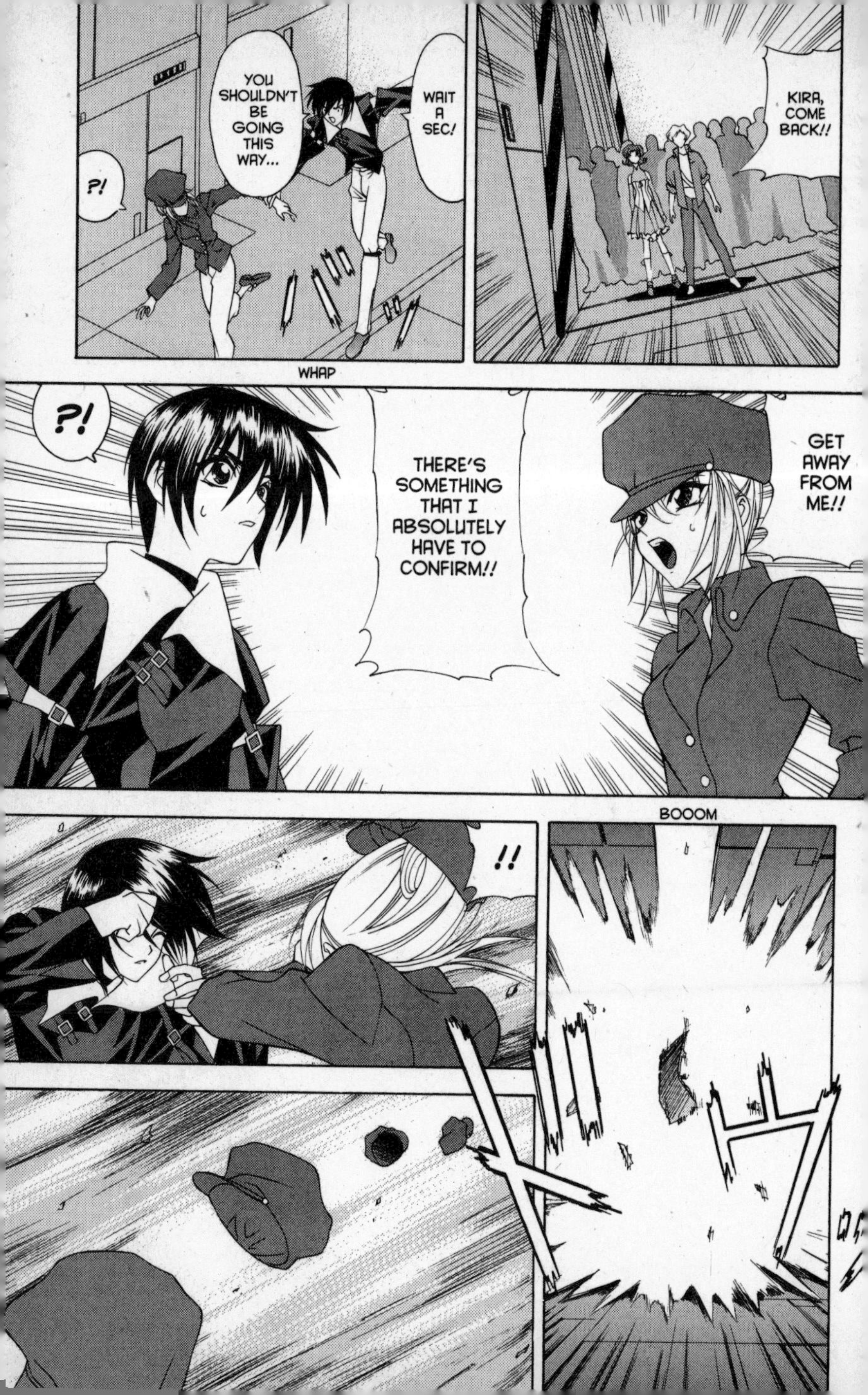
KIRA, COME BACK!!
WAIT A SEC!
YOU SHOULDN'T BE GOING THIS WAY...
?!
WHAP
GET AWAY FROM ME!!
THERE'S SOMETHING THAT I ABSOLUTELY HAVE TO CONFIRM!!
?!
BOOOM
!!

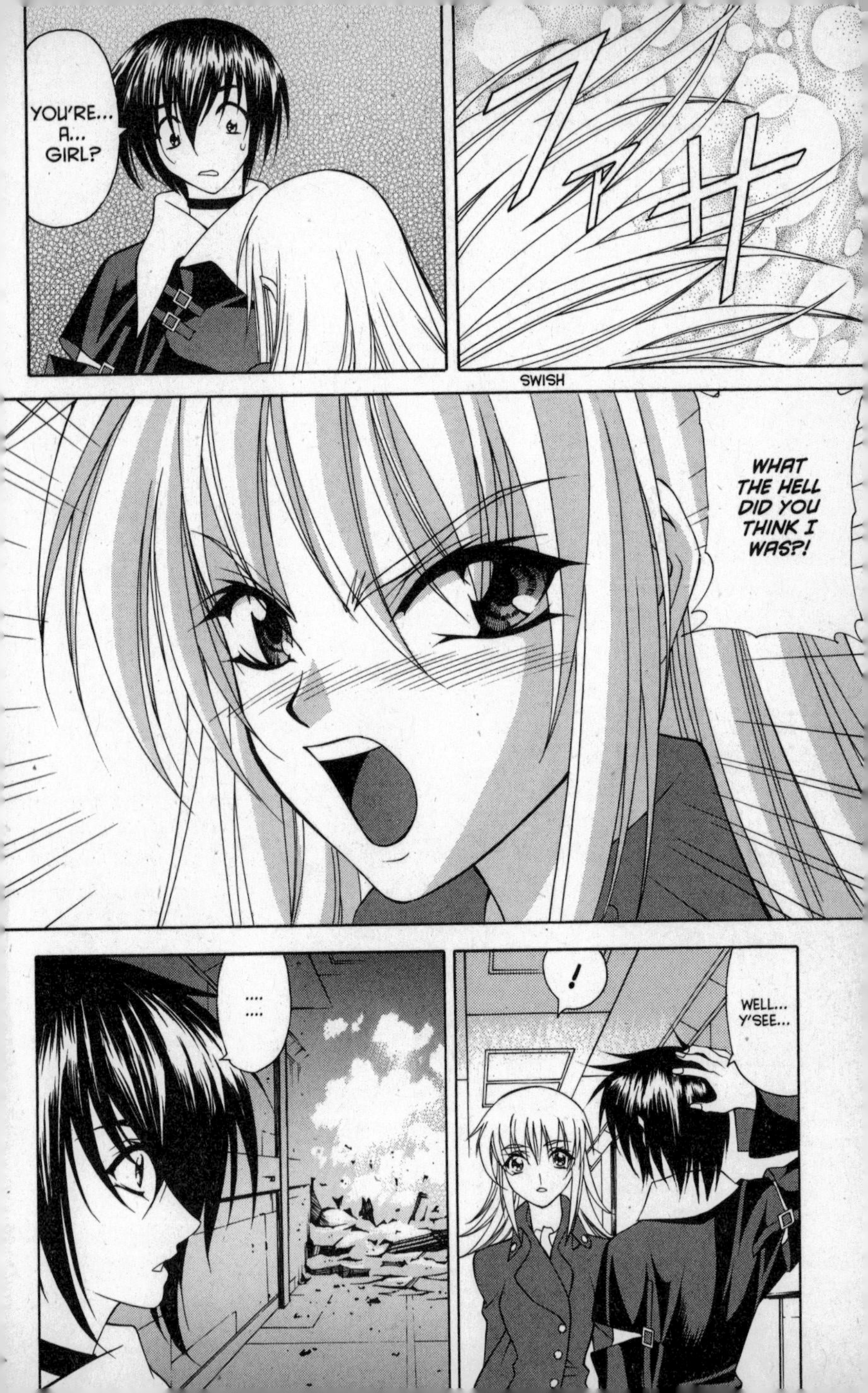
ファサ
SWISH
YOU'RE... A... GIRL?
WHAT THE HELL DID YOU THINK I WAS?!
WELL... Y'SEE...
!
....
....

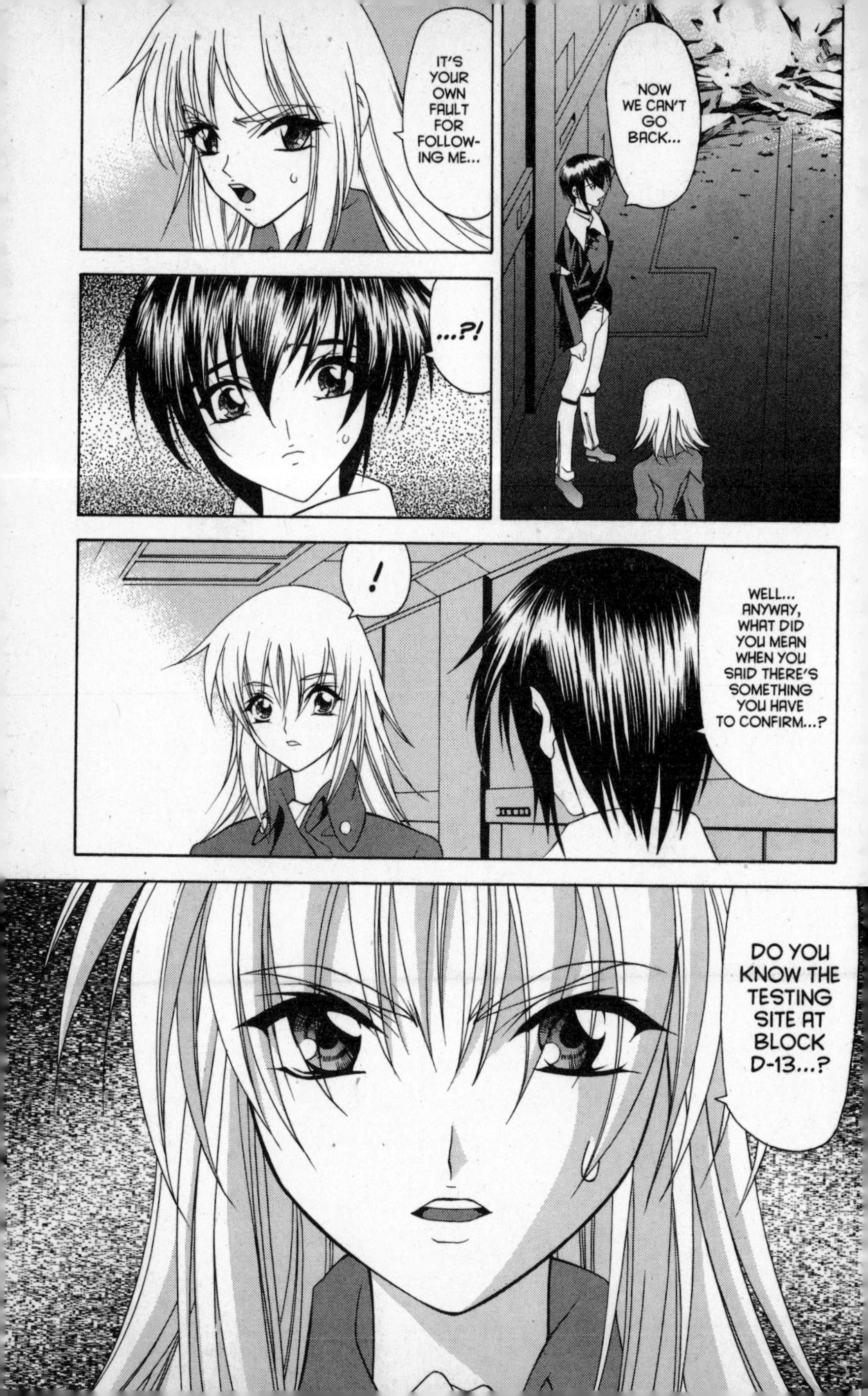
NOW WE CAN'T GO BACK...
IT'S YOUR OWN FAULT FOR FOLLOW-ING ME...
...?!
WELL... ANYWAY, WHAT DID YOU MEAN WHEN YOU SAID THERE'S SOMETHING YOU HAVE TO CONFIRM...?
!
DO YOU KNOW THE TESTING SITE AT BLOCK D-13...?

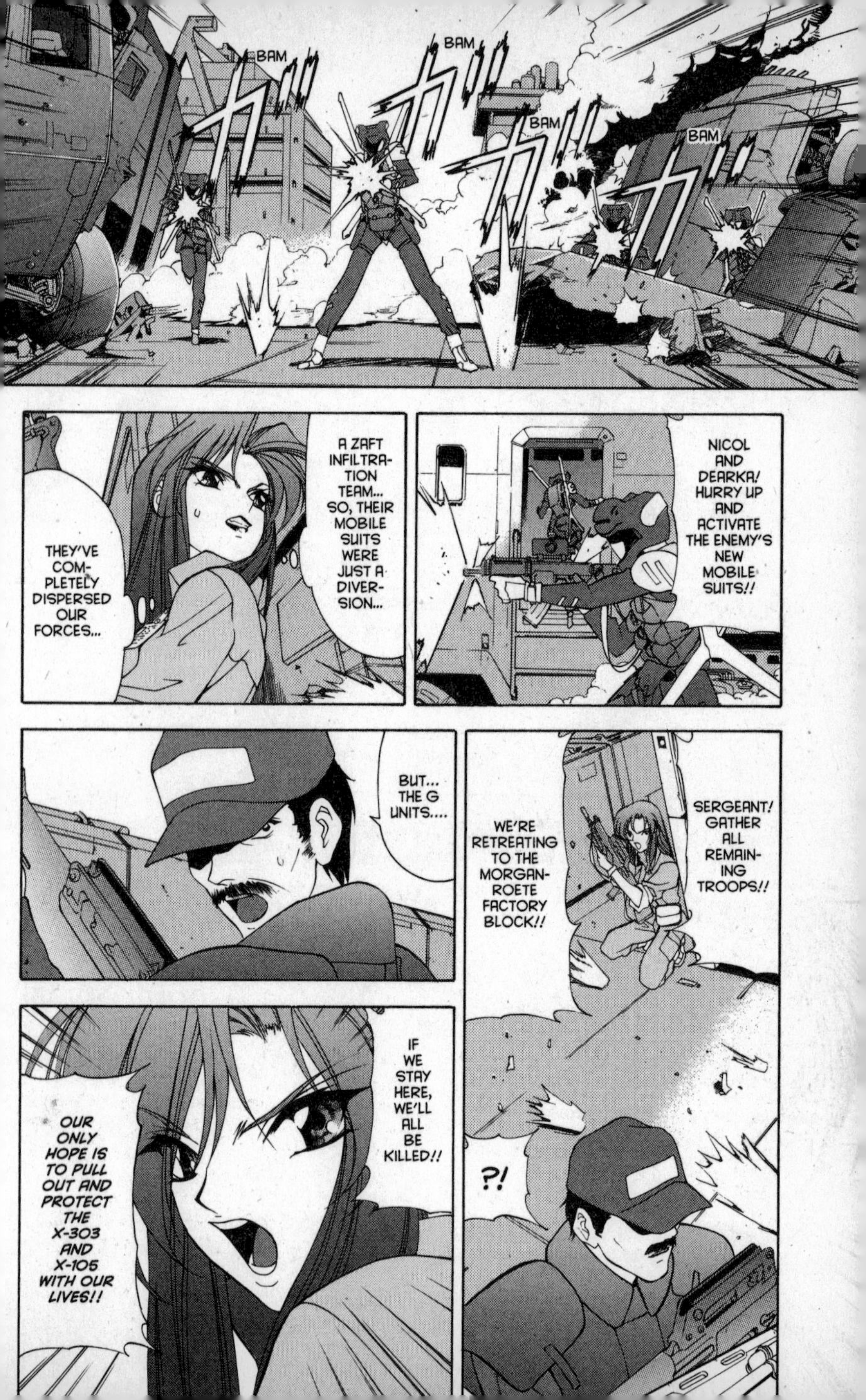
BAM
BAM
BAM
BAM
NICOL AND DEARKA! HURRY UP AND ACTIVATE THE ENEMY'S NEW MOBILE SUITS!!
A ZAFT INFILTRATION TEAM... SO, THEIR MOBILE SUITS WERE JUST A DIVERSION...
THEY'VE COMPLETELY DISPERSED OUR FORCES...
SERGEANT! GATHER ALL REMAINING TROOPS!!
WE'RE RETREATING TO THE MORGANROETE FACTORY BLOCK!!
BUT... THE G UNITS....
?!
IF WE STAY HERE, WE'LL ALL BE KILLED!!
OUR ONLY HOPE IS TO PULL OUT AND PROTECT THE X-303 AND X-105 WITH OUR LIVES!!

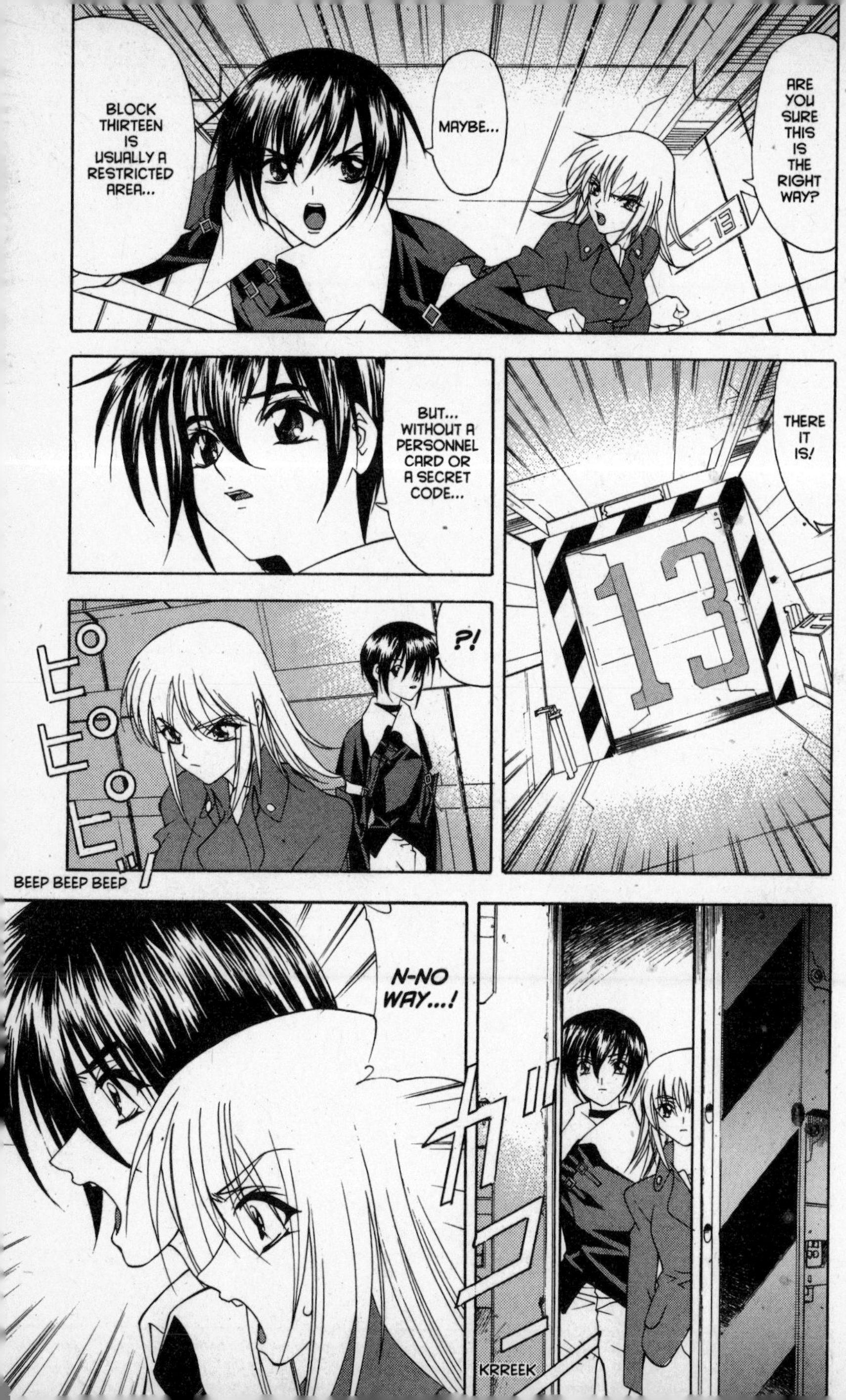
ARE YOU SURE THIS IS THE RIGHT WAY?
MAYBE...
BLOCK THIRTEEN IS USUALLY A RESTRICTED AREA...
THERE IT IS!
BUT... WITHOUT A PERSONNEL CARD OR A SECRET CODE...
?!
BEEP BEEP BEEP
KRREEK
N-NO WAY...!

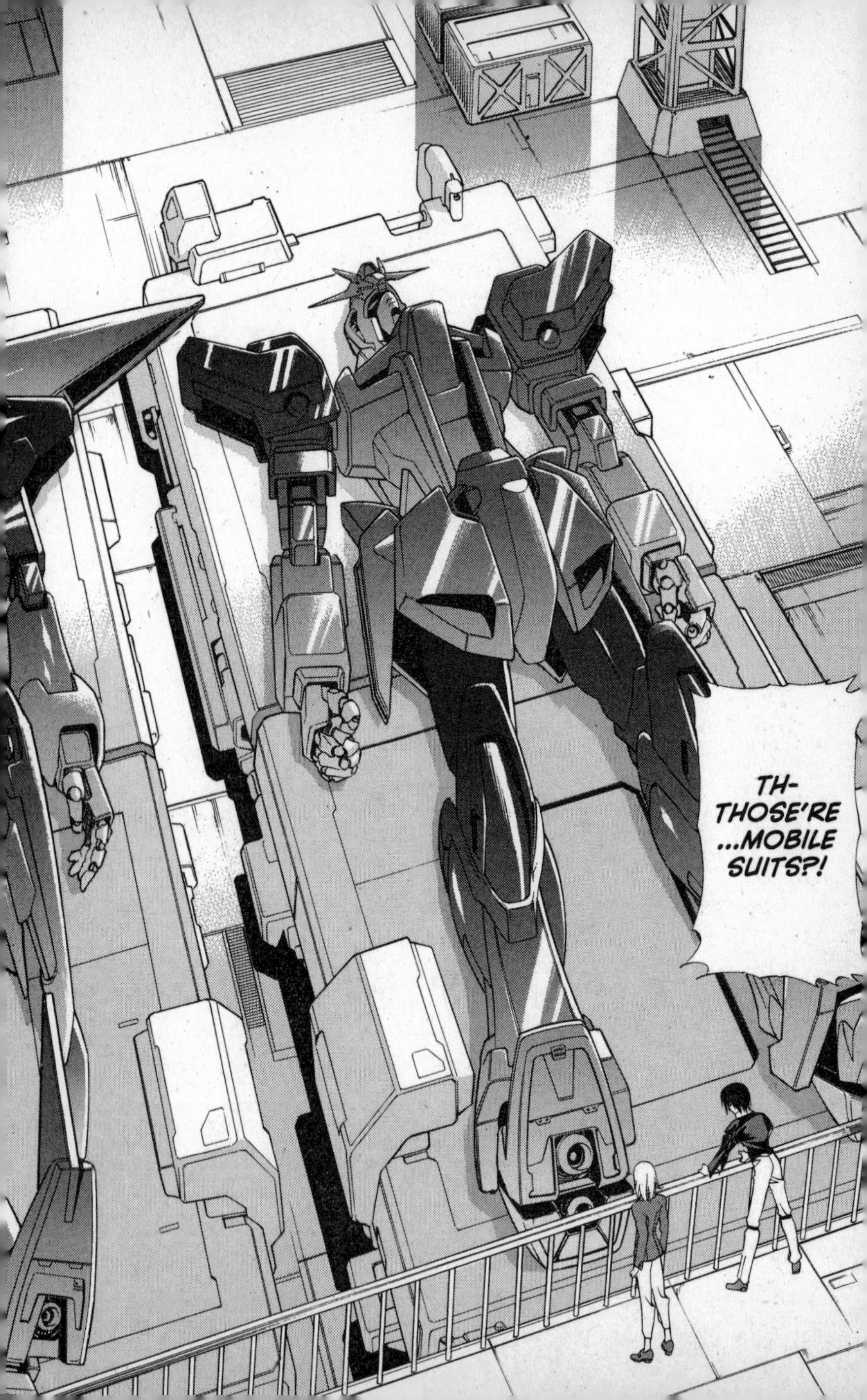
TH-
THOSE'RE
...MOBILE
SUITS?!

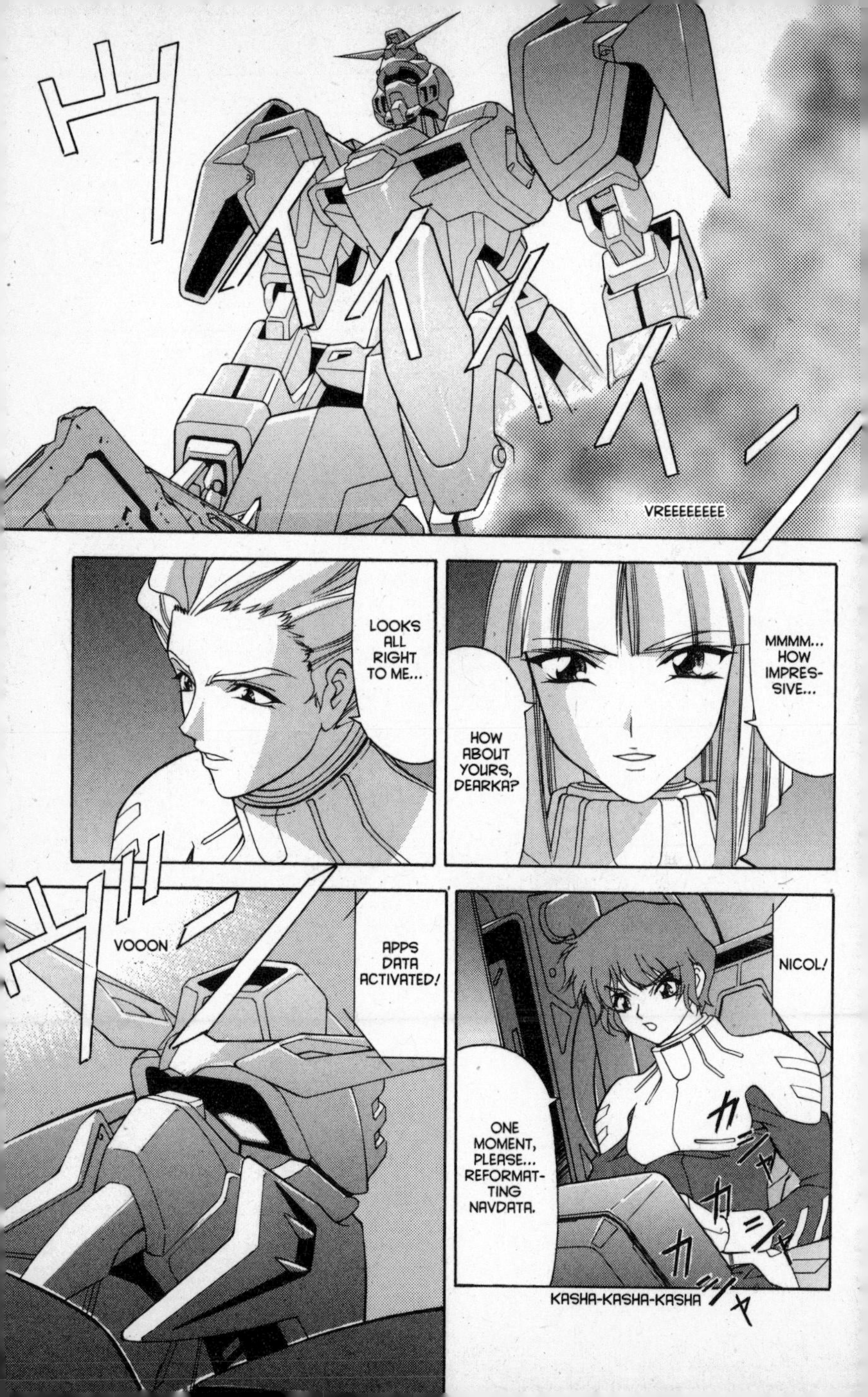
VREEEEEEEE
MMMM... HOW IMPRESSIVE...
HOW ABOUT YOURS, DEARKA?
LOOKS ALL RIGHT TO ME...
NICOL!
ONE MOMENT, PLEASE... REFORMATTING NAVDATA.
KASHA-KASHA-KASHA
APPS DATA ACTIVATED!
VOOON

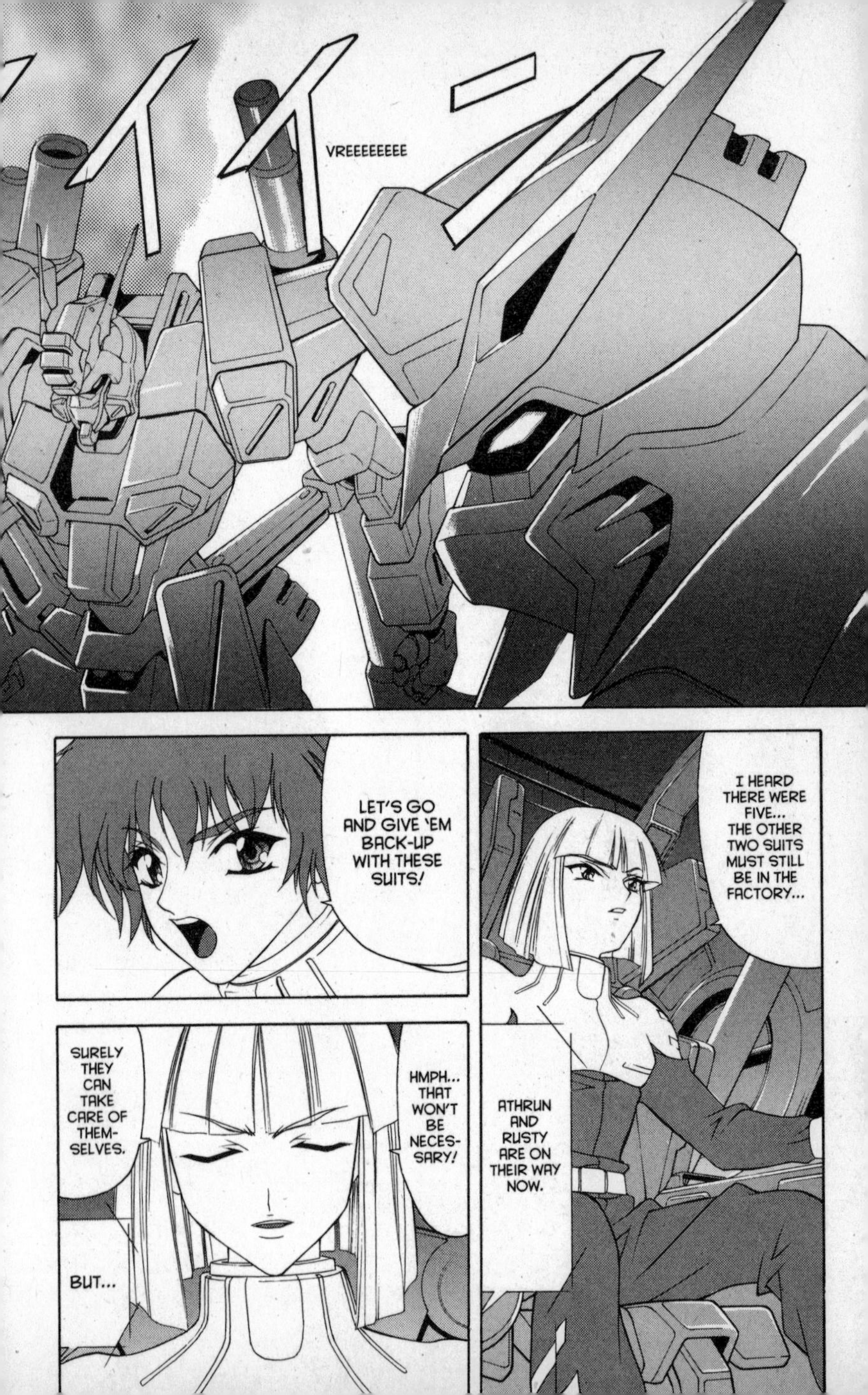
VREEEEEEEE
I HEARD THERE WERE FIVE... THE OTHER TWO SUITS MUST STILL BE IN THE FACTORY...
ATHRUN AND RUSTY ARE ON THEIR WAY NOW.
LET'S GO AND GIVE 'EM BACK-UP WITH THESE SUITS!
HMPH... THAT WON'T BE NECES-SARY!
SURELY THEY CAN TAKE CARE OF THEM-SELVES.
BUT...

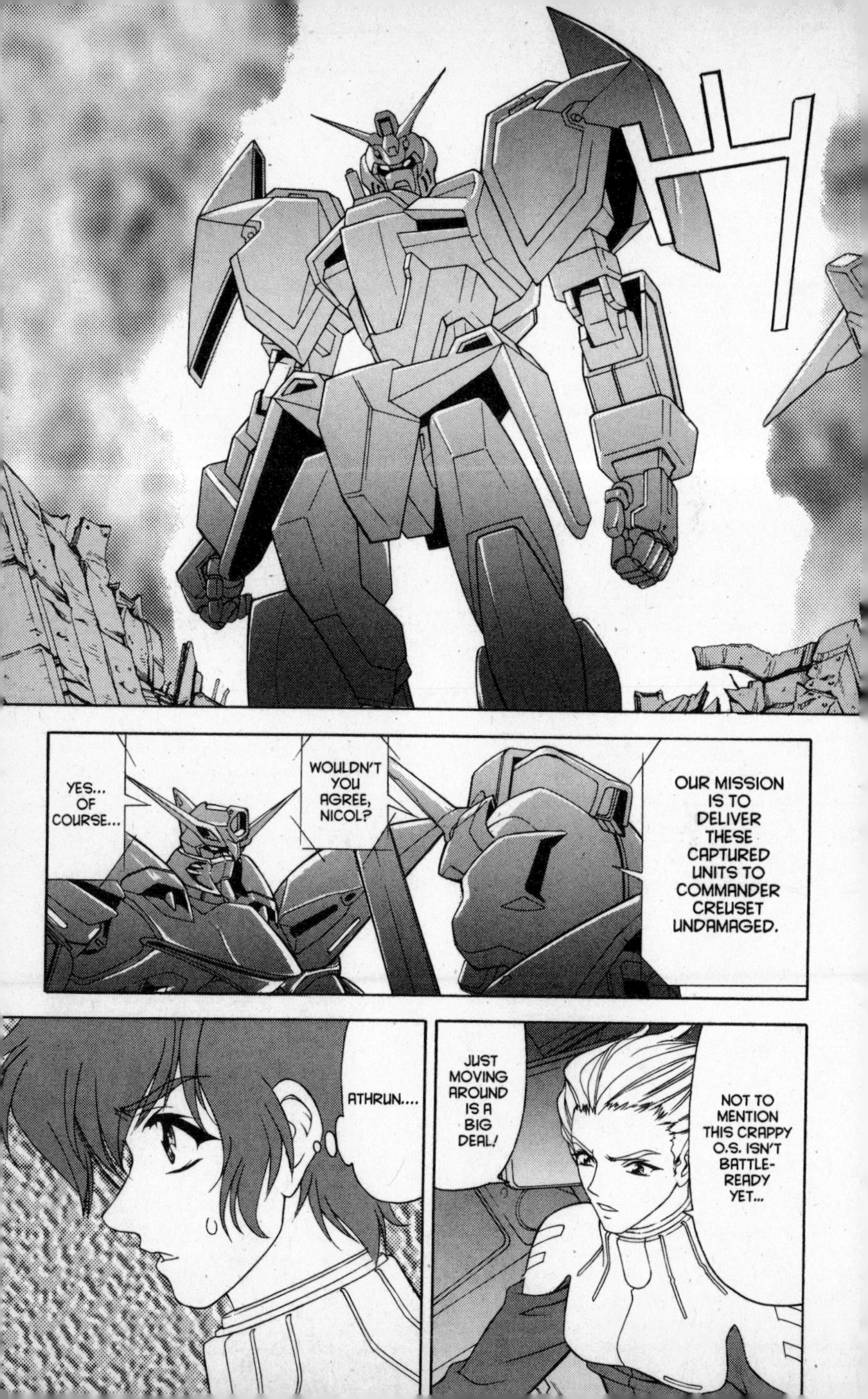
OUR MISSION IS TO DELIVER THESE CAPTURED UNITS TO COMMANDER CREUSET UNDAMAGED.
WOULDN'T YOU AGREE, NICOL?
YES... OF COURSE...
NOT TO MENTION THIS CRAPPY O.S. ISN'T BATTLE-READY YET...
JUST MOVING AROUND IS A BIG DEAL!
ATHRUN....

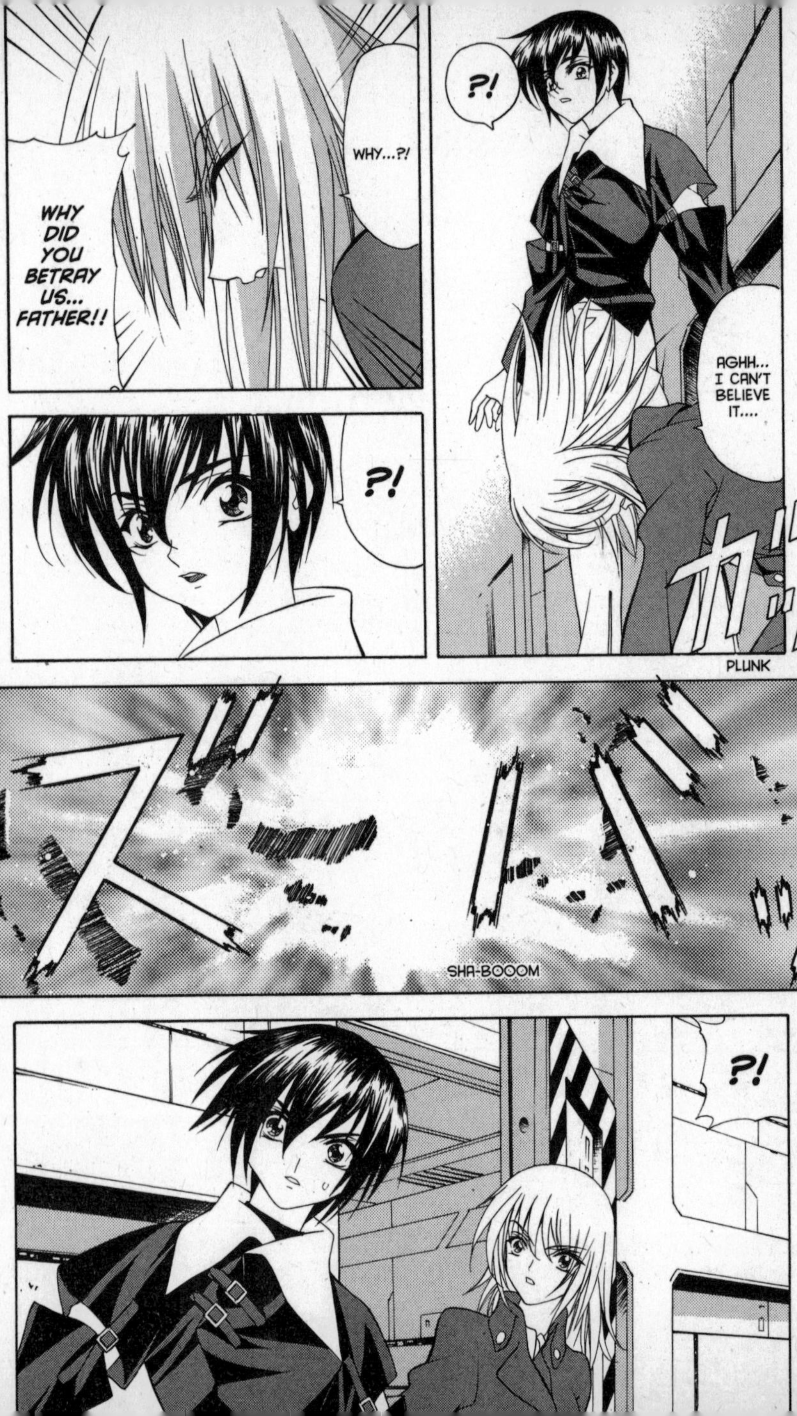
?!
AGHH... I CAN'T BELIEVE IT....
PLUNK
WHY...?!
WHY DID YOU BETRAY US... FATHER!!
?!
SHA-BOOOM
?!

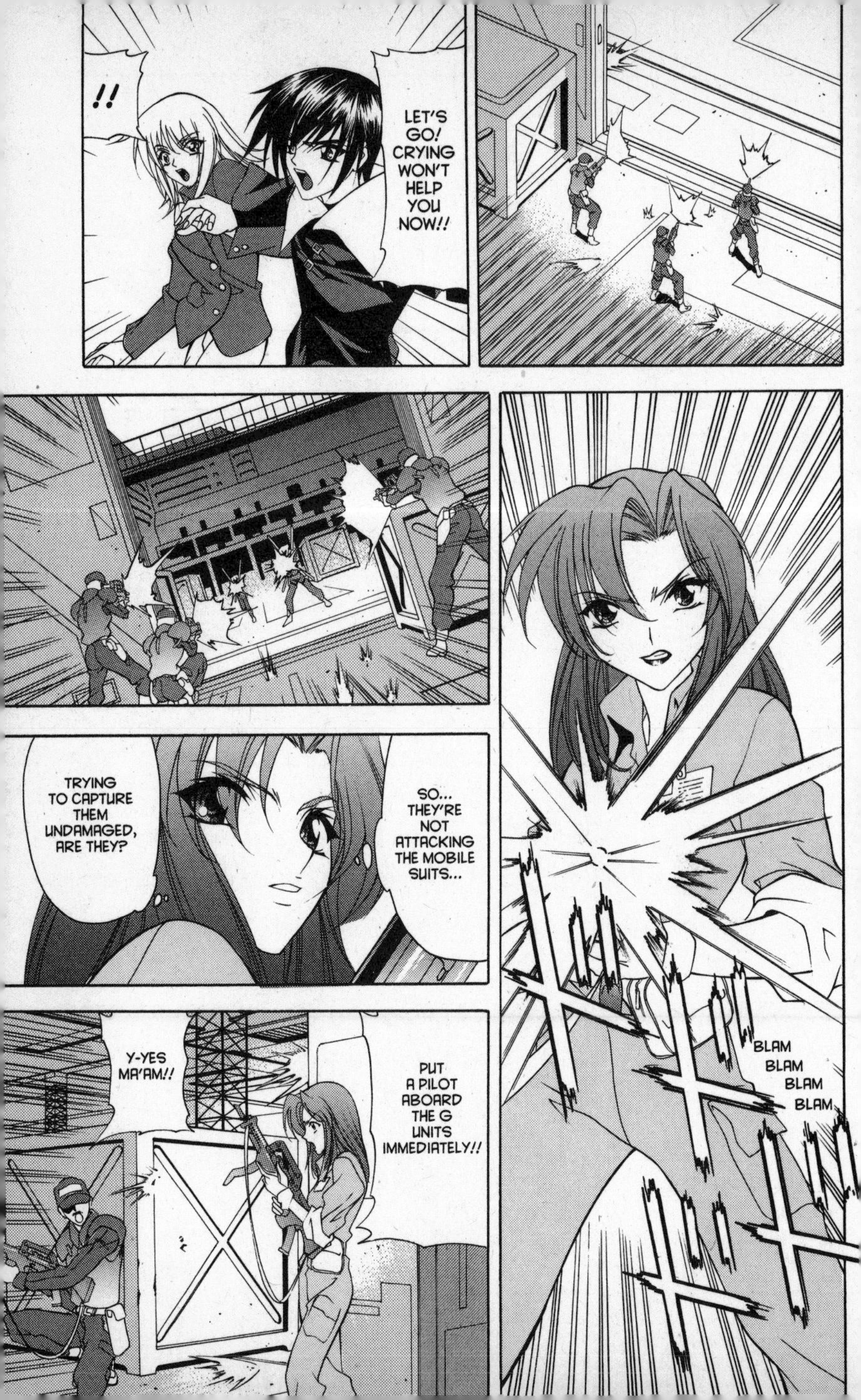
LET'S GO! CRYING WON'T HELP YOU NOW!!
!!
BLAM
BLAM
BLAM
BLAM
SO... THEY'RE NOT ATTACKING THE MOBILE SUITS...
TRYING TO CAPTURE THEM UNDAMAGED, ARE THEY?
PUT A PILOT ABOARD THE G UNITS IMMEDIATELY!!
Y-YES MA'AM!!

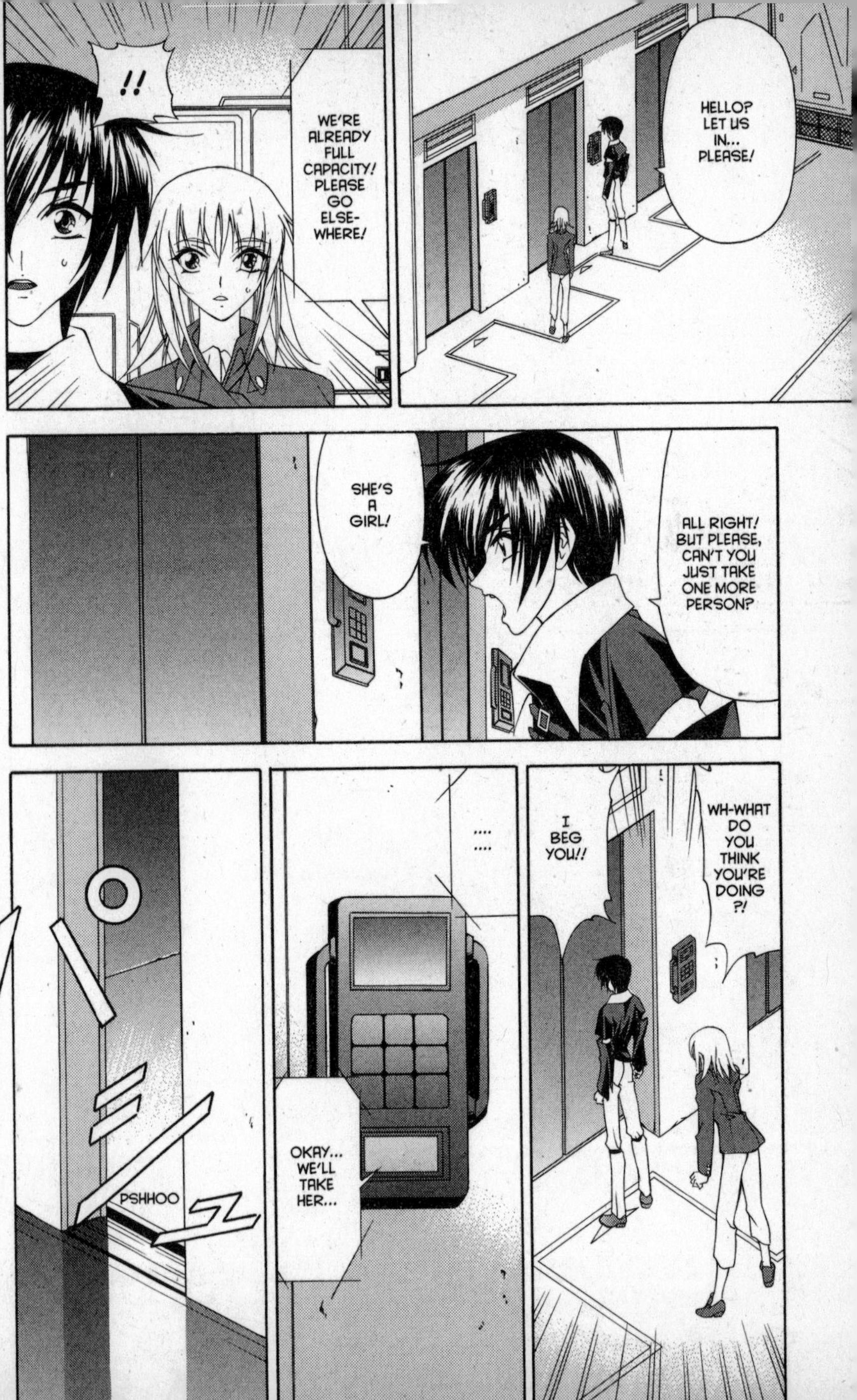
HELLO? LET US IN... PLEASE!
!!
WE'RE ALREADY FULL CAPACITY! PLEASE GO ELSE-WHERE!
ALL RIGHT! BUT PLEASE, CAN'T YOU JUST TAKE ONE MORE PERSON?
SHE'S A GIRL!
WH-WHAT DO YOU THINK YOU'RE DOING?!
I BEG YOU!!
....
....
OKAY... WE'LL TAKE HER...
PSHHOO

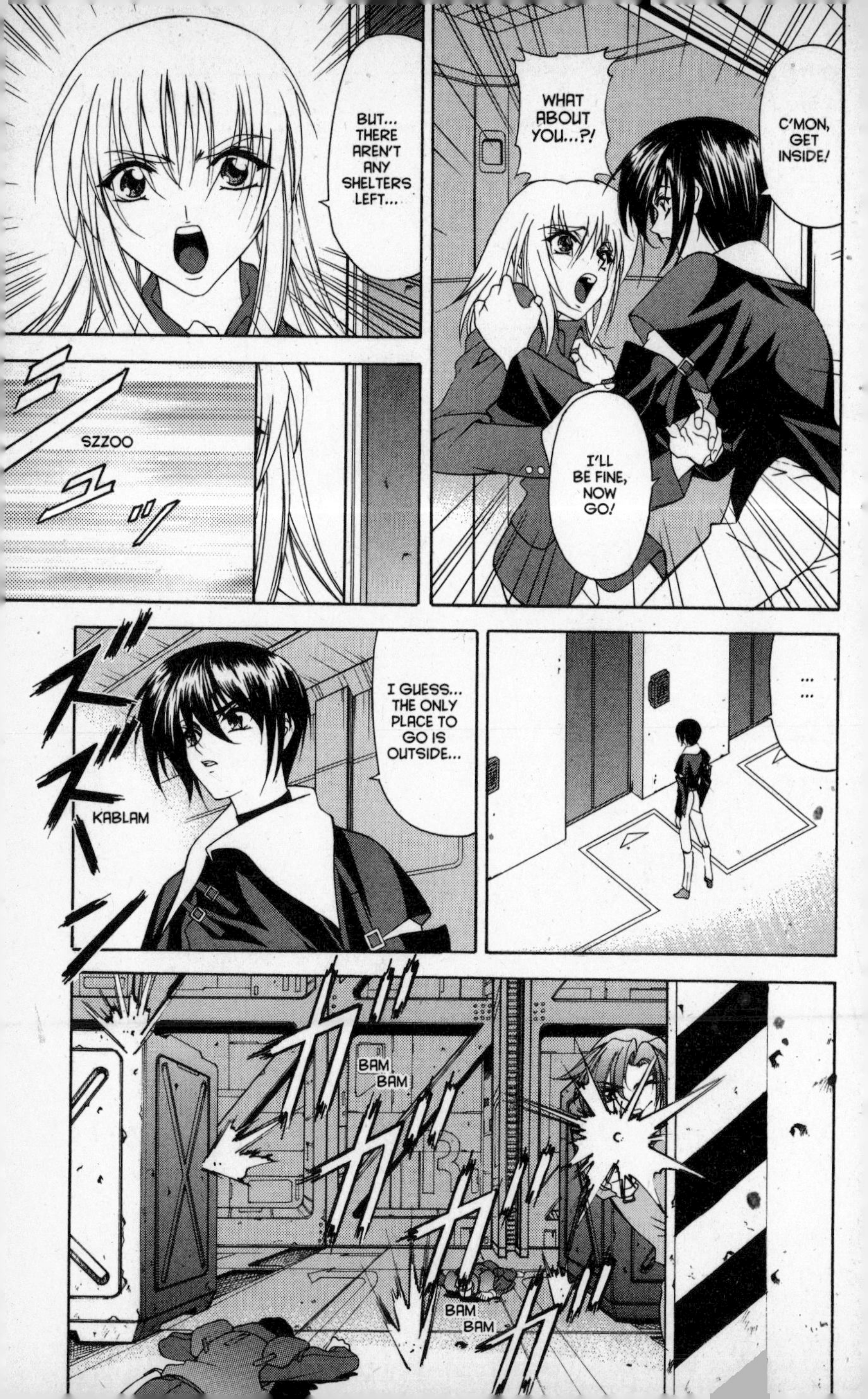
C'MON, GET INSIDE!
WHAT ABOUT YOU...?!
I'LL BE FINE, NOW GO!
BUT... THERE AREN'T ANY SHELTERS LEFT...
SZZOO
...
...
I GUESS... THE ONLY PLACE TO GO IS OUTSIDE...
KABLAM
BAM BAM
BAM BAM

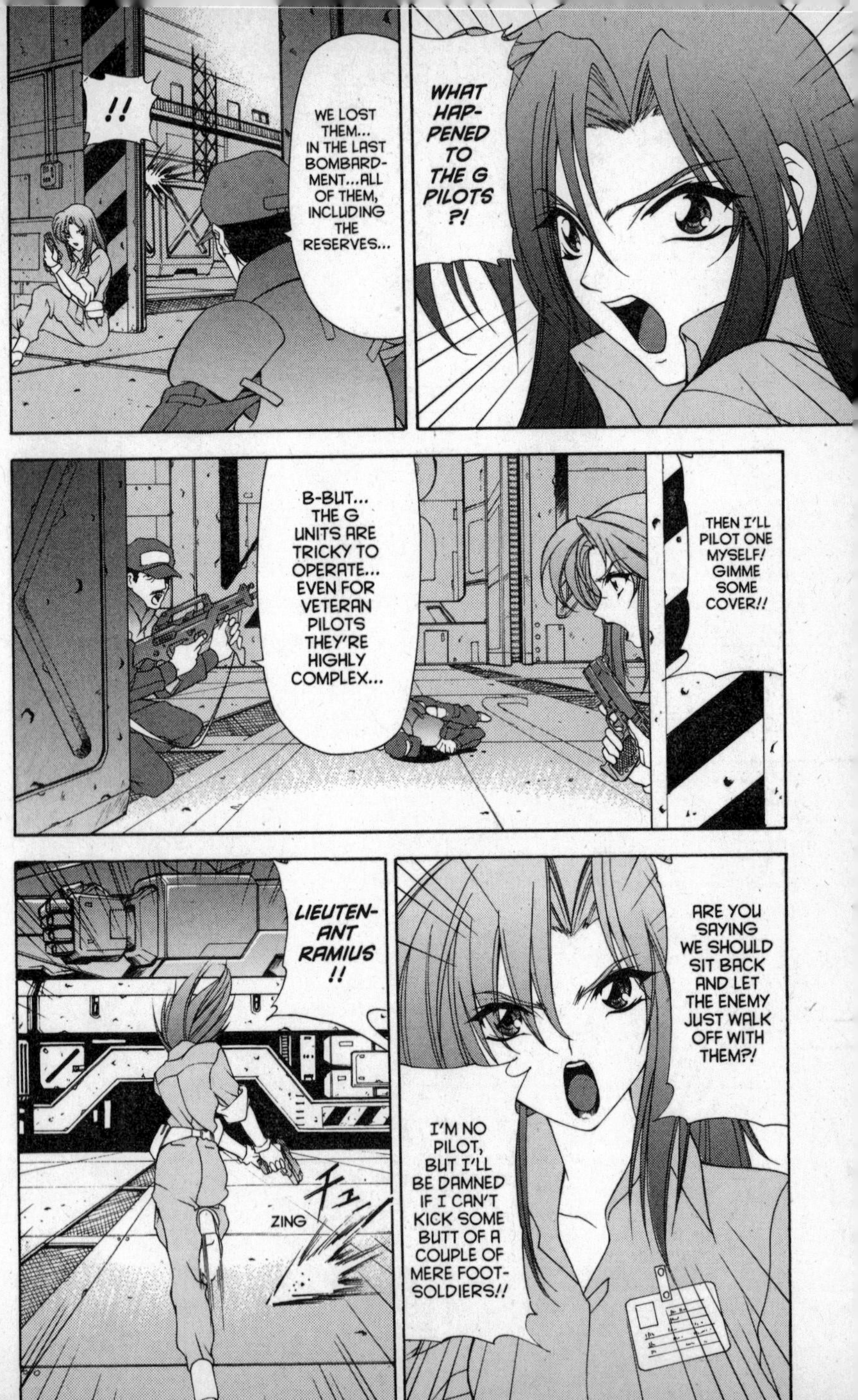
WHAT HAPPENED TO THE G PILOTS?!
WE LOST THEM... IN THE LAST BOMBARDMENT...ALL OF THEM, INCLUDING THE RESERVES...
!!
THEN I'LL PILOT ONE MYSELF! GIMME SOME COVER!!
B-BUT... THE G UNITS ARE TRICKY TO OPERATE... EVEN FOR VETERAN PILOTS THEY'RE HIGHLY COMPLEX...
ARE YOU SAYING WE SHOULD SIT BACK AND LET THE ENEMY JUST WALK OFF WITH THEM?!
I'M NO PILOT, BUT I'LL BE DAMNED IF I CAN'T KICK SOME BUTT OF A COUPLE OF MERE FOOT-SOLDIERS!!
LIEUTENANT RAMIUS!!
チュ
ZING

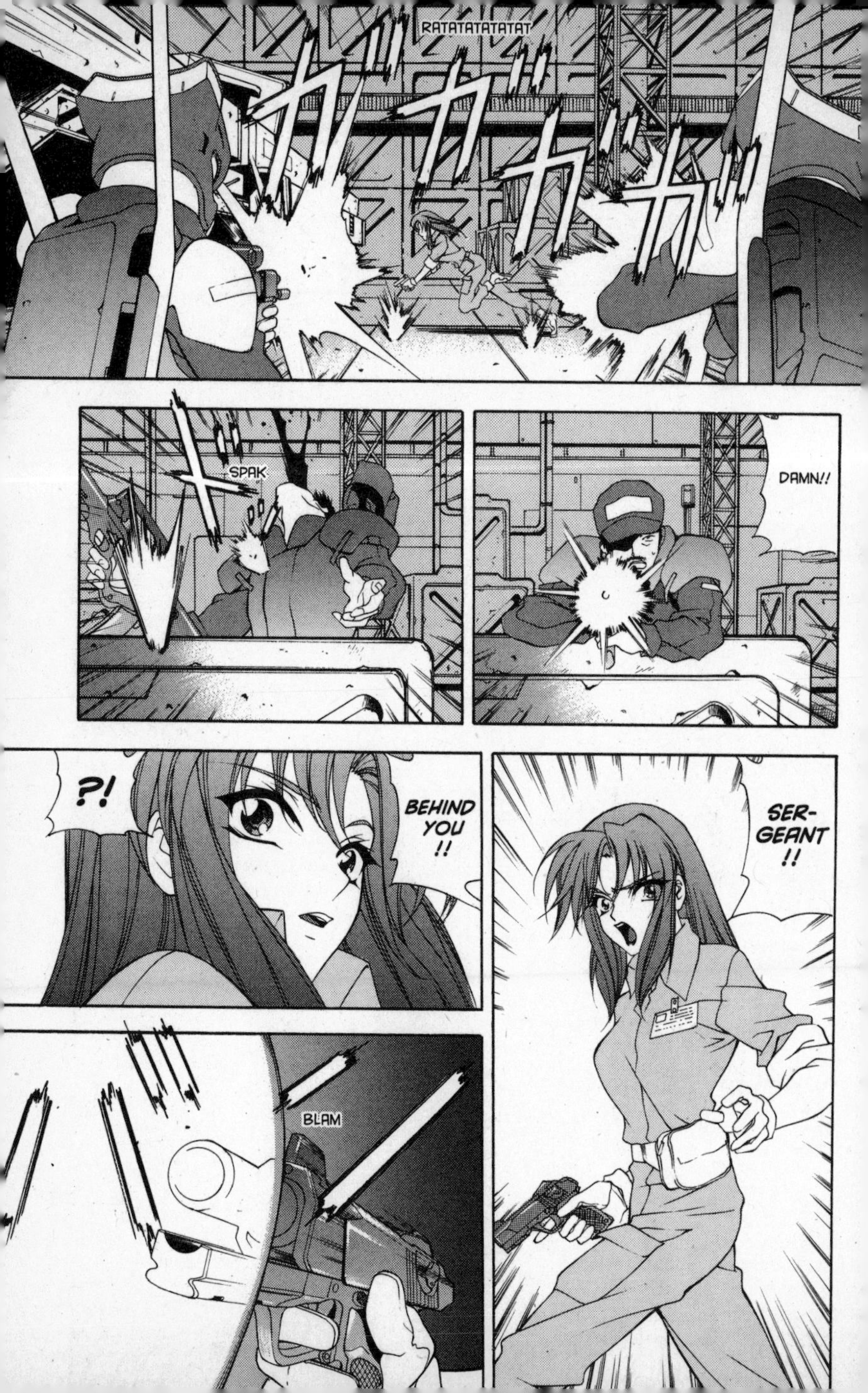
RATATATATATAT
DAMN!!
SPAK
SER-GEANT!!
BEHIND YOU!!
?!
BLAM

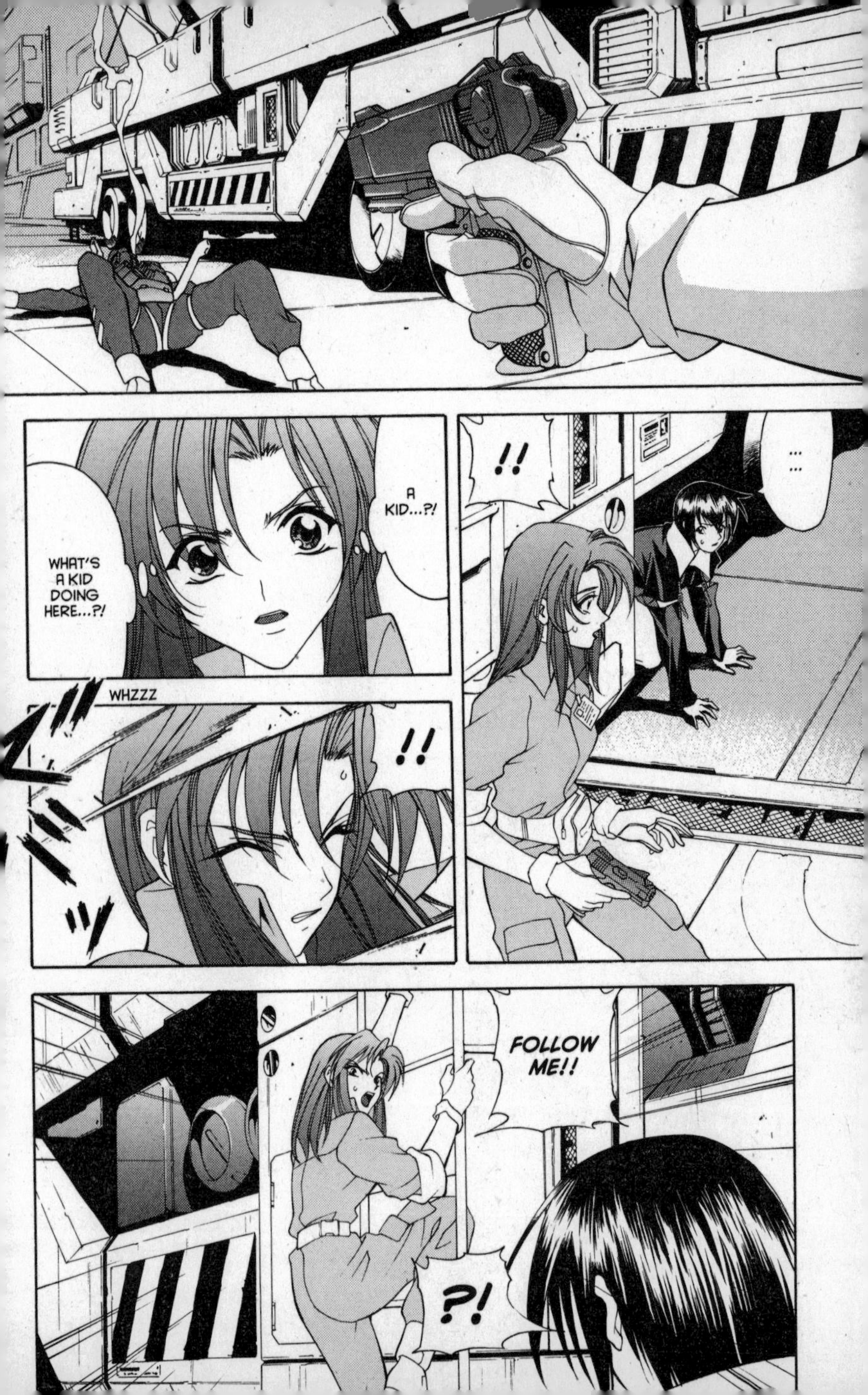

......
!!
A KID...?!
WHAT'S A KID DOING HERE...?!
WHZZZ
!!
FOLLOW ME!!
?!

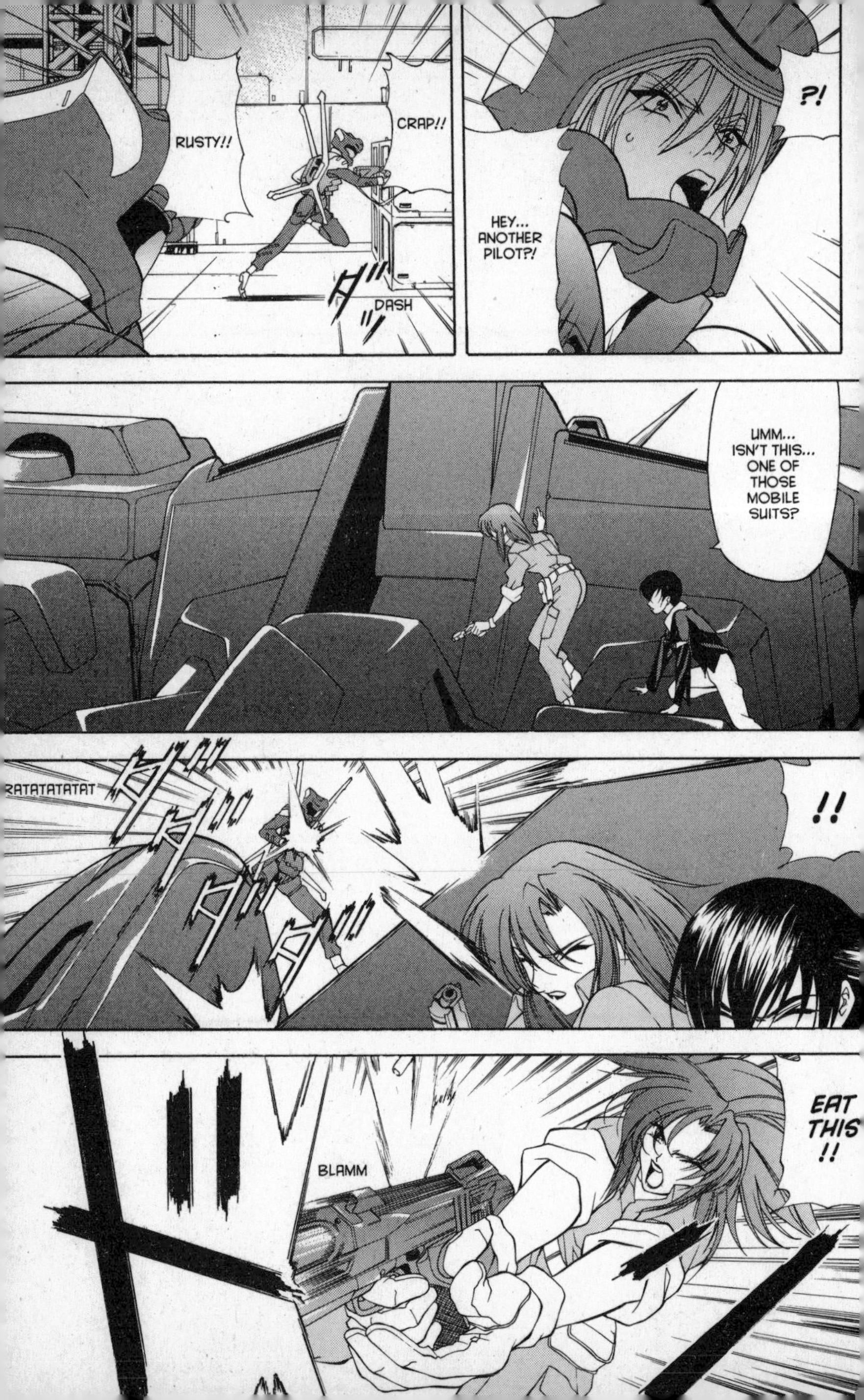
?!
HEY... ANOTHER PILOT?!
CRAP!!
RUSTY!!
DASH
UMM... ISN'T THIS... ONE OF THOSE MOBILE SUITS?
!!
RATATATATAT
EAT THIS !!
BLAMM

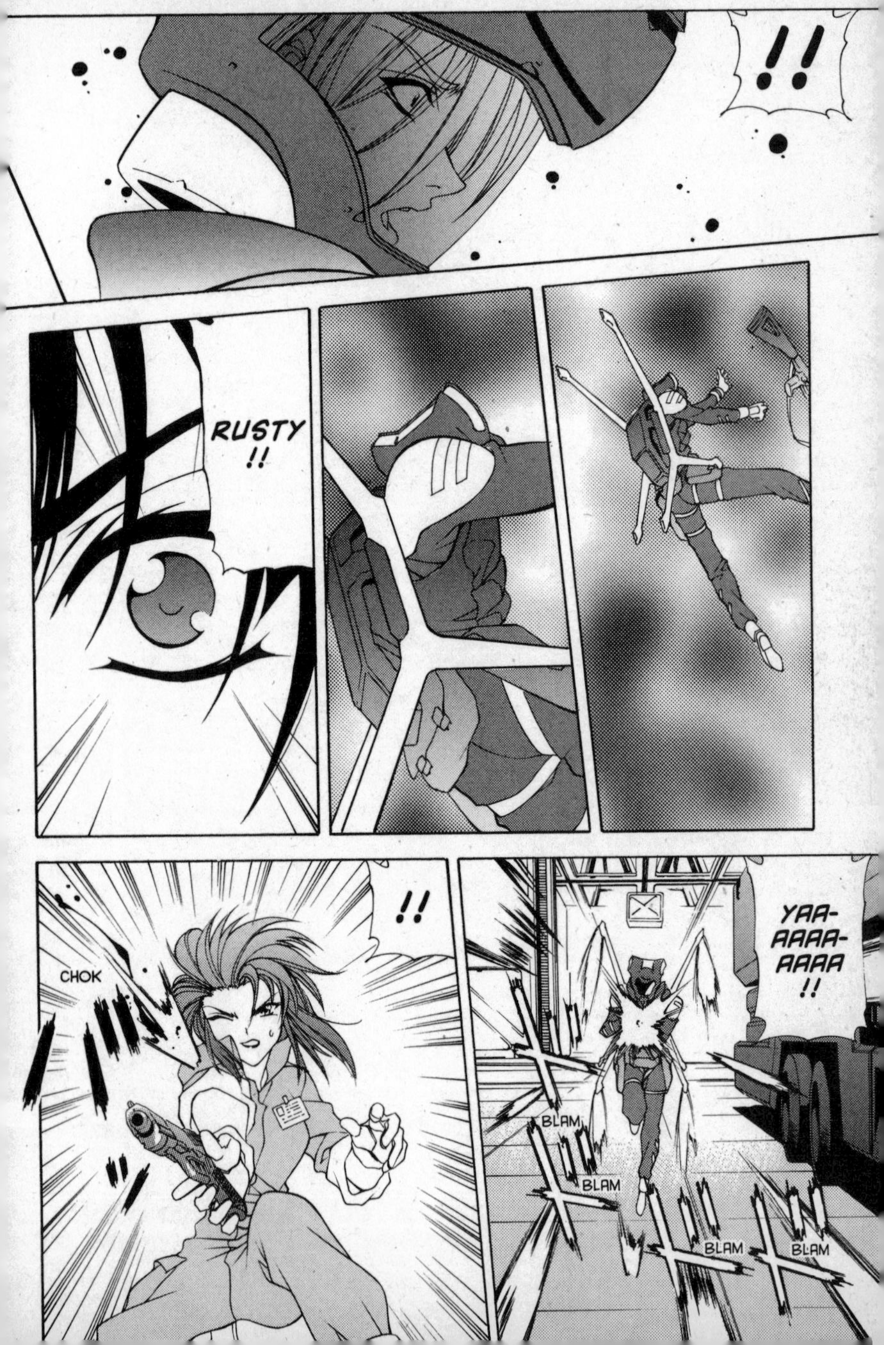
!!
RUSTY !!
YAA-AAAA-AAAA !!
BLAM
BLAM
BLAM
BLAM
!!
CHOK

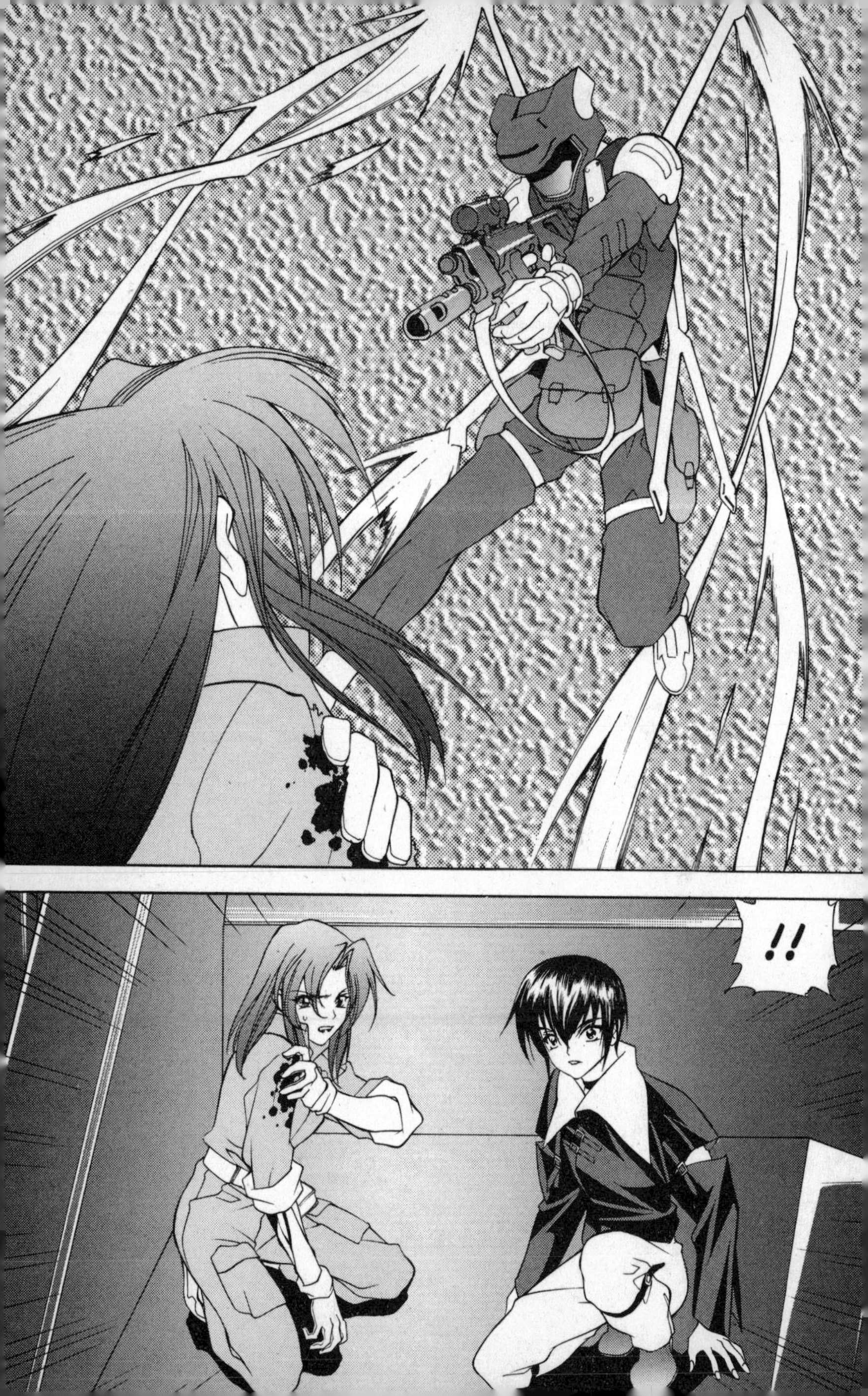
!!

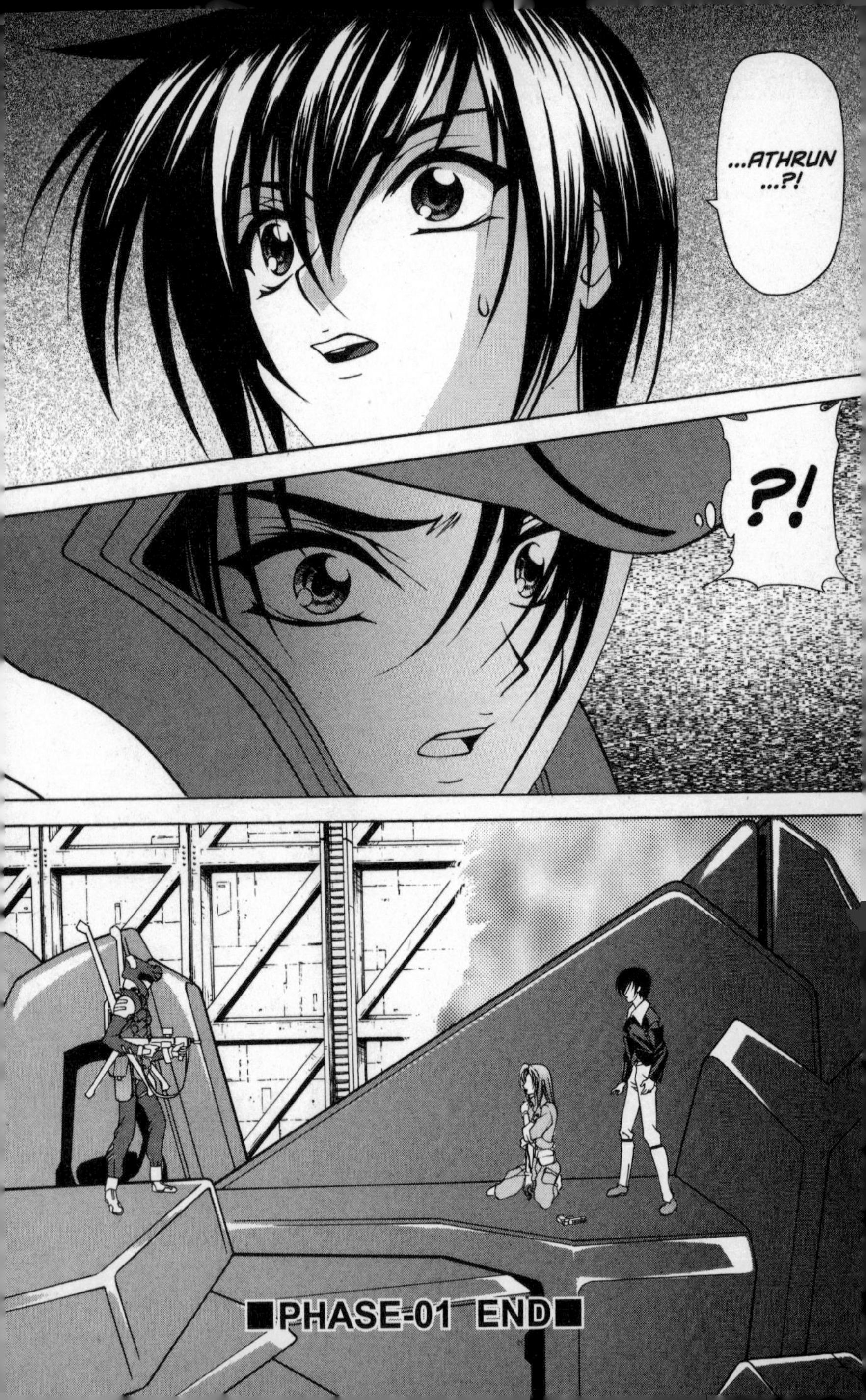
...ATHRUN ...?!
?!
■PHASE-01 END■

C.E. (COSMIC ERA) ~ AN AGE OF WIDESPREAD SPACE EXPLORATION

GEORGE GLENN, THE FIRST COORDINATOR, WAS CREATED THROUGH GENETIC ENGINEERING, EXPANDING THE LIMITS OF HUMANKIND. RETURNING FROM THE FIRST MANNED MISSION TO JUPITER, HE CAME BACK WITH "EVIDENCE 01" (OTHERWISE KNOWN AS THE "WHALE STONE"), AN ALIEN FOSSIL WHICH PRECIPITATED MAN'S RAPID EXPANSON THROUGH SPACE. THIS RESULTED IN THE CONSTRUCTION OF MASSIVE SPACE COLONIES WITHIN THE GRAVITATIONAL FIELDS OF EARTH AND THE MOON IN ADDITION TO THE COLONIES BUILT BY AND FOR THE NATURALS, COLONIES COLLECTIVELY KNOWN AS "THE PLANT" WERE BUILT PRIMARILY FOR COORDINATORS. BUT THE EARTH ALLIANCE DEMANDED EXCESSIVE COMPENSATION FOR ASSISTING THE COORDINATORS IN DEVELOPING THESE PLANT COLONIES. THIS AROUSED GREAT RESENTMENT AMONG THE COORDINATORS, RESULTING IN THE PRESENT CONFLICT. THE FOLLOWING IS A SPACE CHART FOR THE YEAR 71 C.E. EARTH ALLIANCE AND PLANT COLONIES ARE SITUATED ON GRAVITATIONALLY STABLE SECTORS KNOWN AS "LAGRANGE POINTS."

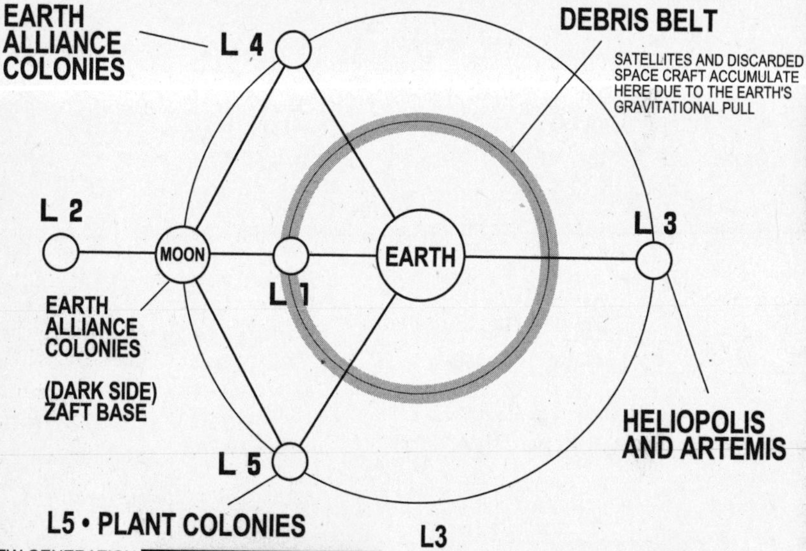
EARTH ALLIANCE COLONIES
L 4
DEBRIS BELT
SATELLITES AND DISCARDED SPACE CRAFT ACCUMULATE HERE DUE TO THE EARTH'S GRAVITATIONAL PULL
L 2
MOON
L 1
EARTH
L 3
EARTH ALLIANCE COLONIES
(DARK SIDE) ZAFT BASE
HELIOPOLIS AND ARTEMIS
L 5
L5 • PLANT COLONIES

NEW GENERATION SATELLITE CITIES BUILT BY THE COORDINATORS, SPANNING SOME 60 KILOMETERS IN LENGTH. NEARLY 100 COLONIES ARE LOCATED HERE. ZAFT, AN ACRONYM FOR "ZODIAC ALLIANCE OF FREEDOM TREATY," REFERS TO THE PLANT ALLIANCE ARMY, WHICH IS ENTIRELY COMPOSED OF VOLUNTEER SOLDIERS.

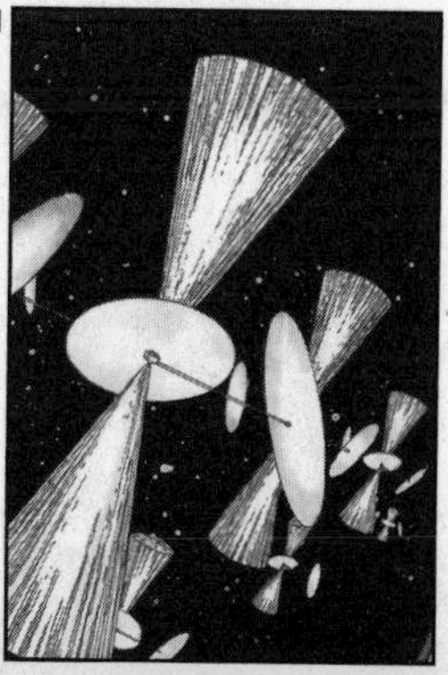

L3

POSITIONED DIRECTLY OPPOSITE THE MOON ON THE OTHER SIDE OF THE EARTH. HELIOPOLIS, AS WELL AS MILITARY SATELLITE ARTEMIS OF THE EURASIAN FEDERATION, ARE LOCATED HERE.

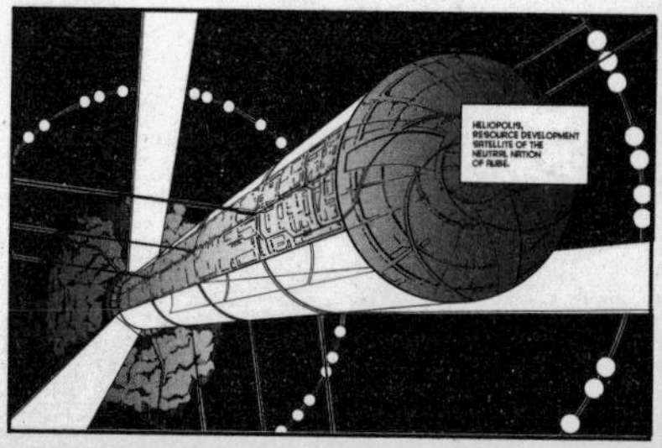
HELIOPOLIS, RESOURCE DEVELOPMENT SATELLITE OF THE NEUTRAL NATION OF AUBE.

PHASE-02: ITS NAME IS GUNDAM

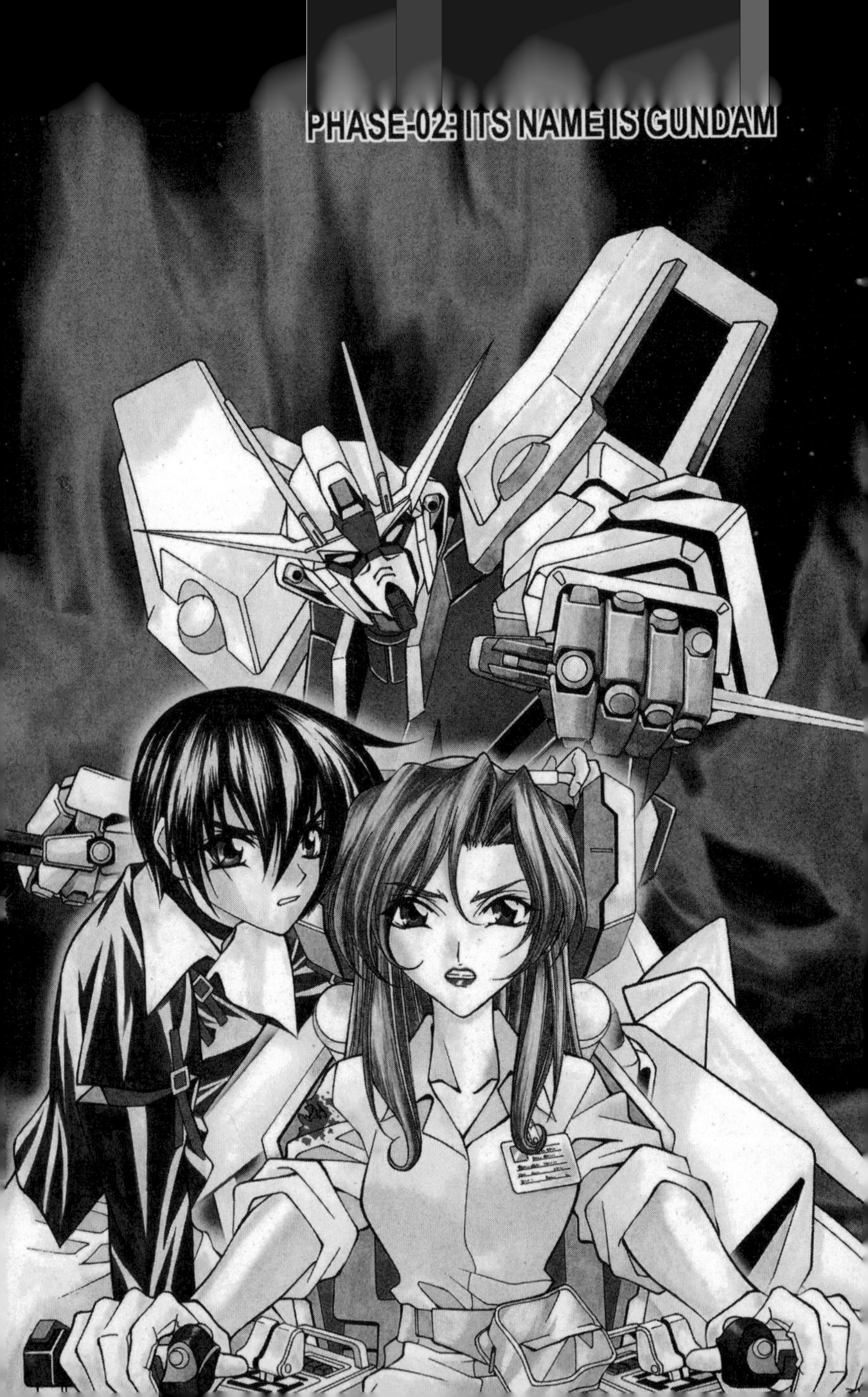

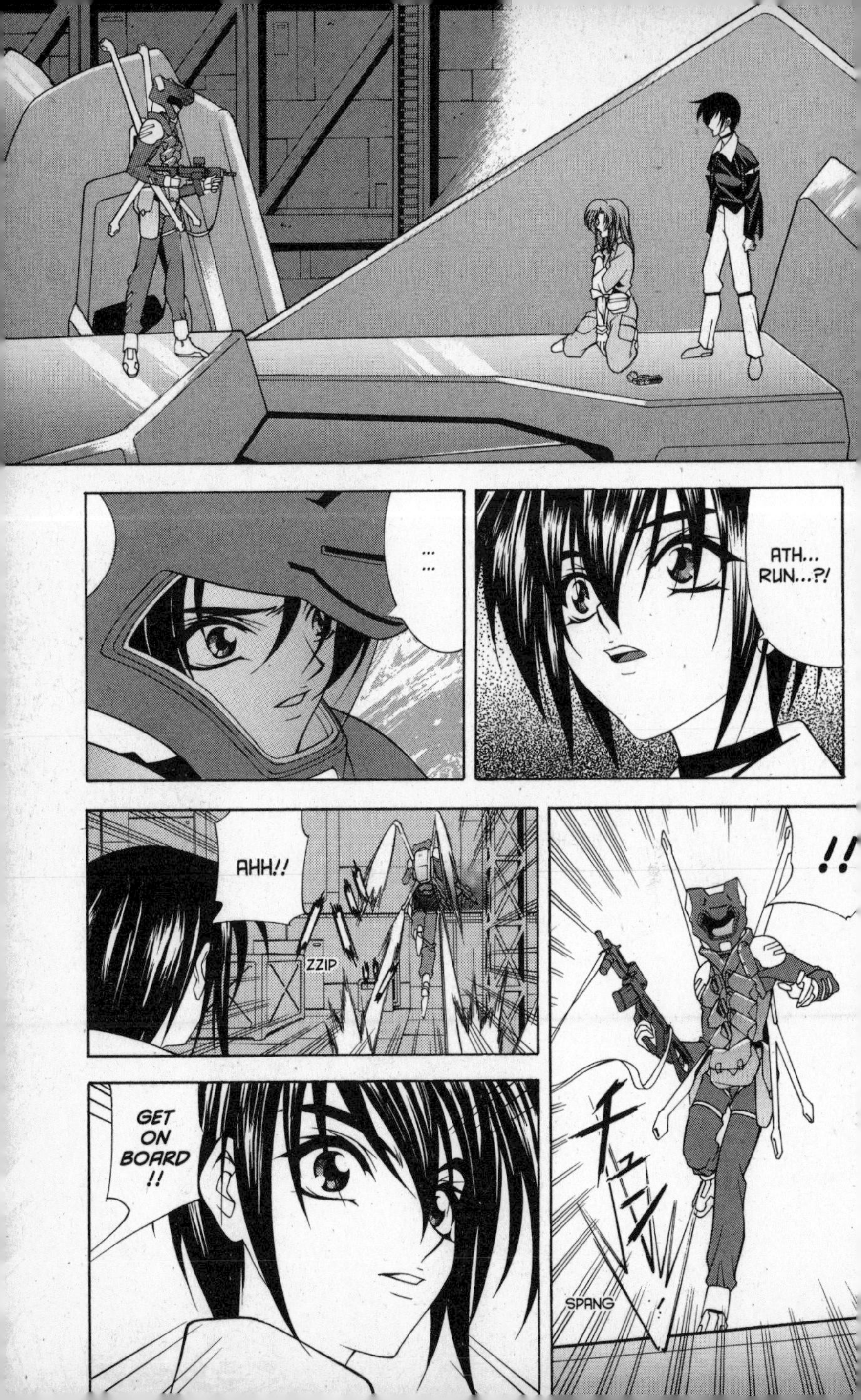
ATH... RUN...?!
... ...
!!
SPANG
AHH!!
ZZIP
GET ON BOARD !!

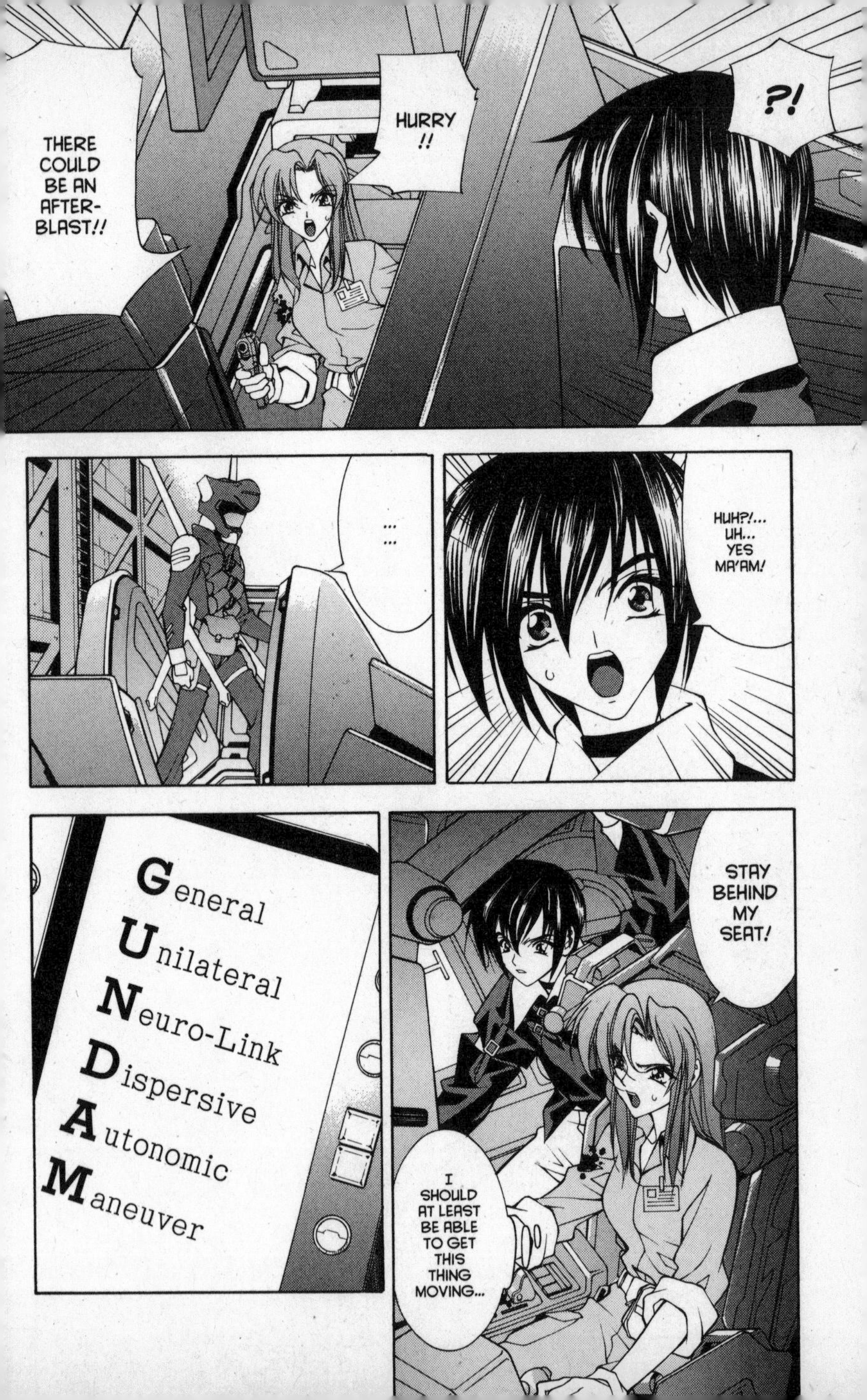
?!
HURRY !!
THERE COULD BE AN AFTER-BLAST!!
HUH?!... UH... YES MA'AM!
... ...
STAY BEHIND MY SEAT!
I SHOULD AT LEAST BE ABLE TO GET THIS THING MOVING...
General
Unilateral
Neuro-Link
Dispersive
Autonomic
Maneuver

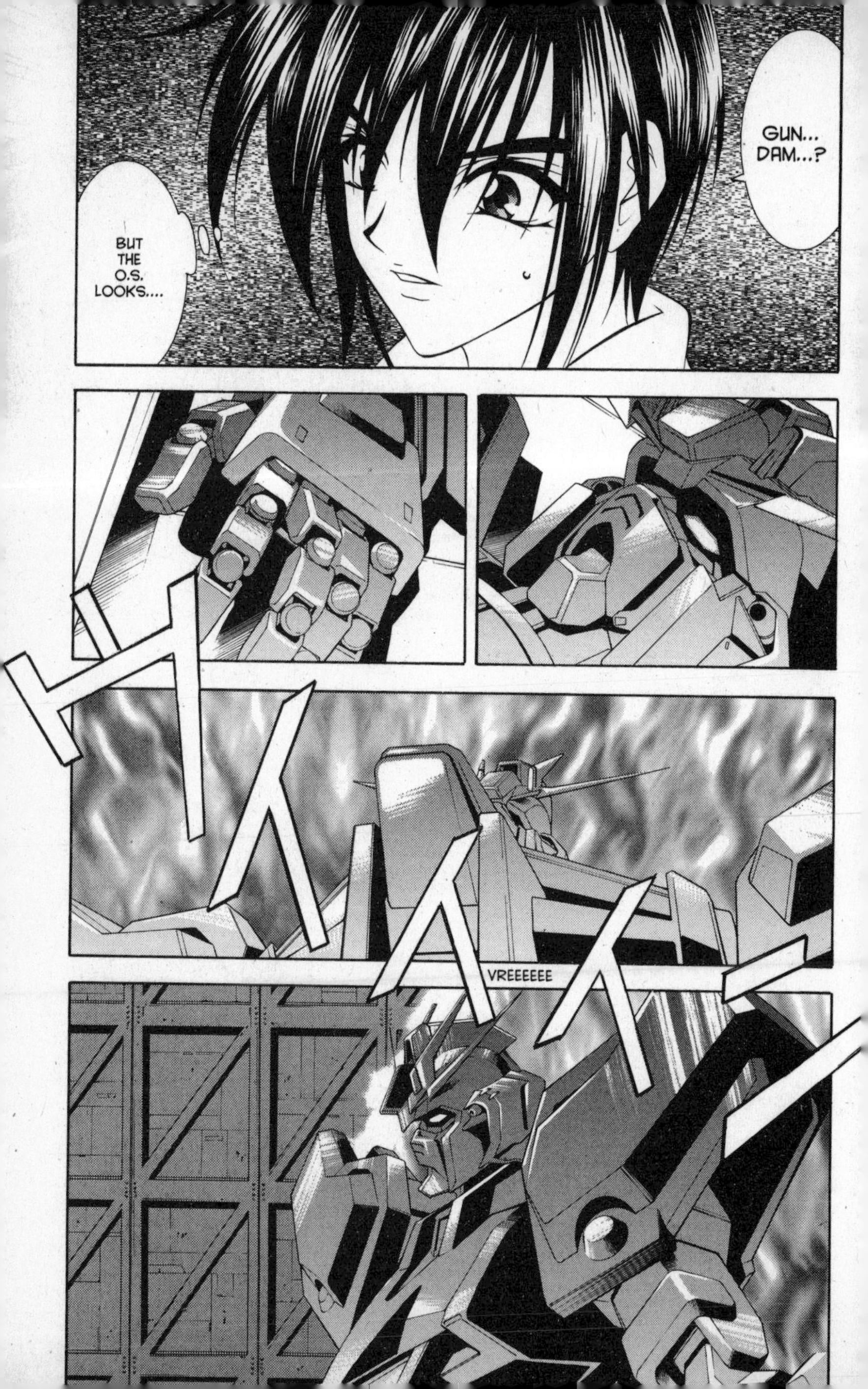
GUN... DAM...?
BUT THE O.S. LOOKS....
VREEEEEE

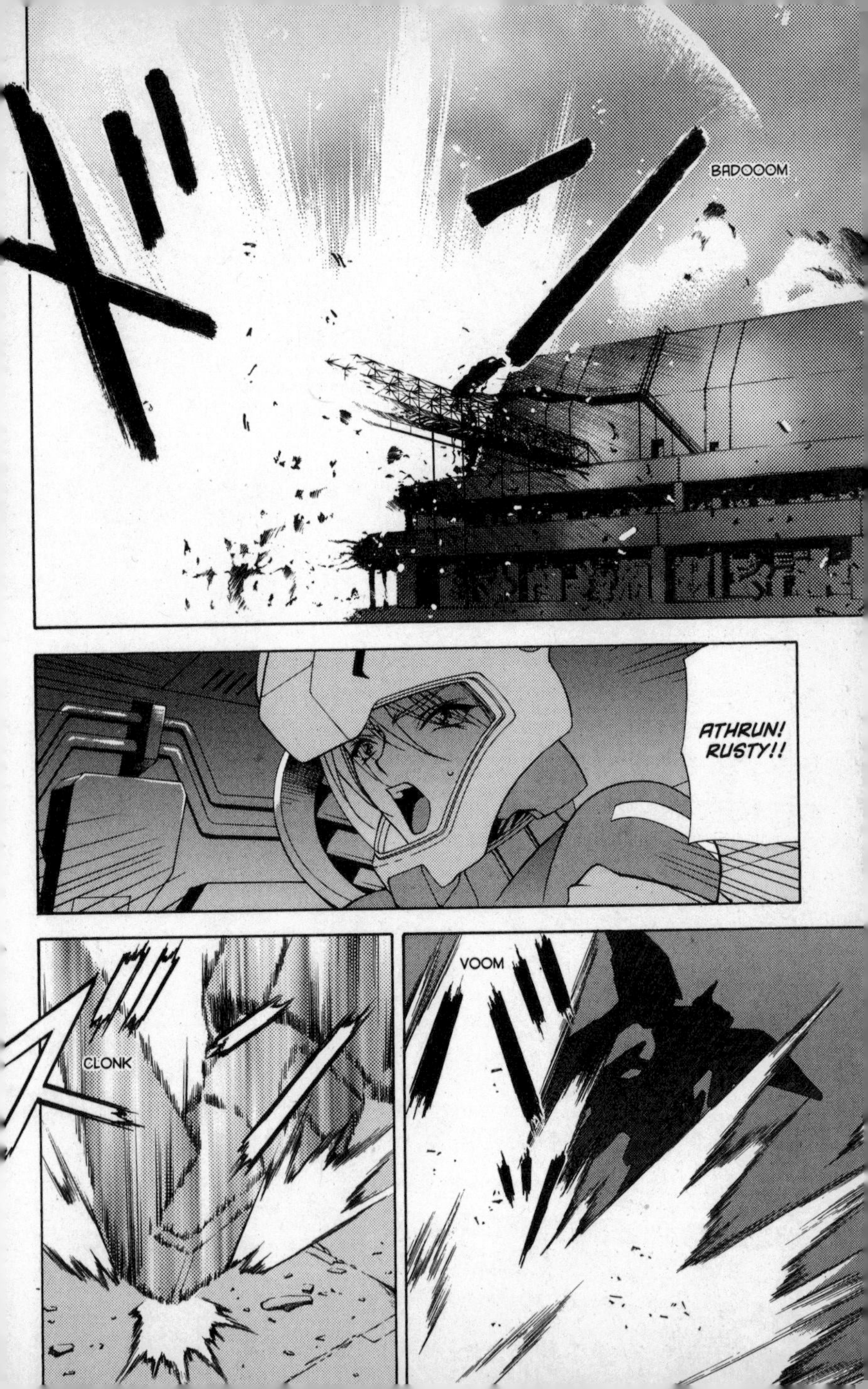
BADOOOM
ATHRUN! RUSTY!!
VOOM
CLONK

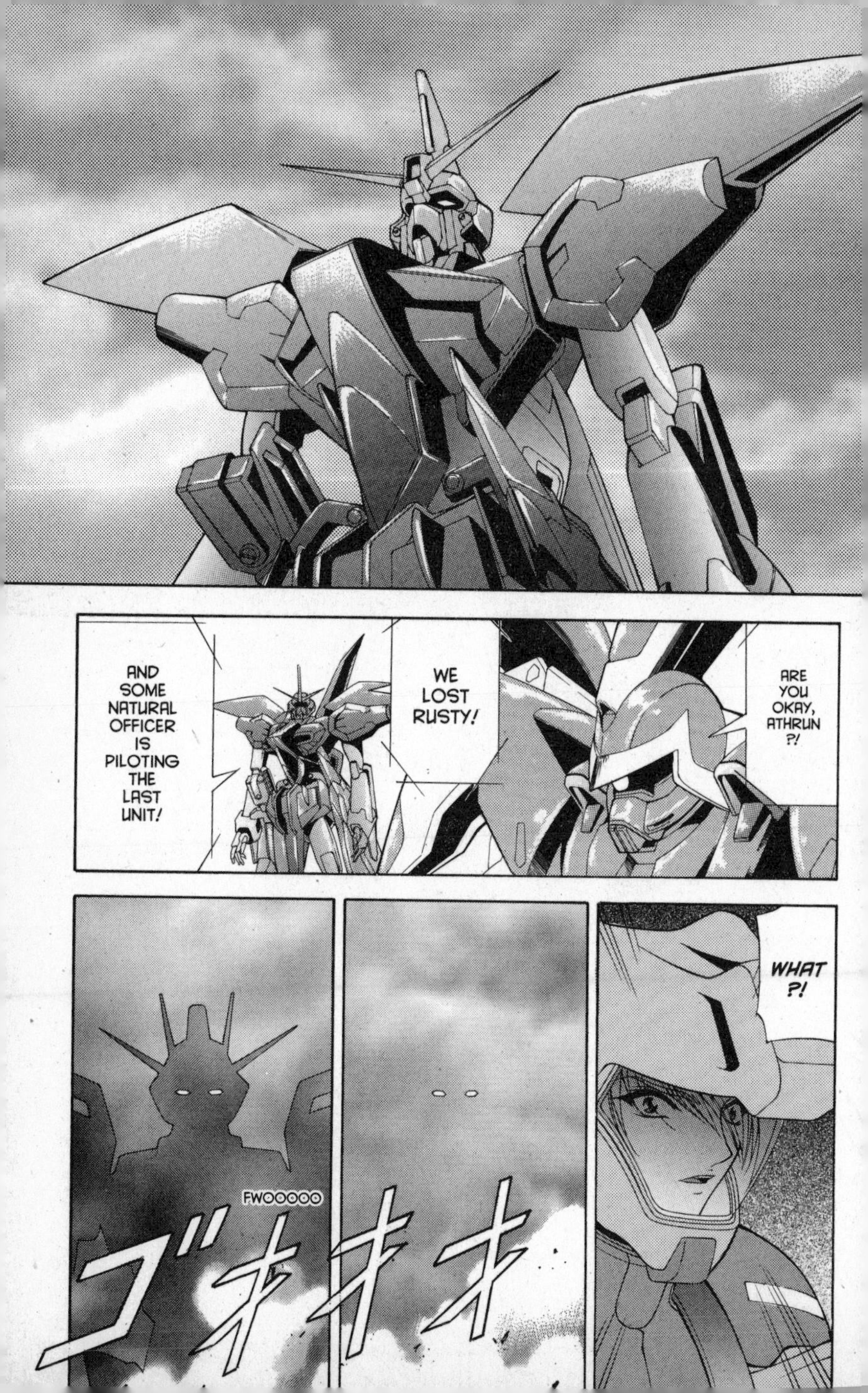
ARE YOU OKAY, ATHRUN?!
WE LOST RUSTY!
AND SOME NATURAL OFFICER IS PILOTING THE LAST UNIT!
WHAT?!
FWOOOOO
ゴオオオ

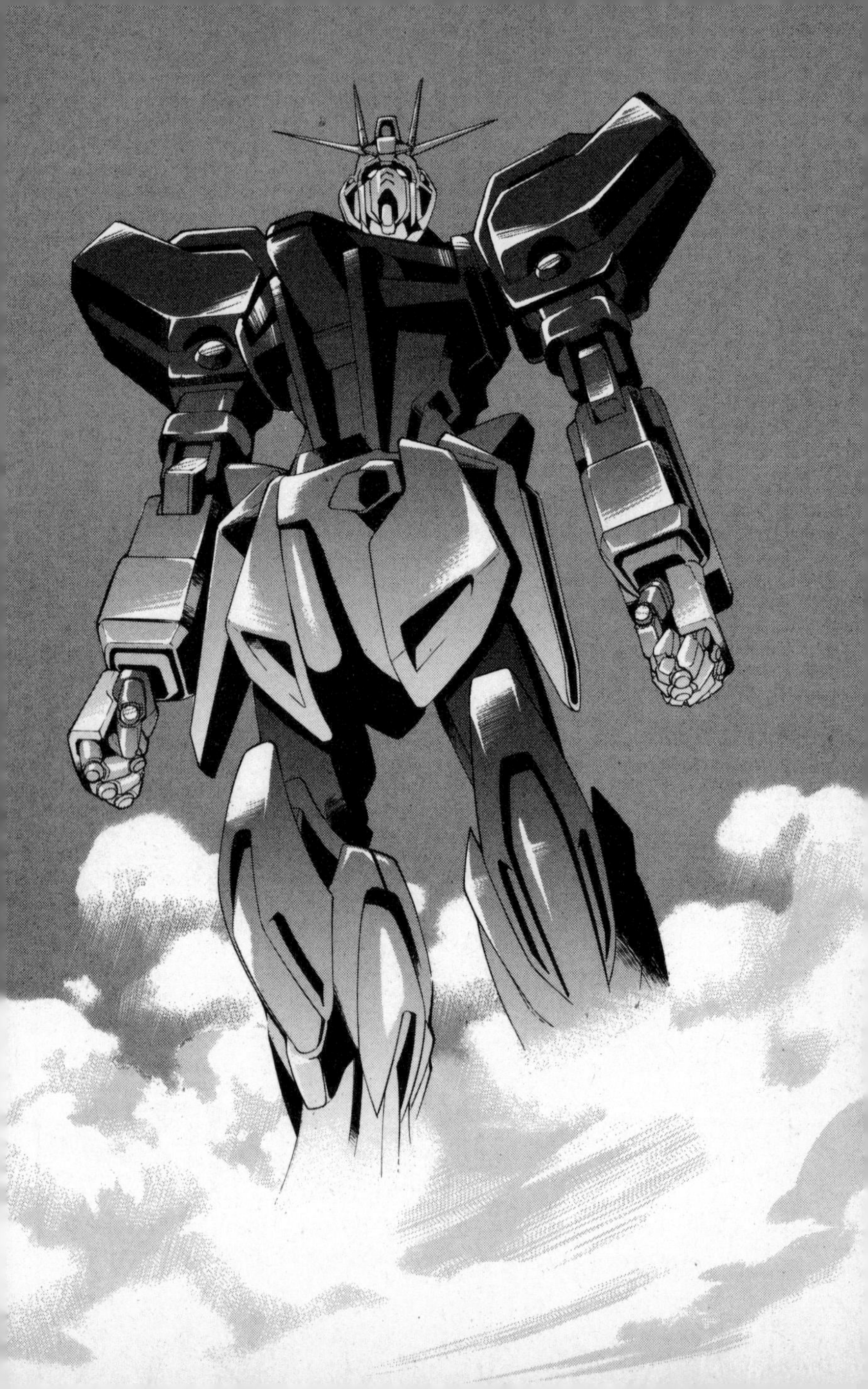

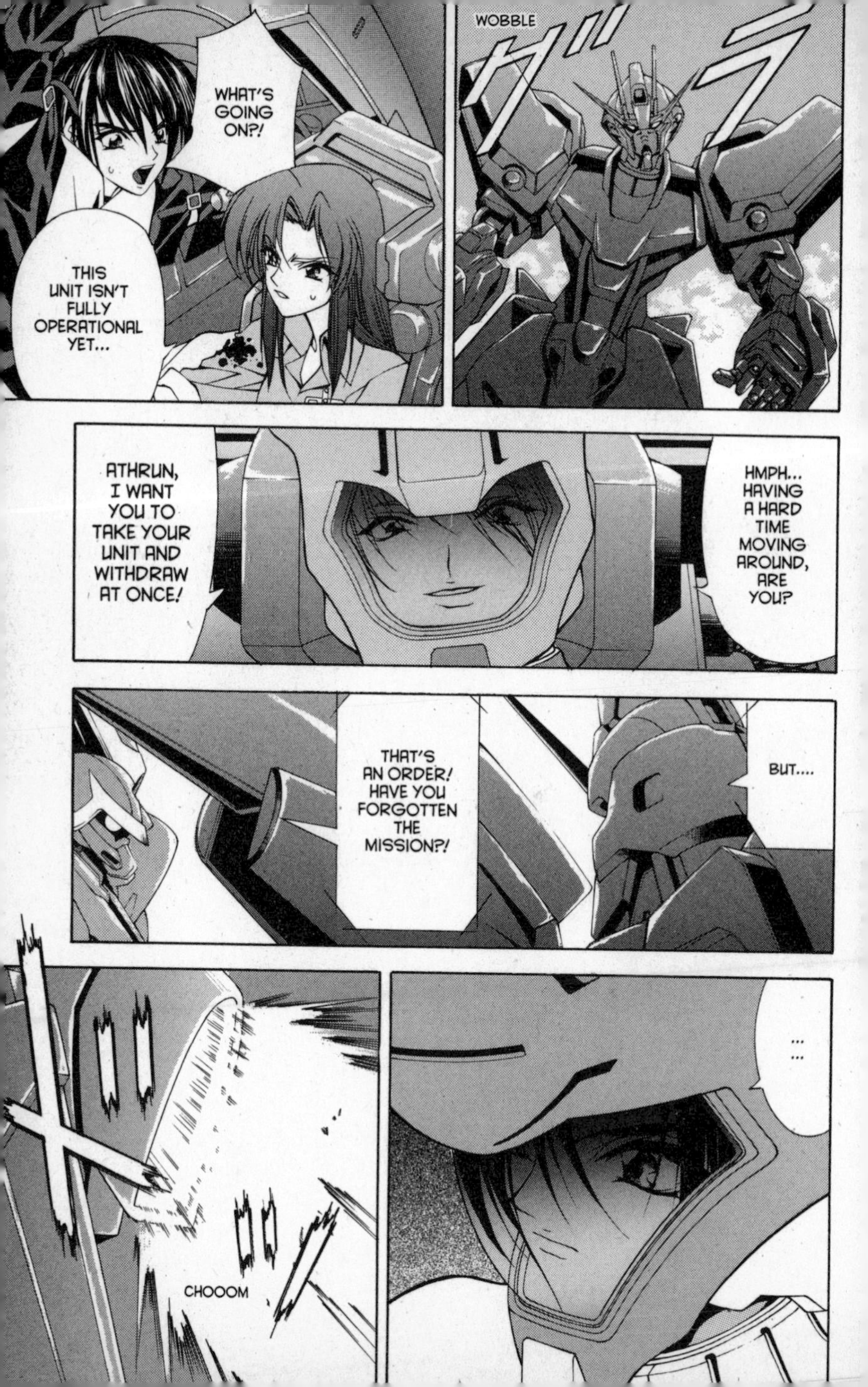
WOBBLE
WHAT'S GOING ON?!
THIS UNIT ISN'T FULLY OPERATIONAL YET...
HMPH... HAVING A HARD TIME MOVING AROUND, ARE YOU?
ATHRUN, I WANT YOU TO TAKE YOUR UNIT AND WITHDRAW AT ONCE!
BUT....
THAT'S AN ORDER! HAVE YOU FORGOTTEN THE MISSION?!
... ...
CHOOOM

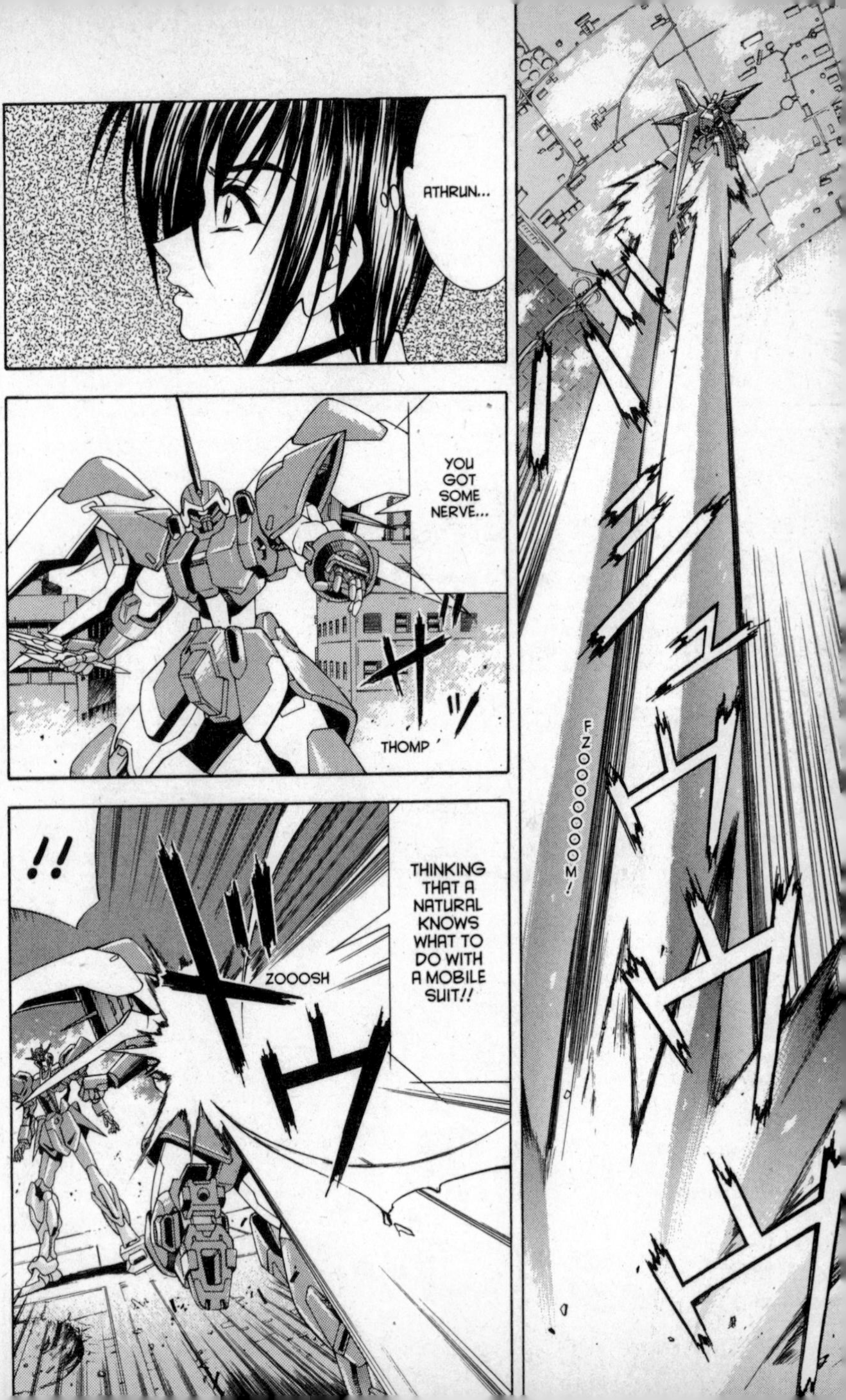
FZOOOOOOOOM!
ATHRUN...
YOU GOT SOME NERVE...
THOMP
!!
THINKING THAT A NATURAL KNOWS WHAT TO DO WITH A MOBILE SUIT!!
ZOOOSH

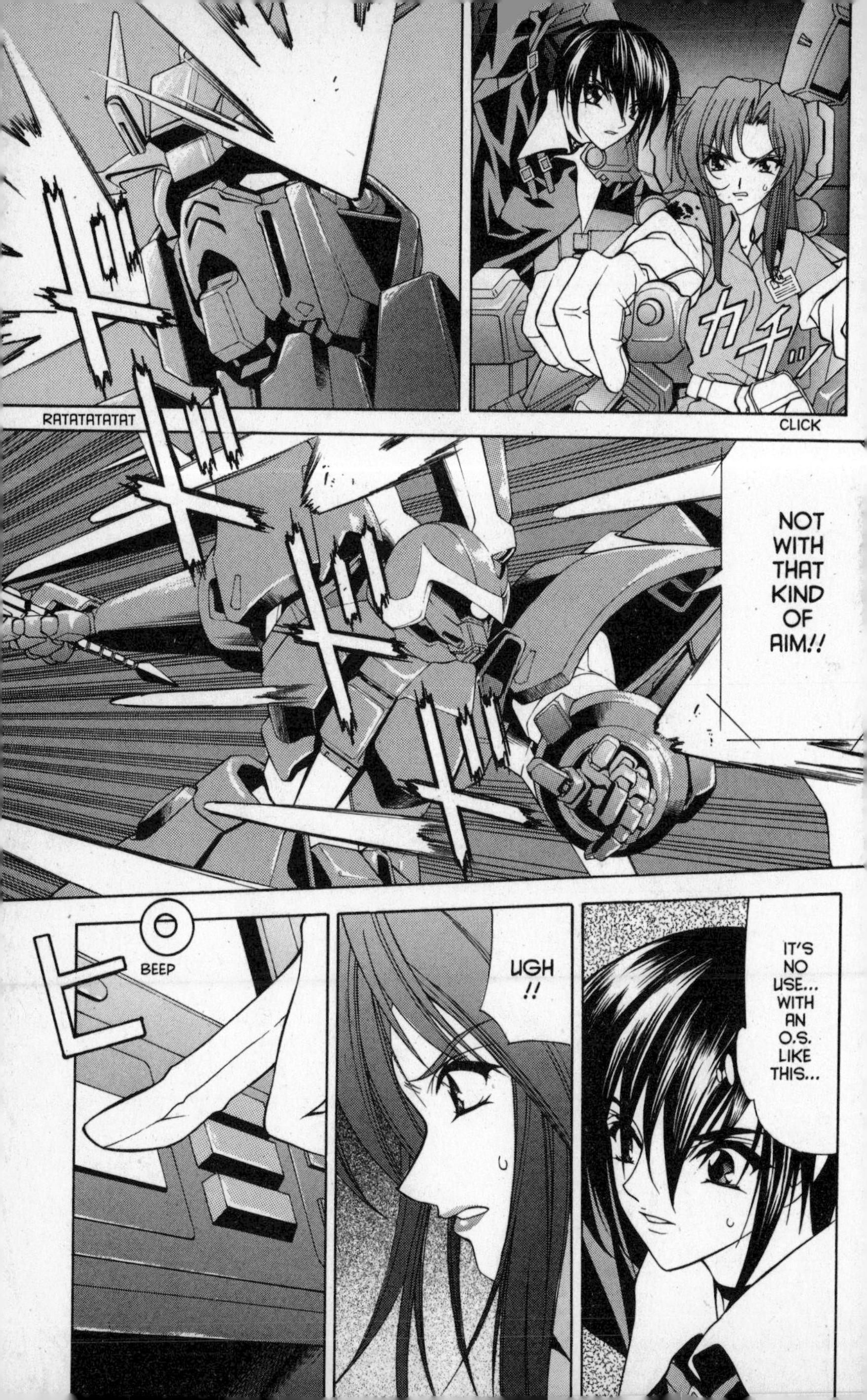

カチッ
CLICK
RATATATATAT
NOT WITH THAT KIND OF AIM!!
IT'S NO USE... WITH AN O.S. LIKE THIS...
UGH !!
BEEP

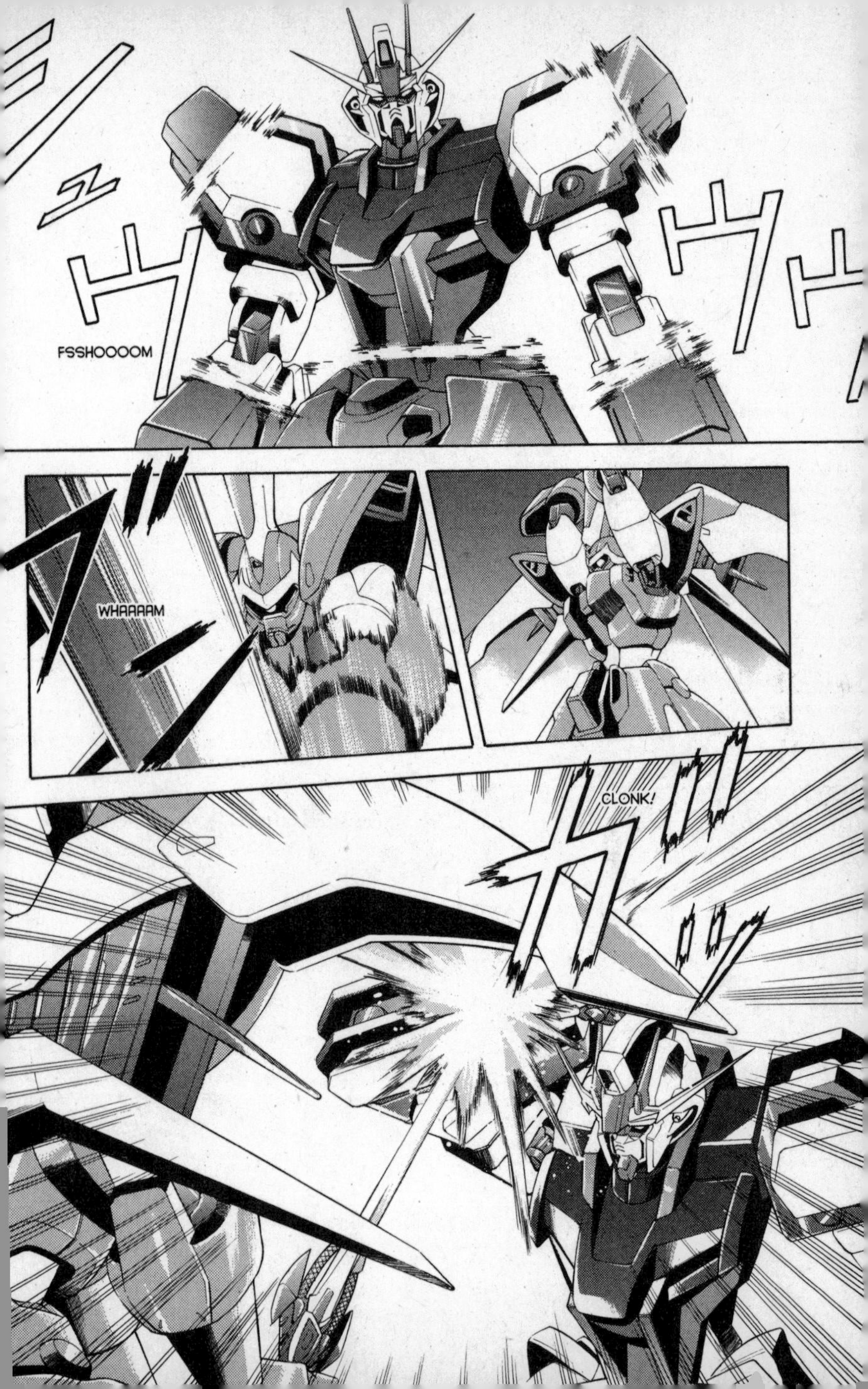
FSSHOOOOM
WHAAAAM
CLONK!

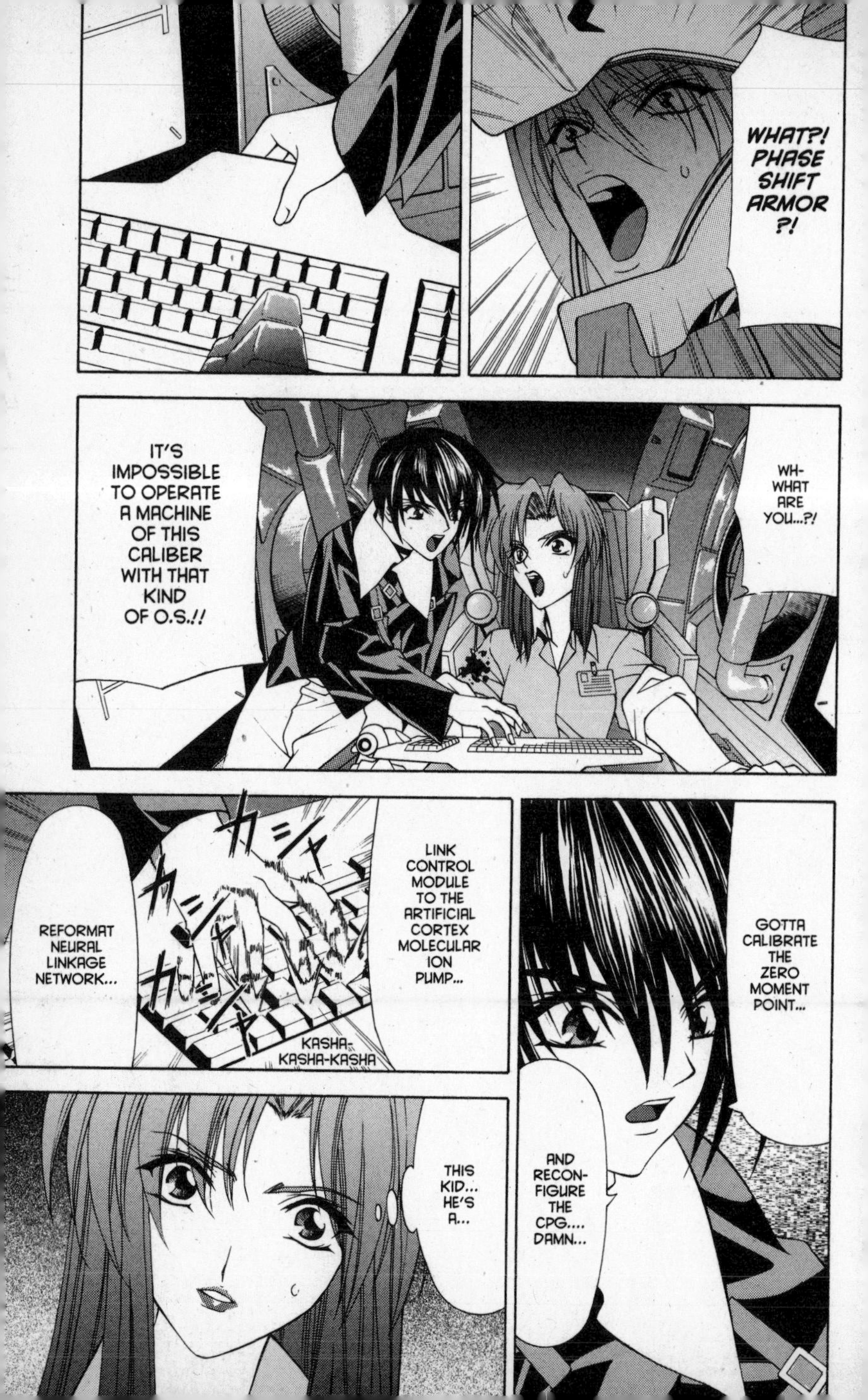
WHAT?! PHASE SHIFT ARMOR ?!
WH- WHAT ARE YOU...?!
IT'S IMPOSSIBLE TO OPERATE A MACHINE OF THIS CALIBER WITH THAT KIND OF O.S.!!
GOTTA CALIBRATE THE ZERO MOMENT POINT...
AND RECONFIGURE THE CPG.... DAMN...
LINK CONTROL MODULE TO THE ARTIFICIAL CORTEX MOLECULAR ION PUMP...
REFORMAT NEURAL LINKAGE NETWORK...
KASHA-KASHA-KASHA
THIS KID... HE'S A...

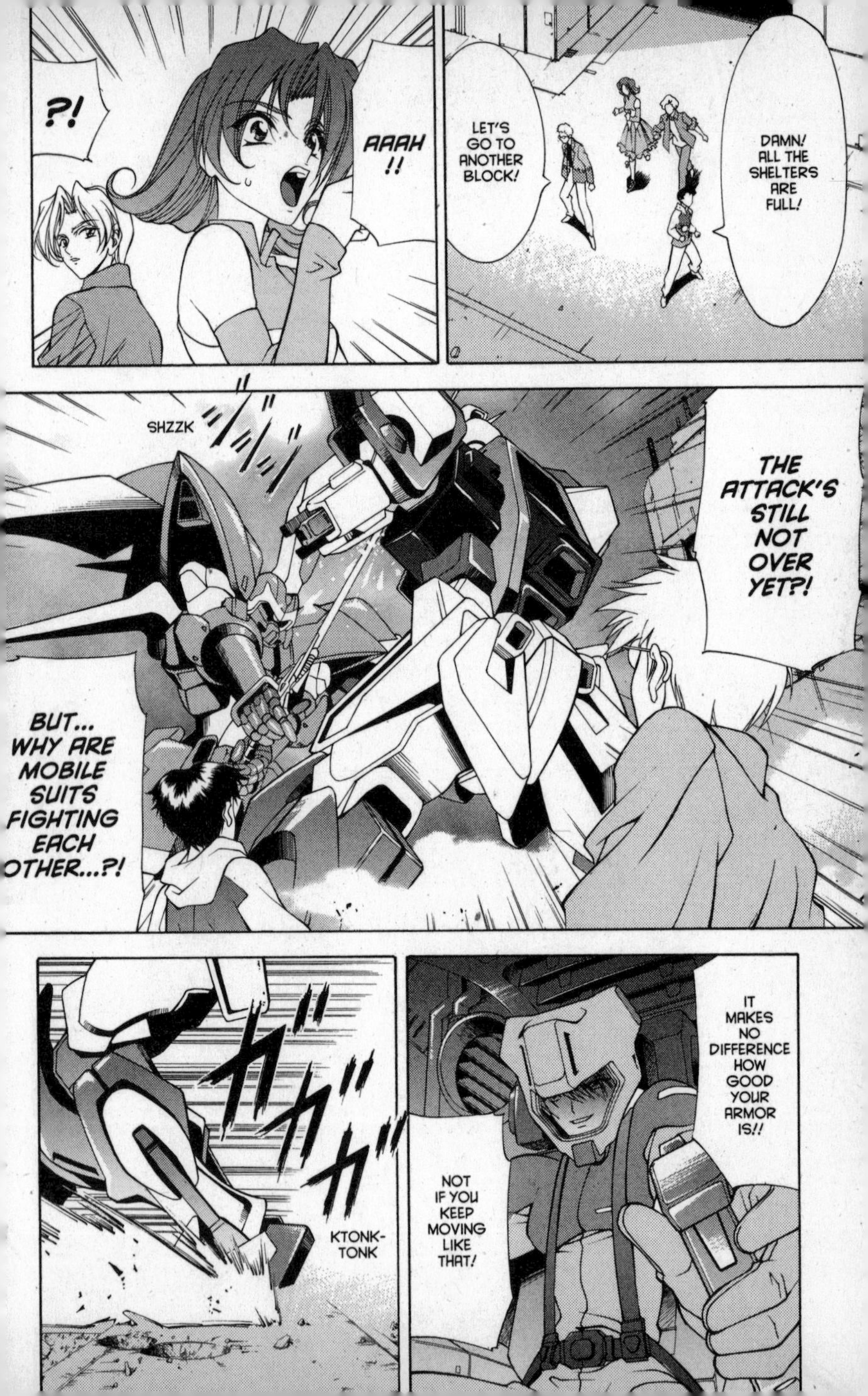
DAMN! ALL THE SHELTERS ARE FULL!
LET'S GO TO ANOTHER BLOCK!
AAAH!!
?!
THE ATTACK'S STILL NOT OVER YET?!
SHZZK
BUT... WHY ARE MOBILE SUITS FIGHTING EACH OTHER...?!
IT MAKES NO DIFFERENCE HOW GOOD YOUR ARMOR IS!!
NOT IF YOU KEEP MOVING LIKE THAT!
KTONK-TONK

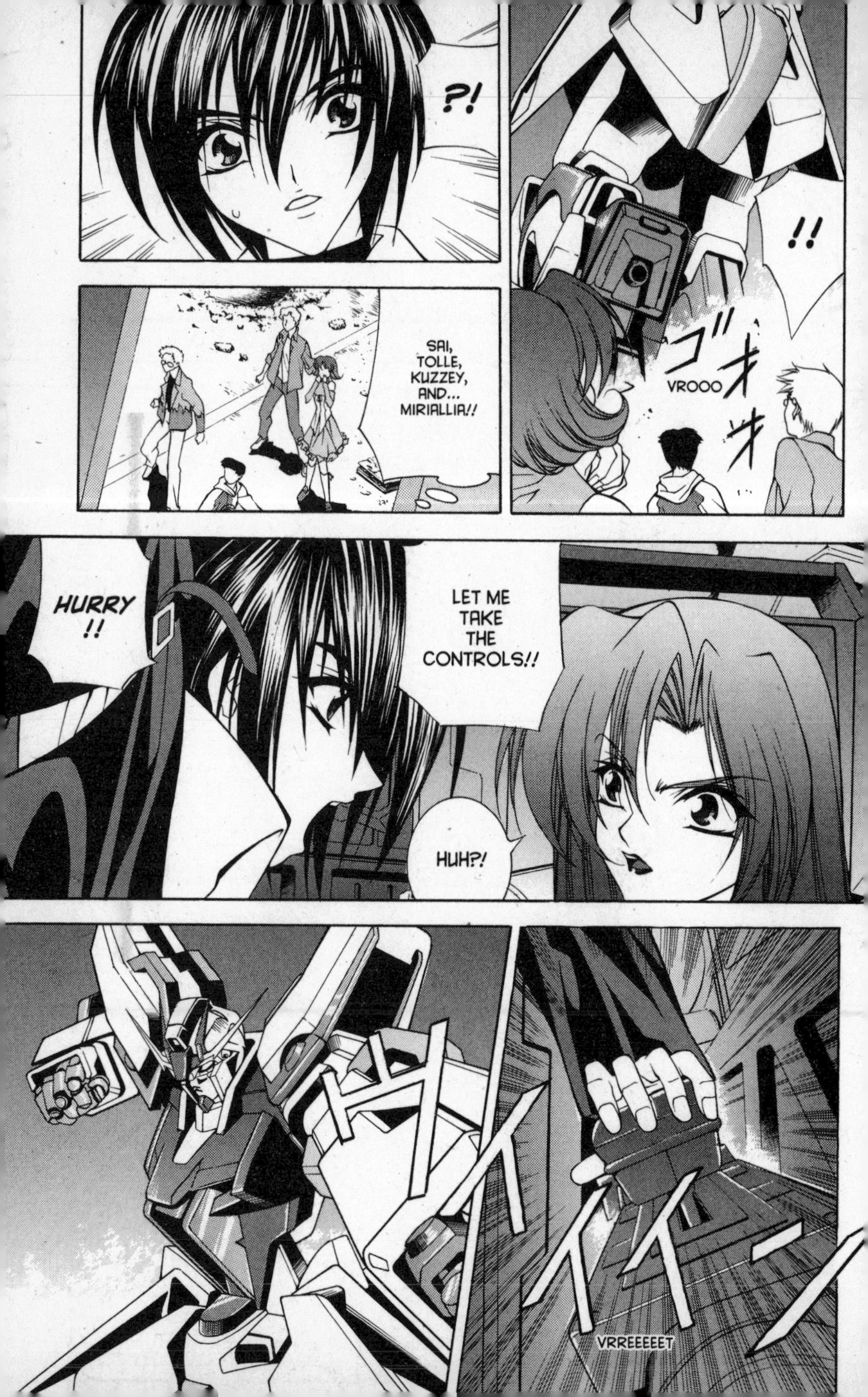
!!
VROOO
?!
SAI, TOLLE, KUZZEY, AND... MIRIALLIA!!
LET ME TAKE THE CONTROLS!!
HURRY !!
HUH?!
VRREEEEET

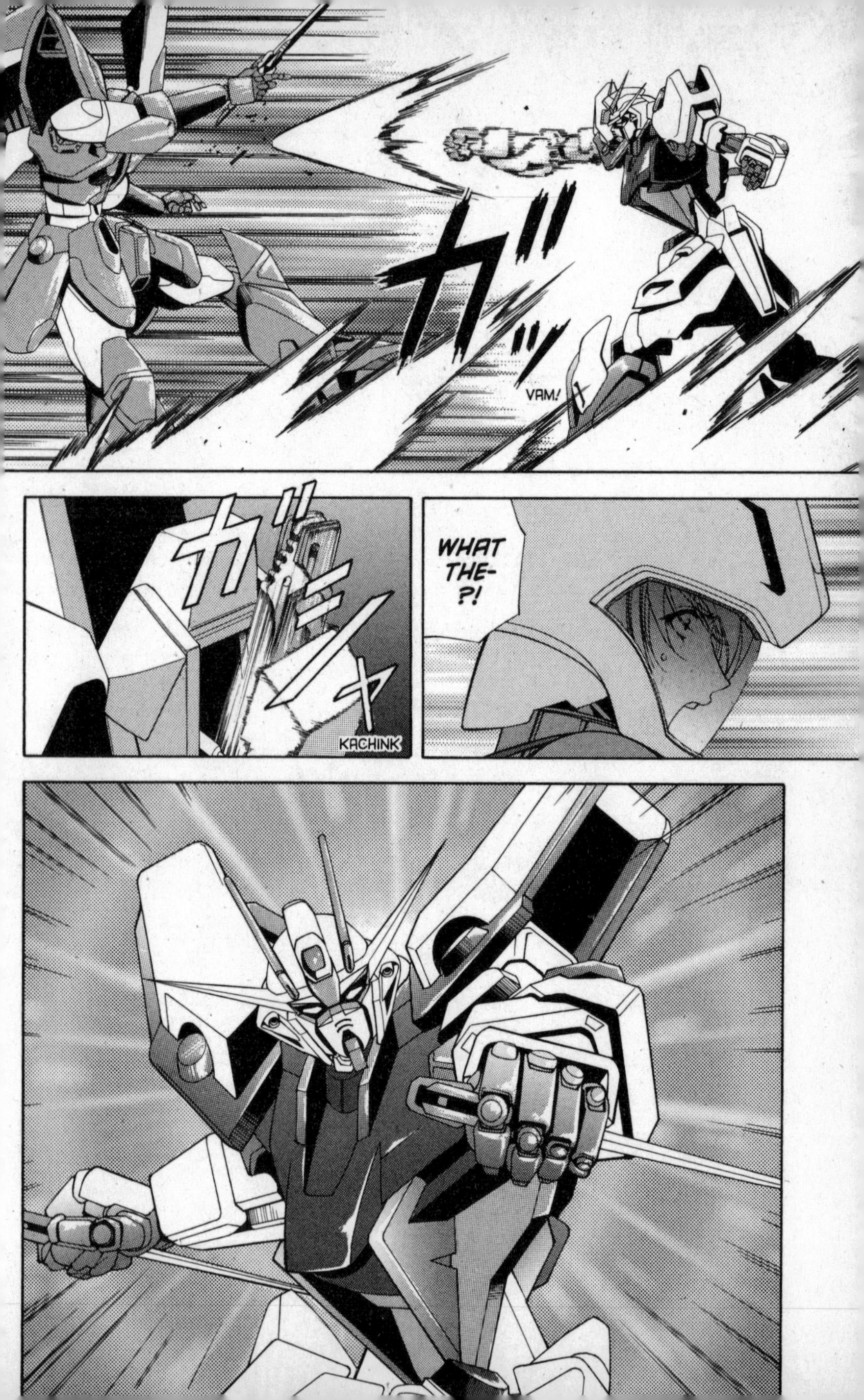
ガッ
VAM!
WHAT THE-?!
KACHINK

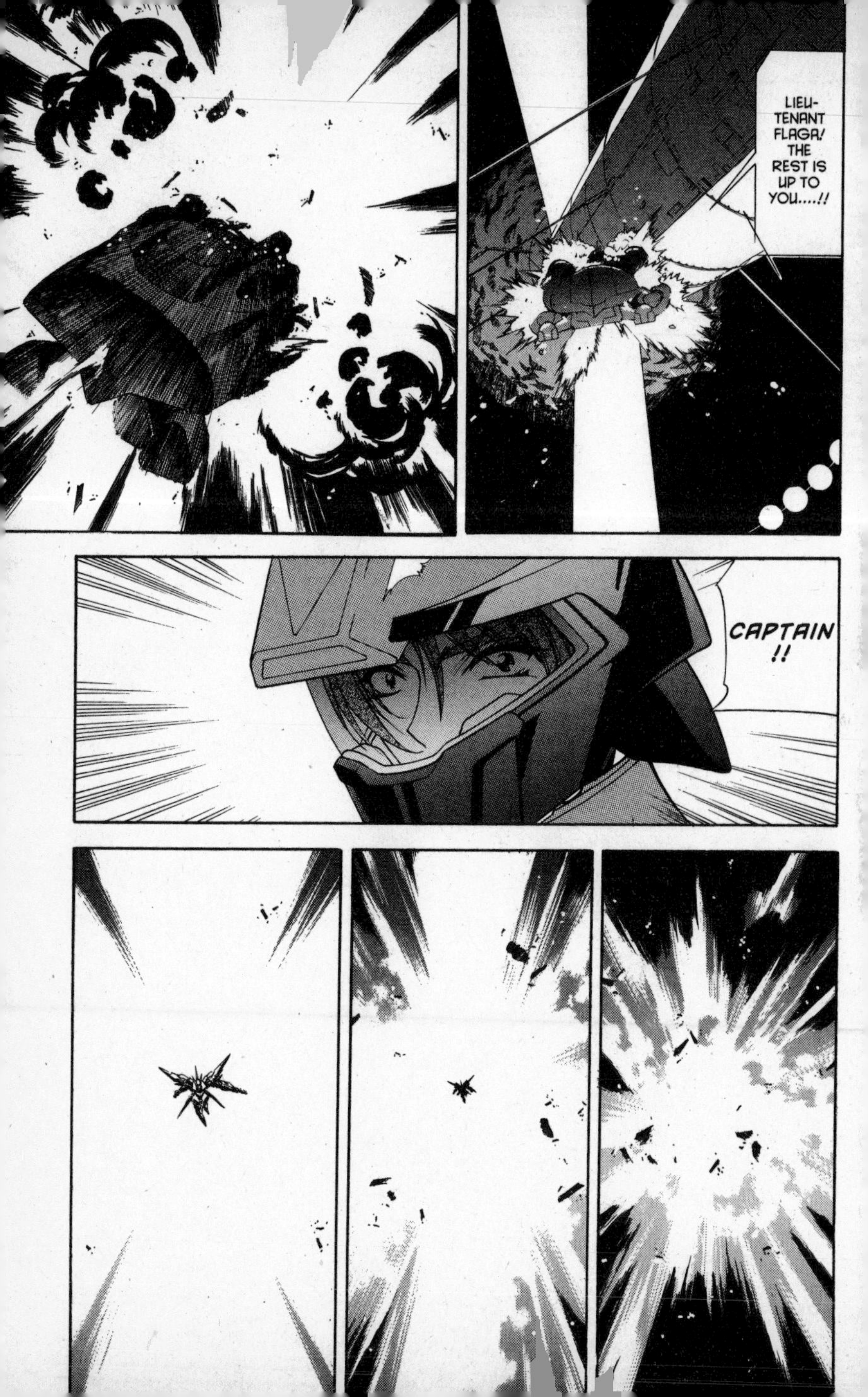
LIEU-TENANT FLAGA! THE REST IS UP TO YOU....!!
CAPTAIN !!

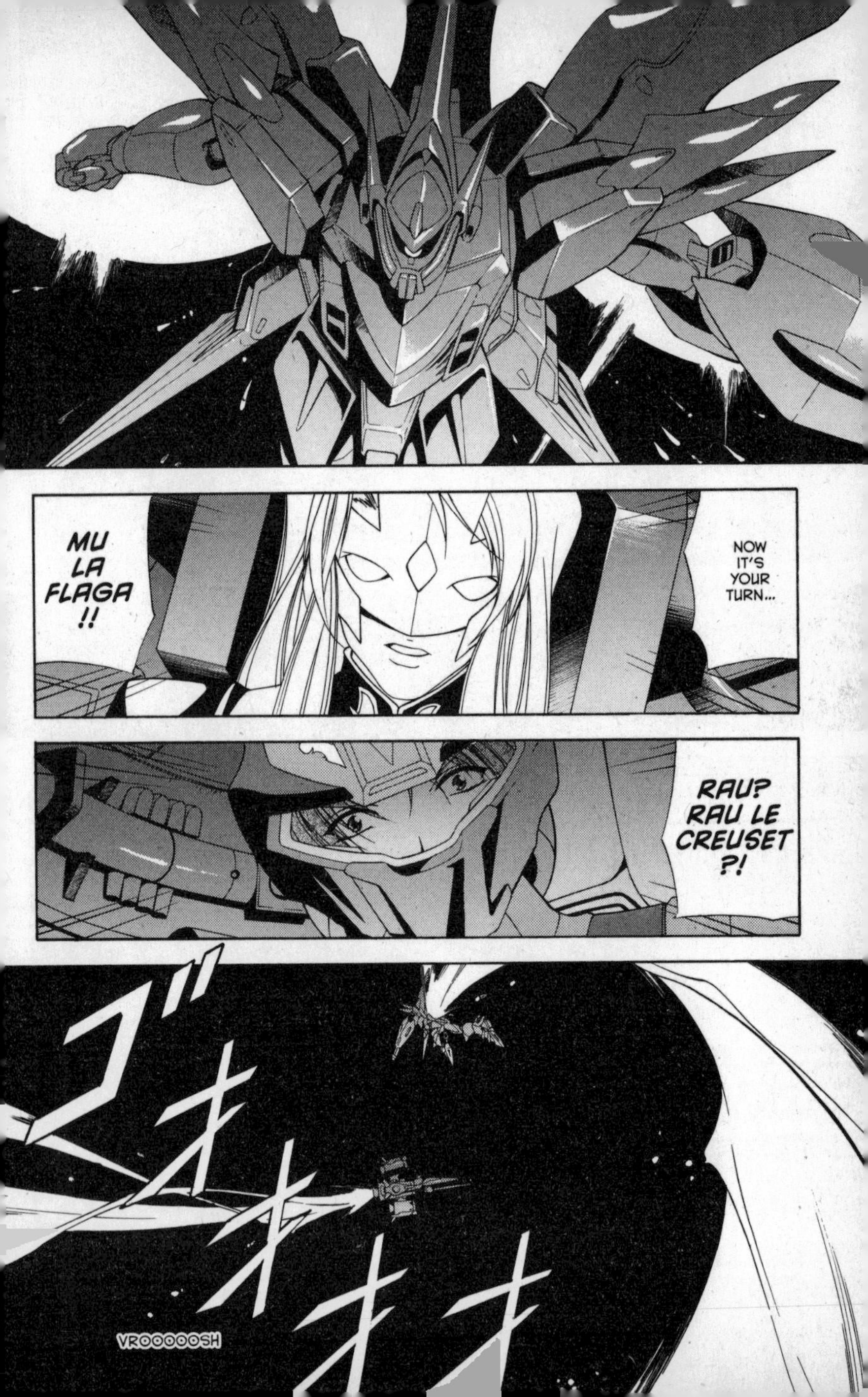
NOW IT'S YOUR TURN...
MU LA FLAGA!!
RAU? RAU LE CREUSET?!
ゴオオオ
VROOOOOSH

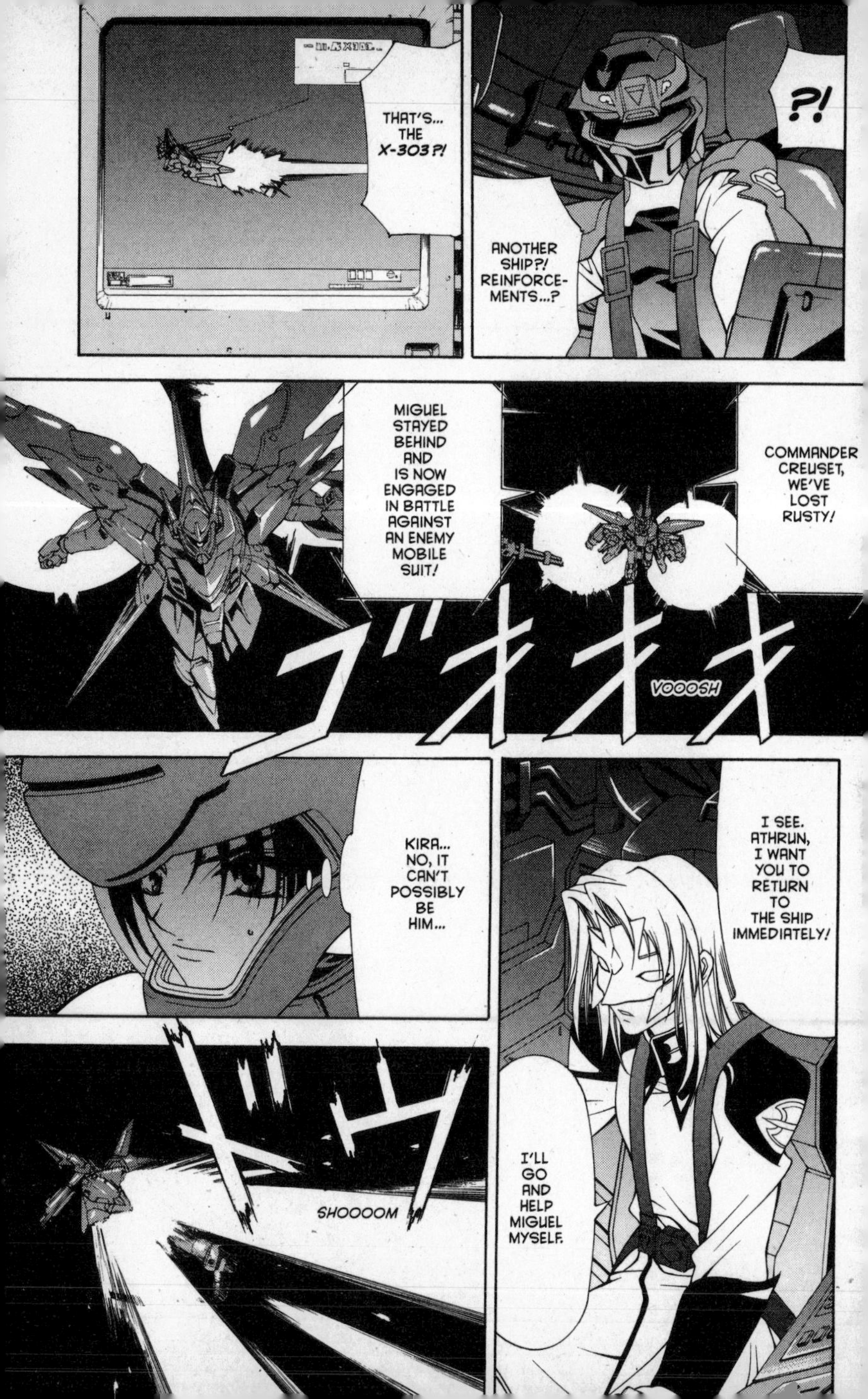
?!
ANOTHER SHIP?! REINFORCE- MENTS...?
THAT'S... THE X-303?!
COMMANDER CREUSET, WE'VE LOST RUSTY!
MIGUEL STAYED BEHIND AND IS NOW ENGAGED IN BATTLE AGAINST AN ENEMY MOBILE SUIT!
ゴオオオ
VOOOSH
I SEE. ATHRUN, I WANT YOU TO RETURN TO THE SHIP IMMEDIATELY!
I'LL GO AND HELP MIGUEL MYSELF.
KIRA... NO, IT CAN'T POSSIBLY BE HIM...
SHOOOOM

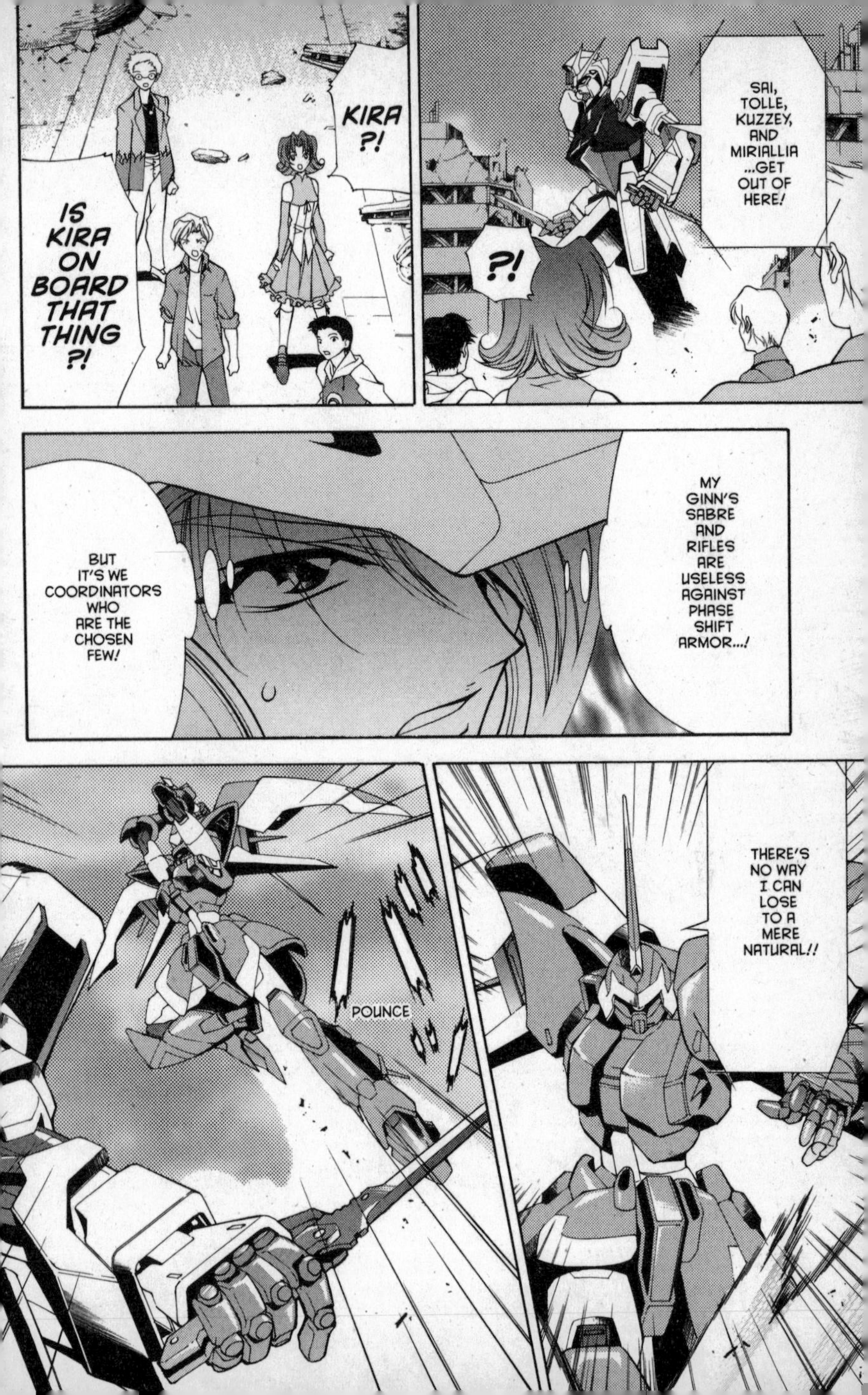
SAI, TOLLE, KUZZEY, AND MIRIALLIA ...GET OUT OF HERE!
?!
KIRA ?!
IS KIRA ON BOARD THAT THING ?!
MY GINN'S SABRE AND RIFLES ARE USELESS AGAINST PHASE SHIFT ARMOR...!
BUT IT'S WE COORDINATORS WHO ARE THE CHOSEN FEW!
THERE'S NO WAY I CAN LOSE TO A MERE NATURAL!!
POUNCE

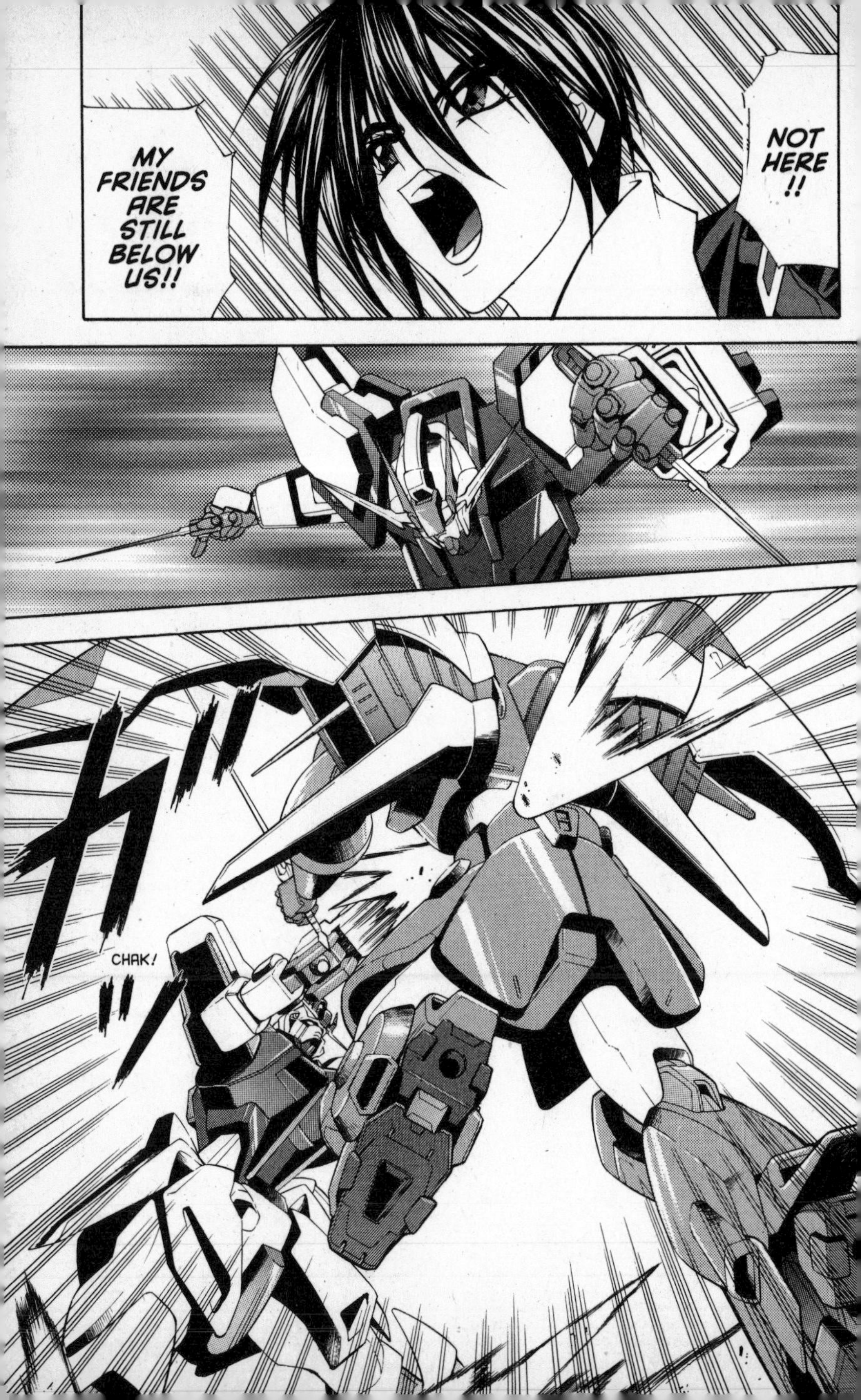
NOT HERE!!
MY FRIENDS ARE STILL BELOW US!!
CHAK!

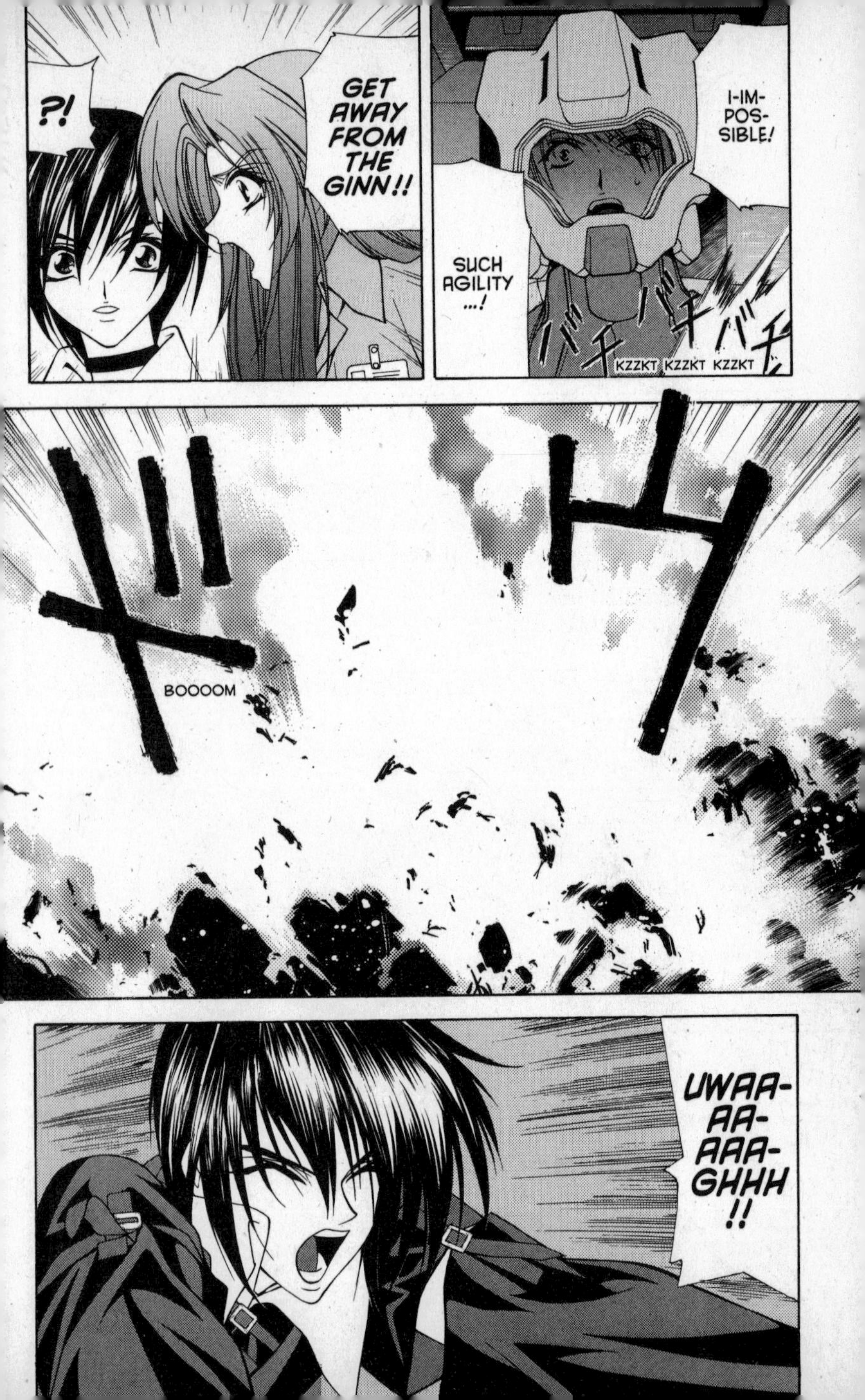
I-IM-POS-SIBLE!
SUCH AGILITY ...!
KZZKT KZZKT KZZKT
GET AWAY FROM THE GINN!!
?!
BOOOOM
UWAA-AA-AAA-GHHH!!

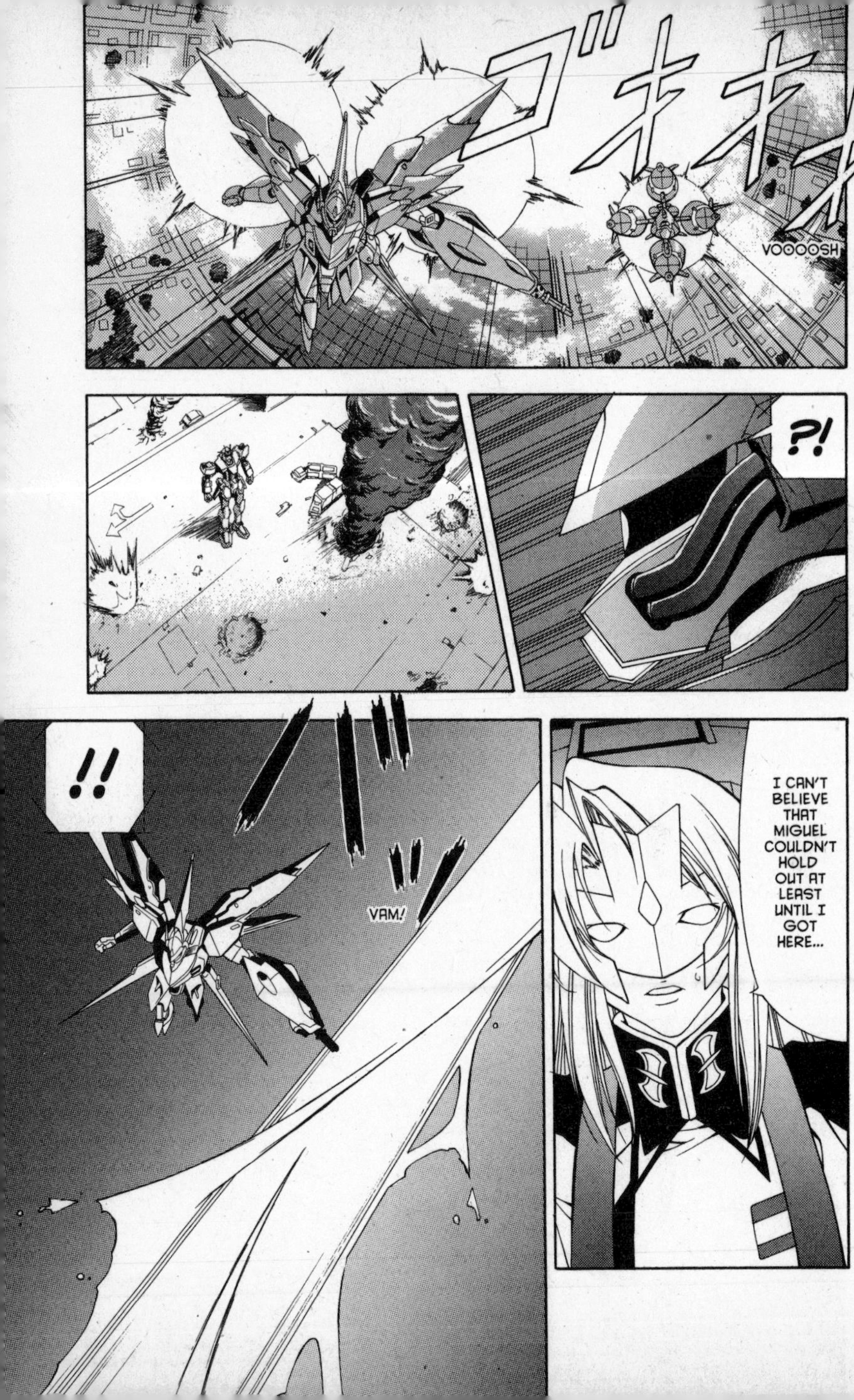
ゴオオオ
VOOOOSH
?!
I CAN'T BELIEVE THAT MIGUEL COULDN'T HOLD OUT AT LEAST UNTIL I GOT HERE...
!!
VAM!

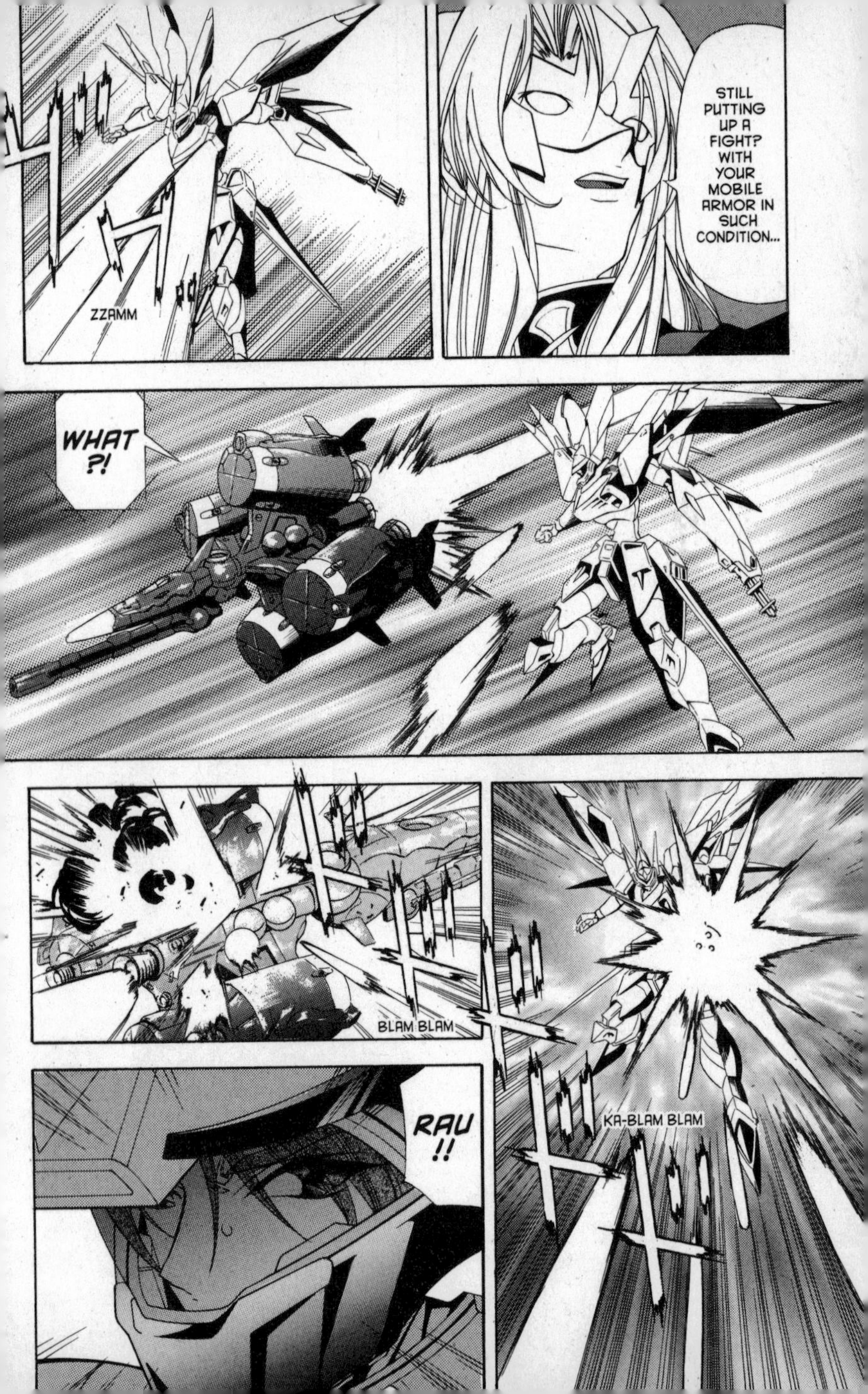
STILL PUTTING UP A FIGHT? WITH YOUR MOBILE ARMOR IN SUCH CONDITION...
ZZAMM
WHAT ?!
KA-BLAM BLAM
BLAM BLAM
RAU !!

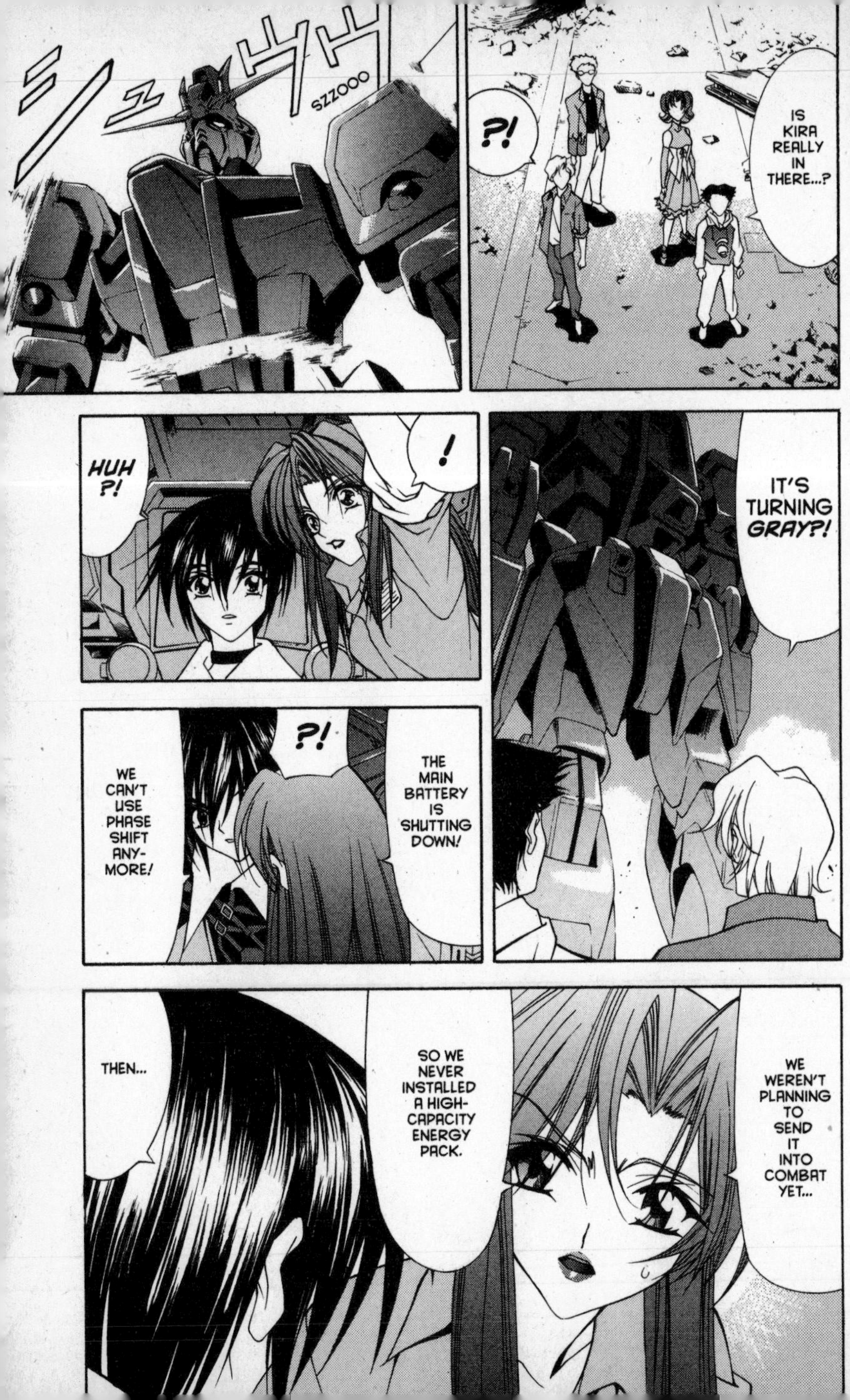
IS KIRA REALLY IN THERE...?
?!
SZZOOO
IT'S TURNING *GRAY?!*
!
HUH ?!
?!
THE MAIN BATTERY IS SHUTTING DOWN!
WE CAN'T USE PHASE SHIFT ANYMORE!
WE WEREN'T PLANNING TO SEND IT INTO COMBAT YET...
SO WE NEVER INSTALLED A HIGH-CAPACITY ENERGY PACK.
THEN...

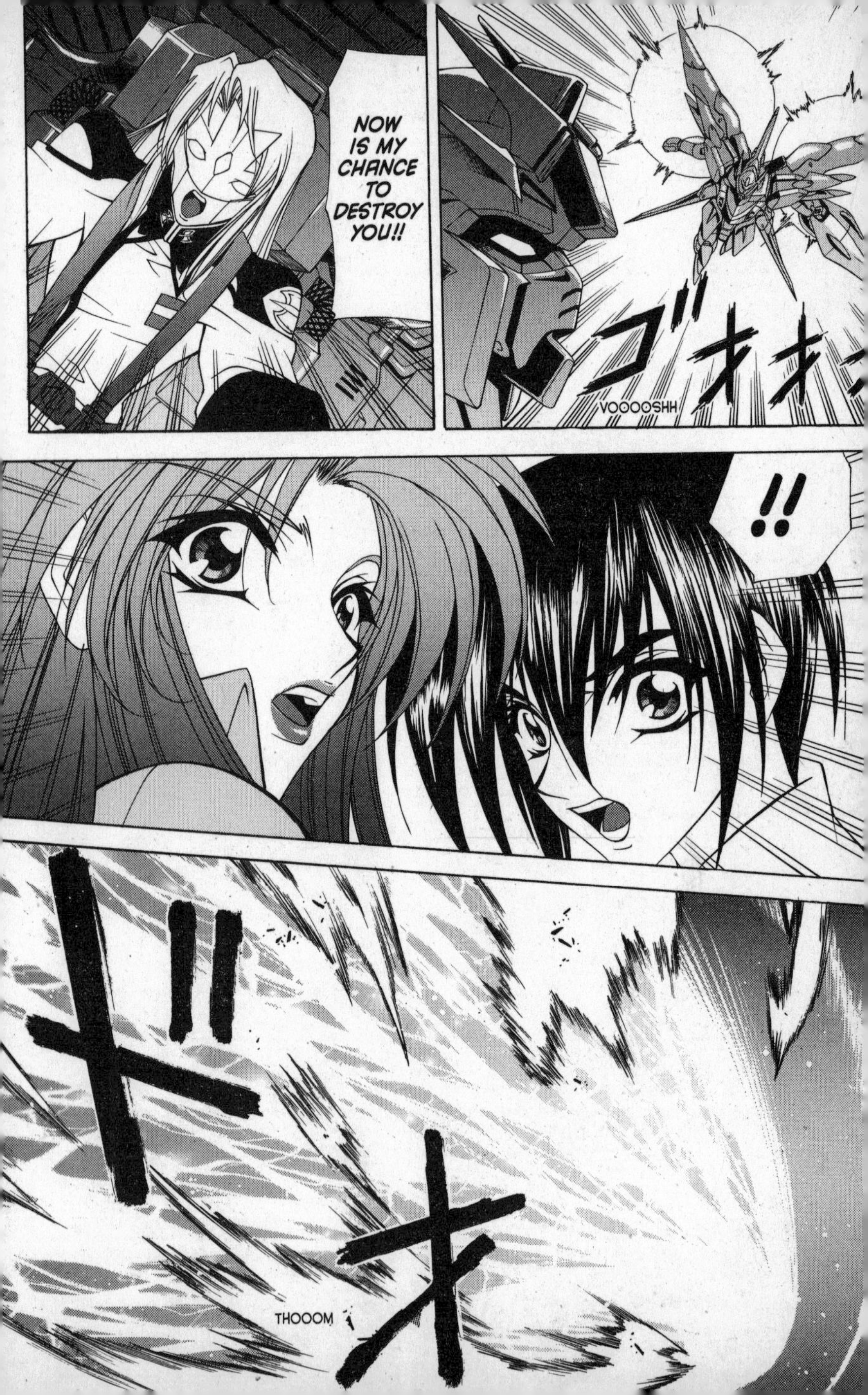
VOOOOSHH
NOW IS MY CHANCE TO DESTROY YOU!!
!!
THOOOM

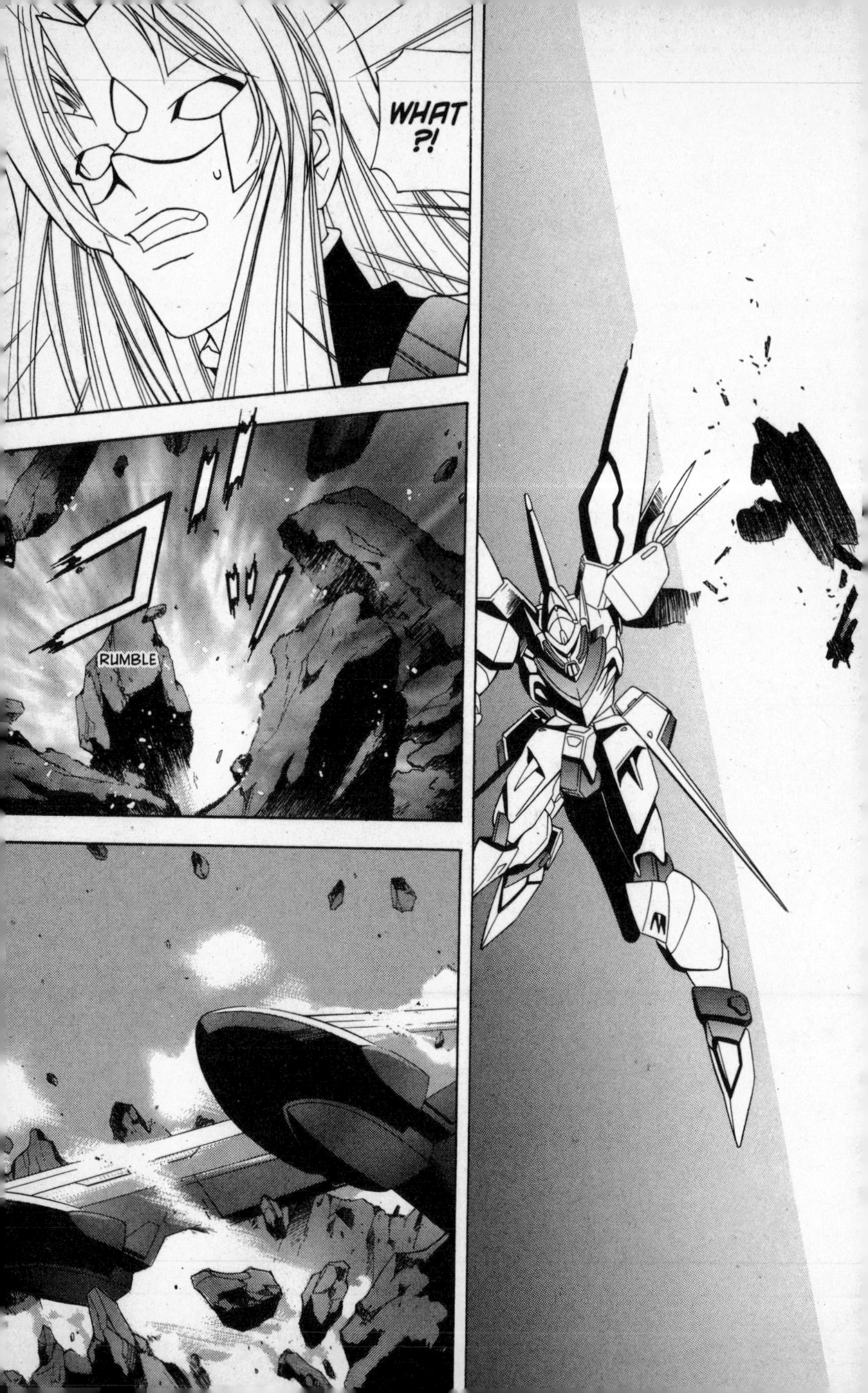
WHAT ?!
RUMBLE

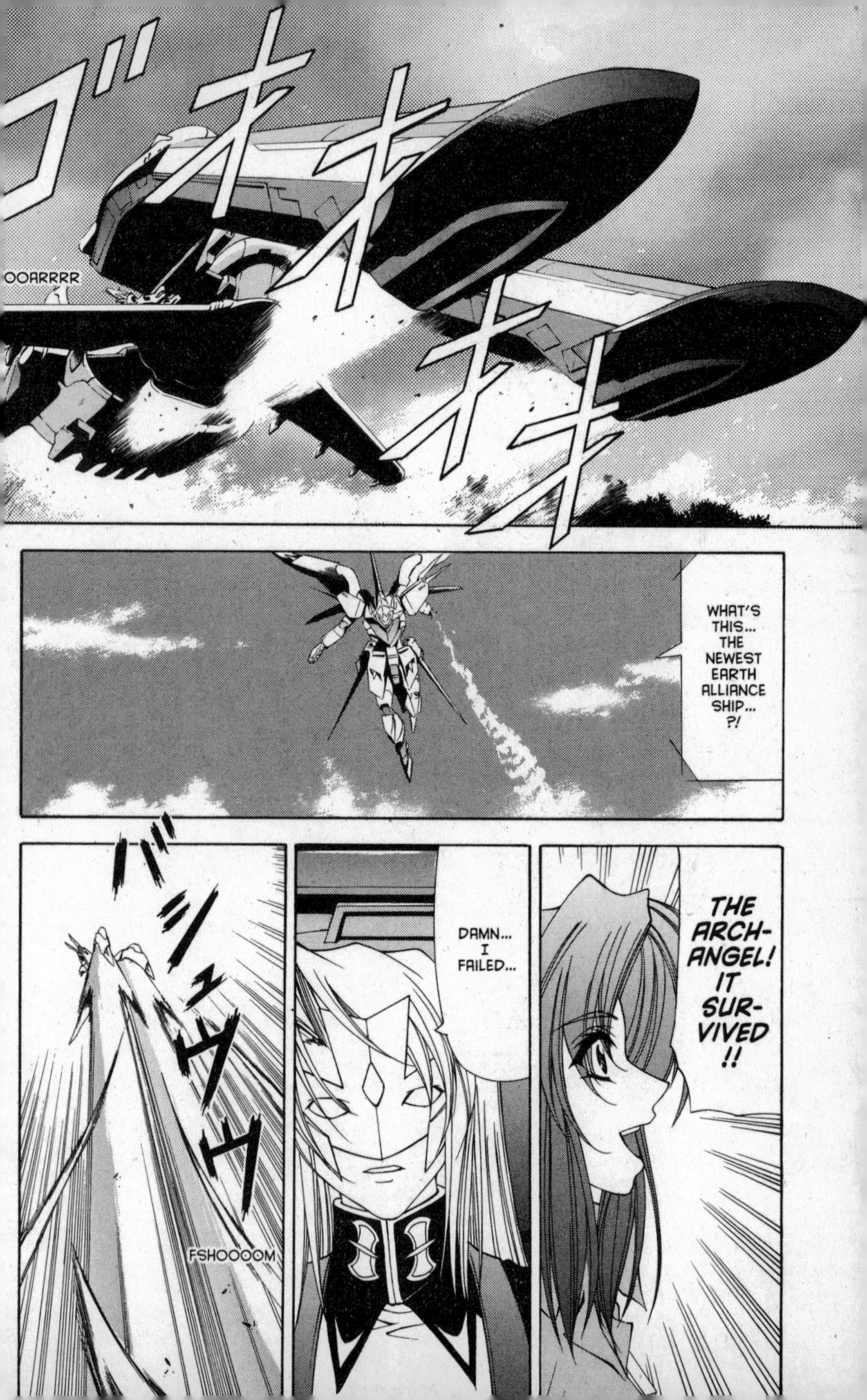
ゴオオオオ
OOARRRR
WHAT'S THIS... THE NEWEST EARTH ALLIANCE SHIP...?!
THE ARCH-ANGEL! IT SUR-VIVED!!
DAMN... I FAILED...
バシュウウ
FSHOOOOM

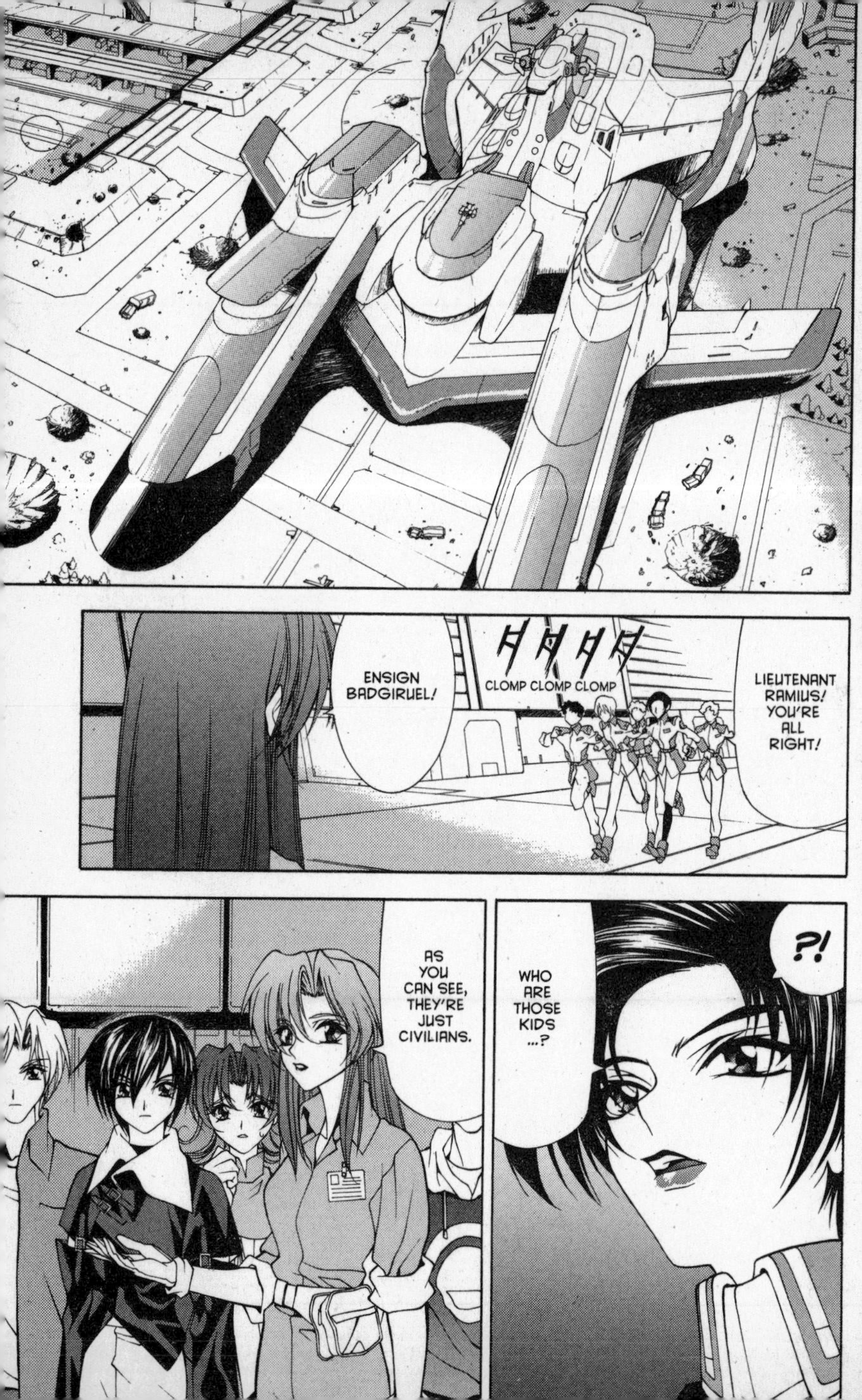
LIEUTENANT RAMIUS! YOU'RE ALL RIGHT!
CLOMP CLOMP CLOMP
ENSIGN BADGIRUEL!
?!
WHO ARE THOSE KIDS ...?
AS YOU CAN SEE, THEY'RE JUST CIVILIANS.

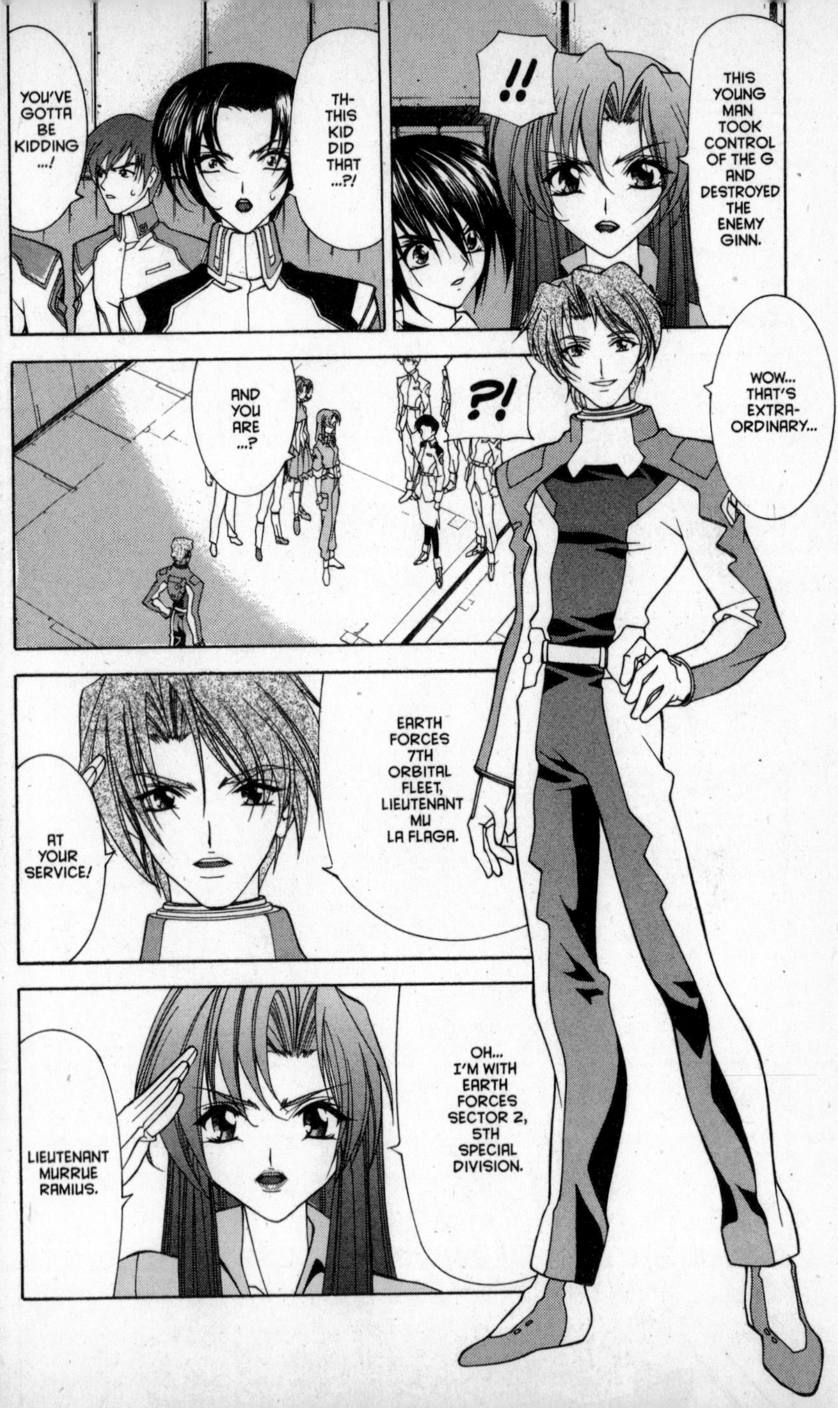
!!
THIS YOUNG MAN TOOK CONTROL OF THE G AND DESTROYED THE ENEMY GINN.
TH-THIS KID DID THAT ...?!
YOU'VE GOTTA BE KIDDING ...!
WOW... THAT'S EXTRA-ORDINARY...
?!
AND YOU ARE ...?
EARTH FORCES 7TH ORBITAL FLEET, LIEUTENANT MU LA FLAGA.
AT YOUR SERVICE!
OH... I'M WITH EARTH FORCES SECTOR 2, 5TH SPECIAL DIVISION.
LIEUTENANT MURRUE RAMIUS.

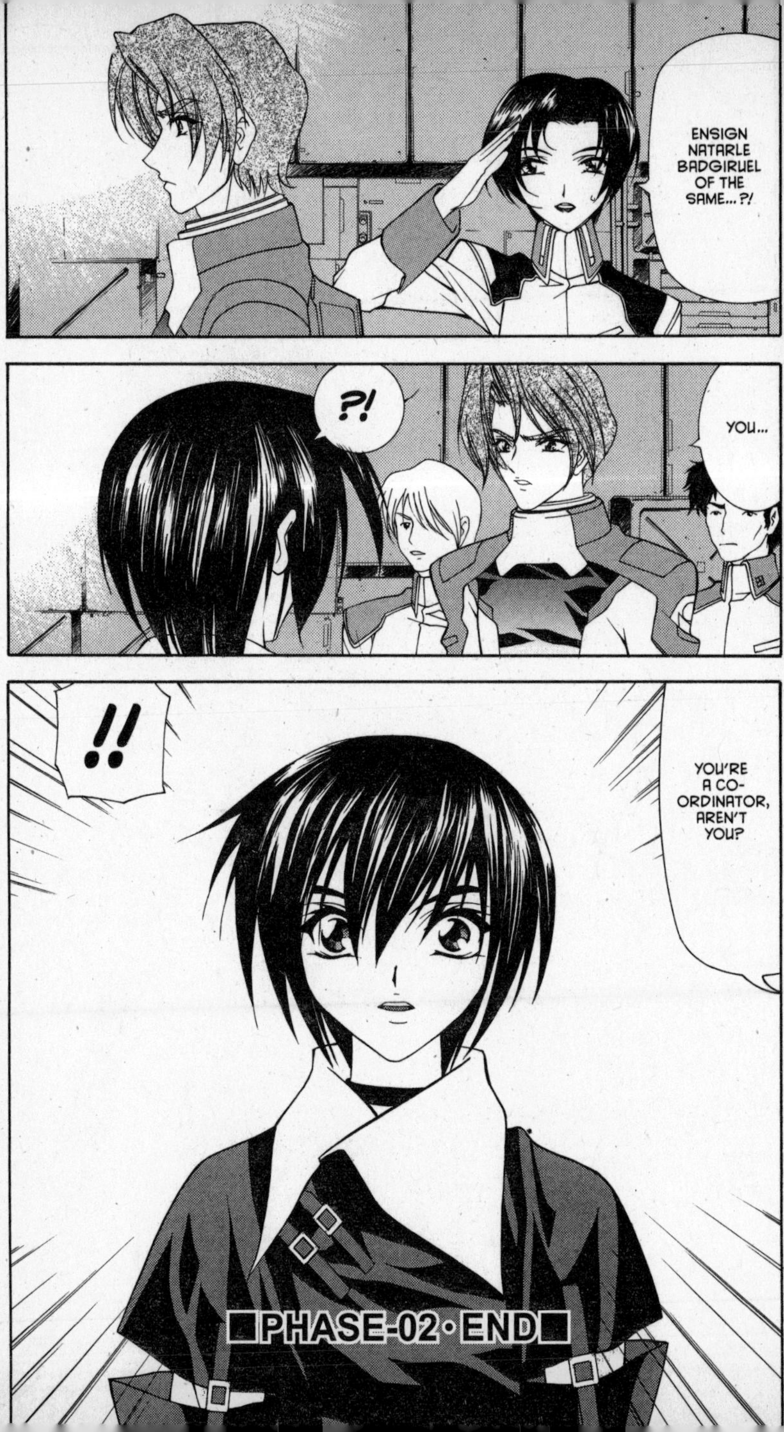
ENSIGN NATARLE BADGIRUEL OF THE SAME...?!
YOU...
?!
YOU'RE A CO-ORDINATOR, AREN'T YOU?
!!
■PHASE-02 • END■

NEW MODEL MOBILE ASSAULT SHIP ARCHANGEL

AS THE WAR REACHED A STALEMATE, IN THE HOPES OF TURNING THE TIDE, THE EARTH FORCES CONSTRUCTED THIS NEW MODEL MOBILE ASSAULT SHIP "ARCHANGEL." ABLE TO TRAVEL AT HIGH SPEEDS, IT WAS BUILT EVEN LARGER THAN PREVIOUS EARTH BATTLESHIPS, FOR THE PURPOSE OF LOADING IT WITH THE NEWLY DEVELOPED MOBILE SUITS. IT IS A HEAVILY ARMED DESTROYER THAT COULD VERY WELL CHANGE THE FACE OF THE WAR.

BADOOM!

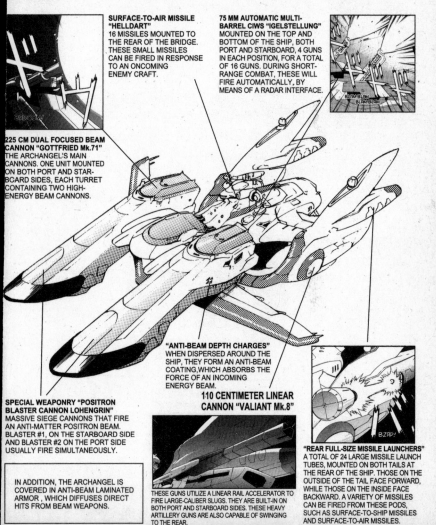

SURFACE-TO-AIR MISSILE "HELLDART"
16 MISSILES MOUNTED TO THE REAR OF THE BRIDGE. THESE SMALL MISSILES CAN BE FIRED IN RESPONSE TO AN ONCOMING ENEMY CRAFT.

75 MM AUTOMATIC MULTI-BARREL CIWS "IGELSTELLUNG"
MOUNTED ON THE TOP AND BOTTOM OF THE SHIP, BOTH PORT AND STARBOARD, 4 GUNS IN EACH POSITION, FOR A TOTAL OF 16 GUNS. DURING SHORT-RANGE COMBAT, THESE WILL FIRE AUTOMATICALLY, BY MEANS OF A RADAR INTERFACE.

BLAM BLAM
BLAM BLAM

225 CM DUAL FOCUSED BEAM CANNON "GOTTFRIED Mk.71"
THE ARCHANGEL'S MAIN CANNONS. ONE UNIT MOUNTED ON BOTH PORT AND STARBOARD SIDES, EACH TURRET CONTAINING TWO HIGH-ENERGY BEAM CANNONS.

"ANTI-BEAM DEPTH CHARGES"
WHEN DISPERSED AROUND THE SHIP, THEY FORM AN ANTI-BEAM COATING,WHICH ABSORBS THE FORCE OF AN INCOMING ENERGY BEAM.

BZAP!

SPECIAL WEAPONRY "POSITRON BLASTER CANNON LOHENGRIN"
MASSIVE SIEGE CANNONS THAT FIRE AN ANTI-MATTER POSITRON BEAM. BLASTER #1, ON THE STARBOARD SIDE AND BLASTER #2 ON THE PORT SIDE USUALLY FIRE SIMULTANEOUSLY.

110 CENTIMETER LINEAR CANNON "VALIANT Mk.8"

THESE GUNS UTILIZE A LINEAR RAIL ACCELERATOR TO FIRE LARGE-CALIBER SLUGS. THEY ARE BUILT-IN ON BOTH PORT AND STARBOARD SIDES. THESE HEAVY ARTILLERY GUNS ARE ALSO CAPABLE OF SWINGING TO THE REAR.

"REAR FULL-SIZE MISSILE LAUNCHERS"
A TOTAL OF 24 LARGE MISSILE LAUNCH TUBES, MOUNTED ON BOTH TAILS AT THE REAR OF THE SHIP. THOSE ON THE OUTSIDE OF THE TAIL FACE FORWARD, WHILE THOSE ON THE INSIDE FACE BACKWARD. A VARIETY OF MISSILES CAN BE FIRED FROM THESE PODS, SUCH AS SURFACE-TO-SHIP MISSILES AND SURFACE-TO-AIR MISSILES.

IN ADDITION, THE ARCHANGEL IS COVERED IN ANTI-BEAM LAMINATED ARMOR , WHICH DIFFUSES DIRECT HITS FROM BEAM WEAPONS.

PHASE-03: COLLAPSING HOMELAND

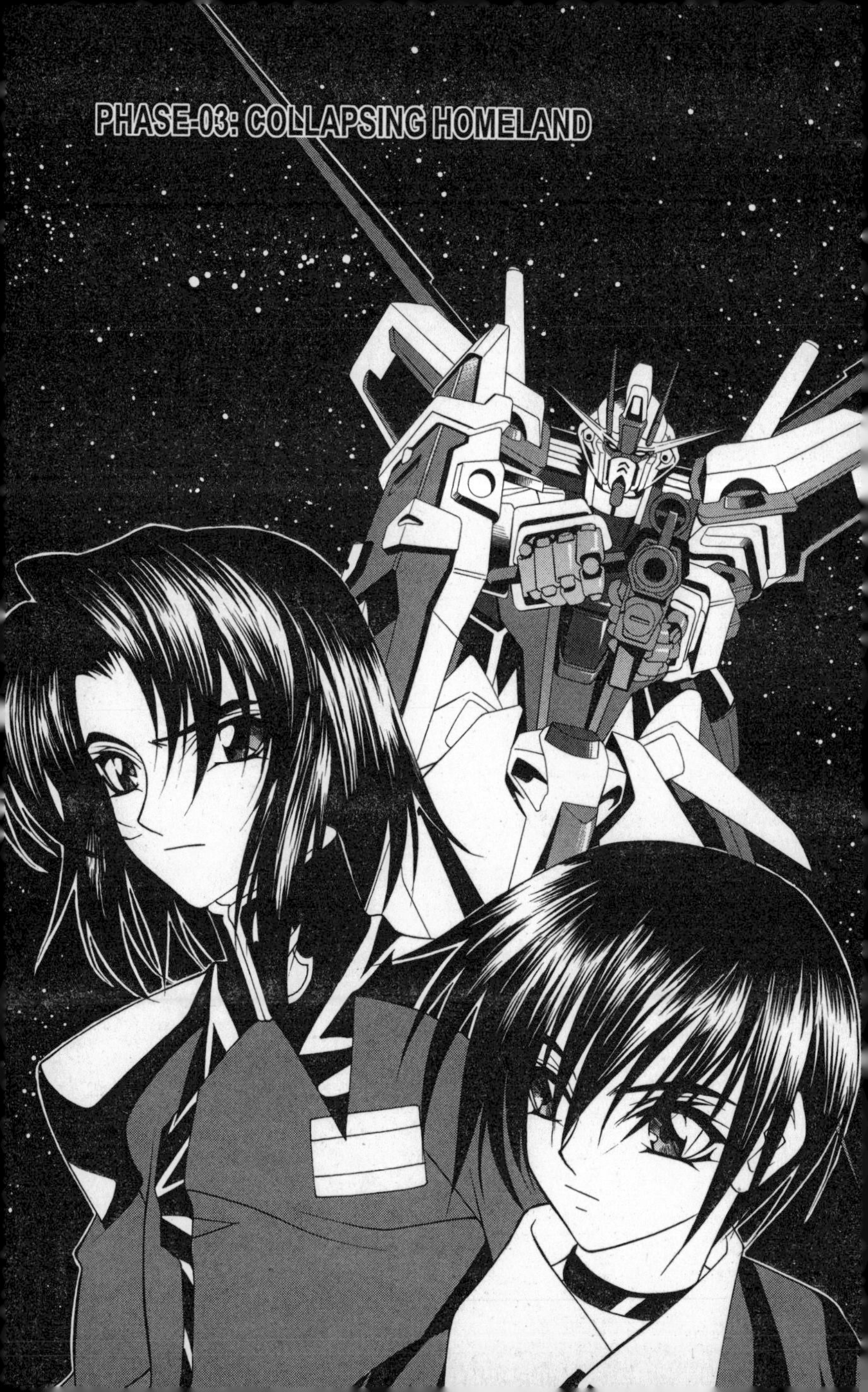

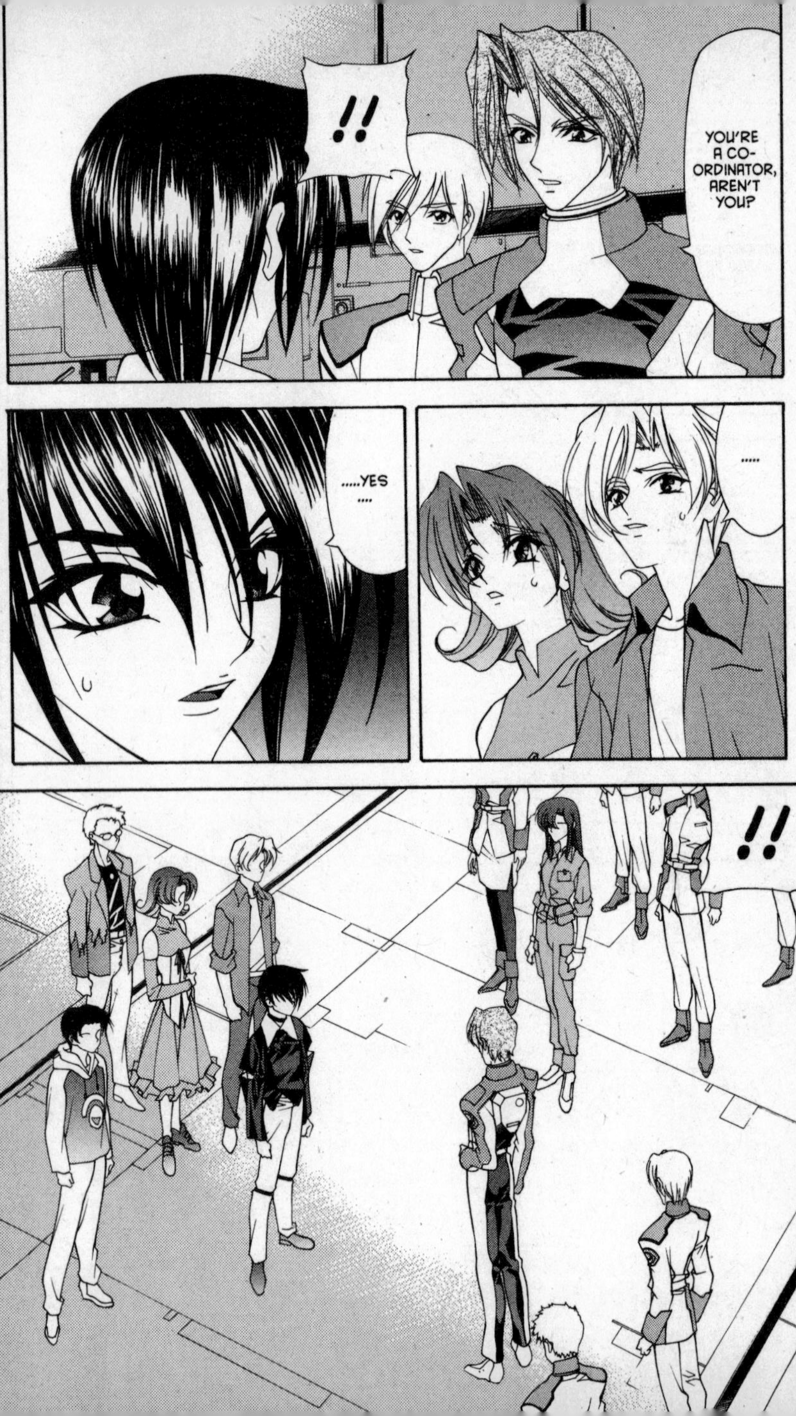
YOU'RE A CO-ORDINATOR, AREN'T YOU?
!!
.....
.....YES ....
!!

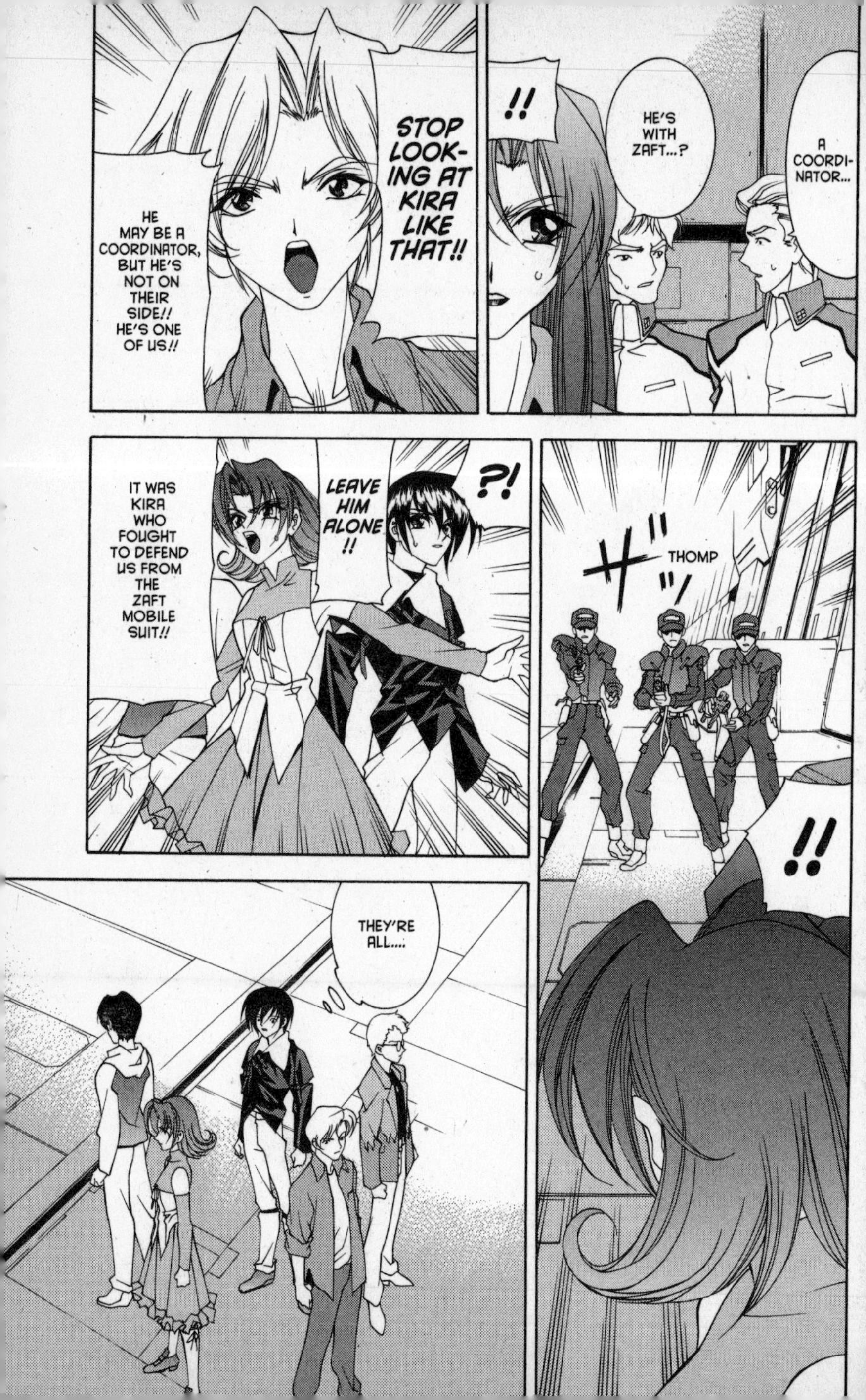
A COORDINATOR...
HE'S WITH ZAFT...?
!!
STOP LOOKING AT KIRA LIKE THAT!!
HE MAY BE A COORDINATOR, BUT HE'S NOT ON THEIR SIDE!! HE'S ONE OF US!!
THOMP
?!
LEAVE HIM ALONE!!
IT WAS KIRA WHO FOUGHT TO DEFEND US FROM THE ZAFT MOBILE SUIT!!
!!
THEY'RE ALL....

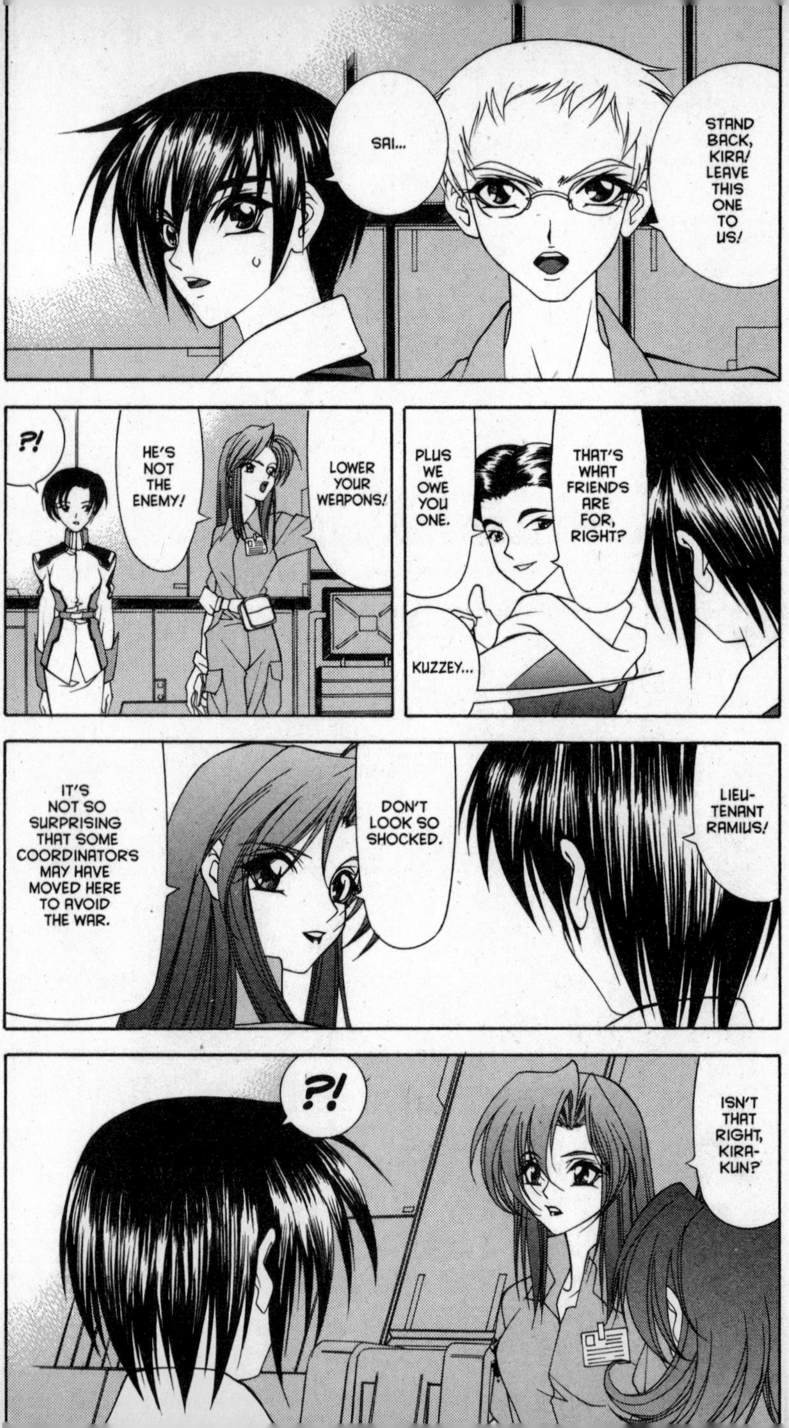
STAND BACK, KIRA! LEAVE THIS ONE TO US!
SAI...
THAT'S WHAT FRIENDS ARE FOR, RIGHT?
PLUS WE OWE YOU ONE.
KUZZEY...
LOWER YOUR WEAPONS!
HE'S NOT THE ENEMY!
?!
LIEU-TENANT RAMIUS!
DON'T LOOK SO SHOCKED.
IT'S NOT SO SURPRISING THAT SOME COORDINATORS MAY HAVE MOVED HERE TO AVOID THE WAR.
ISN'T THAT RIGHT, KIRA-KUN?
?!

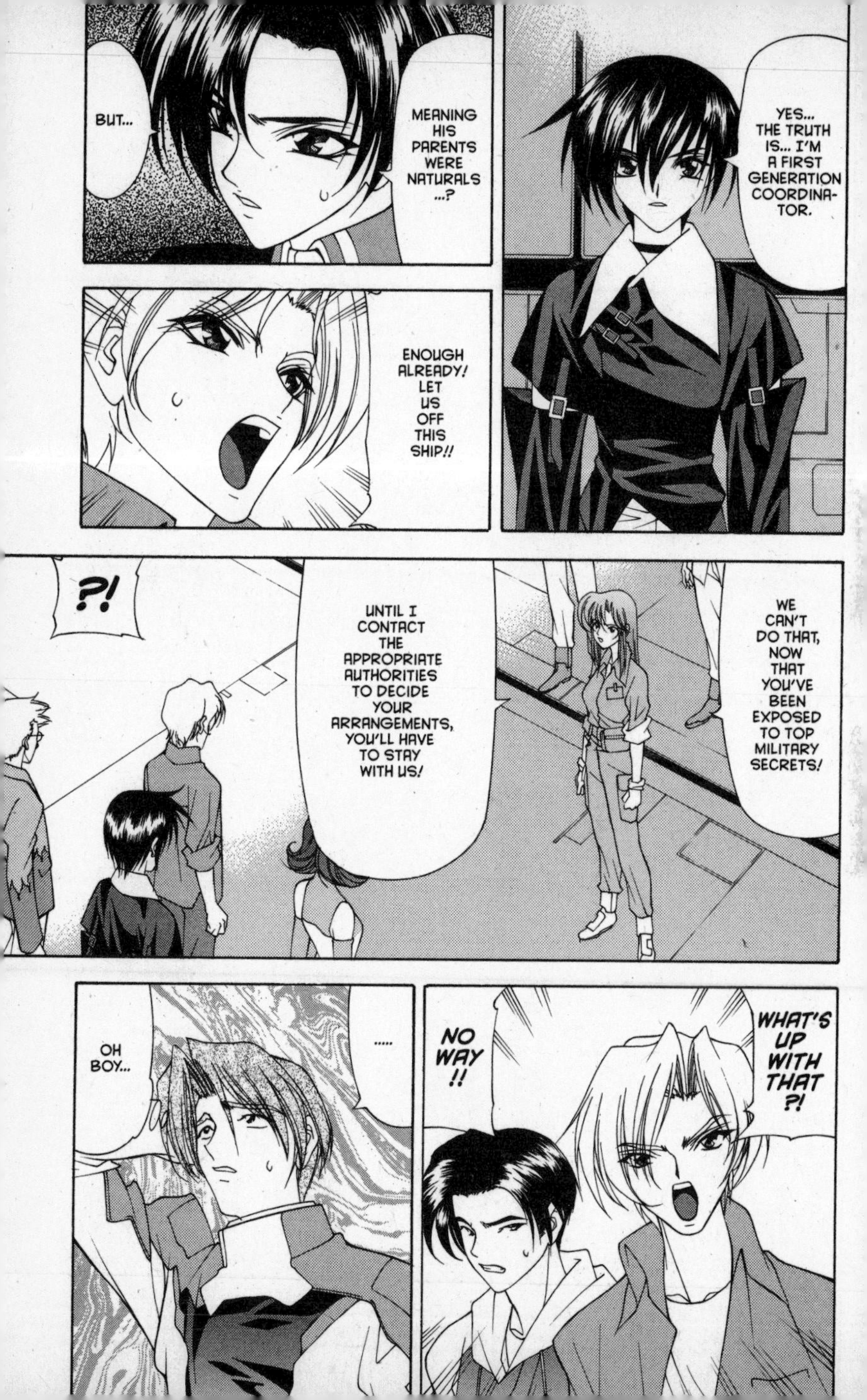
YES... THE TRUTH IS... I'M A FIRST GENERATION COORDINATOR.
MEANING HIS PARENTS WERE NATURALS ...?
BUT...
ENOUGH ALREADY! LET US OFF THIS SHIP!!
WE CAN'T DO THAT, NOW THAT YOU'VE BEEN EXPOSED TO TOP MILITARY SECRETS!
UNTIL I CONTACT THE APPROPRIATE AUTHORITIES TO DECIDE YOUR ARRANGEMENTS, YOU'LL HAVE TO STAY WITH US!
?!
WHAT'S UP WITH THAT?!
NO WAY!!
.....
OH BOY...

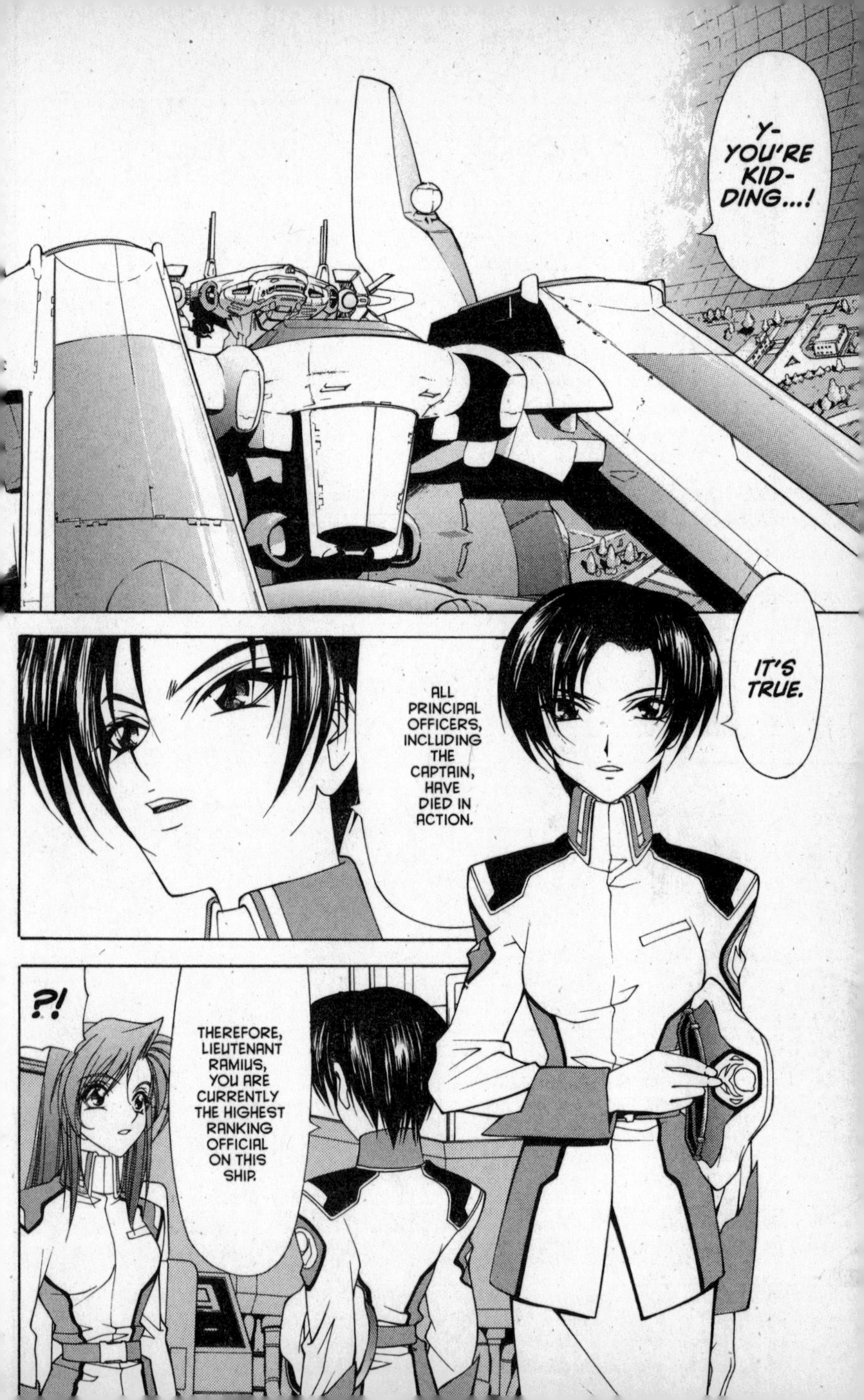

Y-YOU'RE KID-DING...!
IT'S TRUE.
ALL PRINCIPAL OFFICERS, INCLUDING THE CAPTAIN, HAVE DIED IN ACTION.
THEREFORE, LIEUTENANT RAMIUS, YOU ARE CURRENTLY THE HIGHEST RANKING OFFICIAL ON THIS SHIP.
?!

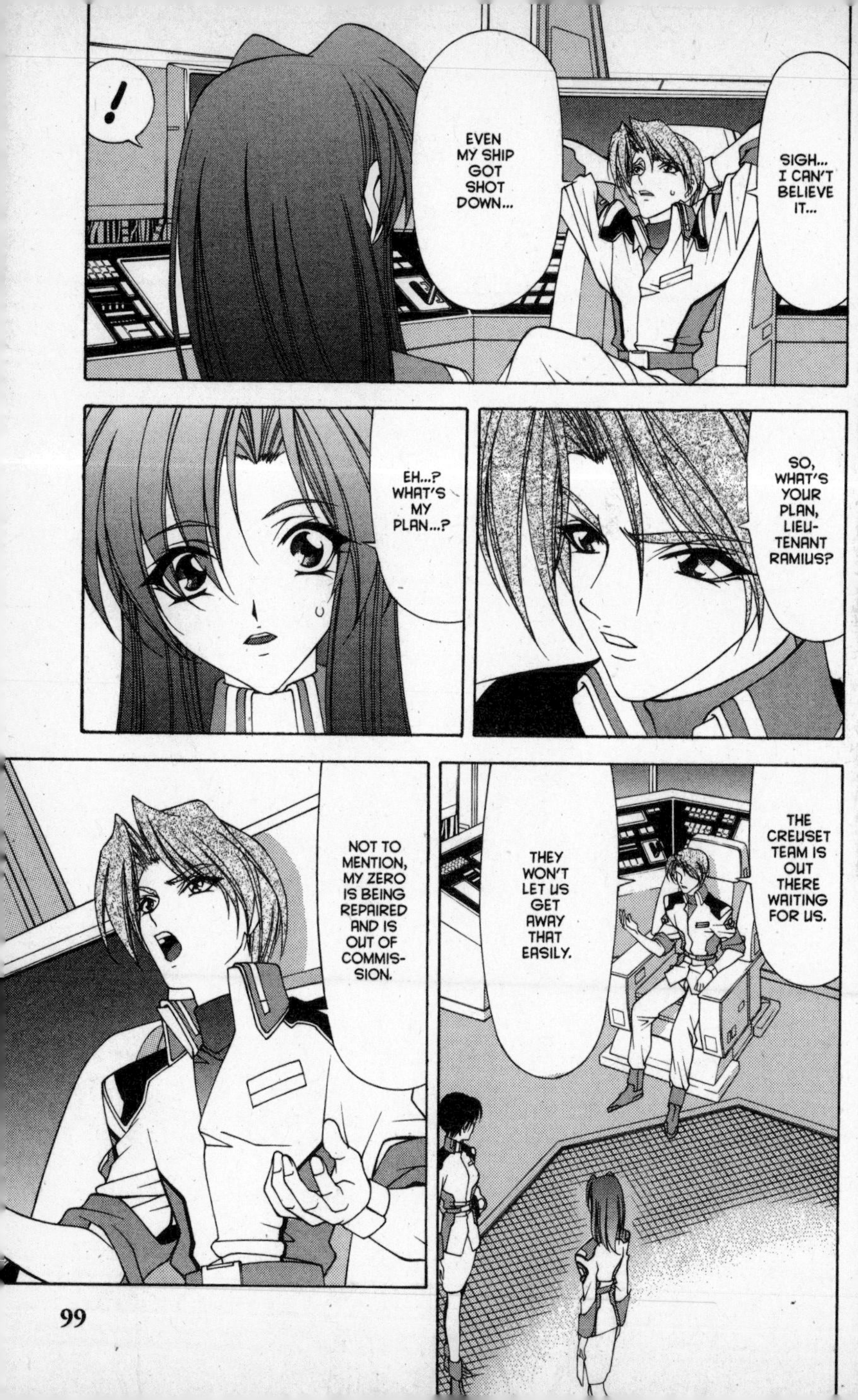
SIGH... I CAN'T BELIEVE IT...
EVEN MY SHIP GOT SHOT DOWN...
!
SO, WHAT'S YOUR PLAN, LIEU-TENANT RAMIUS?
EH...? WHAT'S MY PLAN...?
THE CREUSET TEAM IS OUT THERE WAITING FOR US.
THEY WON'T LET US GET AWAY THAT EASILY.
NOT TO MENTION, MY ZERO IS BEING REPAIRED AND IS OUT OF COMMIS-SION.

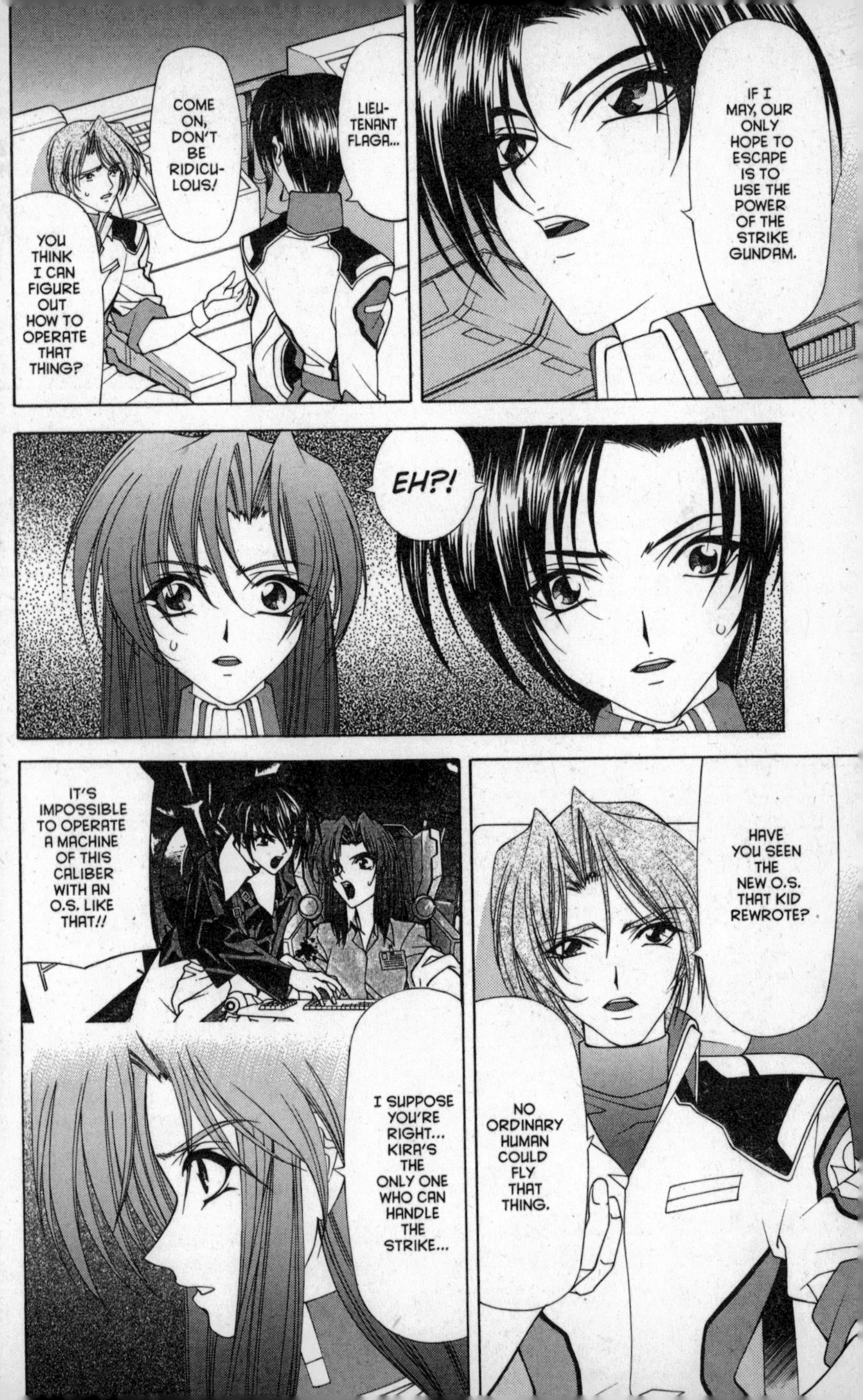
IF I MAY, OUR ONLY HOPE TO ESCAPE IS TO USE THE POWER OF THE STRIKE GUNDAM.
LIEU-TENANT FLAGA...
COME ON, DON'T BE RIDICU-LOUS!
YOU THINK I CAN FIGURE OUT HOW TO OPERATE THAT THING?
EH?!
HAVE YOU SEEN THE NEW O.S. THAT KID REWROTE?
NO ORDINARY HUMAN COULD FLY THAT THING.
IT'S IMPOSSIBLE TO OPERATE A MACHINE OF THIS CALIBER WITH AN O.S. LIKE THAT!!
I SUPPOSE YOU'RE RIGHT... KIRA'S THE ONLY ONE WHO CAN HANDLE THE STRIKE...

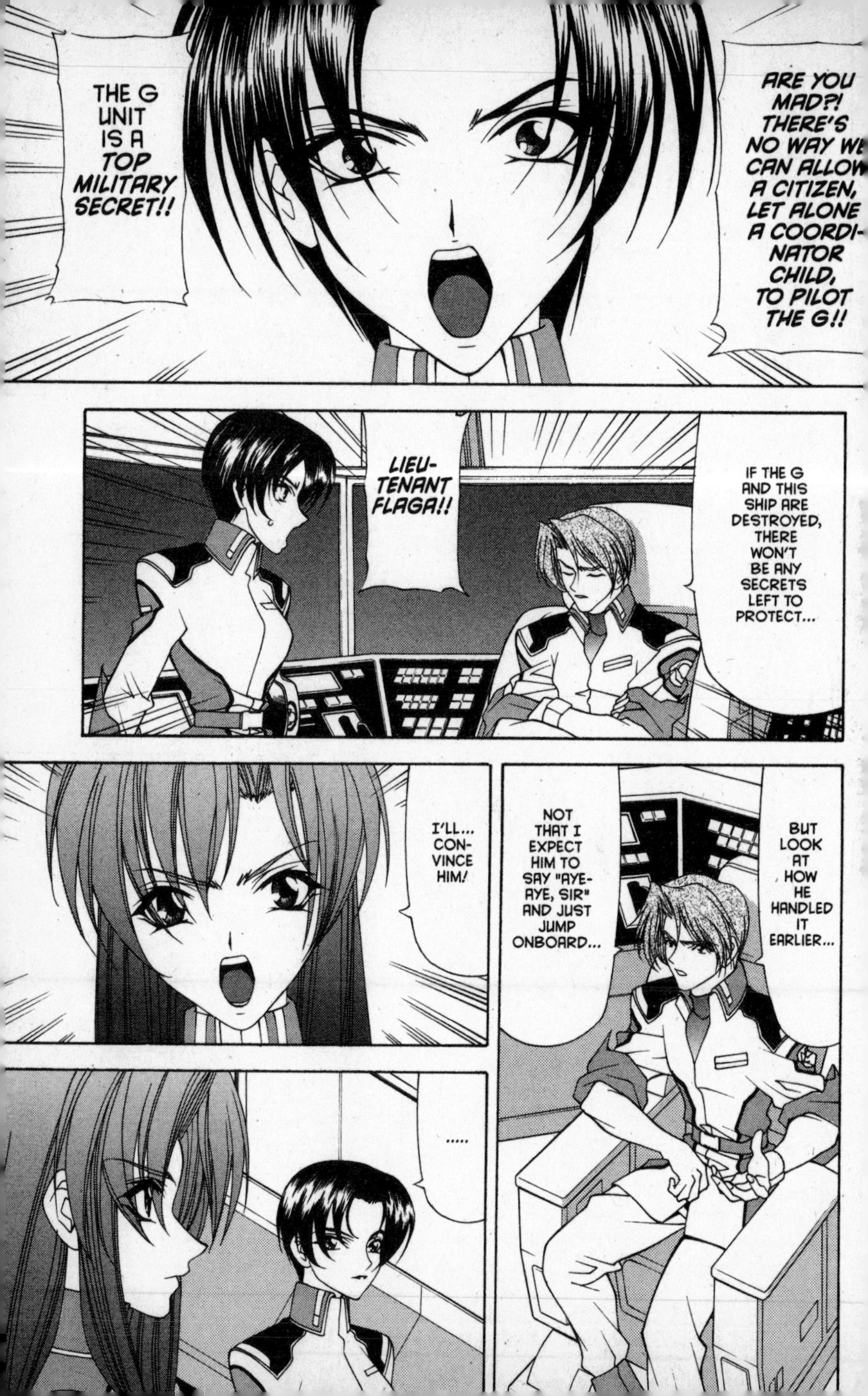

ARE YOU MAD?! THERE'S NO WAY WE CAN ALLOW A CITIZEN, LET ALONE A COORDINATOR CHILD, TO PILOT THE G!!
THE G UNIT IS A TOP MILITARY SECRET!!
IF THE G AND THIS SHIP ARE DESTROYED, THERE WON'T BE ANY SECRETS LEFT TO PROTECT...
LIEUTENANT FLAGA!!
BUT LOOK AT HOW HE HANDLED IT EARLIER...
NOT THAT I EXPECT HIM TO SAY "AYE-AYE, SIR" AND JUST JUMP ONBOARD...
I'LL... CONVINCE HIM!
.....

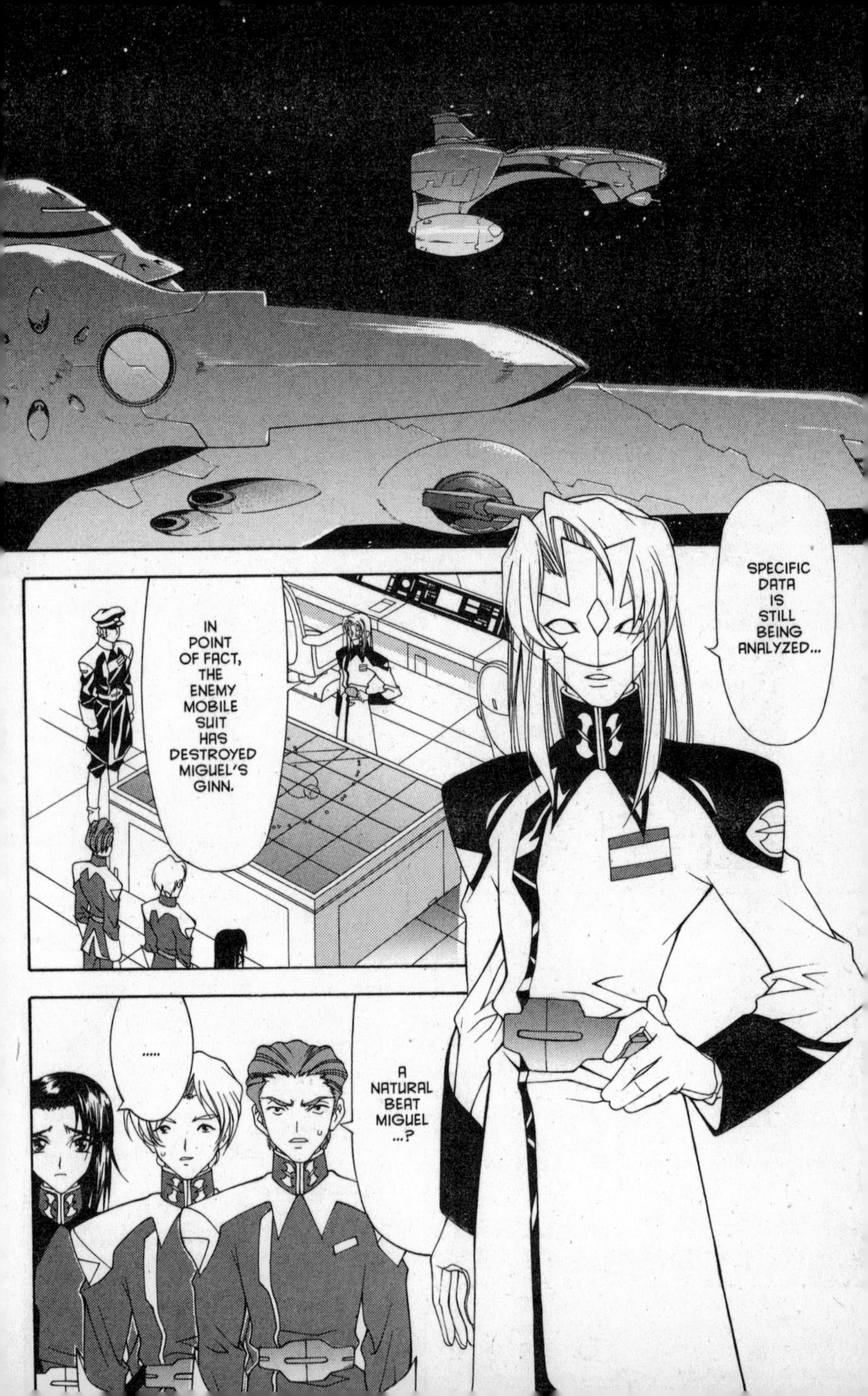
SPECIFIC DATA IS STILL BEING ANALYZED...
IN POINT OF FACT, THE ENEMY MOBILE SUIT HAS DESTROYED MIGUEL'S GINN.
A NATURAL BEAT MIGUEL ...?
.....

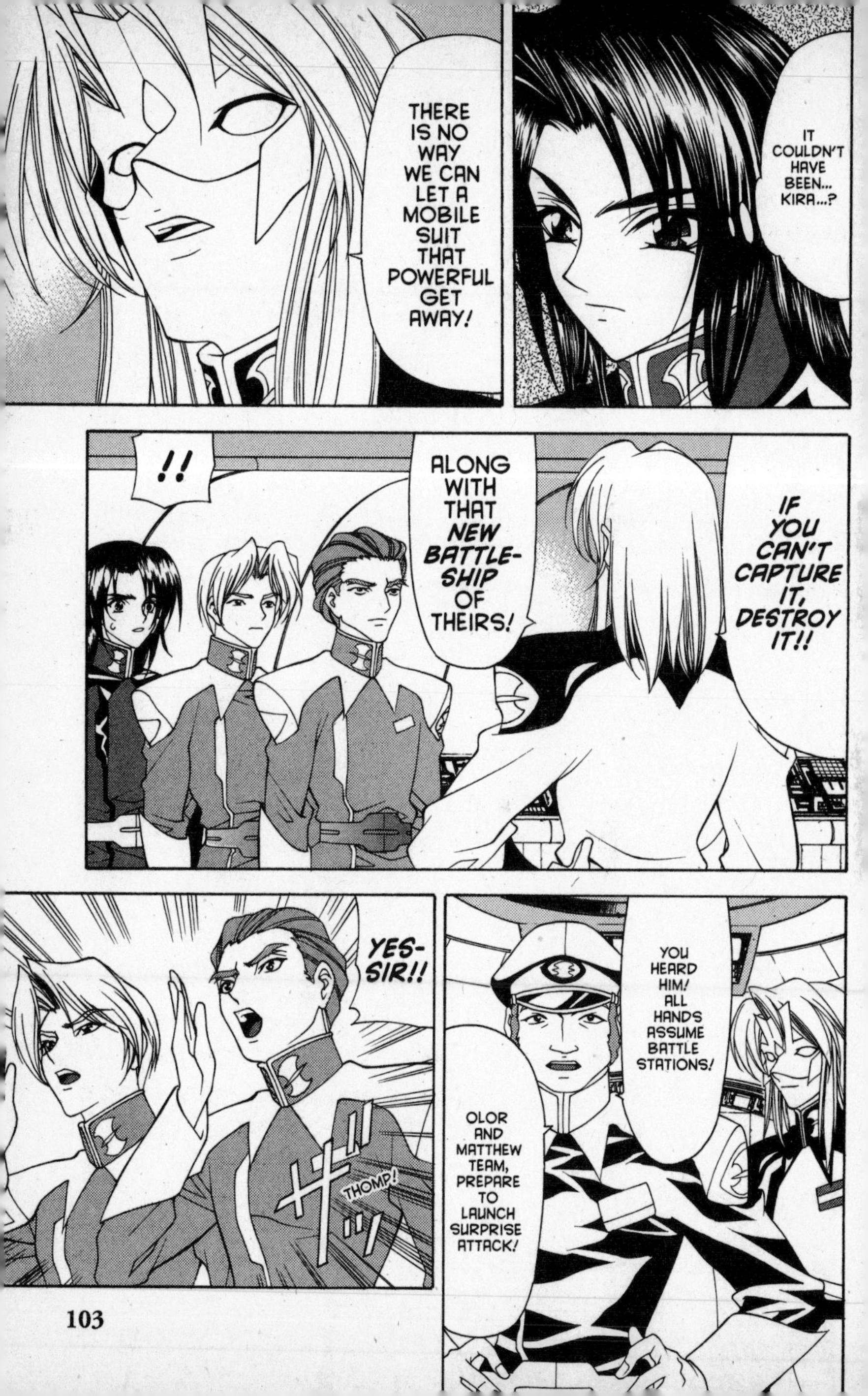
IT COULDN'T HAVE BEEN... KIRA...?
THERE IS NO WAY WE CAN LET A MOBILE SUIT THAT POWERFUL GET AWAY!
IF YOU CAN'T CAPTURE IT, DESTROY IT!!
ALONG WITH THAT NEW BATTLESHIP OF THEIRS!
!!
YOU HEARD HIM! ALL HANDS ASSUME BATTLE STATIONS!
OLOR AND MATTHEW TEAM, PREPARE TO LAUNCH SURPRISE ATTACK!
YES-SIR!!
THOMP!

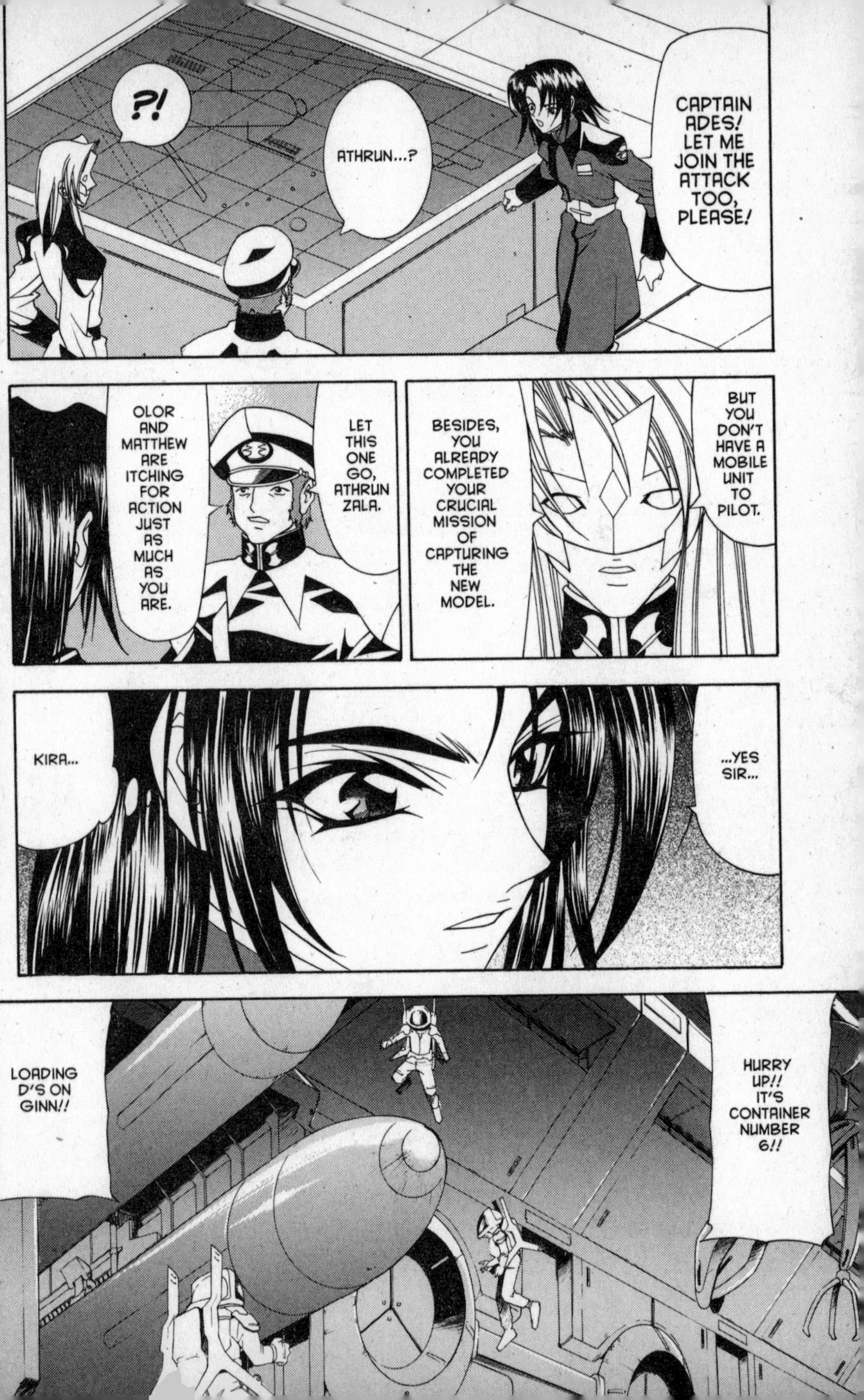
CAPTAIN ADES! LET ME JOIN THE ATTACK TOO, PLEASE!
ATHRUN...?
?!
BUT YOU DON'T HAVE A MOBILE UNIT TO PILOT.
BESIDES, YOU ALREADY COMPLETED YOUR CRUCIAL MISSION OF CAPTURING THE NEW MODEL.
LET THIS ONE GO, ATHRUN ZALA.
OLOR AND MATTHEW ARE ITCHING FOR ACTION JUST AS MUCH AS YOU ARE.
...YES SIR...
KIRA...
HURRY UP!! IT'S CONTAINER NUMBER 6!!
LOADING D'S ON GINN!!

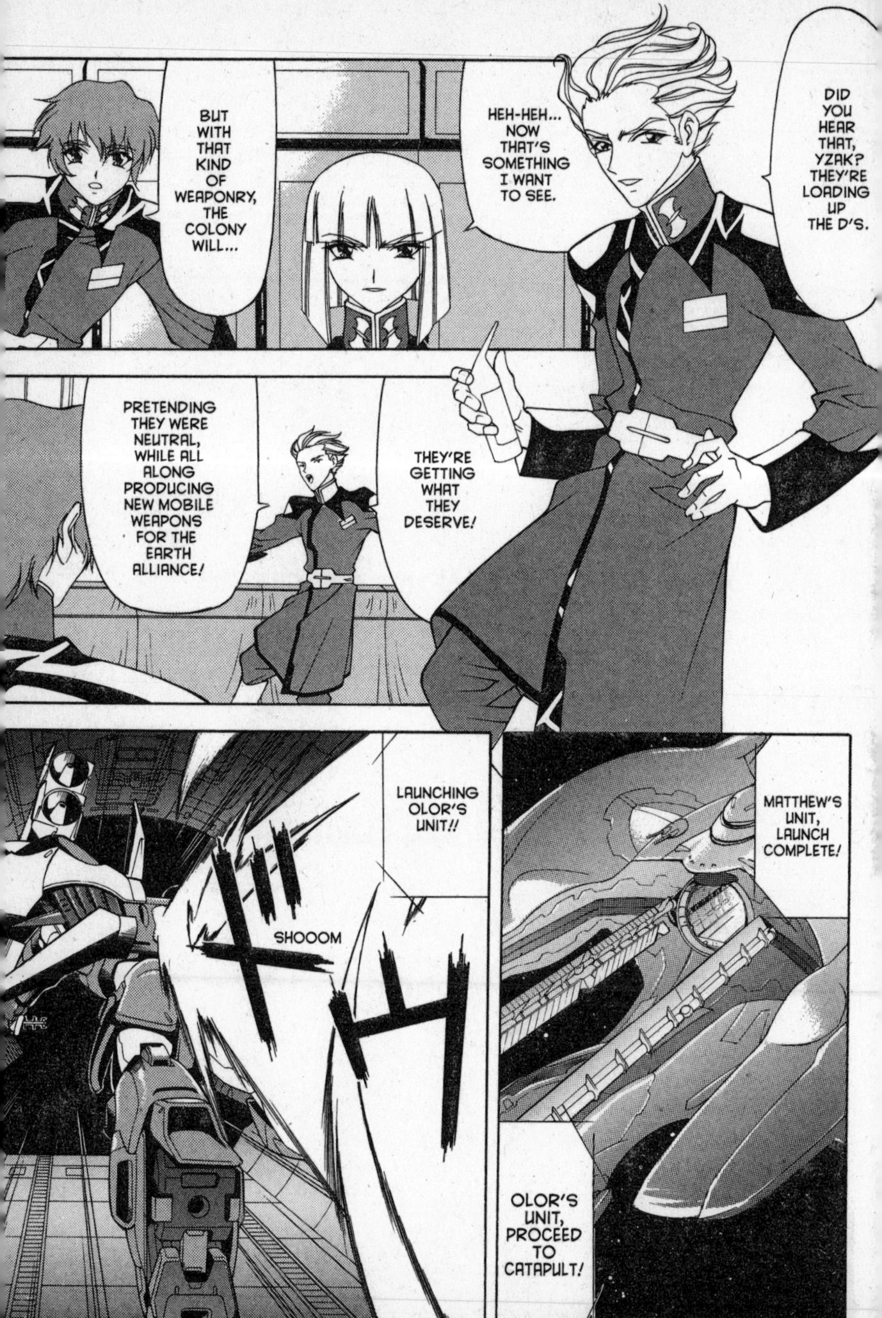
DID YOU HEAR THAT, YZAK? THEY'RE LOADING UP THE D'S.
HEH-HEH... NOW THAT'S SOMETHING I WANT TO SEE.
BUT WITH THAT KIND OF WEAPONRY, THE COLONY WILL...
THEY'RE GETTING WHAT THEY DESERVE!
PRETENDING THEY WERE NEUTRAL, WHILE ALL ALONG PRODUCING NEW MOBILE WEAPONS FOR THE EARTH ALLIANCE!
MATTHEW'S UNIT, LAUNCH COMPLETE!
OLOR'S UNIT, PROCEED TO CATAPULT!
LAUNCHING OLOR'S UNIT!!
SHOOOM

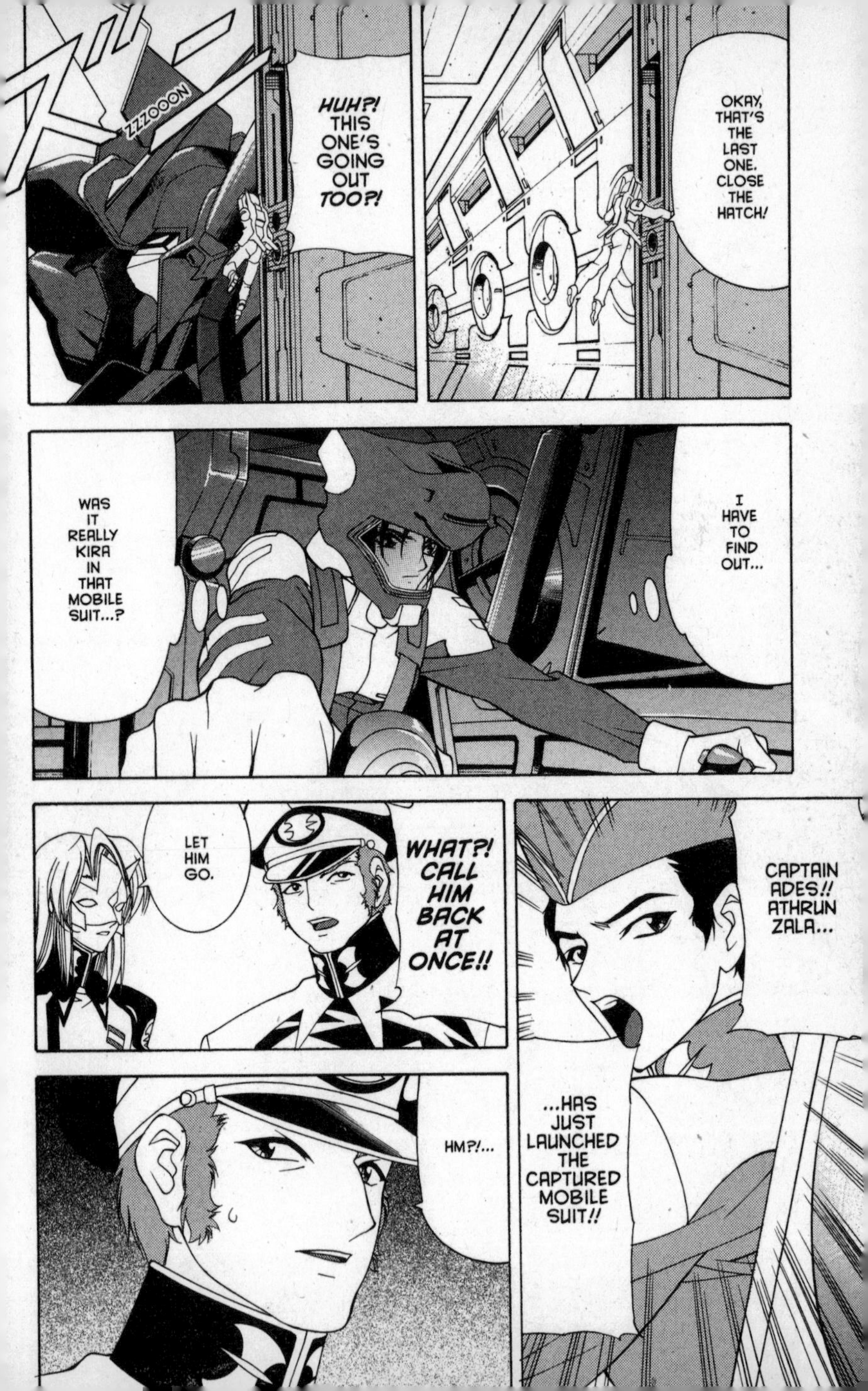
OKAY, THAT'S THE LAST ONE. CLOSE THE HATCH!
ZZZOOON
HUH?! THIS ONE'S GOING OUT TOO?!
I HAVE TO FIND OUT...
WAS IT REALLY KIRA IN THAT MOBILE SUIT...?
CAPTAIN ADES!! ATHRUN ZALA...
...HAS JUST LAUNCHED THE CAPTURED MOBILE SUIT!!
WHAT?! CALL HIM BACK AT ONCE!!
LET HIM GO.
HM?!...

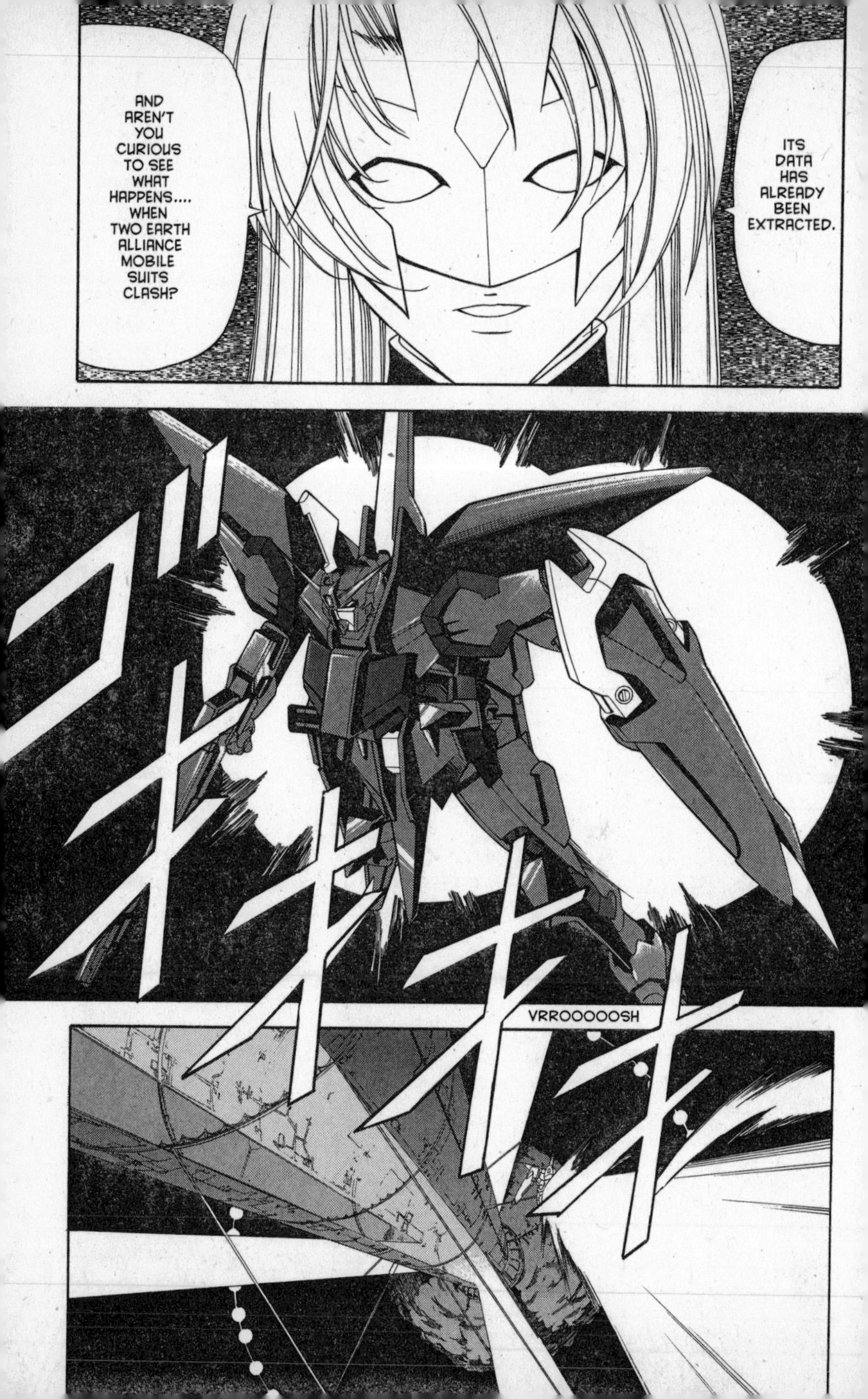
ITS DATA HAS ALREADY BEEN EXTRACTED.
AND AREN'T YOU CURIOUS TO SEE WHAT HAPPENS.... WHEN TWO EARTH ALLIANCE MOBILE SUITS CLASH?
ゴオオオオ
VRROOOOOSH

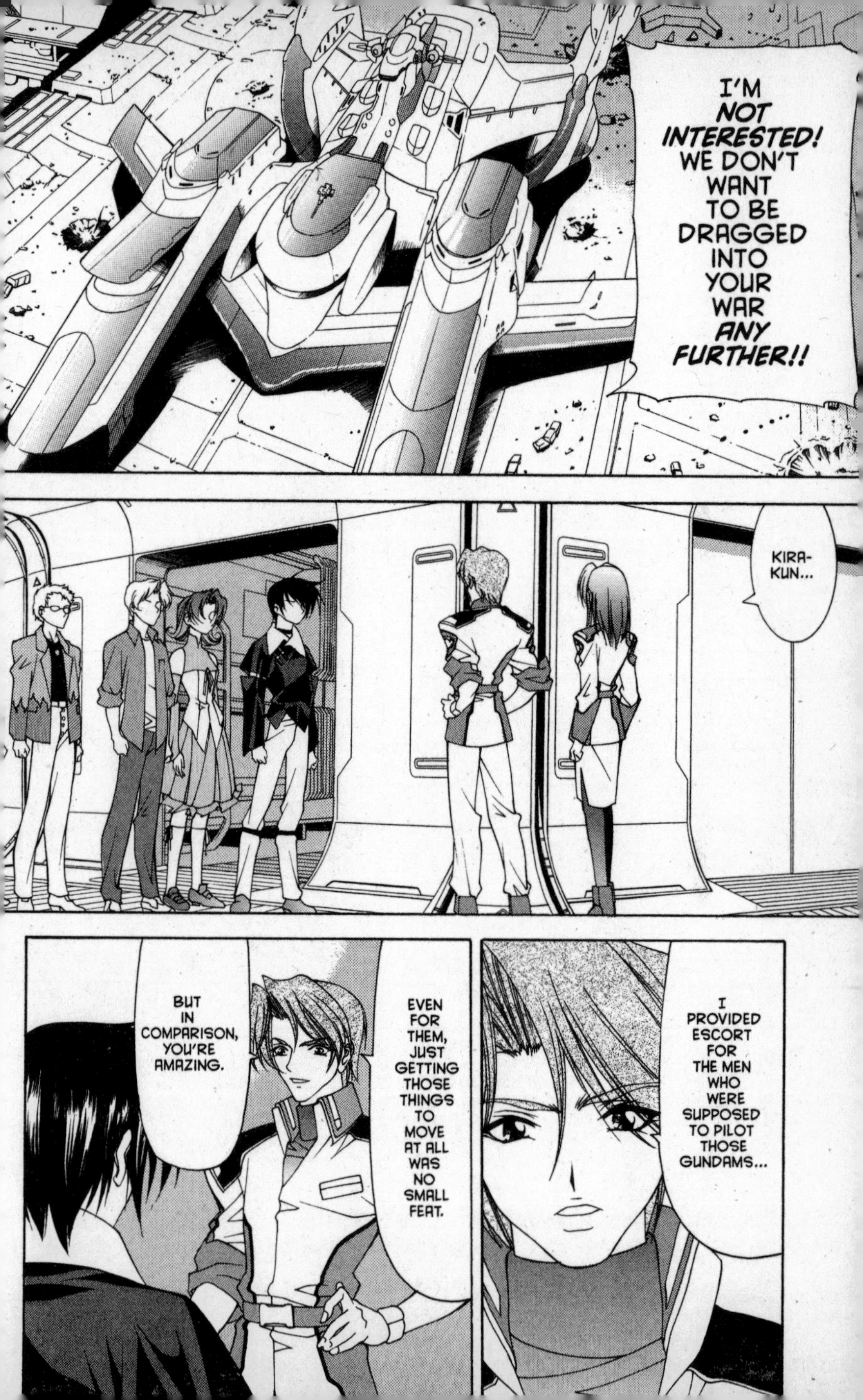
I'M NOT INTERESTED! WE DON'T WANT TO BE DRAGGED INTO YOUR WAR ANY FURTHER!!
KIRA-KUN...
I PROVIDED ESCORT FOR THE MEN WHO WERE SUPPOSED TO PILOT THOSE GUNDAMS...
EVEN FOR THEM, JUST GETTING THOSE THINGS TO MOVE AT ALL WAS NO SMALL FEAT.
BUT IN COMPARISON, YOU'RE AMAZING.

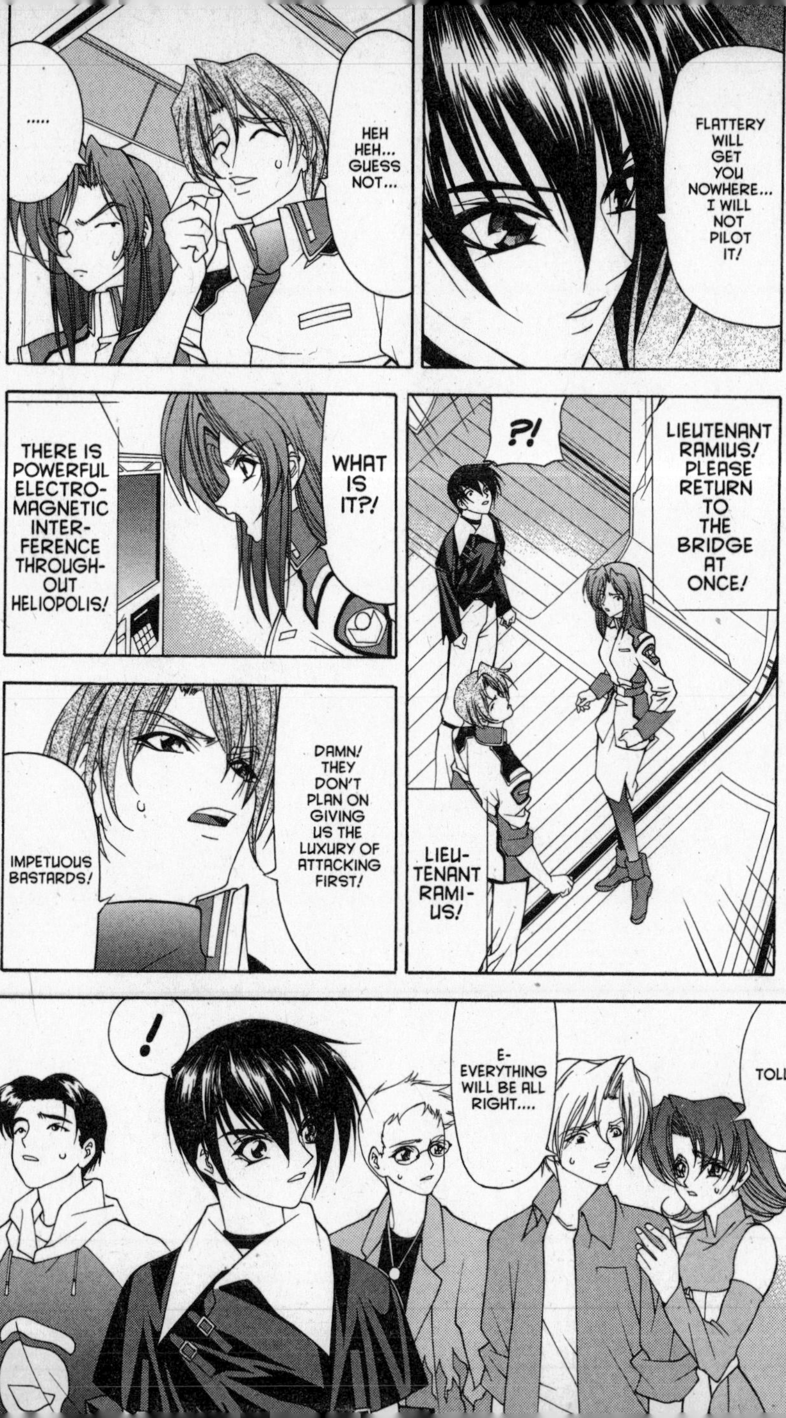
FLATTERY WILL GET YOU NOWHERE... I WILL NOT PILOT IT!
HEH HEH... GUESS NOT...
.....
LIEUTENANT RAMIUS! PLEASE RETURN TO THE BRIDGE AT ONCE!
?!
LIEU-TENANT RAMI-US!
WHAT IS IT?!
THERE IS POWERFUL ELECTRO-MAGNETIC INTER-FERENCE THROUGH-OUT HELIOPOLIS!
DAMN! THEY DON'T PLAN ON GIVING US THE LUXURY OF ATTACKING FIRST!
IMPETUOUS BASTARDS!
TOLLE.
E- EVERYTHING WILL BE ALL RIGHT....
!

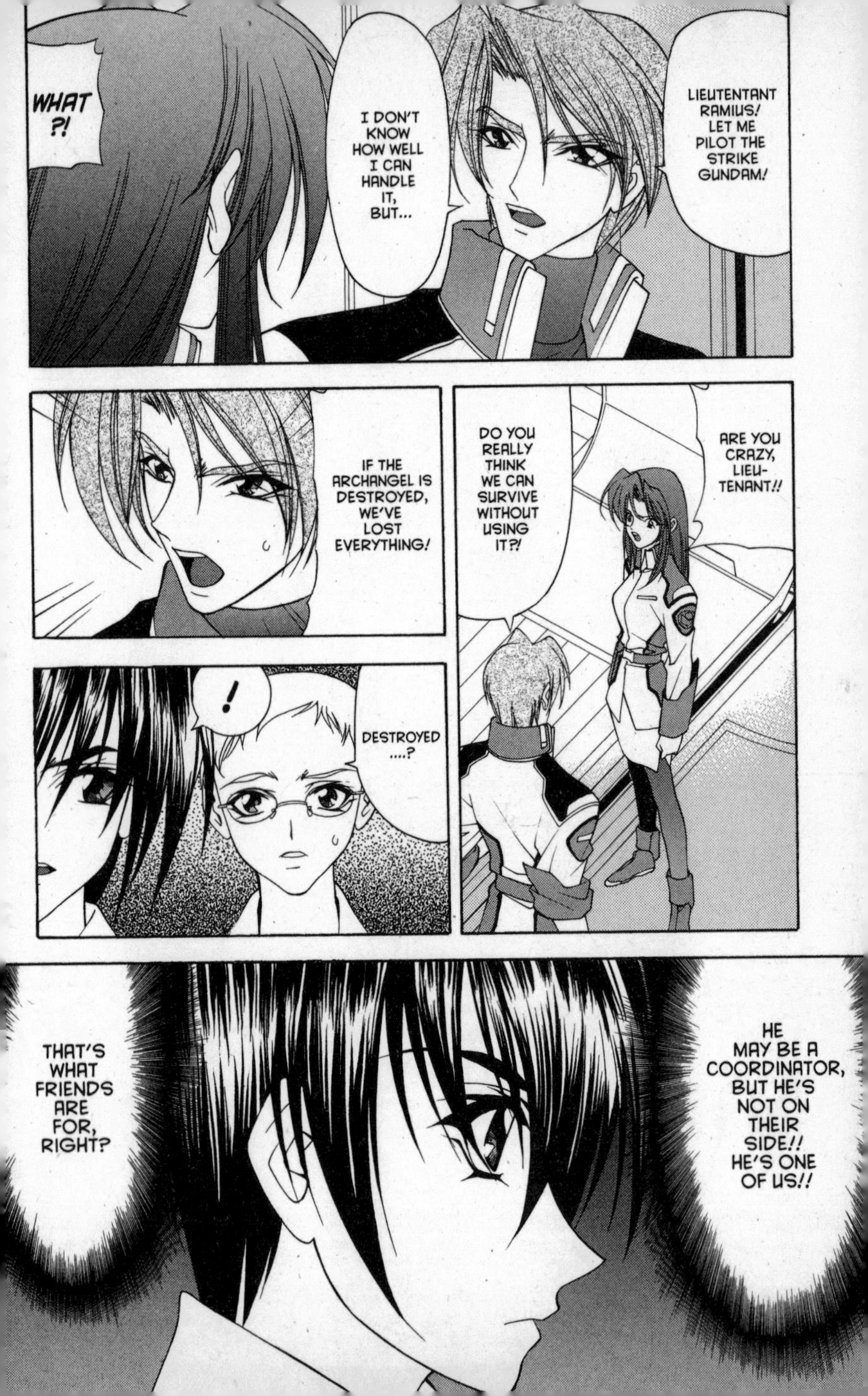
LIEUTENTANT RAMIUS! LET ME PILOT THE STRIKE GUNDAM!
I DON'T KNOW HOW WELL I CAN HANDLE IT, BUT...
WHAT?!
ARE YOU CRAZY, LIEU-TENANT!!
DO YOU REALLY THINK WE CAN SURVIVE WITHOUT USING IT?!
IF THE ARCHANGEL IS DESTROYED, WE'VE LOST EVERYTHING!
!
DESTROYED ....?
HE MAY BE A COORDINATOR, BUT HE'S NOT ON THEIR SIDE!! HE'S ONE OF US!!
THAT'S WHAT FRIENDS ARE FOR, RIGHT?

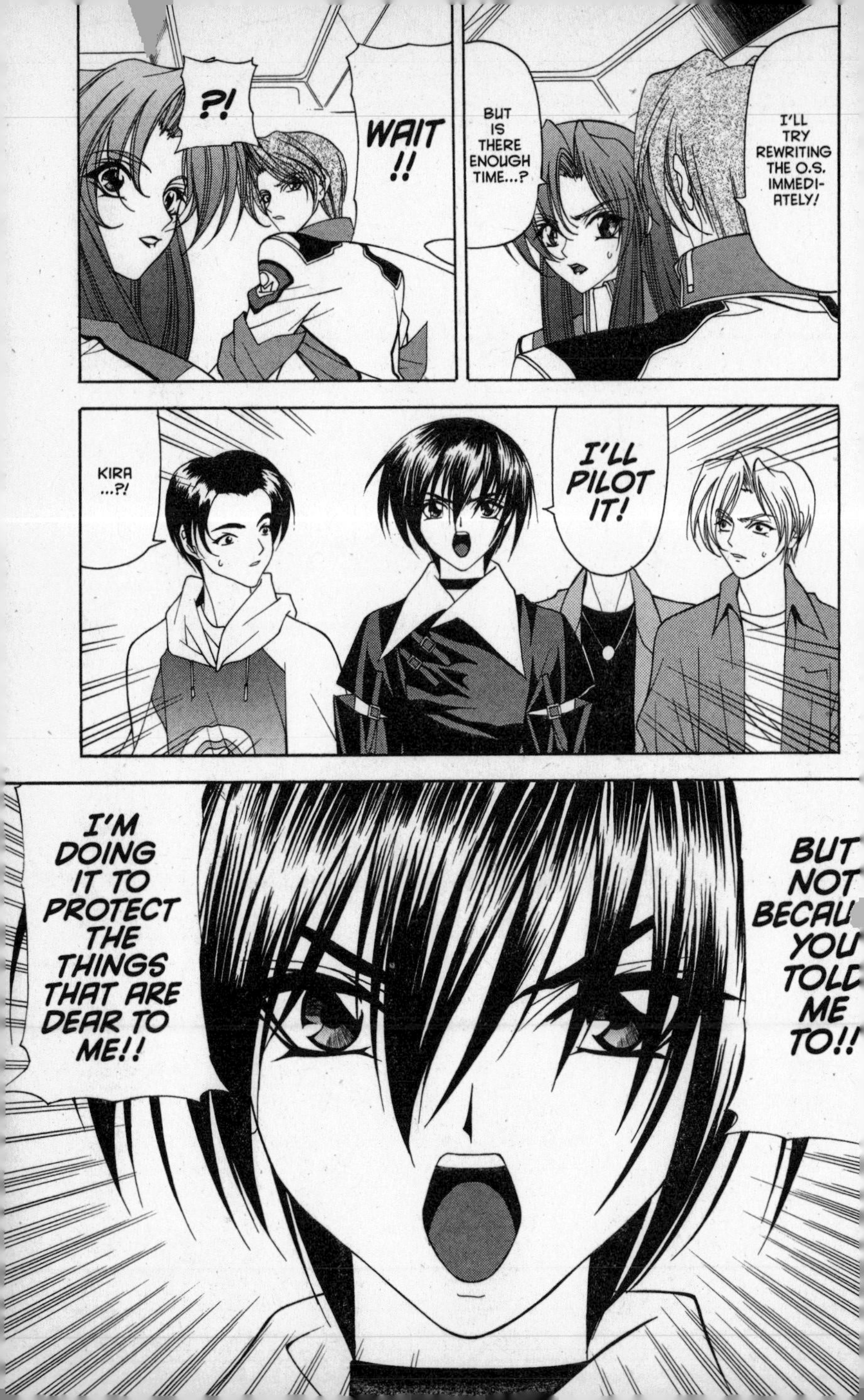
I'LL TRY REWRITING THE O.S. IMMEDIATELY!
BUT IS THERE ENOUGH TIME...?
WAIT!!
?!
I'LL PILOT IT!
KIRA ...?!
BUT NOT BECAU YOU TOLD ME TO!!
I'M DOING IT TO PROTECT THE THINGS THAT ARE DEAR TO ME!!

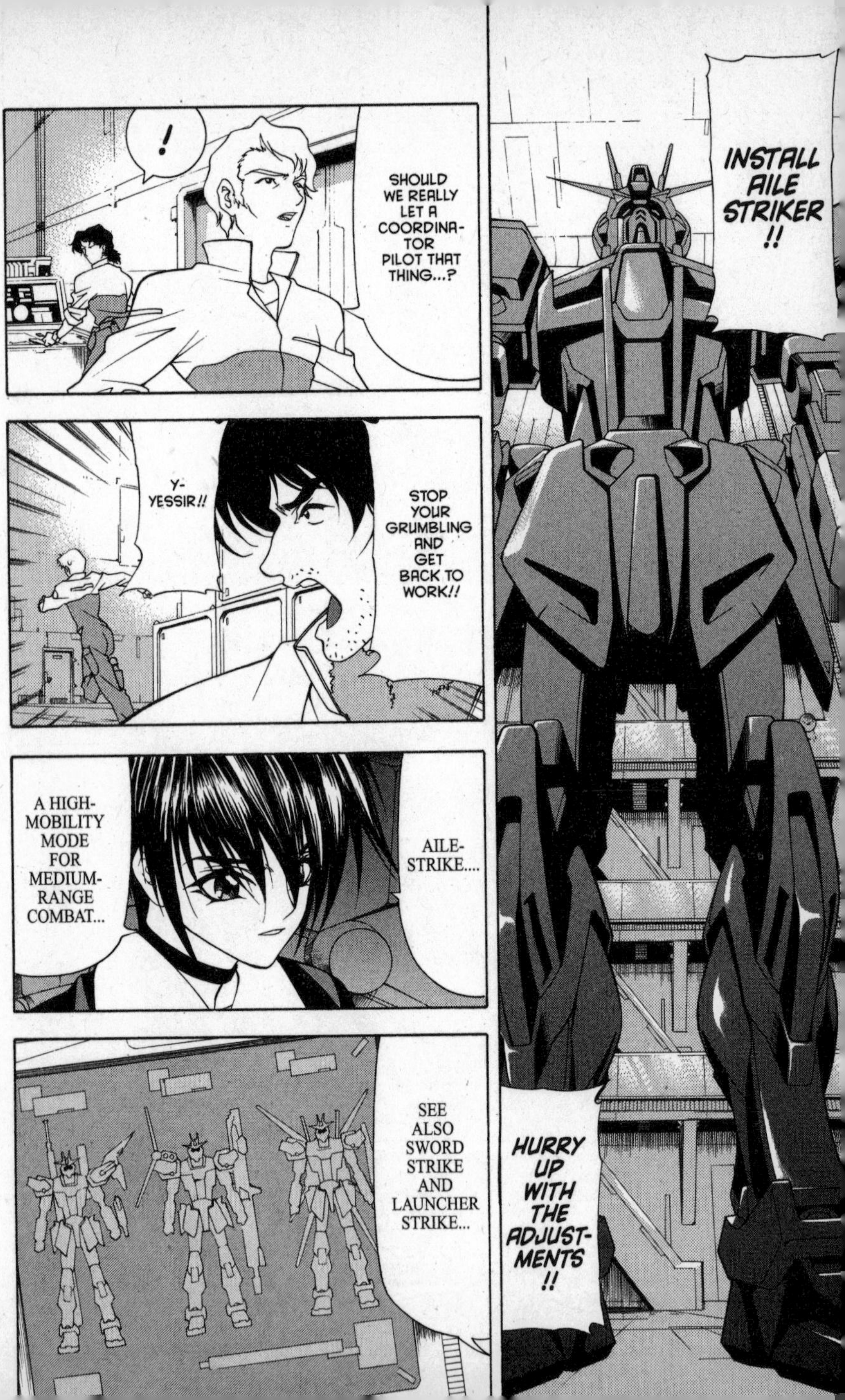
INSTALL AILE STRIKER!!
HURRY UP WITH THE ADJUSTMENTS!!
SHOULD WE REALLY LET A COORDINATOR PILOT THAT THING...?
!
STOP YOUR GRUMBLING AND GET BACK TO WORK!!
Y-YESSIR!!
AILE-STRIKE....
A HIGH-MOBILITY MODE FOR MEDIUM-RANGE COMBAT...
SEE ALSO SWORD STRIKE AND LAUNCHER STRIKE...

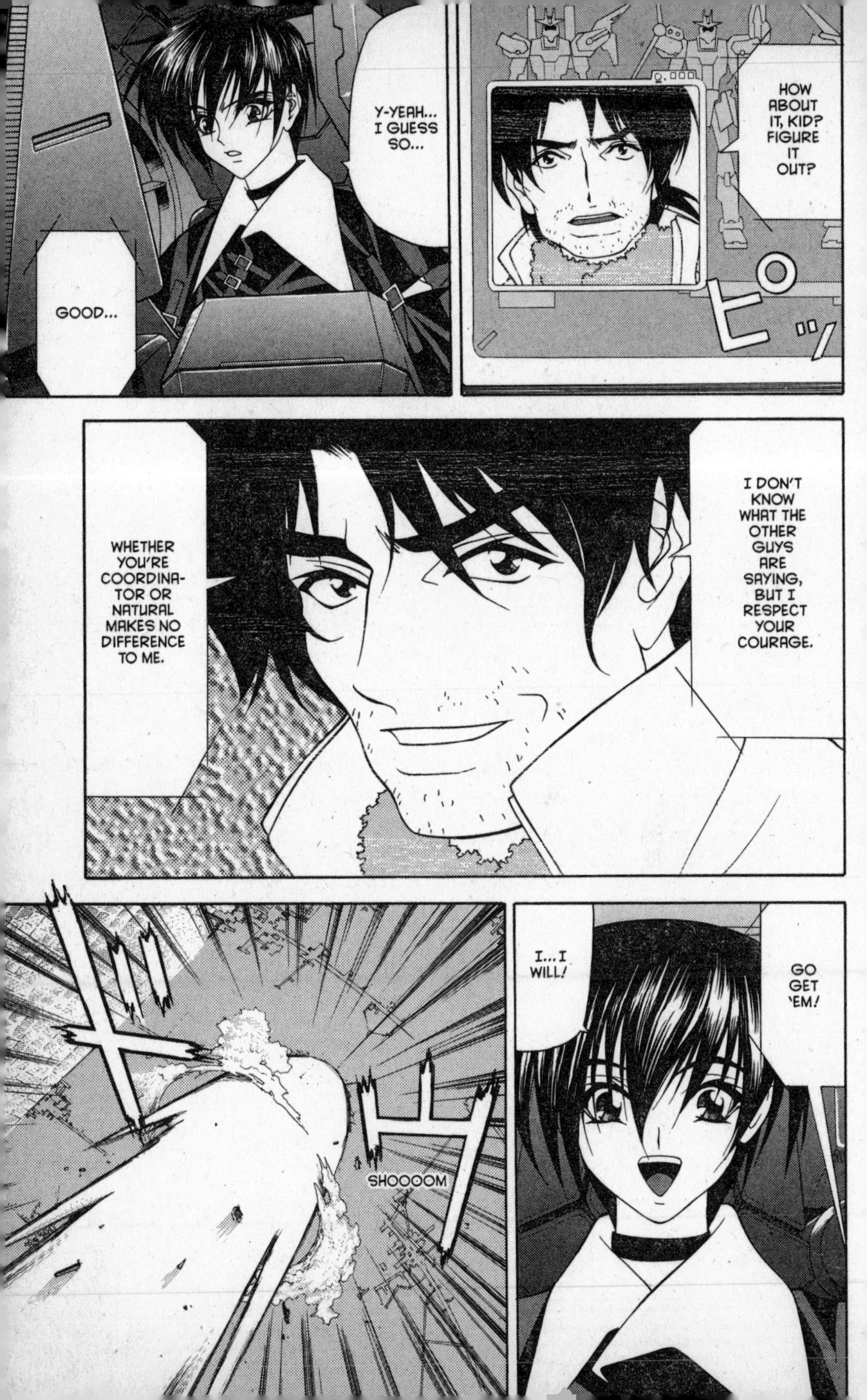
HOW ABOUT IT, KID? FIGURE IT OUT?
Y-YEAH... I GUESS SO...
GOOD...
I DON'T KNOW WHAT THE OTHER GUYS ARE SAYING, BUT I RESPECT YOUR COURAGE.
WHETHER YOU'RE COORDINA-TOR OR NATURAL MAKES NO DIFFERENCE TO ME.
GO GET 'EM!
I... I WILL!
SHOOOOM

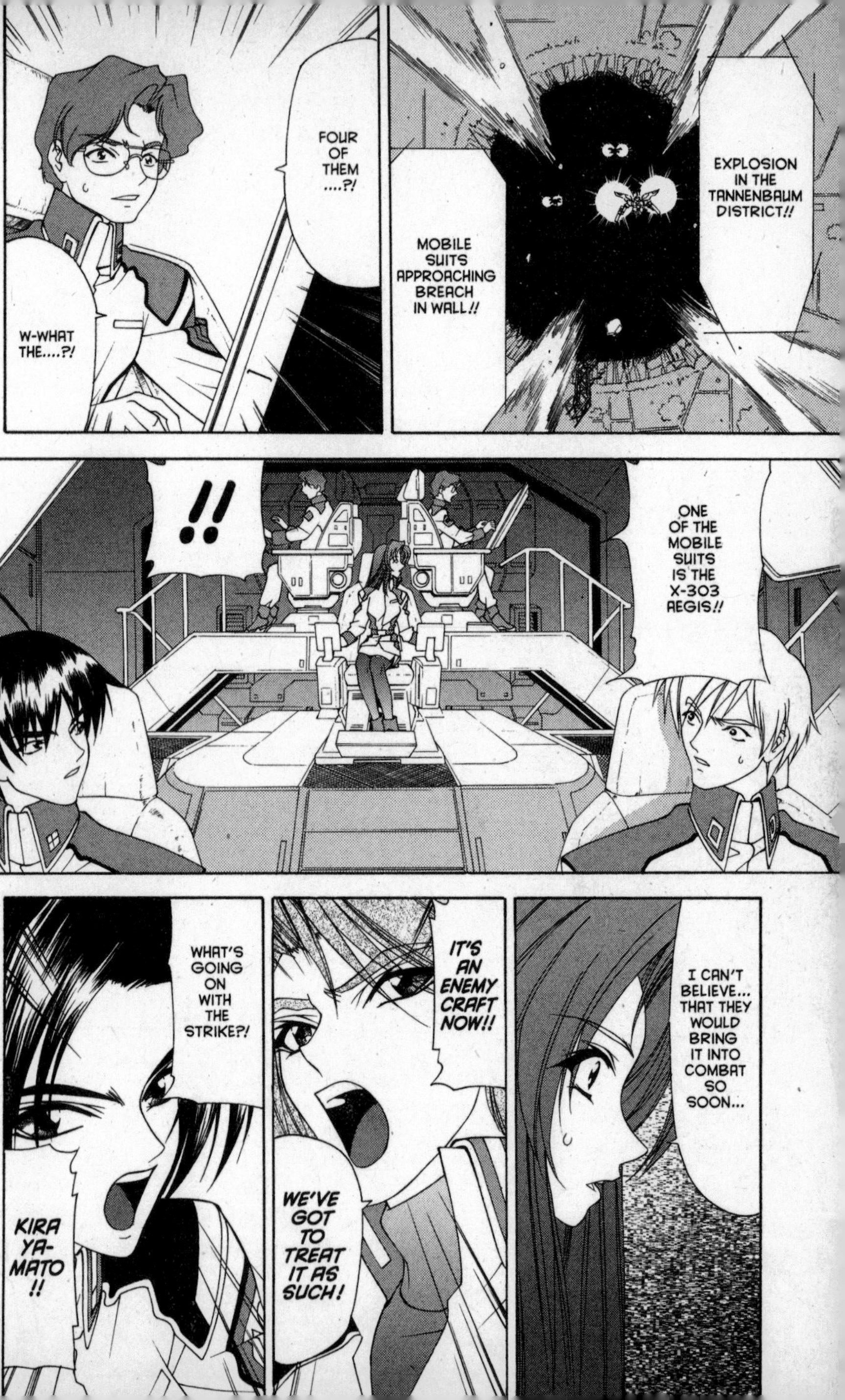
EXPLOSION IN THE TANNENBAUM DISTRICT!!
MOBILE SUITS APPROACHING BREACH IN WALL!!
FOUR OF THEM ....?!
W-WHAT THE....?!
ONE OF THE MOBILE SUITS IS THE X-303 AEGIS!!
!!
I CAN'T BELIEVE... THAT THEY WOULD BRING IT INTO COMBAT SO SOON...
IT'S AN ENEMY CRAFT NOW!!
WE'VE GOT TO TREAT IT AS SUCH!
WHAT'S GOING ON WITH THE STRIKE?!
KIRA YA-MATO!!

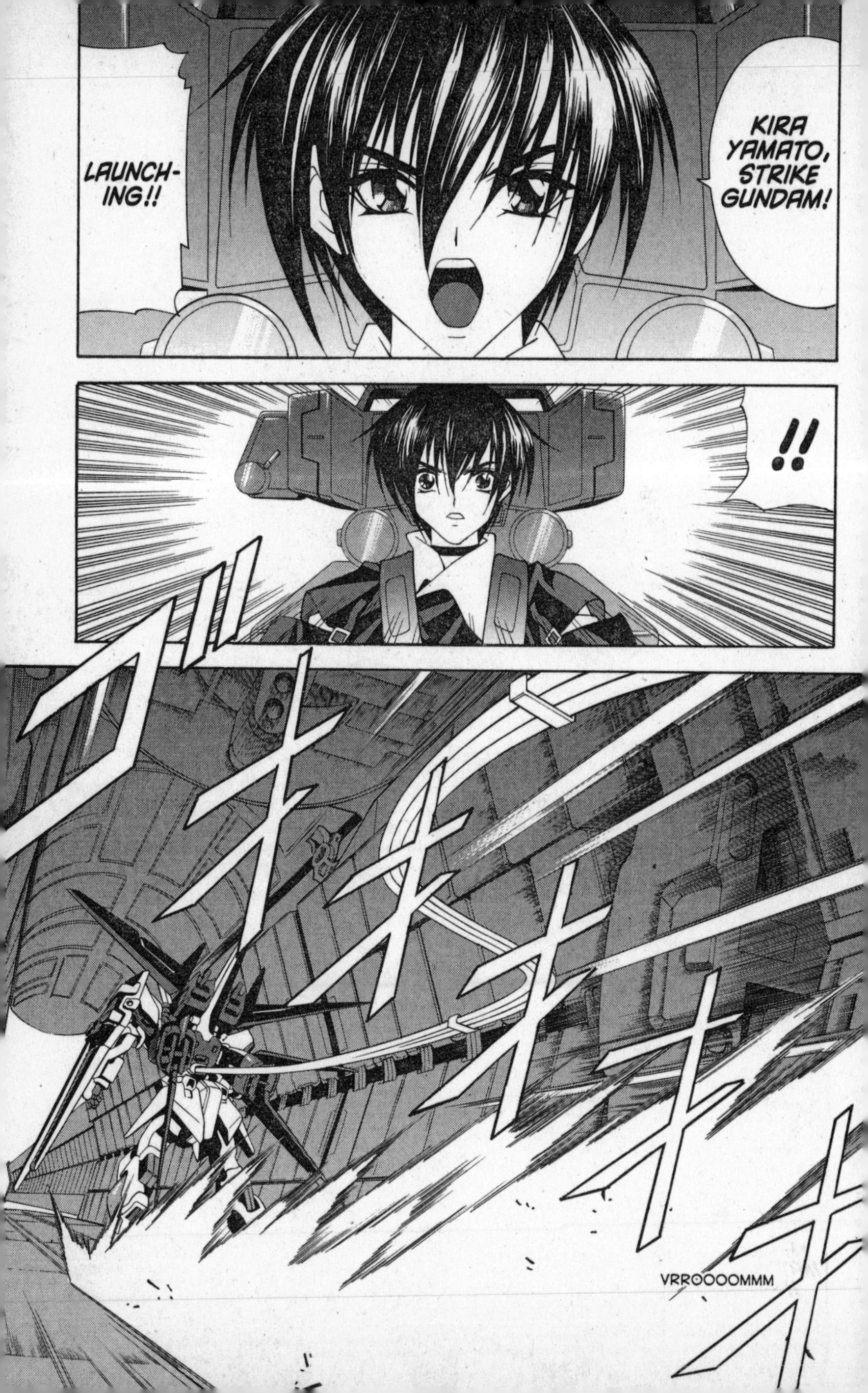
KIRA YAMATO, STRIKE GUNDAM!
LAUNCHING!!
!!
VRROOOOMMM

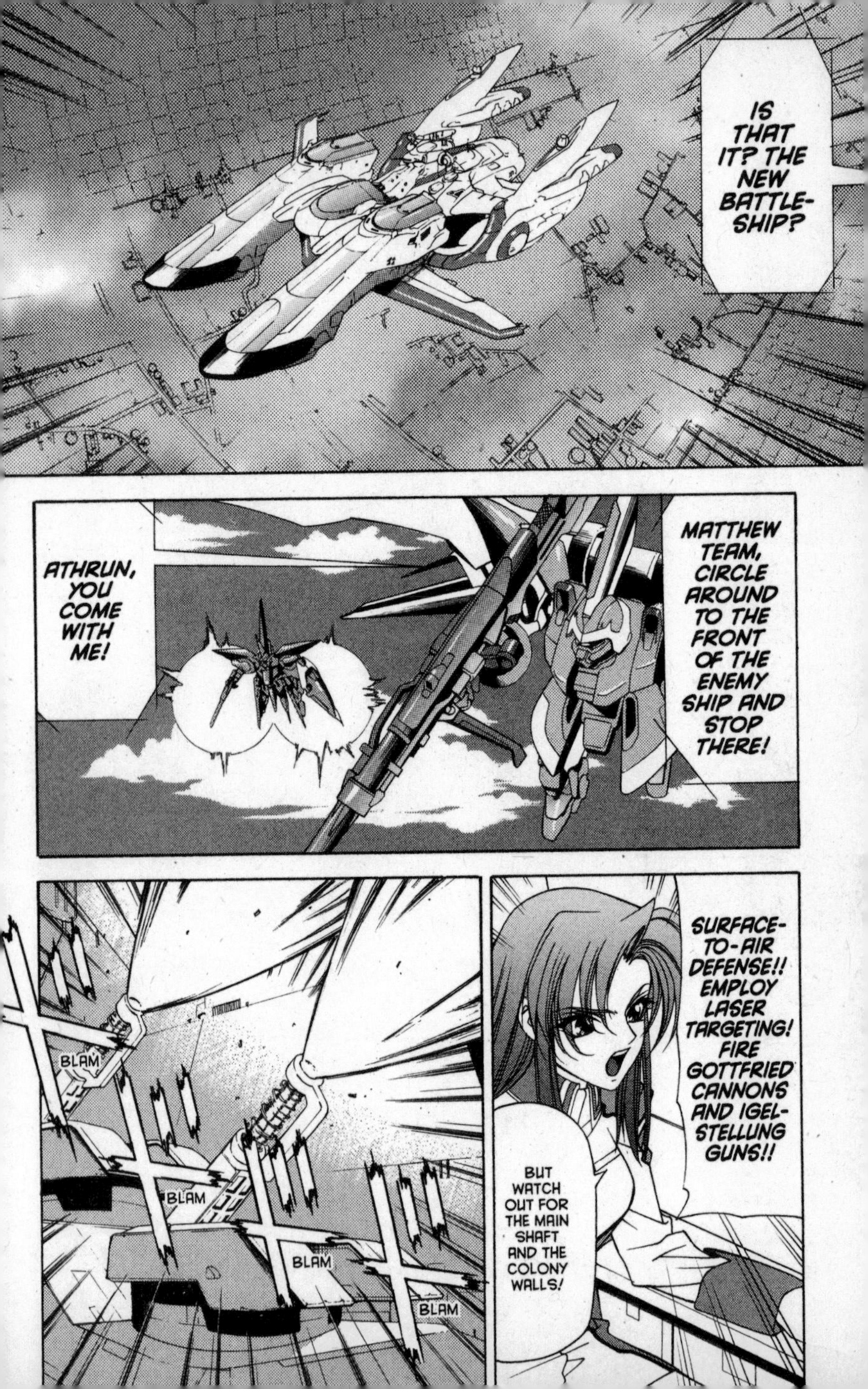
IS THAT IT? THE NEW BATTLE-SHIP?
MATTHEW TEAM, CIRCLE AROUND TO THE FRONT OF THE ENEMY SHIP AND STOP THERE!
ATHRUN, YOU COME WITH ME!
SURFACE-TO-AIR DEFENSE!! EMPLOY LASER TARGETING! FIRE GOTTFRIED CANNONS AND IGEL-STELLUNG GUNS!!
BUT WATCH OUT FOR THE MAIN SHAFT AND THE COLONY WALLS!
BLAM
BLAM
BLAM
BLAM

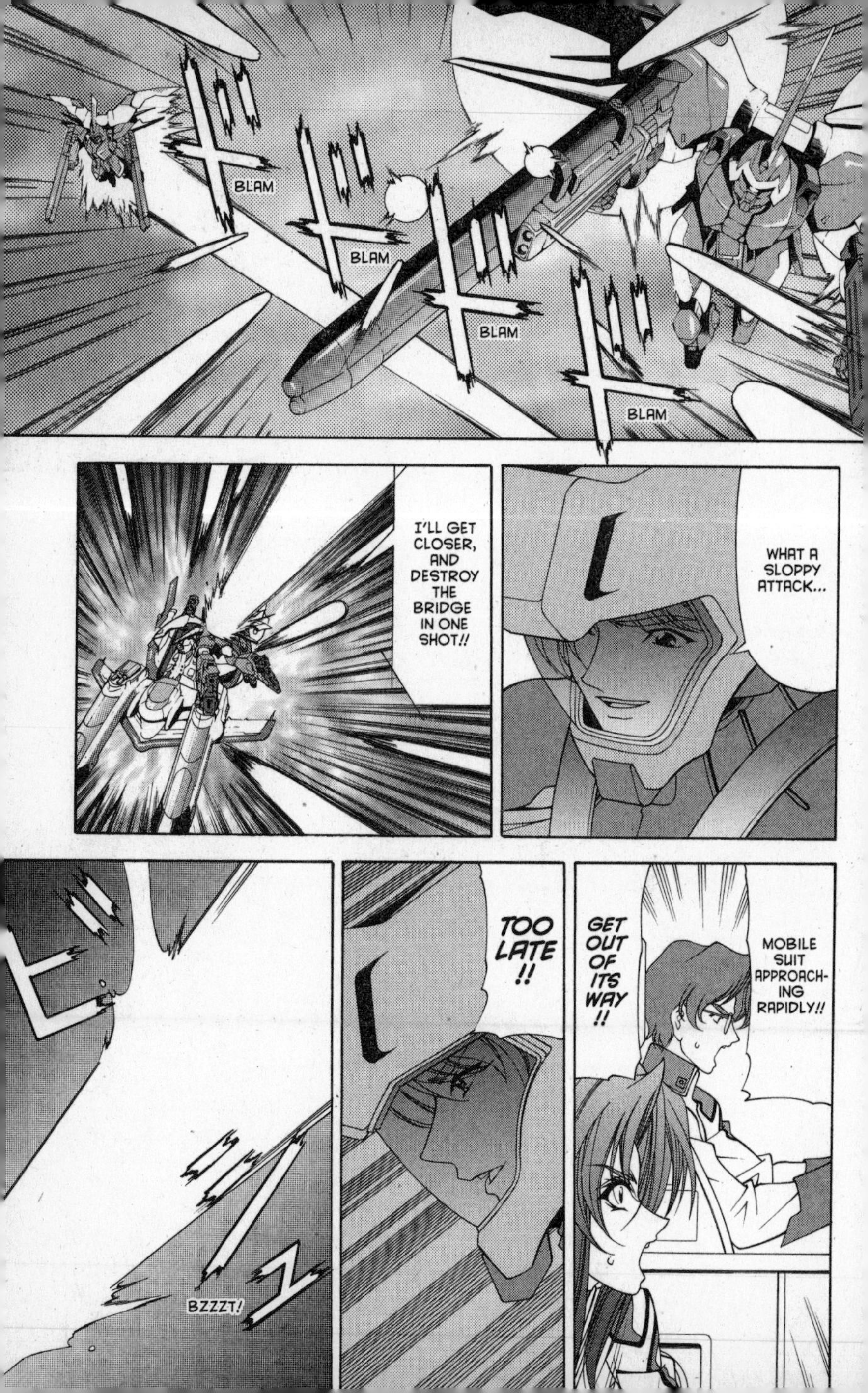
BLAM
BLAM
BLAM
BLAM
WHAT A SLOPPY ATTACK...
I'LL GET CLOSER, AND DESTROY THE BRIDGE IN ONE SHOT!!
MOBILE SUIT APPROACHING RAPIDLY!!
GET OUT OF ITS WAY!!
TOO LATE!!
BZZZT!

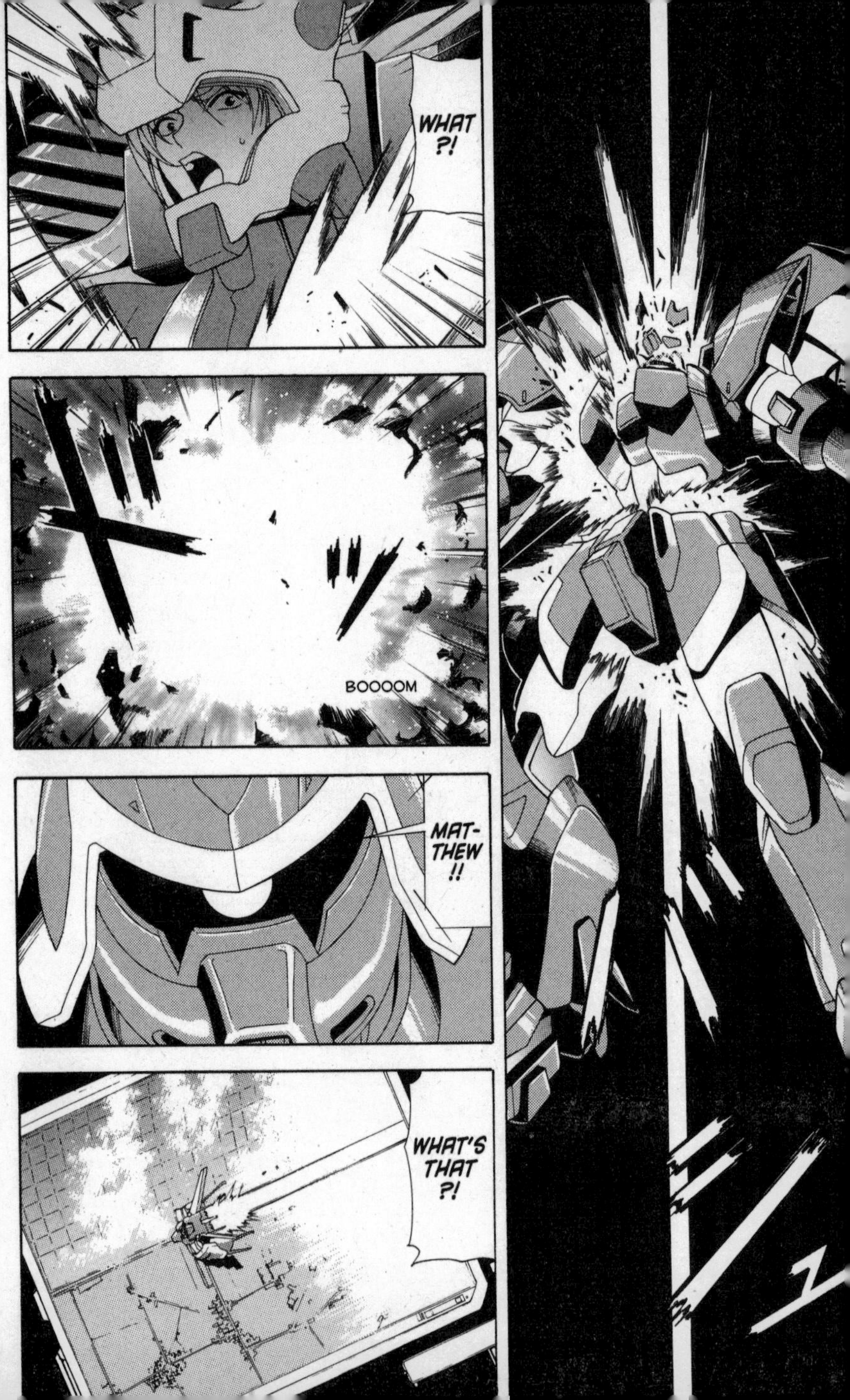
WHAT ?!
BOOOOM
MAT-THEW !!
WHAT'S THAT ?!

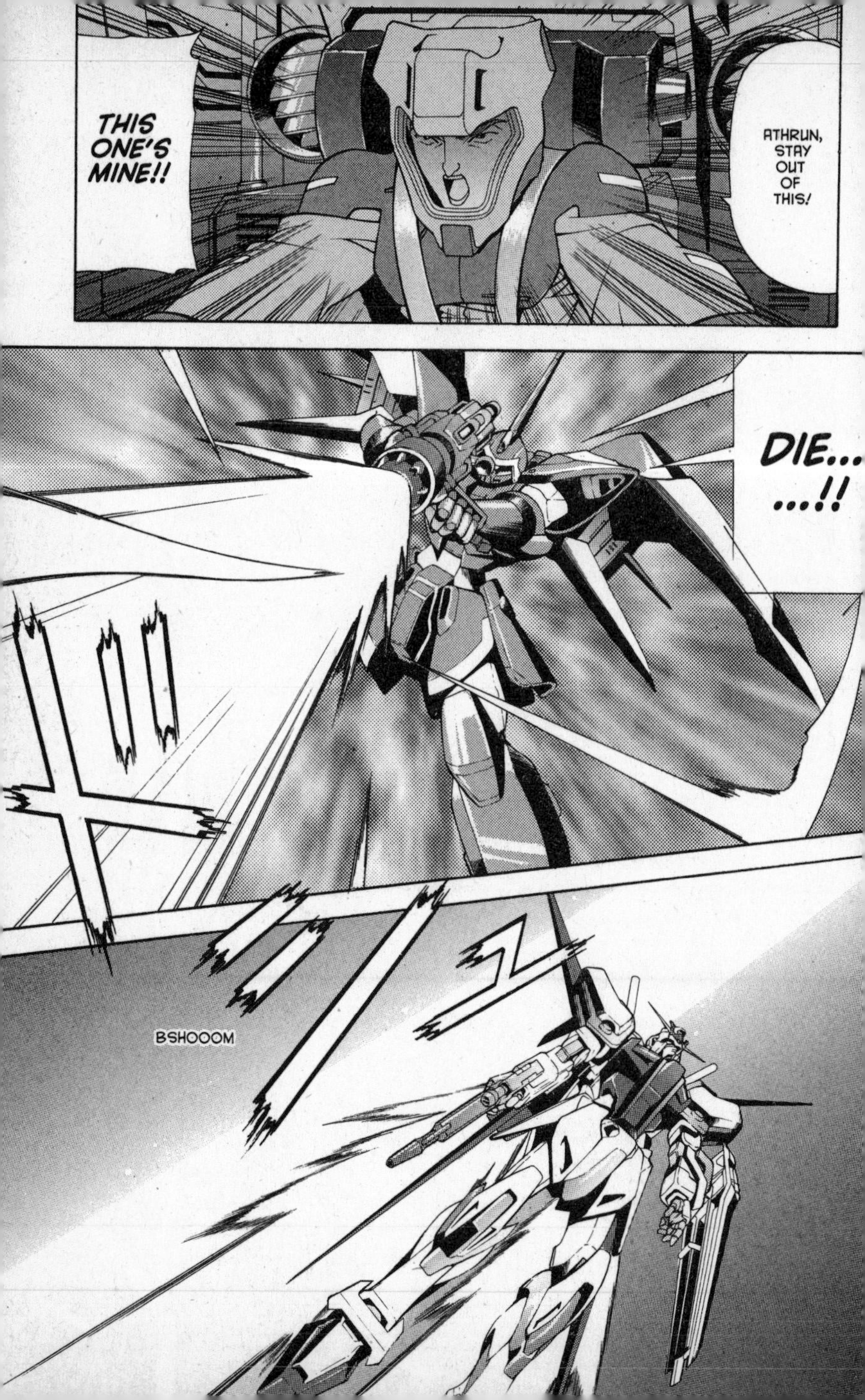
ATHRUN, STAY OUT OF THIS!
THIS ONE'S MINE!!
DIE... ...!!
BSHOOOM

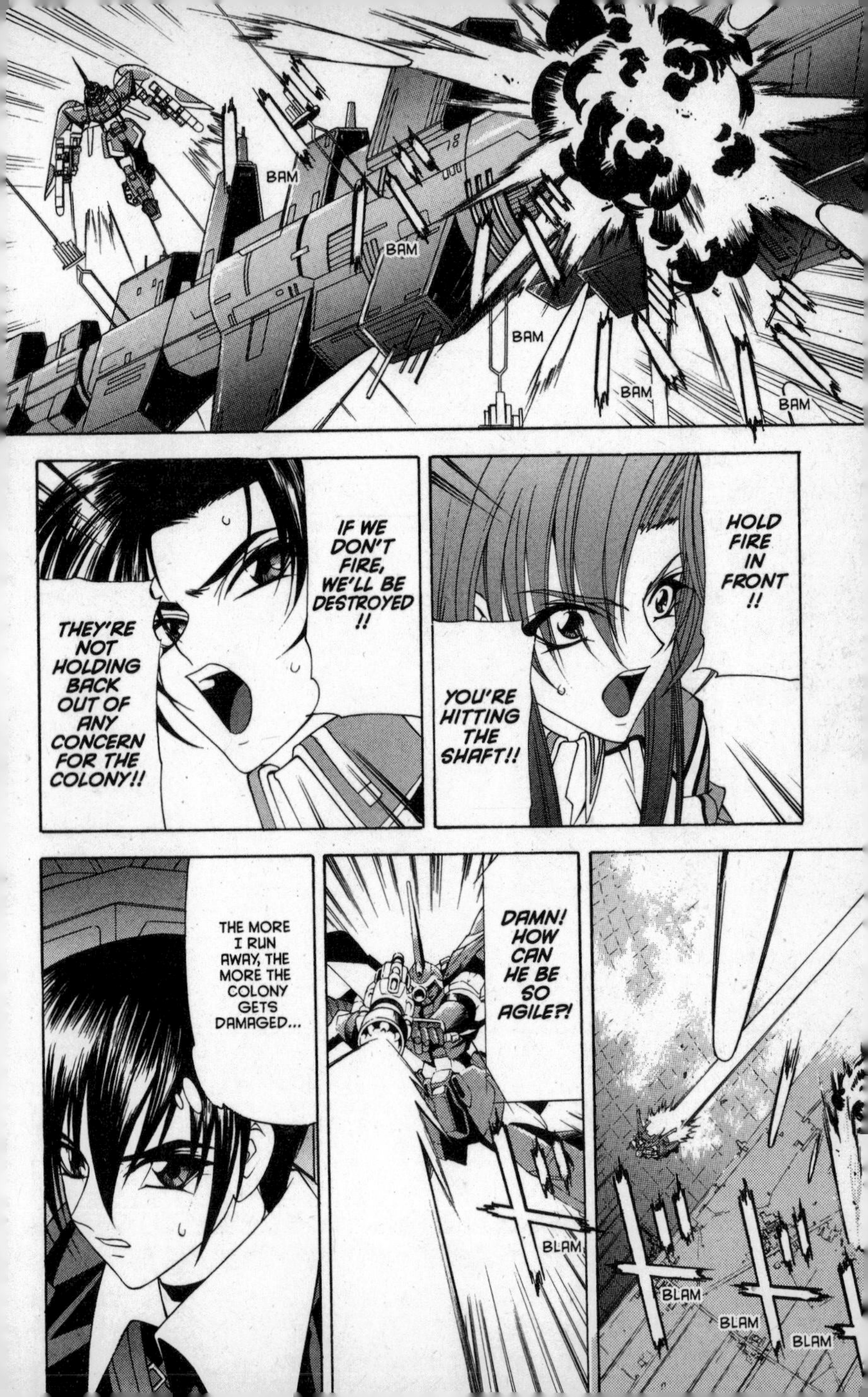
BAM
BAM
BAM
BAM
BAM
HOLD FIRE IN FRONT!!
YOU'RE HITTING THE SHAFT!!
IF WE DON'T FIRE, WE'LL BE DESTROYED!!
THEY'RE NOT HOLDING BACK OUT OF ANY CONCERN FOR THE COLONY!!
BLAM
BLAM
BLAM
DAMN! HOW CAN HE BE SO AGILE?!
BLAM
THE MORE I RUN AWAY, THE MORE THE COLONY GETS DAMAGED...

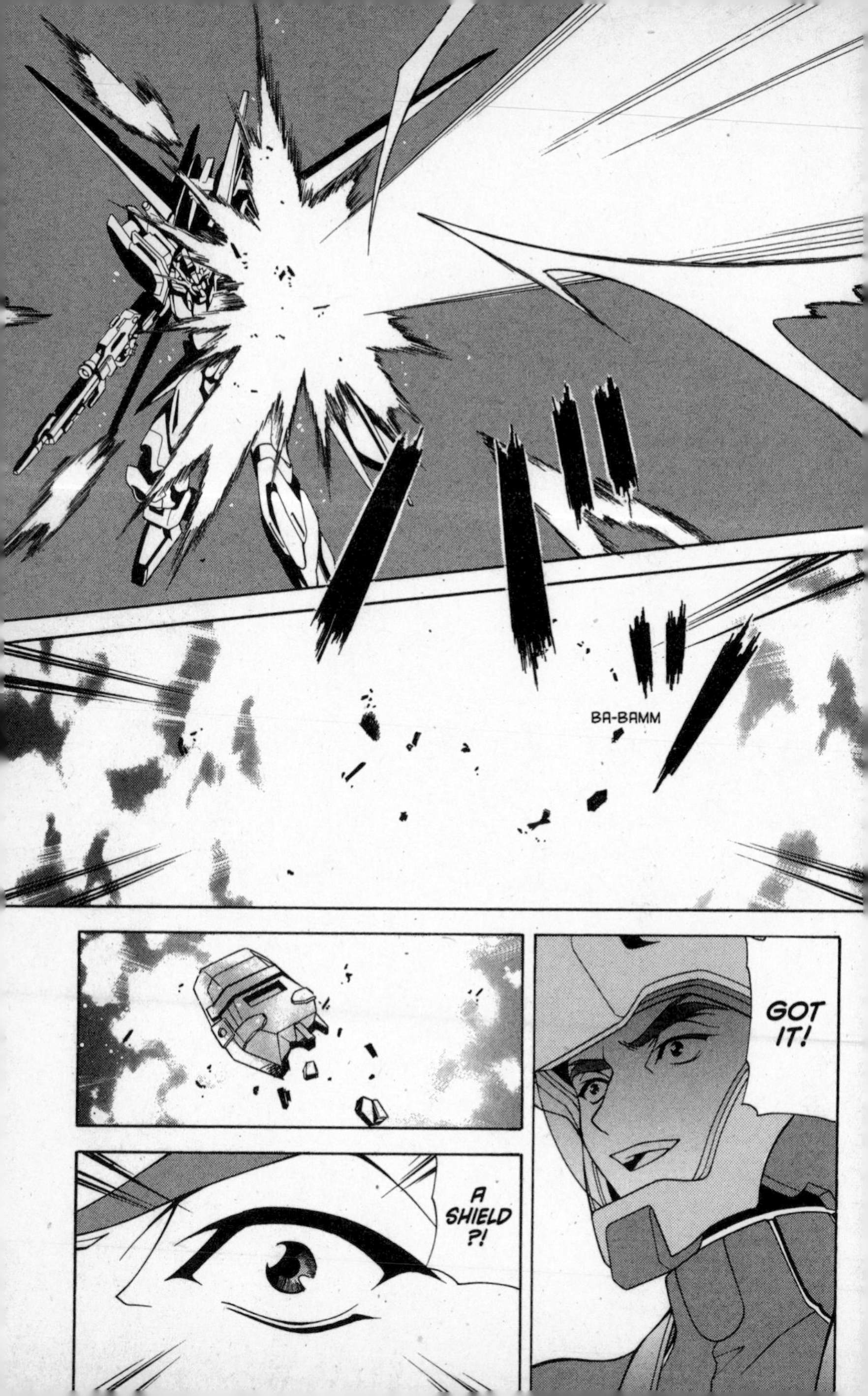
BA-BAMM
GOT IT!
A SHIELD ?!

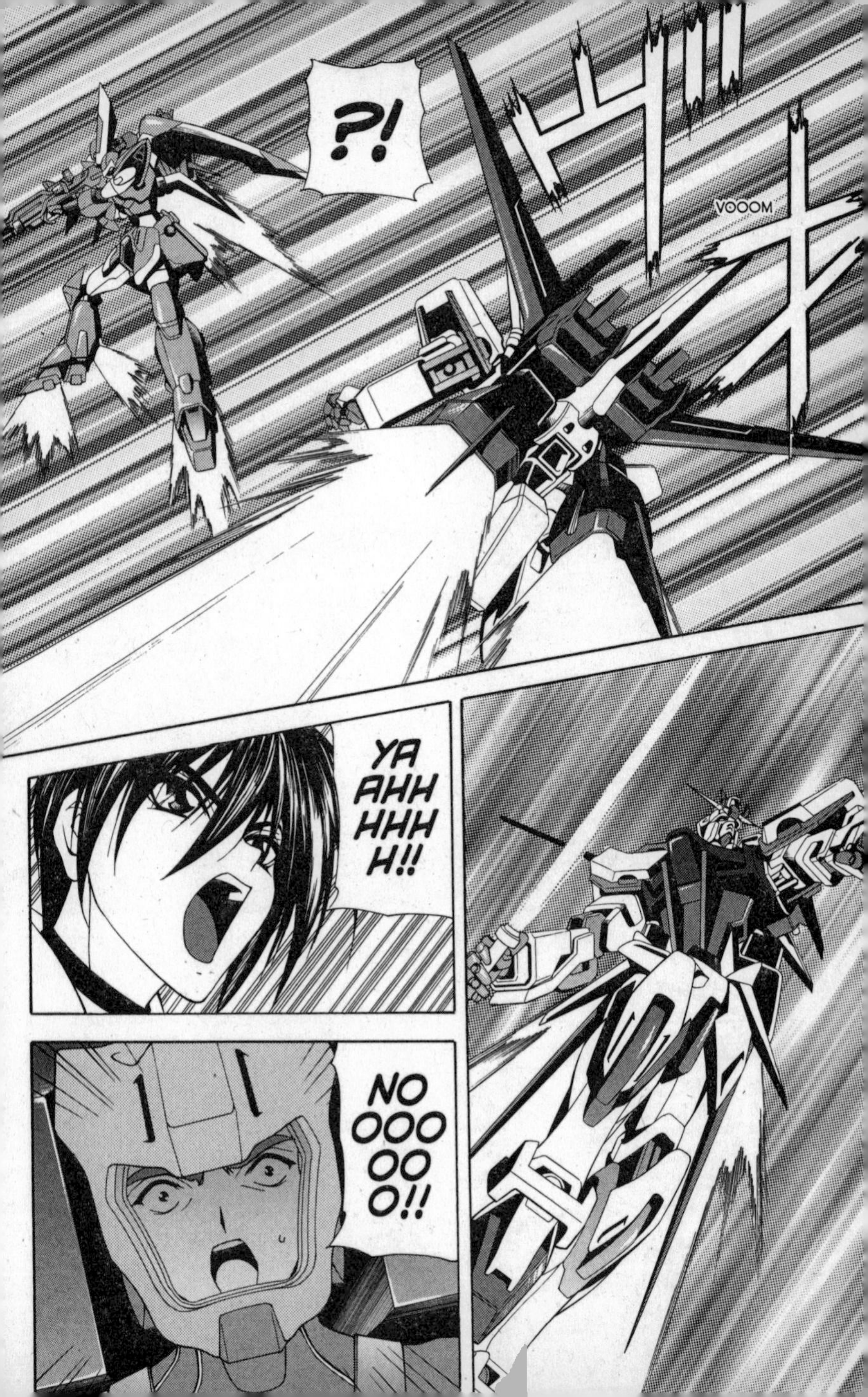
?!
VOOOM
YAAHHHHHH!!
NOOOOOOO!!

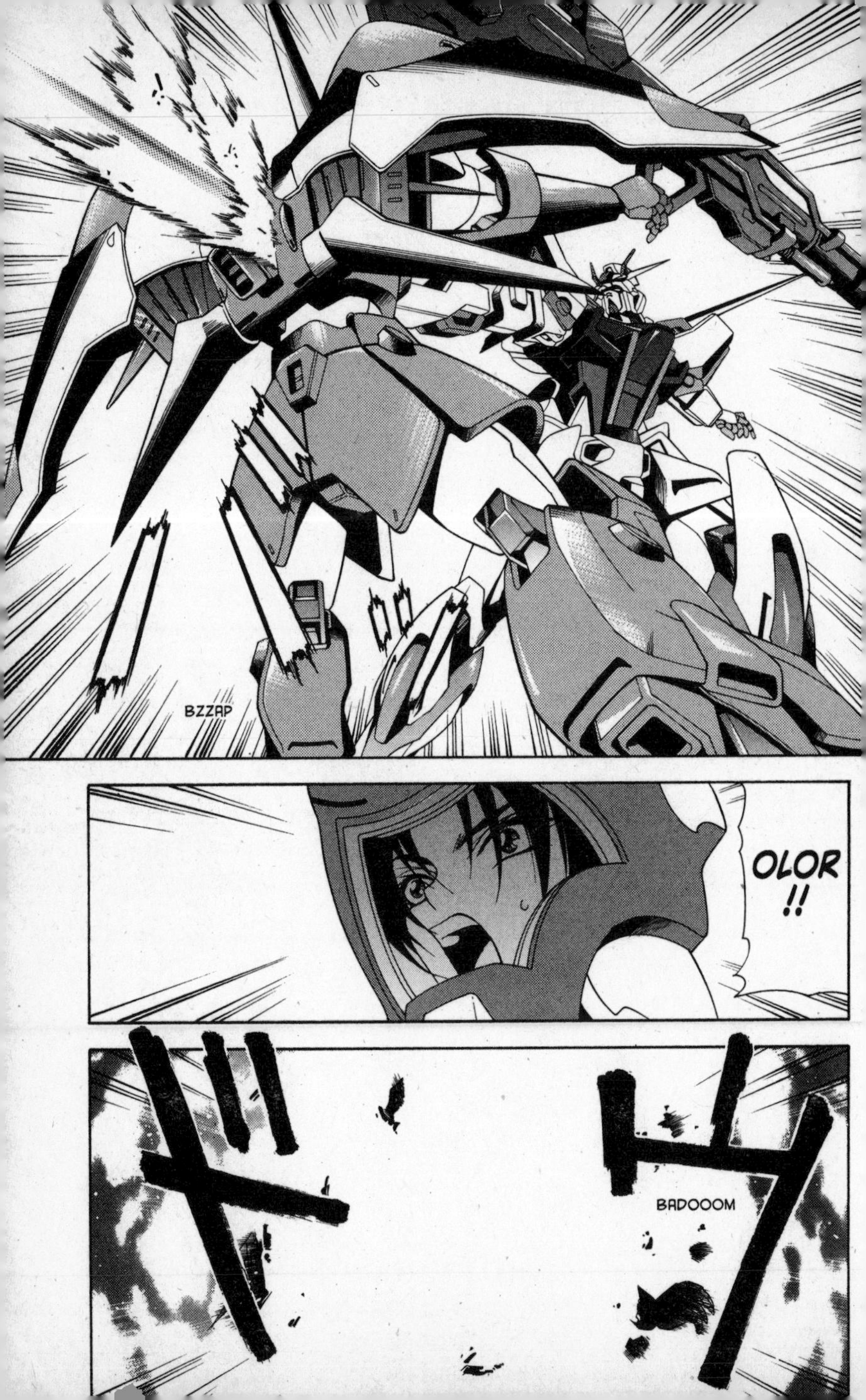
BZZAP
OLOR !!
BADOOOM

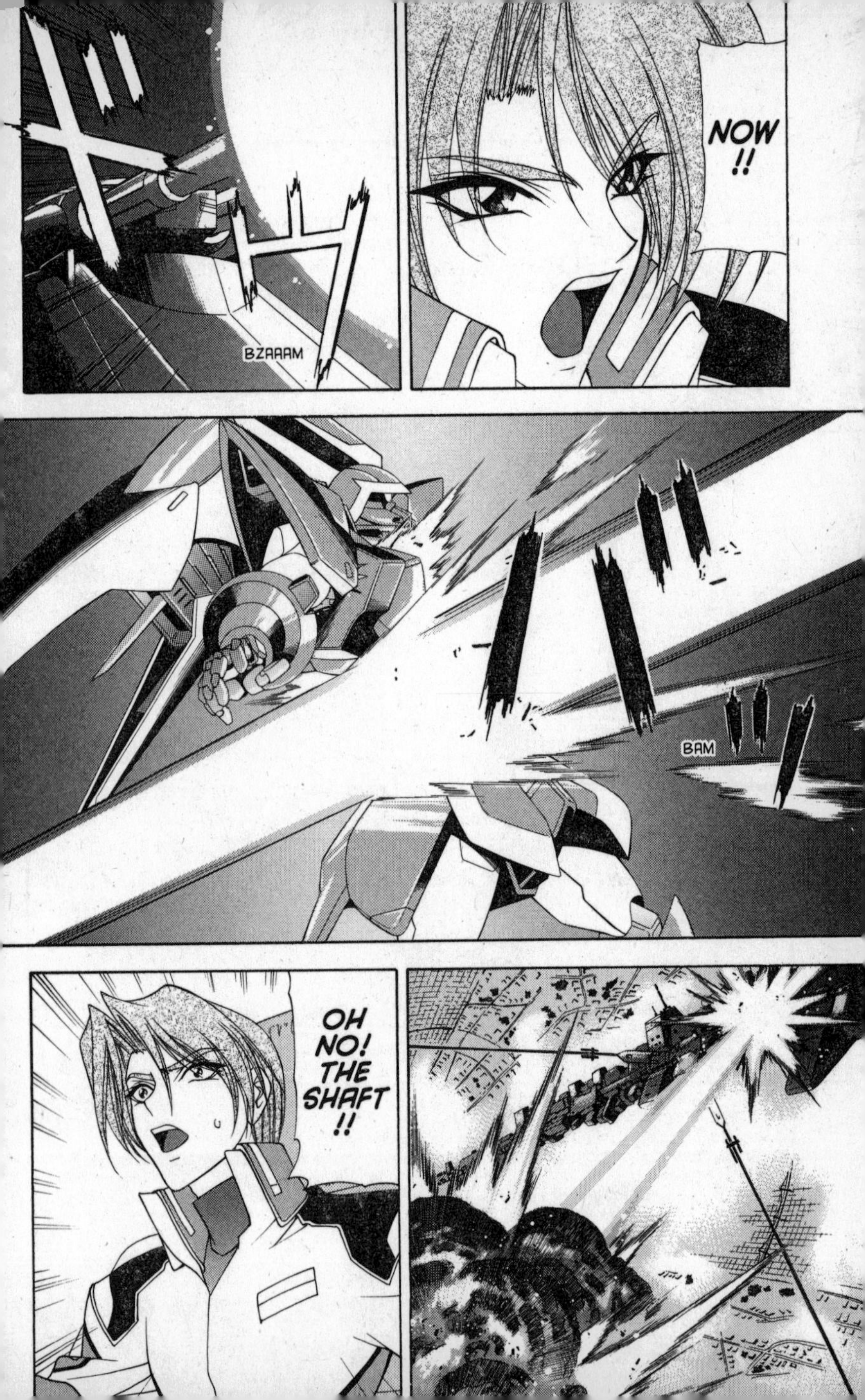
NOW !!
BZAAAM
BAM
OH NO! THE SHAFT !!

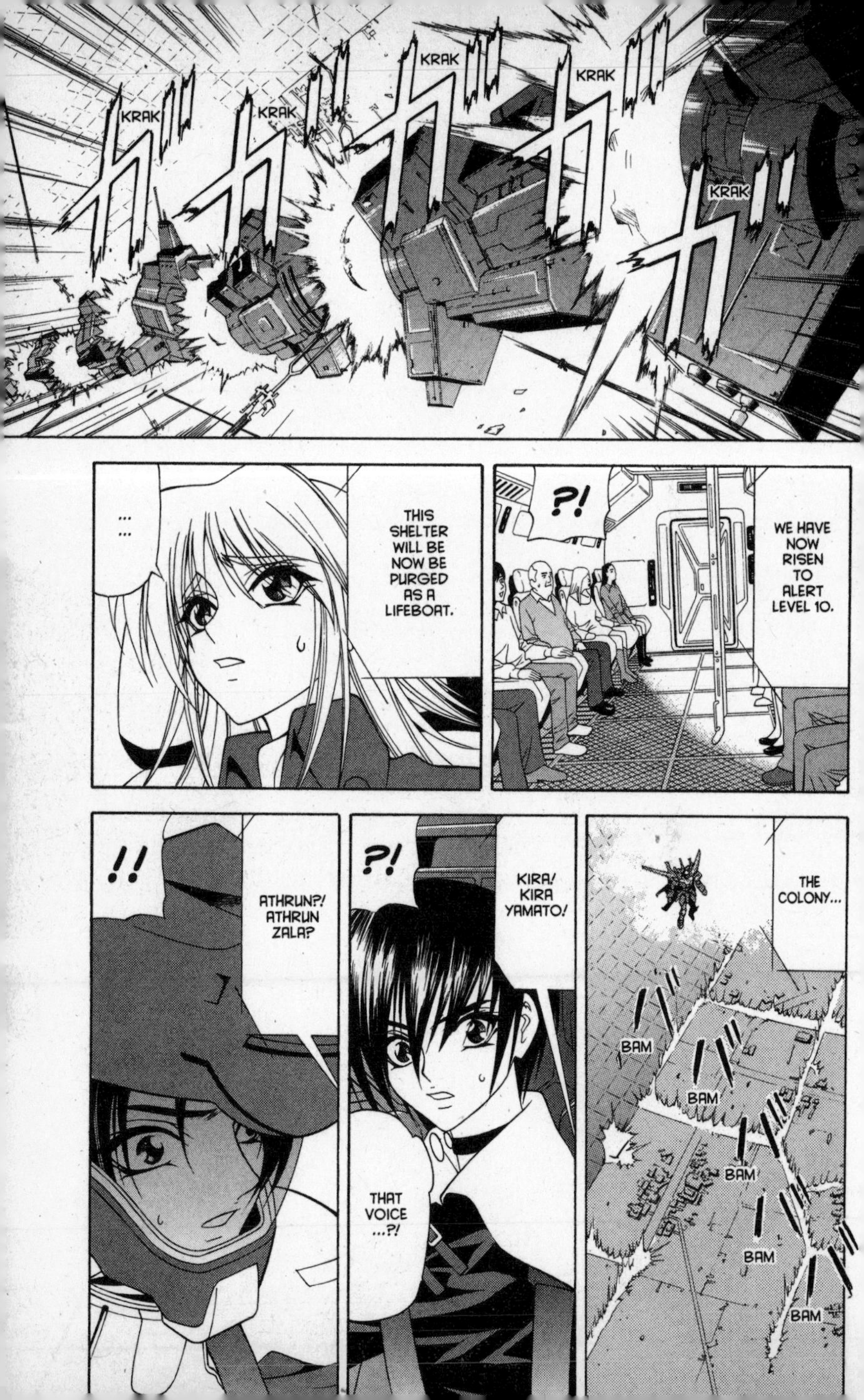
KRAK
KRAK
KRAK
KRAK
KRAK
WE HAVE NOW RISEN TO ALERT LEVEL 10.
?!
THIS SHELTER WILL BE NOW BE PURGED AS A LIFEBOAT.
...
...
THE COLONY...
BAM
BAM
BAM
BAM
BAM
KIRA! KIRA YAMATO!
?!
THAT VOICE ...?!
ATHRUN?! ATHRUN ZALA?
!!

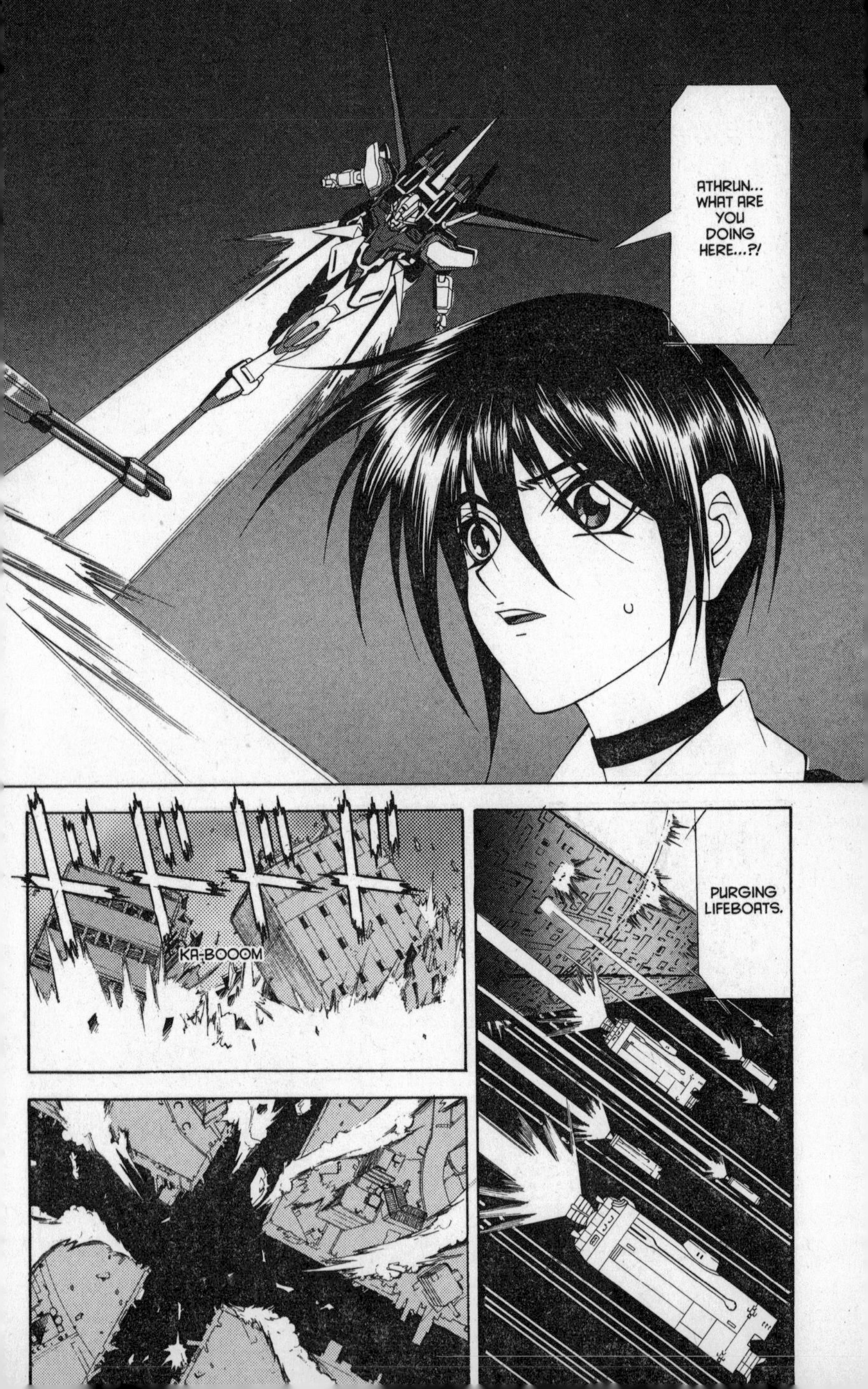
ATHRUN... WHAT ARE YOU DOING HERE...?!
PURGING LIFEBOATS.
KA-BOOOM

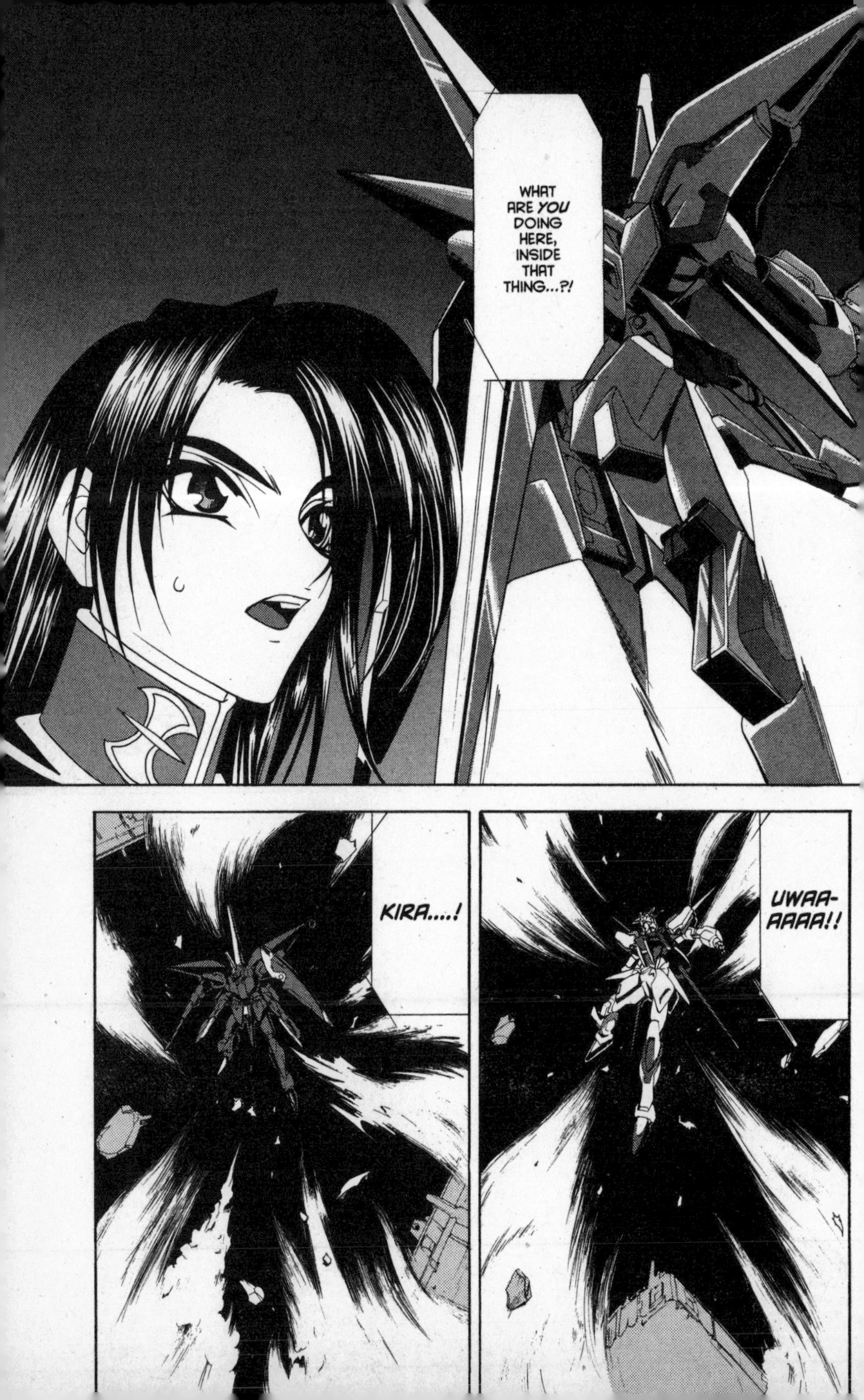
WHAT ARE *YOU* DOING HERE, INSIDE THAT THING...?!
UWAA-AAAA!!
KIRA....!

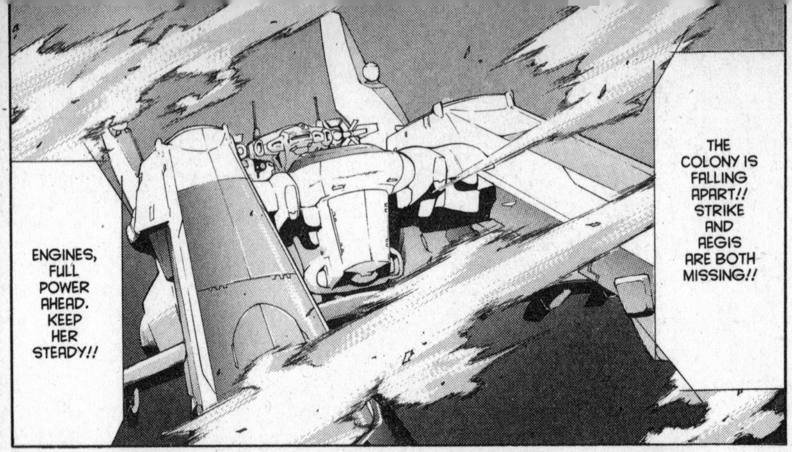
THE COLONY IS FALLING APART!! STRIKE AND AEGIS ARE BOTH MISSING!!
ENGINES, FULL POWER AHEAD. KEEP HER STEADY!!

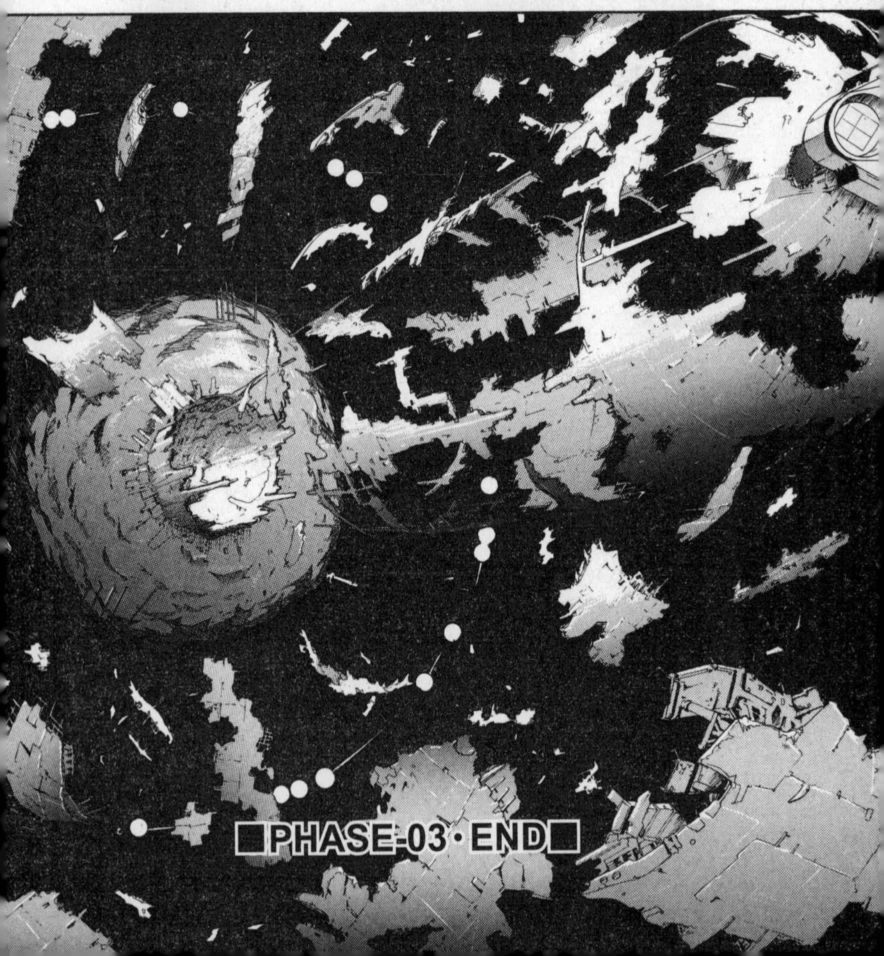
■PHASE-03 · END■

PHASE-04: PHASE-SHIFT DOWN

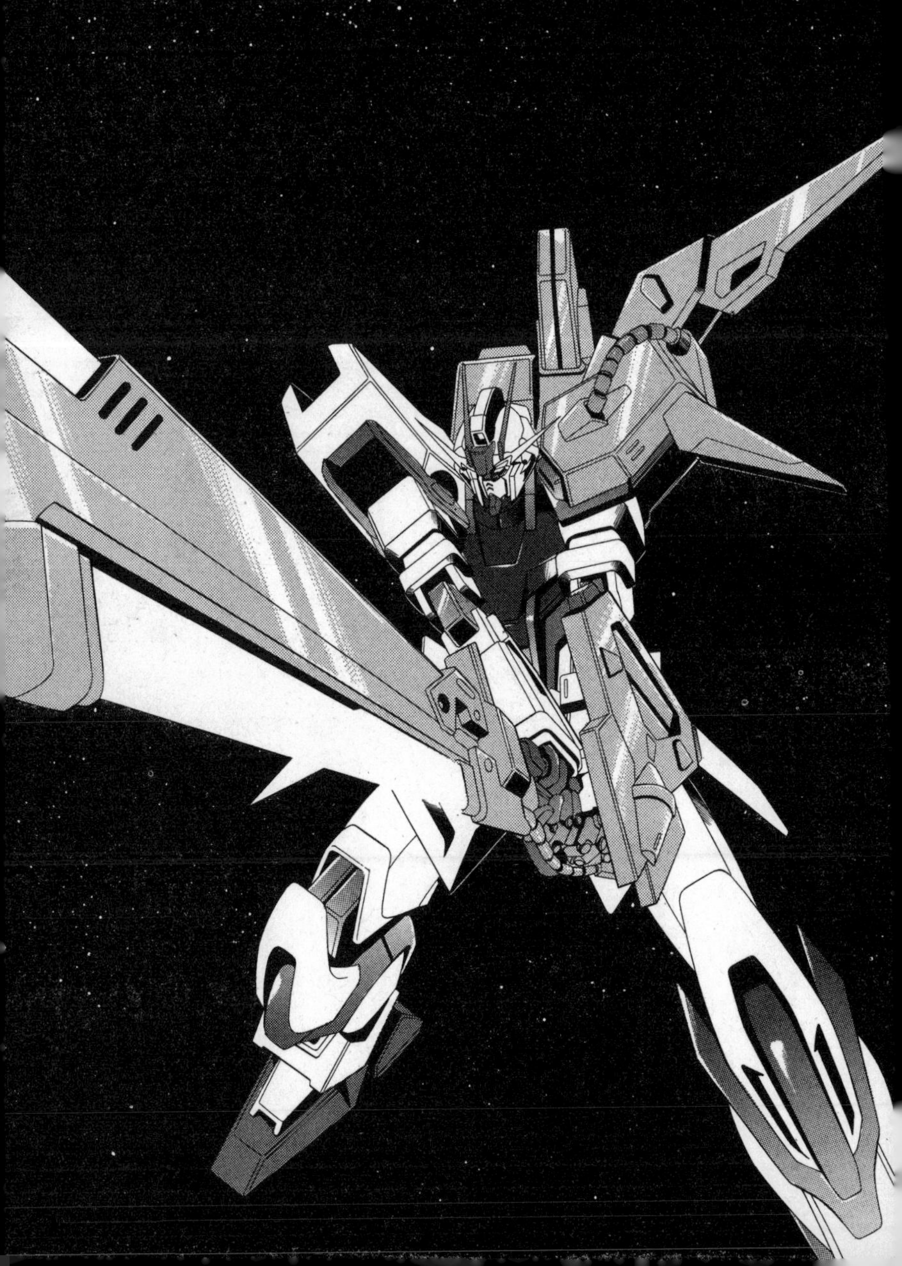

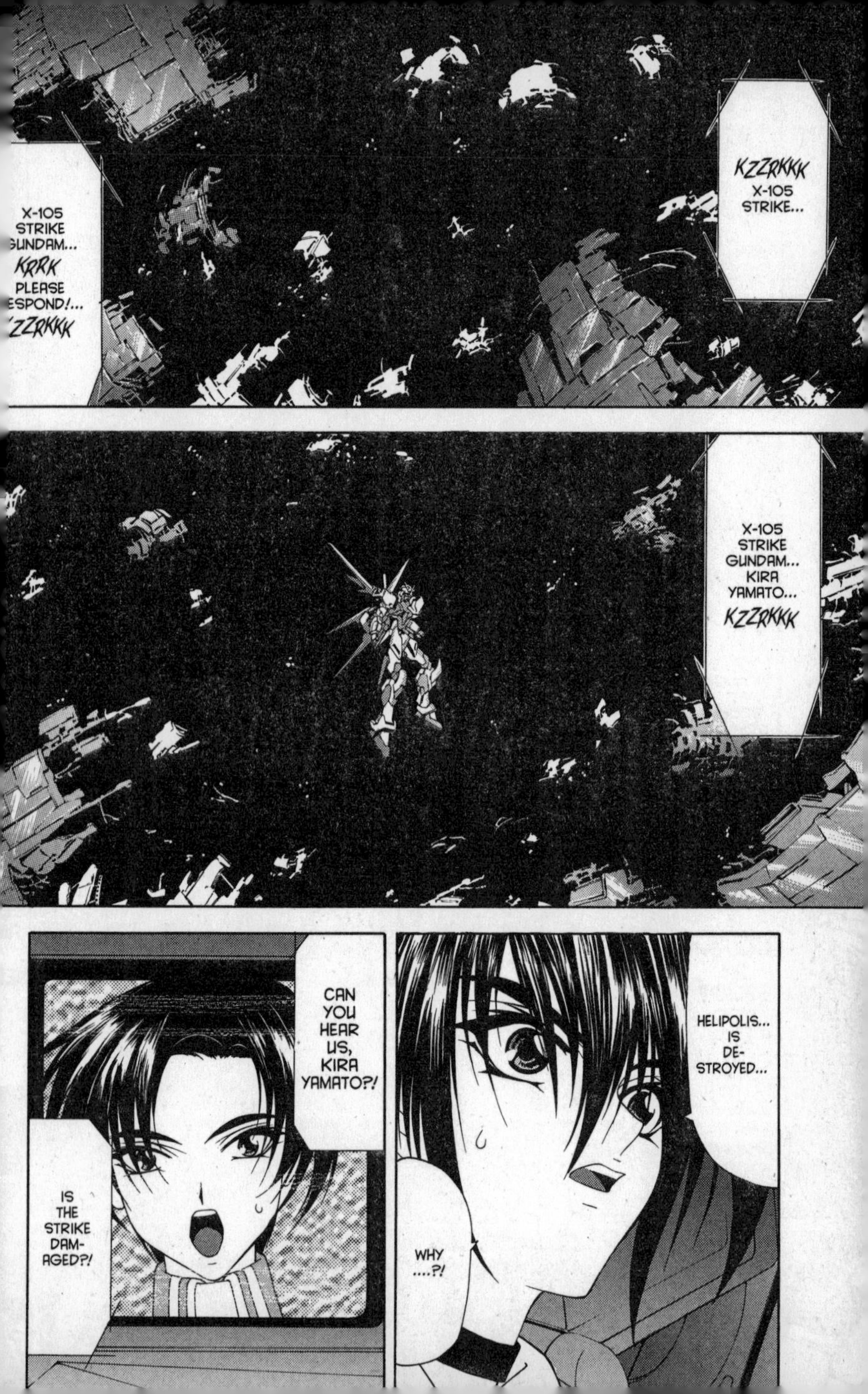
KZZRKKK X-105 STRIKE...
X-105 STRIKE UNDAM... KRRK PLEASE ESPOND!... ZZRKKK
X-105 STRIKE GUNDAM... KIRA YAMATO... KZZRKKK
HELIPOLIS... IS DE-STROYED...
WHY ....?!
CAN YOU HEAR US, KIRA YAMATO?!
IS THE STRIKE DAM-AGED?!

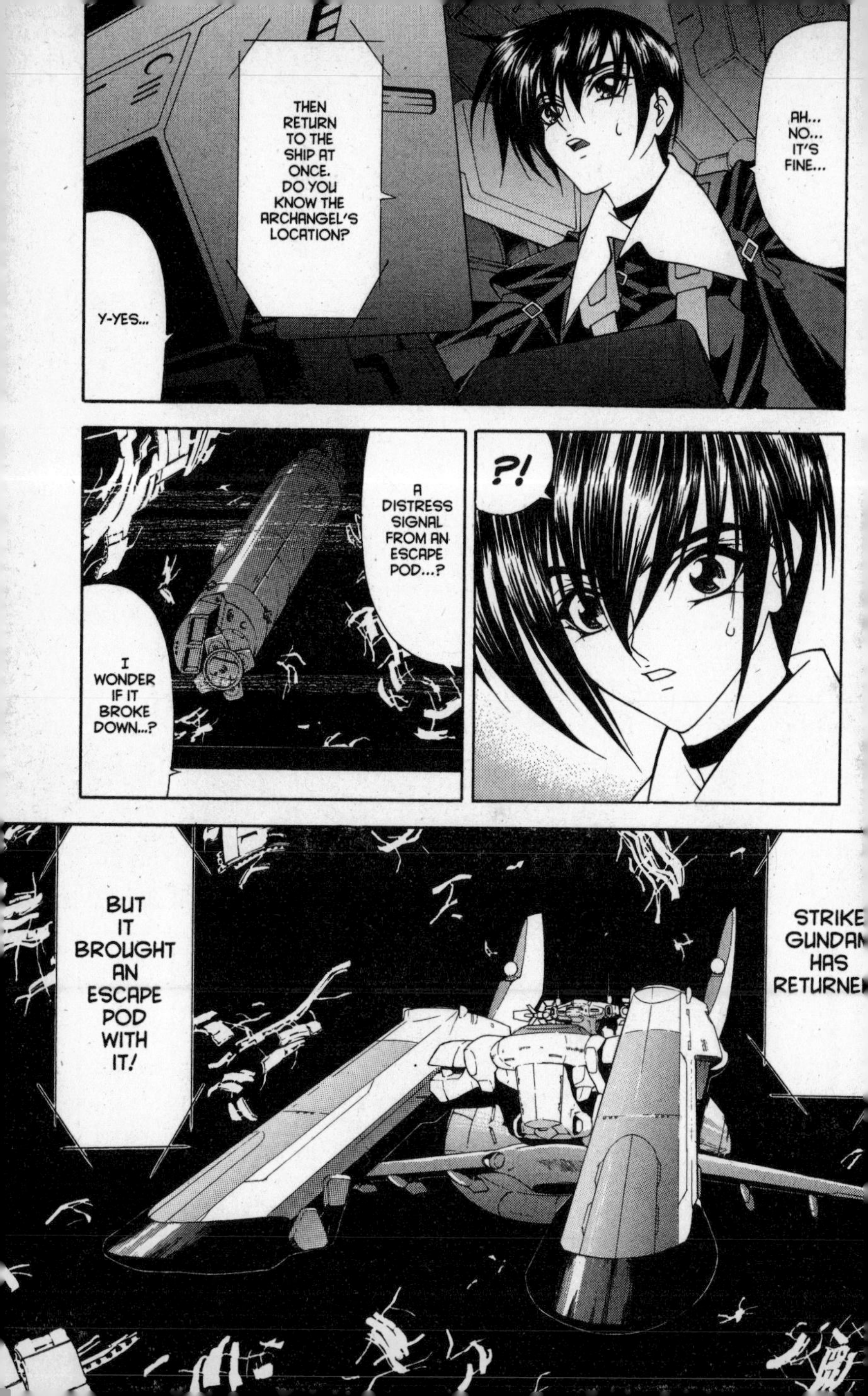
AH... NO... IT'S FINE...
THEN RETURN TO THE SHIP AT ONCE. DO YOU KNOW THE ARCHANGEL'S LOCATION?
Y-YES...
?!
A DISTRESS SIGNAL FROM AN ESCAPE POD...?
I WONDER IF IT BROKE DOWN...?
STRIKE GUNDA HAS RETURNE
BUT IT BROUGHT AN ESCAPE POD WITH IT!

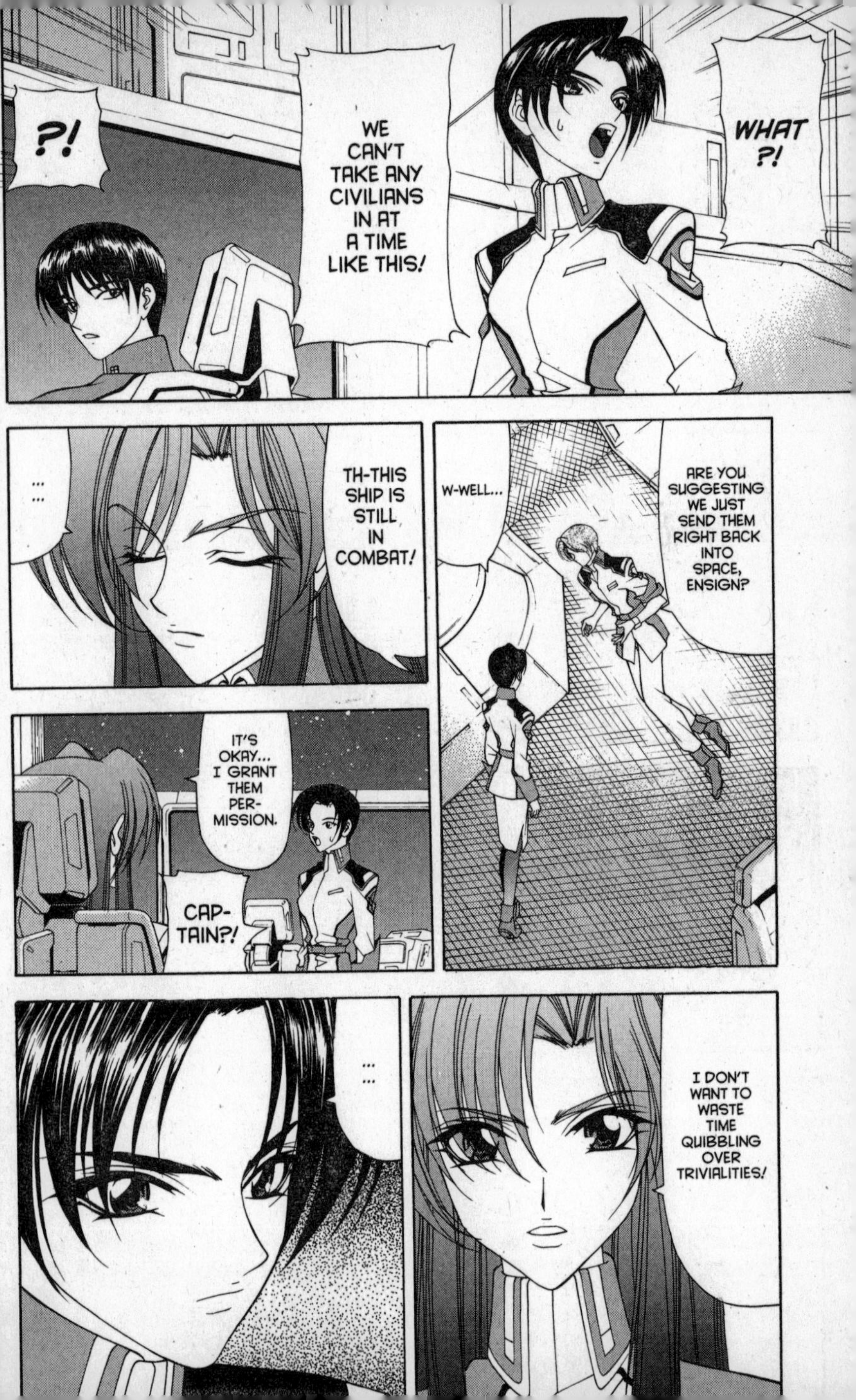
WHAT ?!
WE CAN'T TAKE ANY CIVILIANS IN AT A TIME LIKE THIS!
?!
ARE YOU SUGGESTING WE JUST SEND THEM RIGHT BACK INTO SPACE, ENSIGN?
W-WELL...
TH-THIS SHIP IS STILL IN COMBAT!
......
IT'S OKAY... I GRANT THEM PER-MISSION.
CAP-TAIN?!
I DON'T WANT TO WASTE TIME QUIBBLING OVER TRIVIALITIES!
......

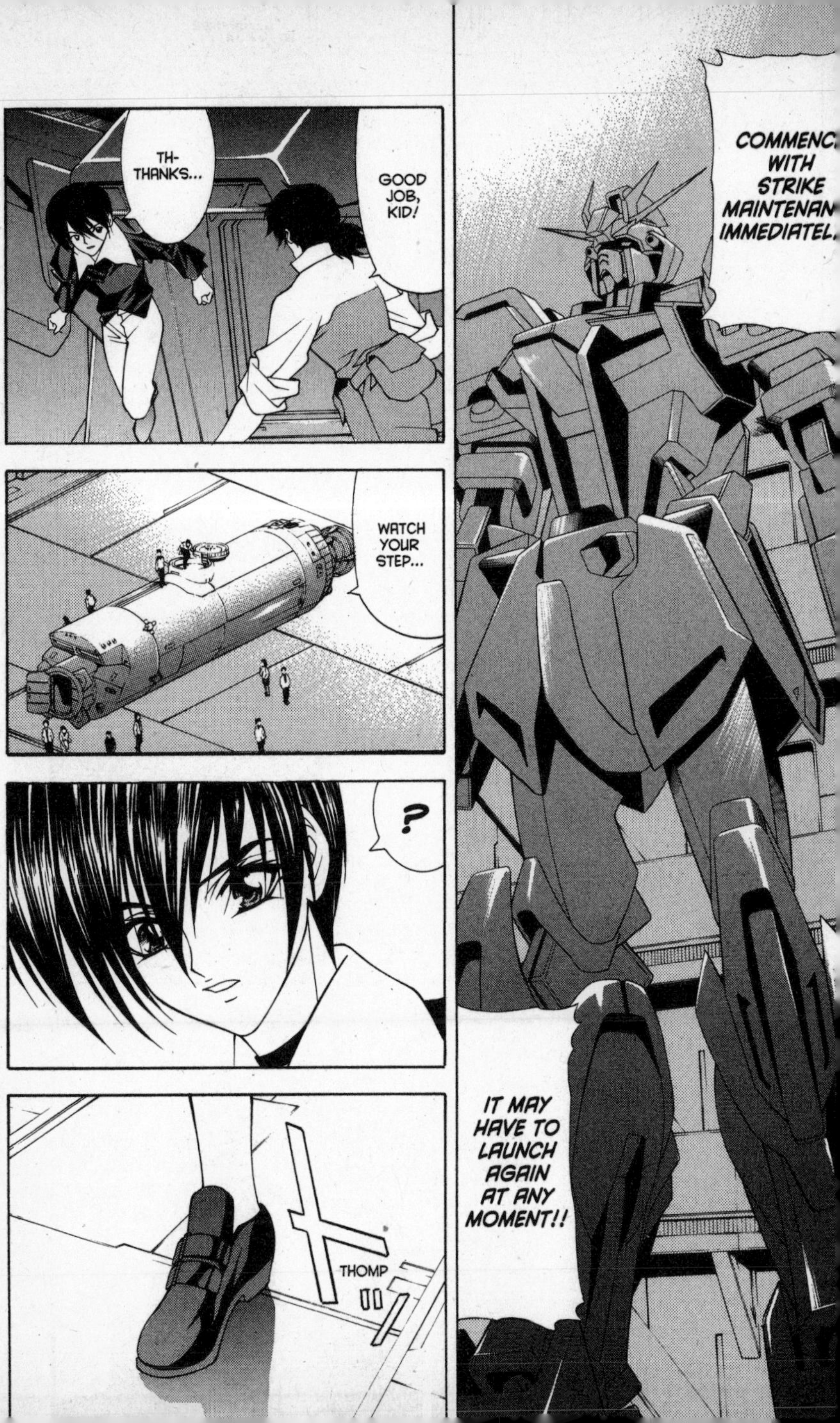
COMMENC WITH STRIKE MAINTENAN IMMEDIATEL
IT MAY HAVE TO LAUNCH AGAIN AT ANY MOMENT!!
GOOD JOB, KID!
TH- THANKS...
WATCH YOUR STEP...
?
THOMP

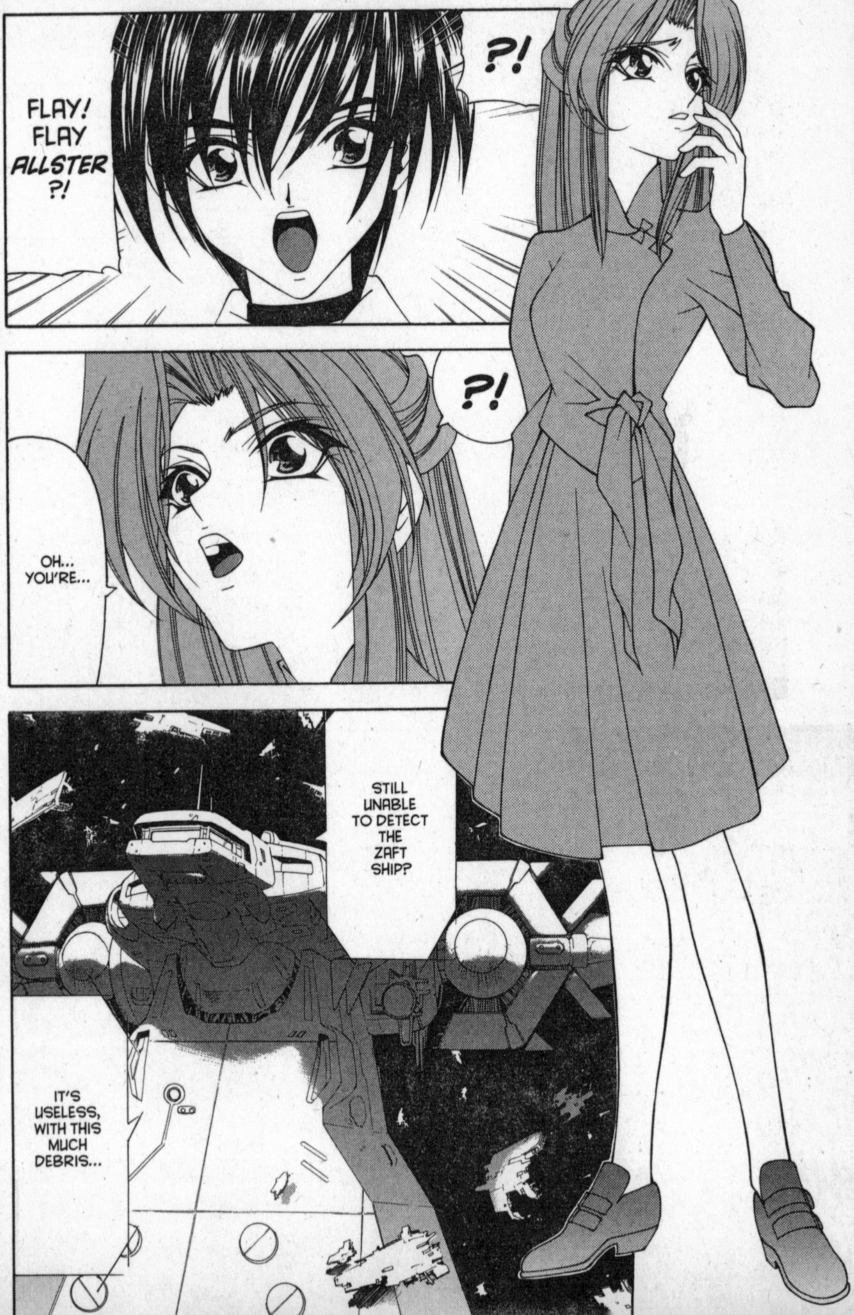
?!
FLAY! FLAY ALLSTER ?!
?!
OH... YOU'RE...
STILL UNABLE TO DETECT THE ZAFT SHIP?
IT'S USELESS, WITH THIS MUCH DEBRIS...

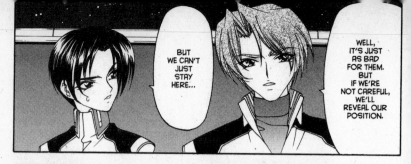

WELL, IT'S JUST AS BAD FOR THEM. BUT IF WE'RE NOT CAREFUL, WE'LL REVEAL OUR POSITION.
BUT WE CAN'T JUST STAY HERE...
IN OUR PRESENT STATE, WE CAN'T HOPE TO MAKE IT TO THE MOON BASE WITHOUT REFUELING.
L4
MOON
L1
EARTH
L3
L5
WHAT IF WE STOP OFF AT ARTEMIS FIRST?
?!
ARTEMIS... WELL, FROM OUR CURRENT LOCATION, IT *IS* THE CLOSEST EARTH ALLIANCE BASE...
L3
HELIOPOLIS
ARCH ANGEL
ARTEMIS

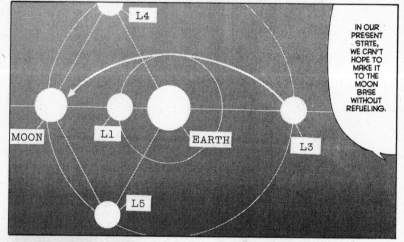

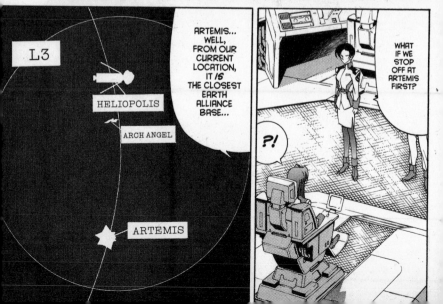

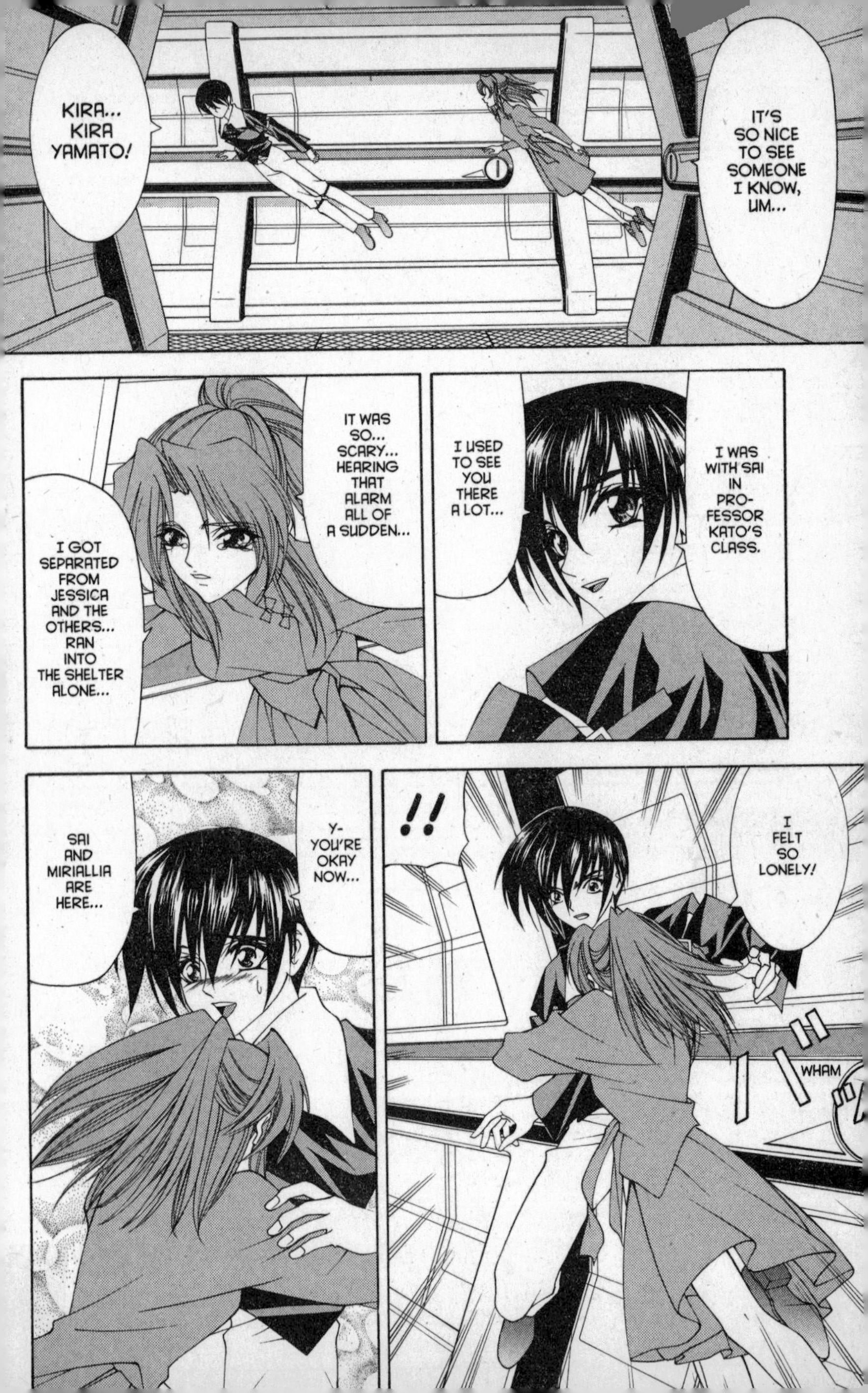
IT'S SO NICE TO SEE SOMEONE I KNOW, UM...
KIRA... KIRA YAMATO!
I WAS WITH SAI IN PRO-FESSOR KATO'S CLASS.
I USED TO SEE YOU THERE A LOT...
IT WAS SO... SCARY... HEARING THAT ALARM ALL OF A SUDDEN...
I GOT SEPARATED FROM JESSICA AND THE OTHERS... RAN INTO THE SHELTER ALONE...
I FELT SO LONELY!
WHAM
!!
Y-YOU'RE OKAY NOW...
SAI AND MIRIALLIA ARE HERE...

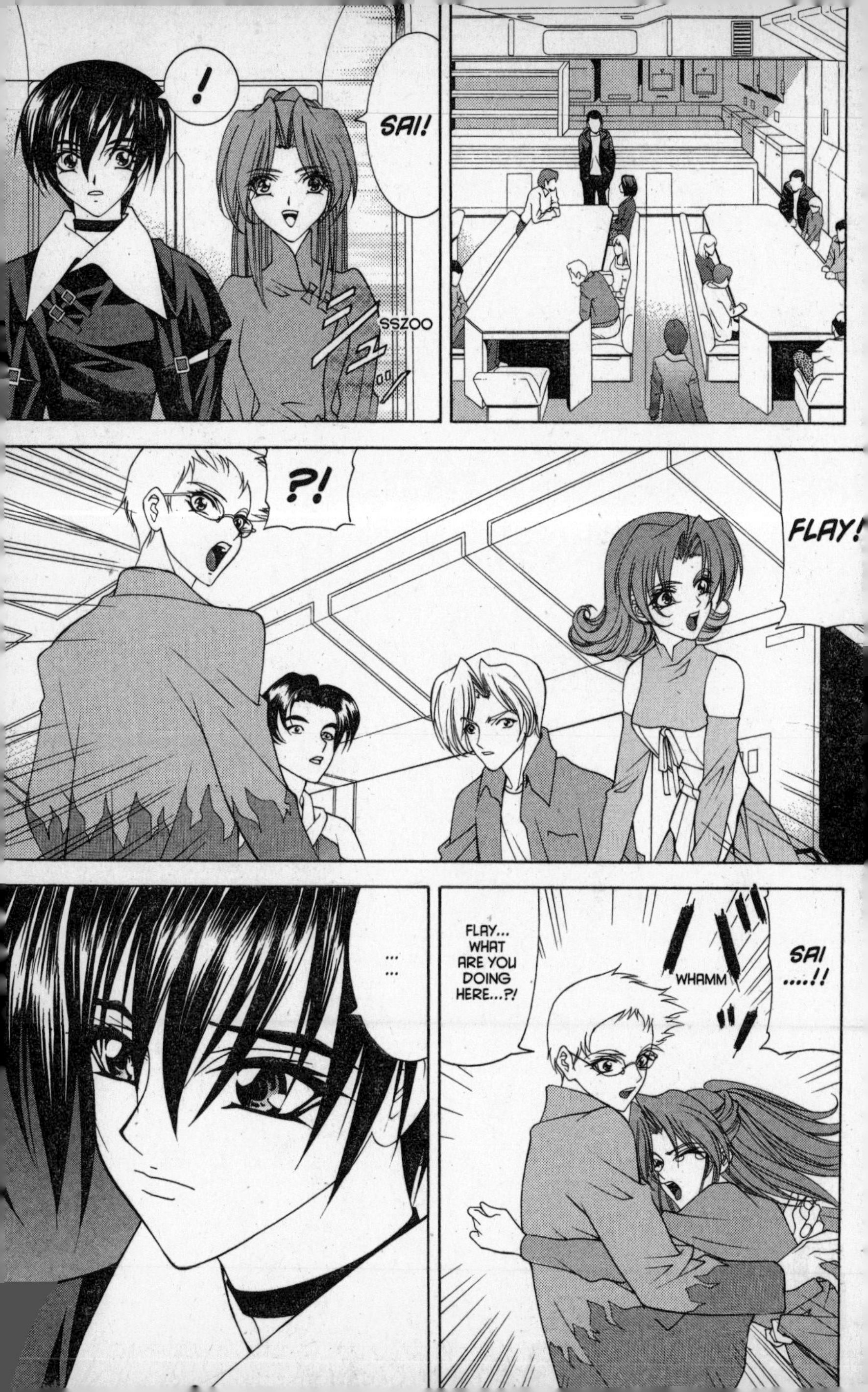
SAI!
!
SSZOO
FLAY!
?!
SAI ....!!
WHAMM
FLAY... WHAT ARE YOU DOING HERE...?!
... ...

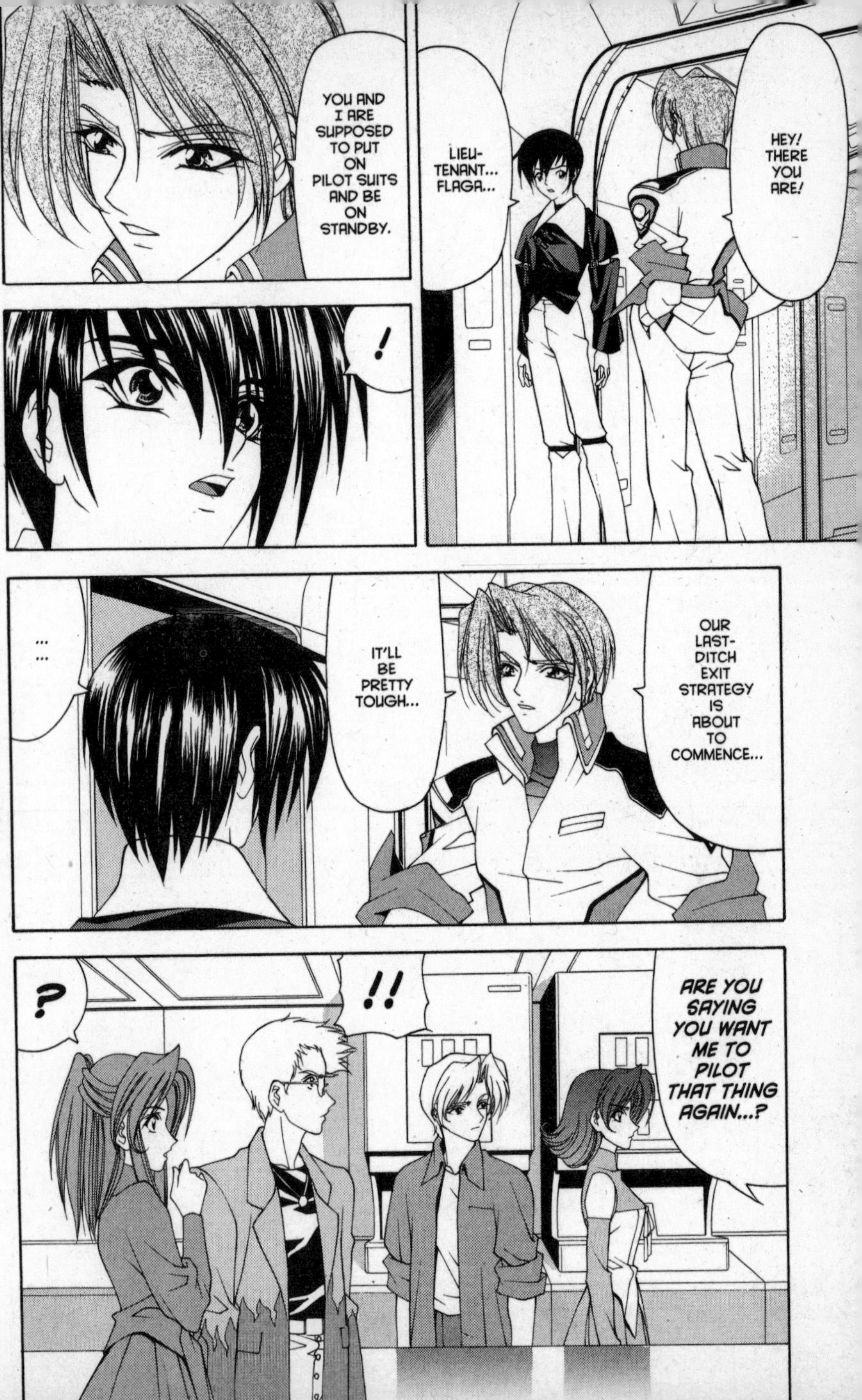
HEY! THERE YOU ARE!
LIEU-TENANT... FLAGA...
YOU AND I ARE SUPPOSED TO PUT ON PILOT SUITS AND BE ON STANDBY.
!
OUR LAST-DITCH EXIT STRATEGY IS ABOUT TO COMMENCE...
IT'LL BE PRETTY TOUGH...
... ...
ARE YOU SAYING YOU WANT ME TO PILOT THAT THING AGAIN...?
!!
?

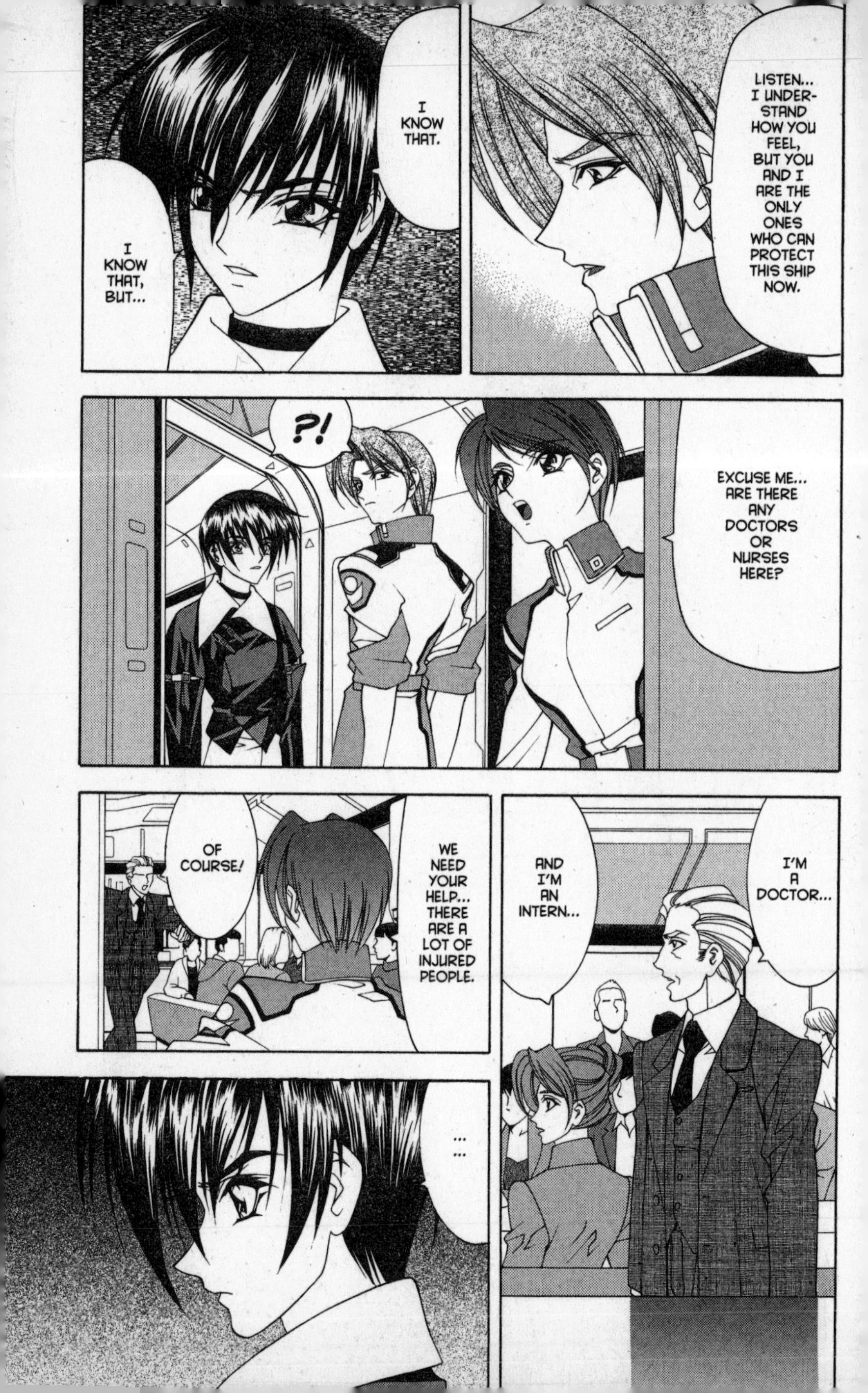
LISTEN... I UNDER-STAND HOW YOU FEEL, BUT YOU AND I ARE THE ONLY ONES WHO CAN PROTECT THIS SHIP NOW.
I KNOW THAT.
I KNOW THAT, BUT...
EXCUSE ME... ARE THERE ANY DOCTORS OR NURSES HERE?
?!
I'M A DOCTOR...
AND I'M AN INTERN...
WE NEED YOUR HELP... THERE ARE A LOT OF INJURED PEOPLE.
OF COURSE!
... ...

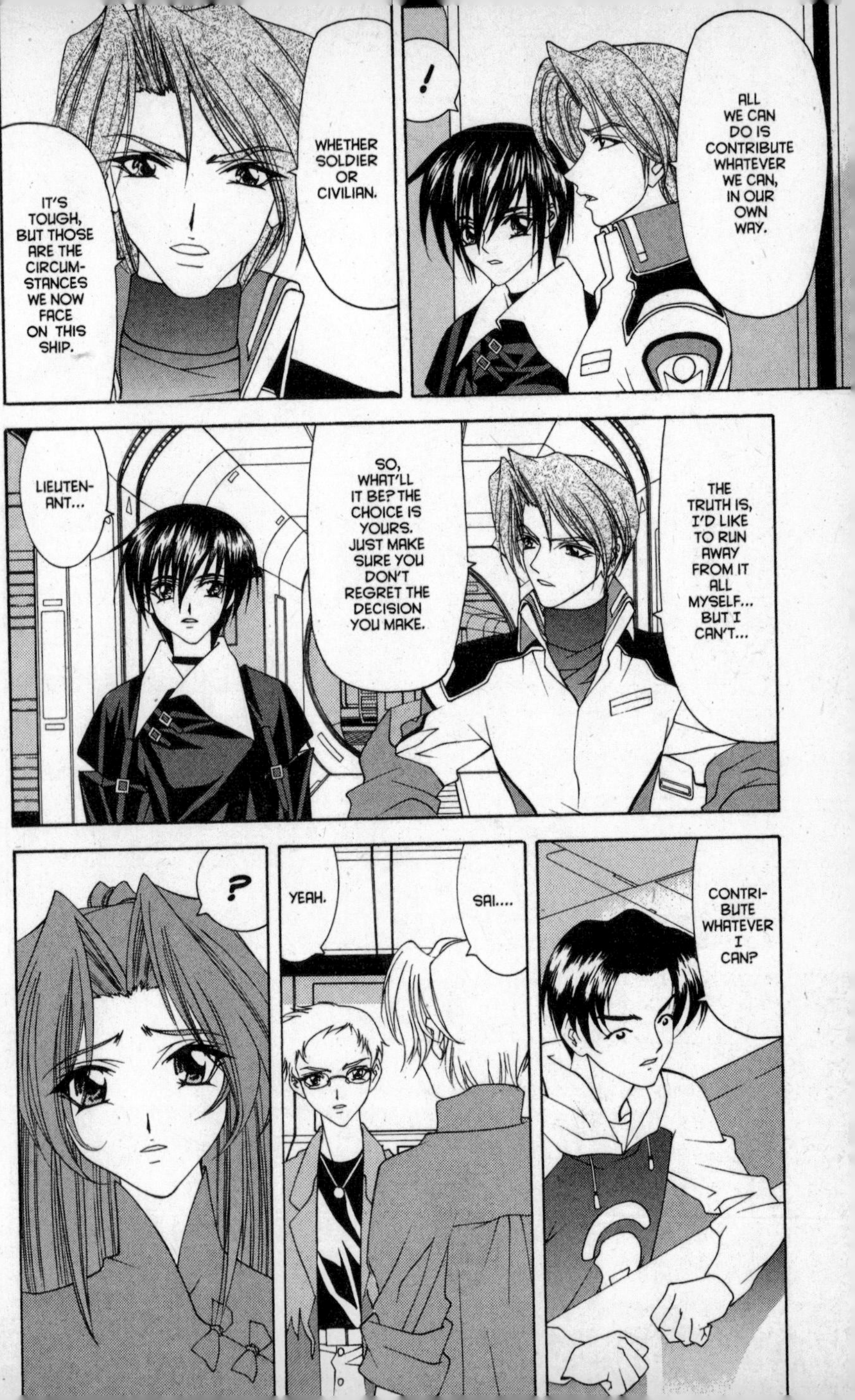
ALL WE CAN DO IS CONTRIBUTE WHATEVER WE CAN, IN OUR OWN WAY.
!
WHETHER SOLDIER OR CIVILIAN.
IT'S TOUGH, BUT THOSE ARE THE CIRCUM-STANCES WE NOW FACE ON THIS SHIP.
THE TRUTH IS, I'D LIKE TO RUN AWAY FROM IT ALL MYSELF... BUT I CAN'T...
SO, WHAT'LL IT BE? THE CHOICE IS YOURS. JUST MAKE SURE YOU DON'T REGRET THE DECISION YOU MAKE.
LIEUTEN-ANT...
CONTRI-BUTE WHATEVER I CAN?
SAI....
YEAH.
?

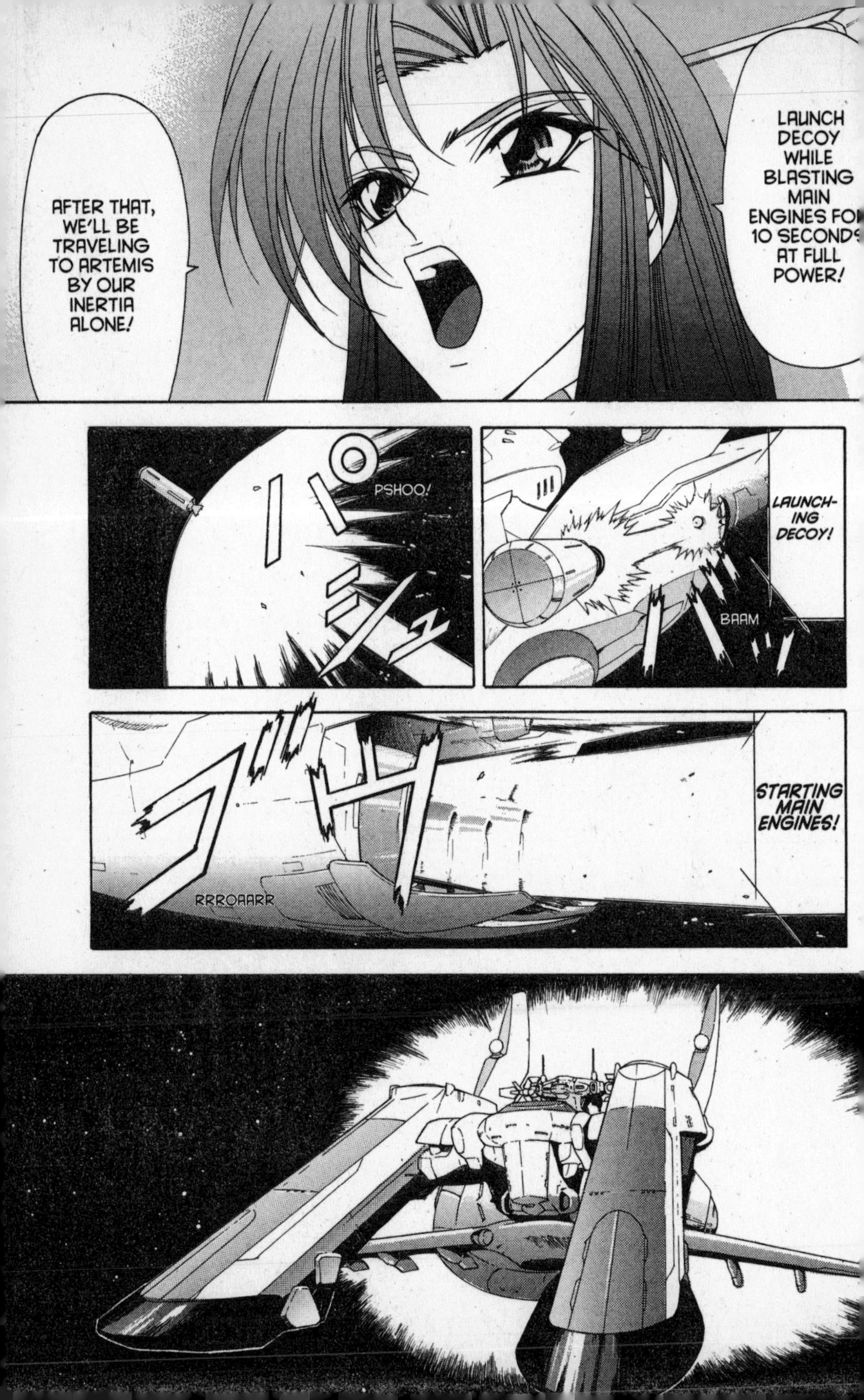
LAUNCH DECOY WHILE BLASTING MAIN ENGINES FO 10 SECOND AT FULL POWER!
AFTER THAT, WE'LL BE TRAVELING TO ARTEMIS BY OUR INERTIA ALONE!
LAUNCHING DECOY!
BAAM
PSHOO!
STARTING MAIN ENGINES!
RRROAARR

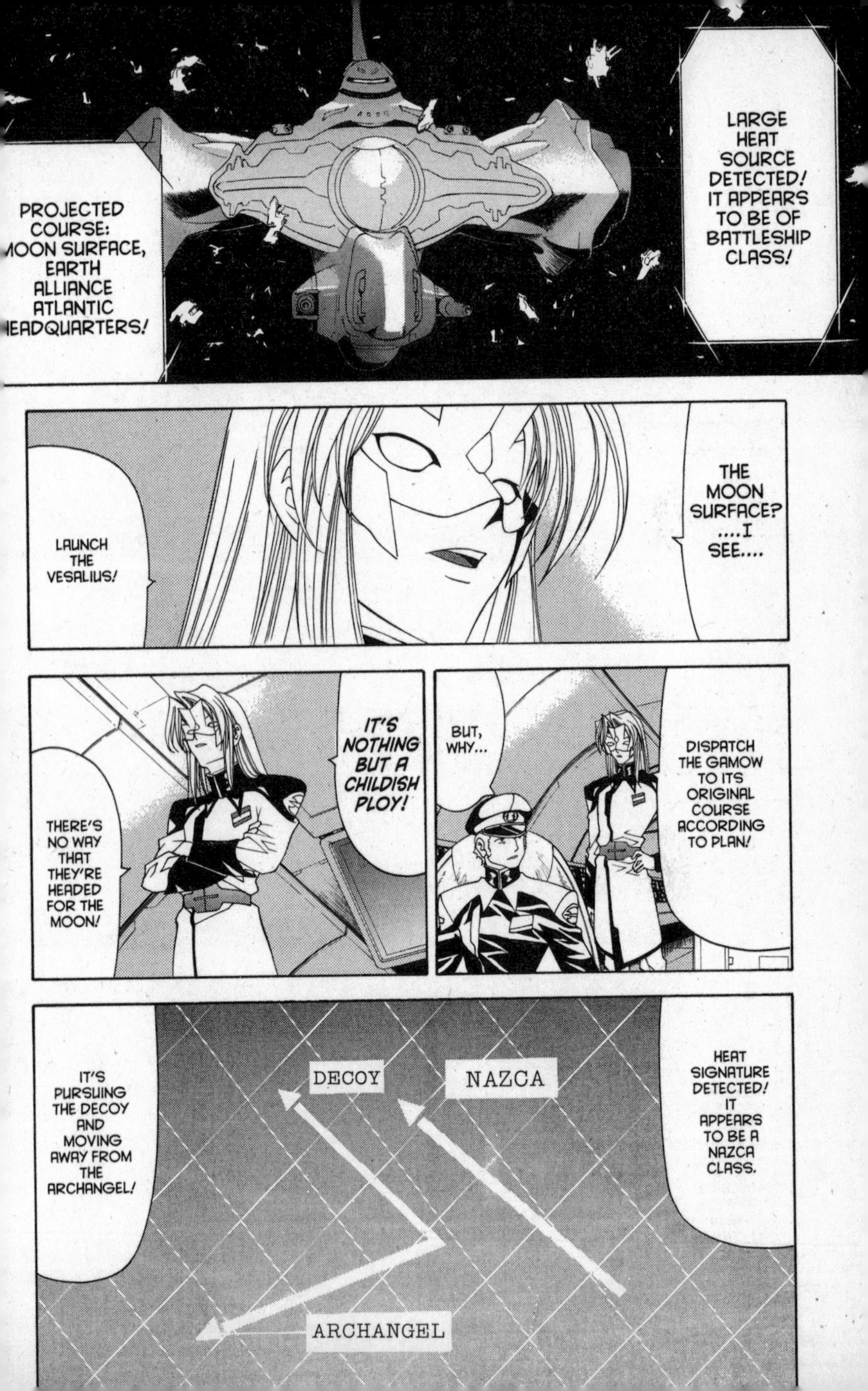
LARGE HEAT SOURCE DETECTED! IT APPEARS TO BE OF BATTLESHIP CLASS!
PROJECTED COURSE: MOON SURFACE, EARTH ALLIANCE ATLANTIC HEADQUARTERS!
THE MOON SURFACE? ....I SEE....
LAUNCH THE VESALIUS!
DISPATCH THE GAMOW TO ITS ORIGINAL COURSE ACCORDING TO PLAN!
BUT, WHY...
IT'S NOTHING BUT A CHILDISH PLOY!
THERE'S NO WAY THAT THEY'RE HEADED FOR THE MOON!
HEAT SIGNATURE DETECTED! IT APPEARS TO BE A NAZCA CLASS.
NAZCA
DECOY
ARCHANGEL
IT'S PURSUING THE DECOY AND MOVING AWAY FROM THE ARCHANGEL!

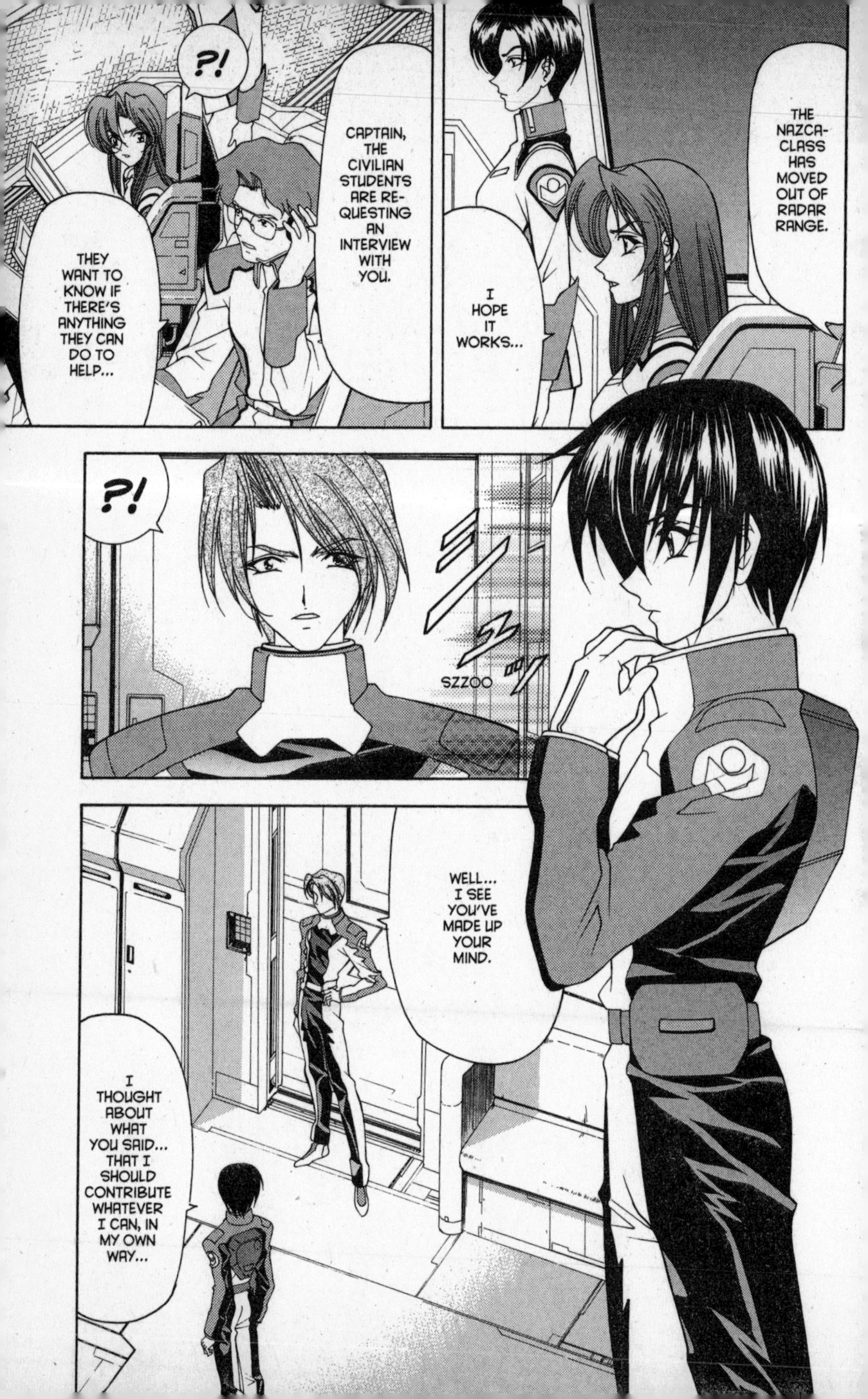
THE NAZCA-CLASS HAS MOVED OUT OF RADAR RANGE.
I HOPE IT WORKS...
?!
CAPTAIN, THE CIVILIAN STUDENTS ARE RE-QUESTING AN INTERVIEW WITH YOU.
THEY WANT TO KNOW IF THERE'S ANYTHING THEY CAN DO TO HELP...
?!
SZZOO
WELL... I SEE YOU'VE MADE UP YOUR MIND.
I THOUGHT ABOUT WHAT YOU SAID... THAT I SHOULD CONTRIBUTE WHATEVER I CAN, IN MY OWN WAY...

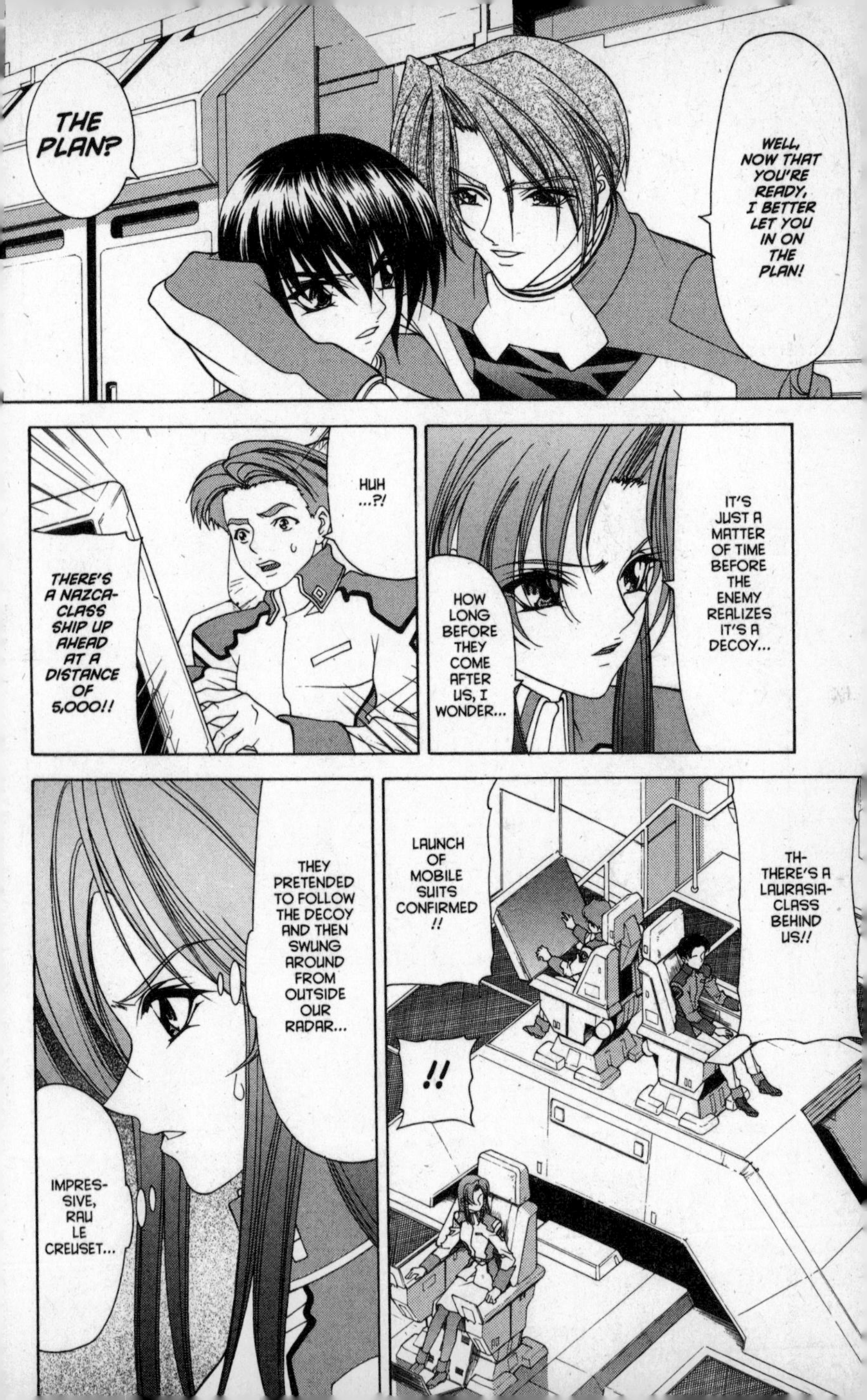
WELL, NOW THAT YOU'RE READY, I BETTER LET YOU IN ON THE PLAN!
THE PLAN?
IT'S JUST A MATTER OF TIME BEFORE THE ENEMY REALIZES IT'S A DECOY...
HOW LONG BEFORE THEY COME AFTER US, I WONDER...
HUH ...?!
THERE'S A NAZCA-CLASS SHIP UP AHEAD AT A DISTANCE OF 5,000!!
TH-THERE'S A LAURASIA-CLASS BEHIND US!!
LAUNCH OF MOBILE SUITS CONFIRMED!!
!!
THEY PRETENDED TO FOLLOW THE DECOY AND THEN SWUNG AROUND FROM OUTSIDE OUR RADAR...
IMPRES-SIVE, RAU LE CREUSET...

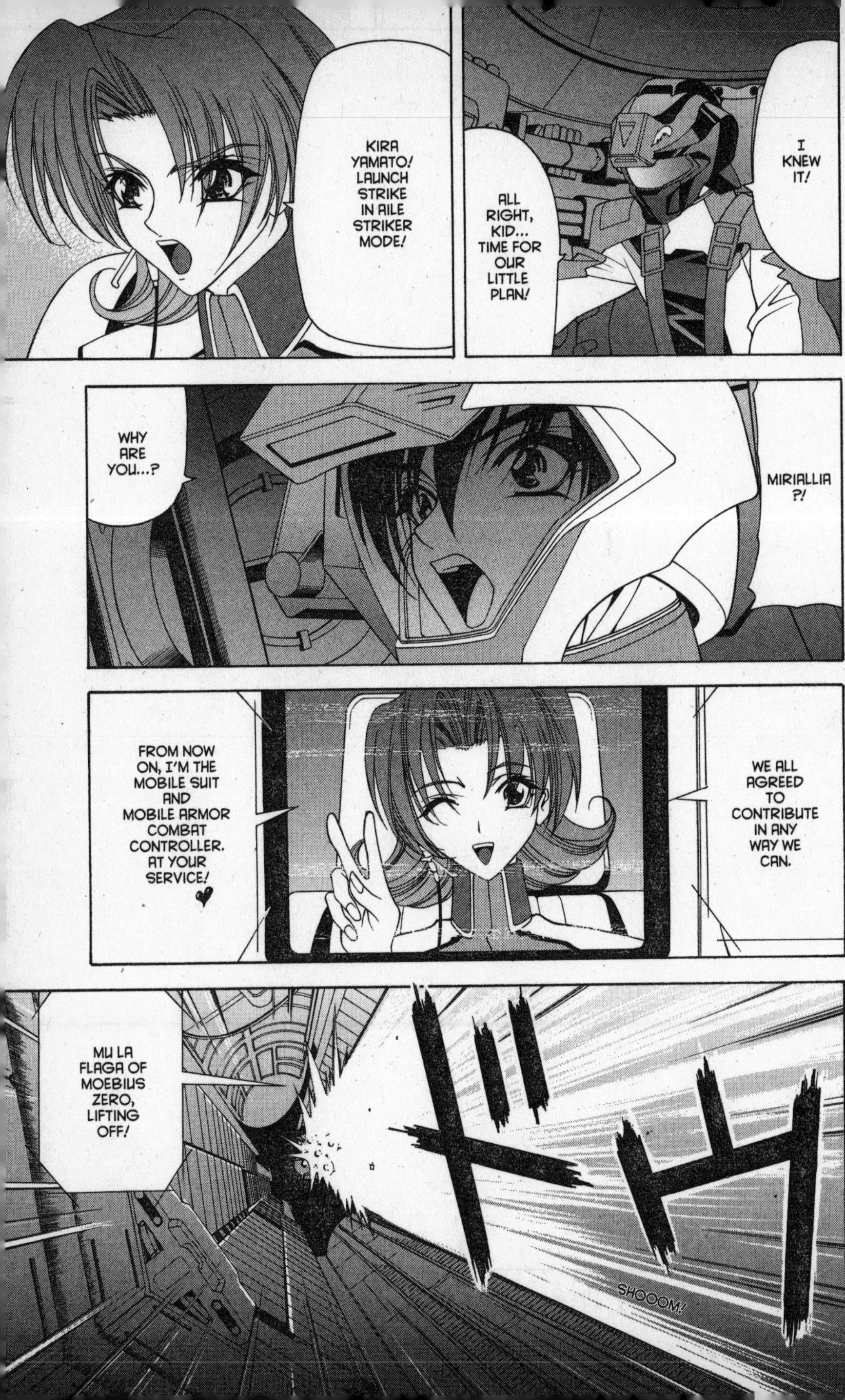
I KNEW IT!
ALL RIGHT, KID... TIME FOR OUR LITTLE PLAN!
KIRA YAMATO! LAUNCH STRIKE IN AILE STRIKER MODE!
MIRIALLIA?!
WHY ARE YOU...?
WE ALL AGREED TO CONTRIBUTE IN ANY WAY WE CAN.
FROM NOW ON, I'M THE MOBILE SUIT AND MOBILE ARMOR COMBAT CONTROLLER. AT YOUR SERVICE! ♥
MU LA FLAGA OF MOEBIUS ZERO, LIFTING OFF!
ドッ
SHOOOM!

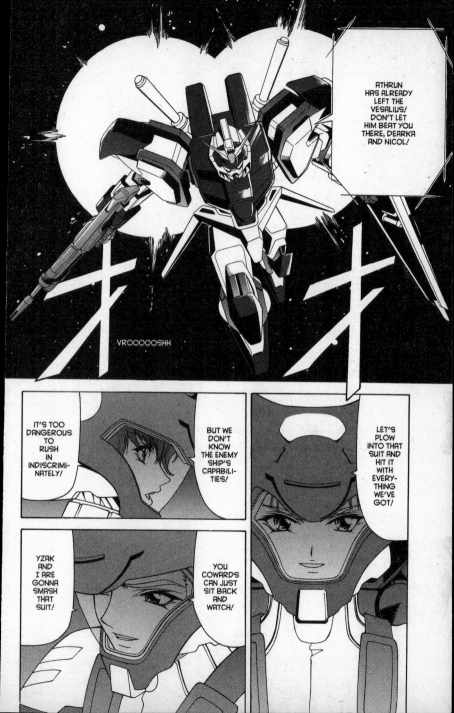

ATHRUN HAS ALREADY LEFT THE VESALIUS! DON'T LET HIM BEAT YOU THERE, DEARKA AND NICOL!

VROOOOOSHH.

IT'S TOO DANGEROUS TO RUSH IN INDISCRIMINATELY!

BUT WE DON'T KNOW THE ENEMY SHIP'S CAPABILITIES!

LET'S PLOW INTO THAT SUIT AND HIT IT WITH EVERYTHING WE'VE GOT!

YZAK AND I ARE GONNA SMASH THAT SUIT!

YOU COWARDS CAN JUST SIT BACK AND WATCH!

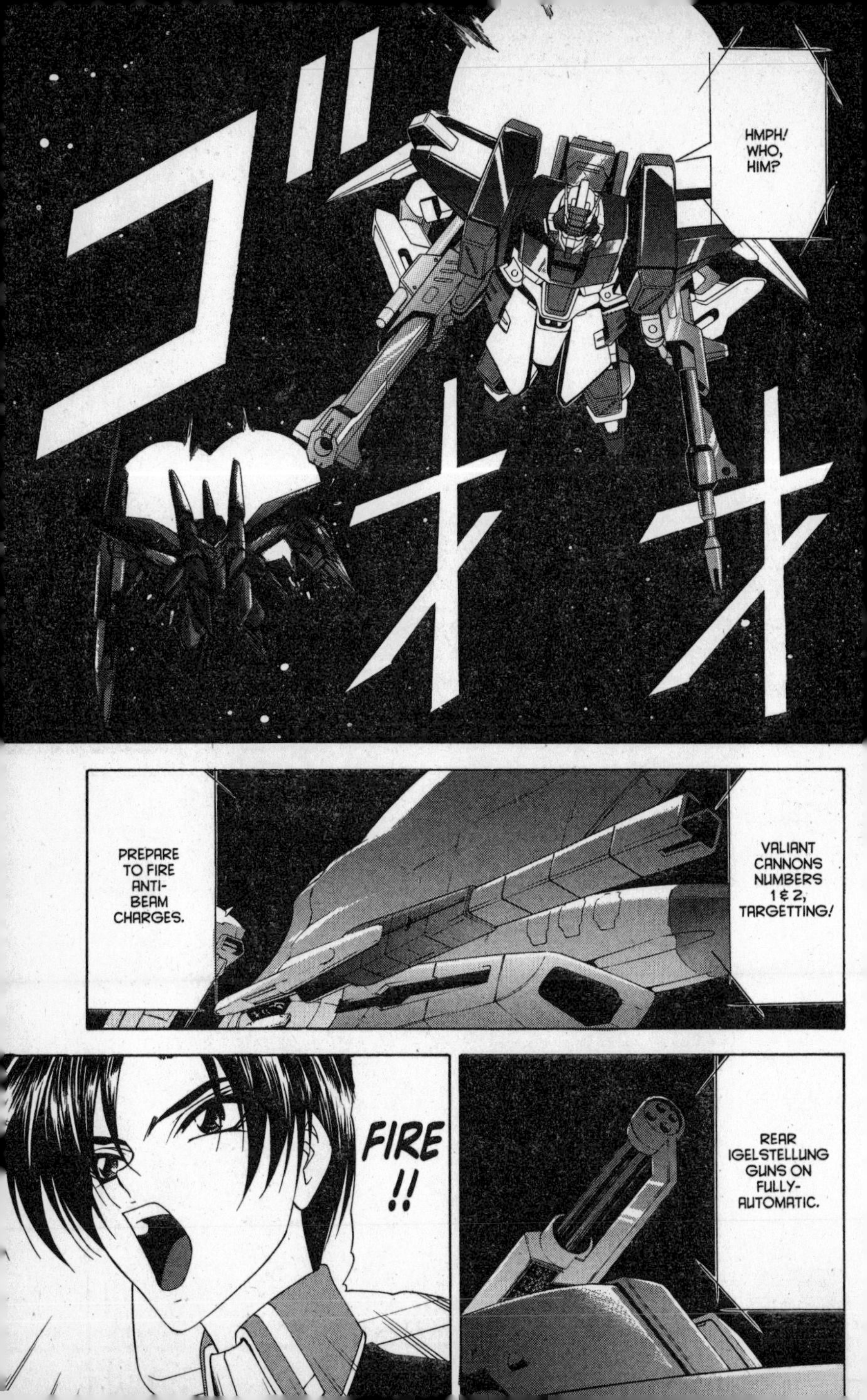

HMPH! WHO, HIM?
ゴオオ
VALIANT CANNONS NUMBERS 1 & 2, TARGETTING!
PREPARE TO FIRE ANTI-BEAM CHARGES.
REAR IGELSTELLUNG GUNS ON FULLY-AUTOMATIC.
FIRE !!

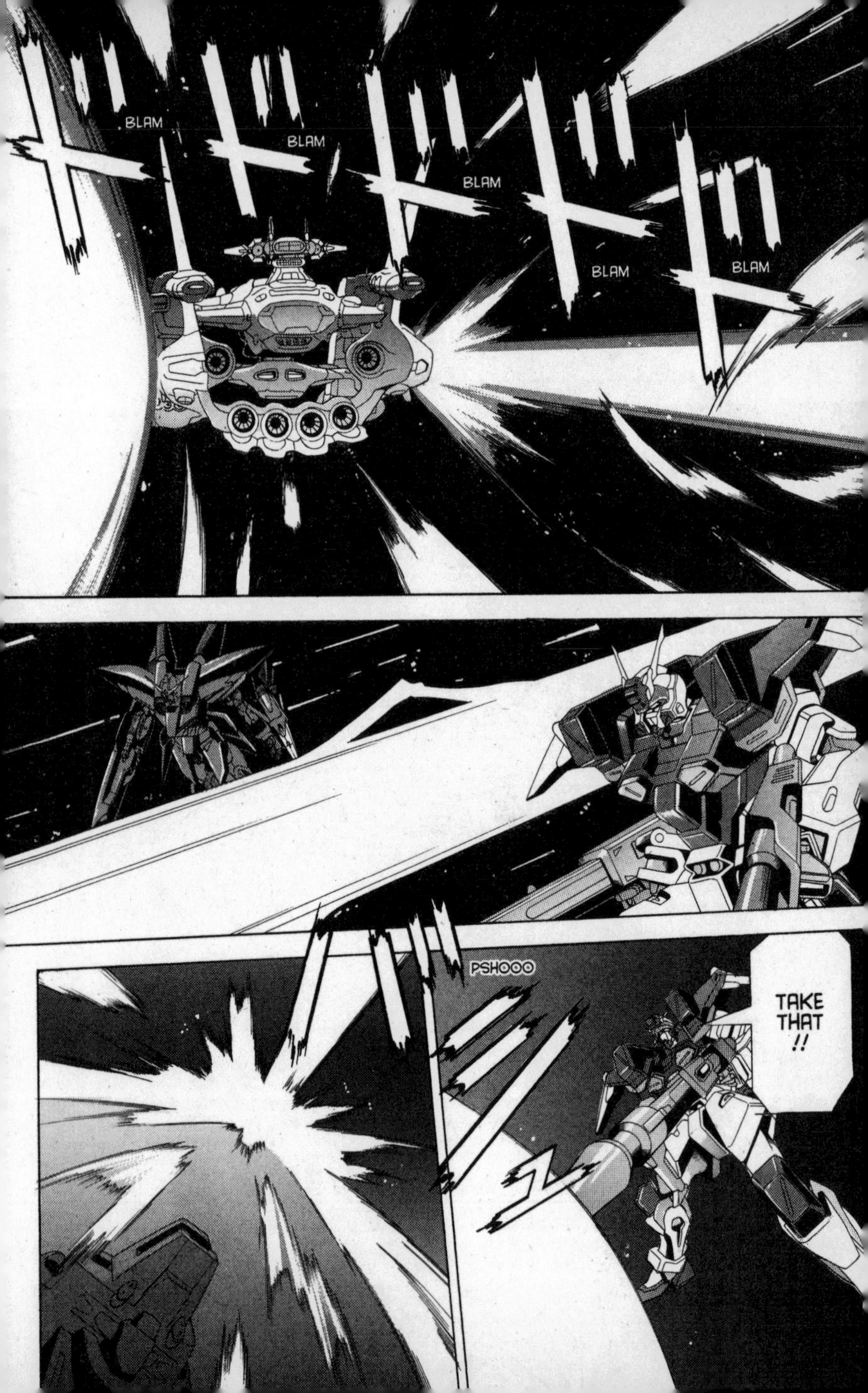
BLAM
BLAM
BLAM
BLAM
BLAM
TAKE THAT!!
PSHOOO

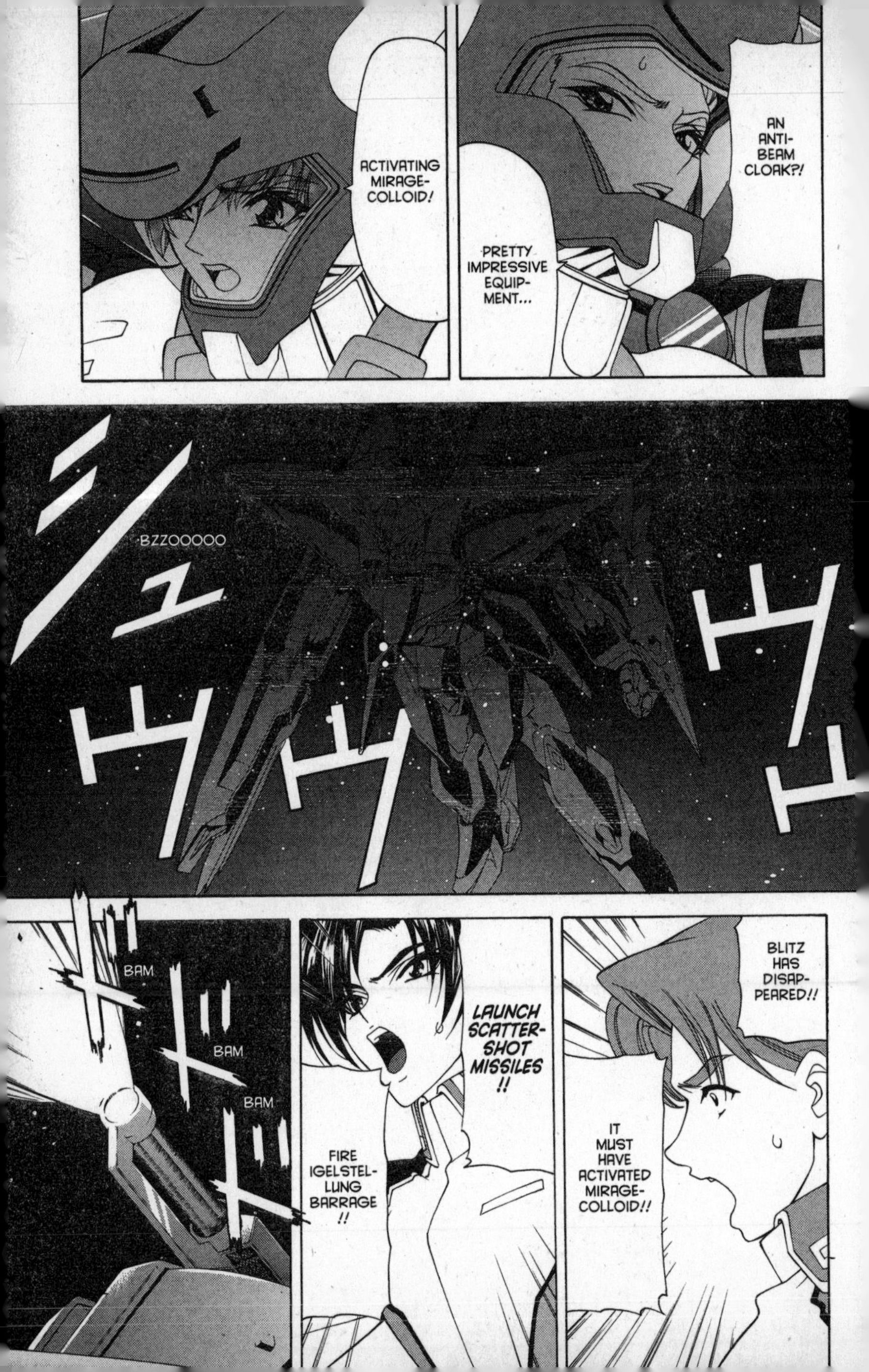
AN ANTI-BEAM CLOAK?!
PRETTY IMPRESSIVE EQUIPMENT...
ACTIVATING MIRAGE-COLLOID!
BZZOOOOO
BLITZ HAS DISAPPEARED!!
IT MUST HAVE ACTIVATED MIRAGE-COLLOID!!
LAUNCH SCATTER-SHOT MISSILES!!
FIRE IGELSTELLUNG BARRAGE!!
BAM
BAM
BAM

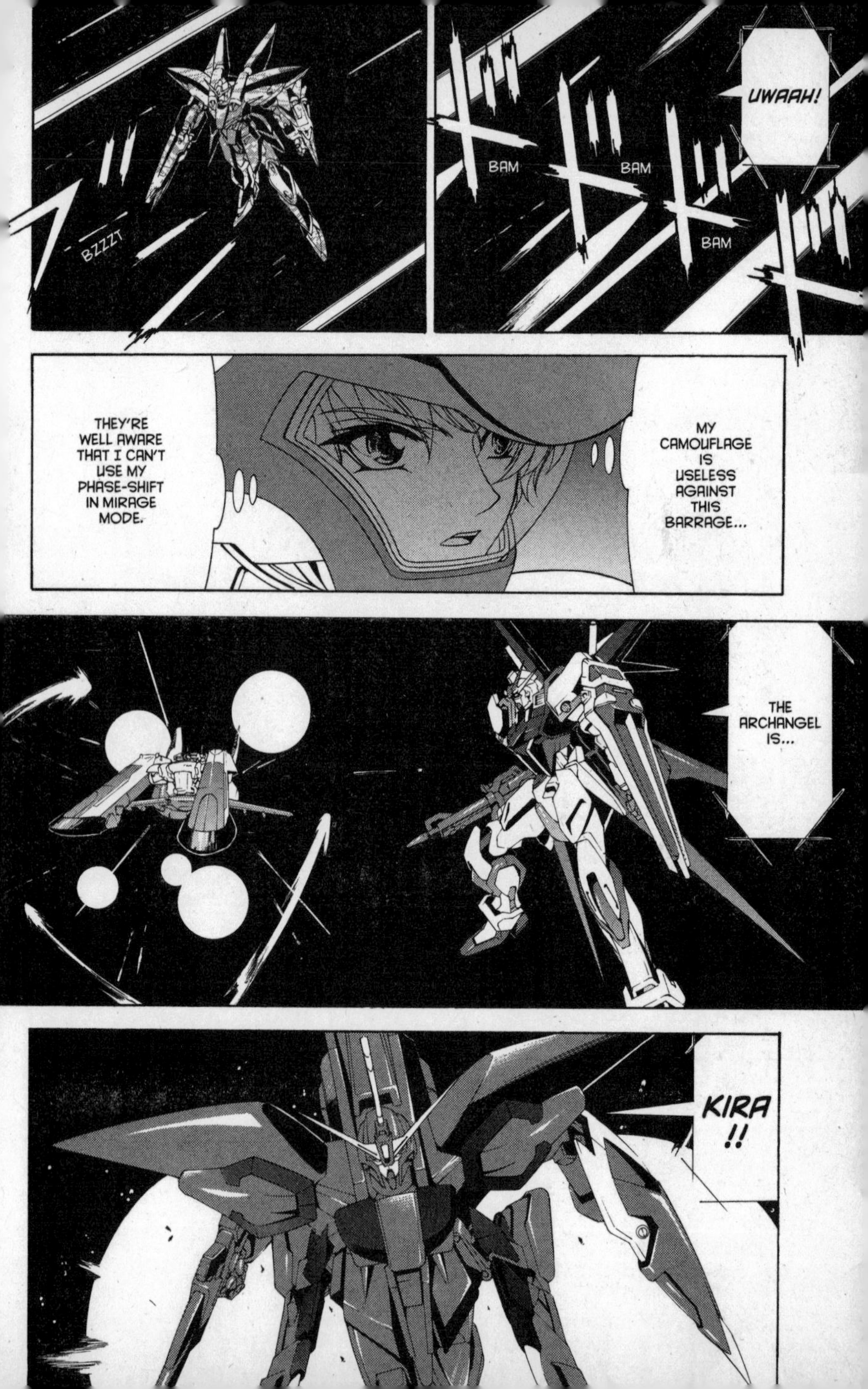
UWAAH!
BAM
BAM
BAM
BZZZT
MY CAMOUFLAGE IS USELESS AGAINST THIS BARRAGE...
THEY'RE WELL AWARE THAT I CAN'T USE MY PHASE-SHIFT IN MIRAGE MODE.
THE ARCHANGEL IS...
KIRA !!

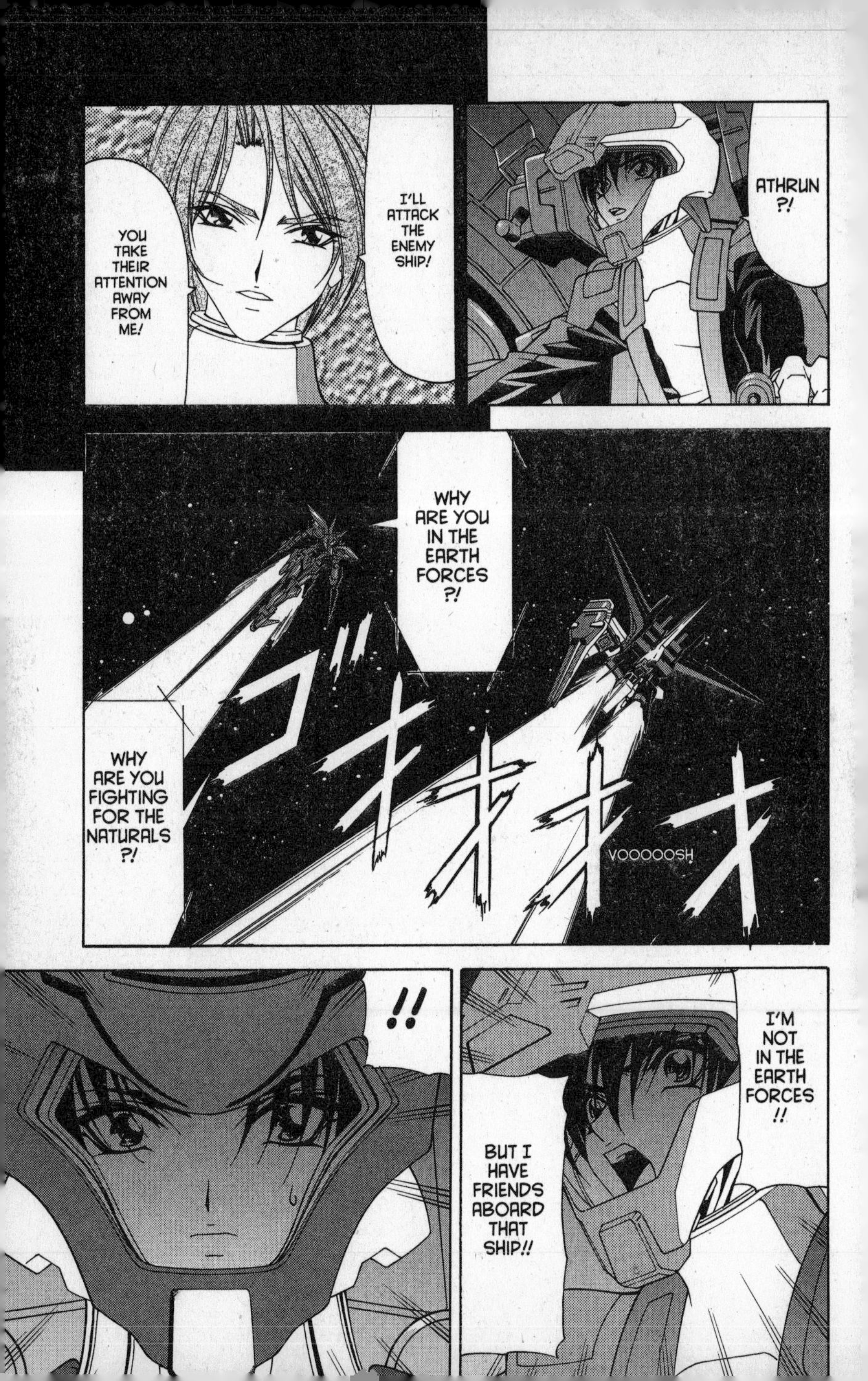
ATHRUN ?!
I'LL ATTACK THE ENEMY SHIP!
YOU TAKE THEIR ATTENTION AWAY FROM ME!
WHY ARE YOU IN THE EARTH FORCES ?!
WHY ARE YOU FIGHTING FOR THE NATURALS ?!
ゴオオオオ
VOOOOOSH
I'M NOT IN THE EARTH FORCES !!
BUT I HAVE FRIENDS ABOARD THAT SHIP!!
!!

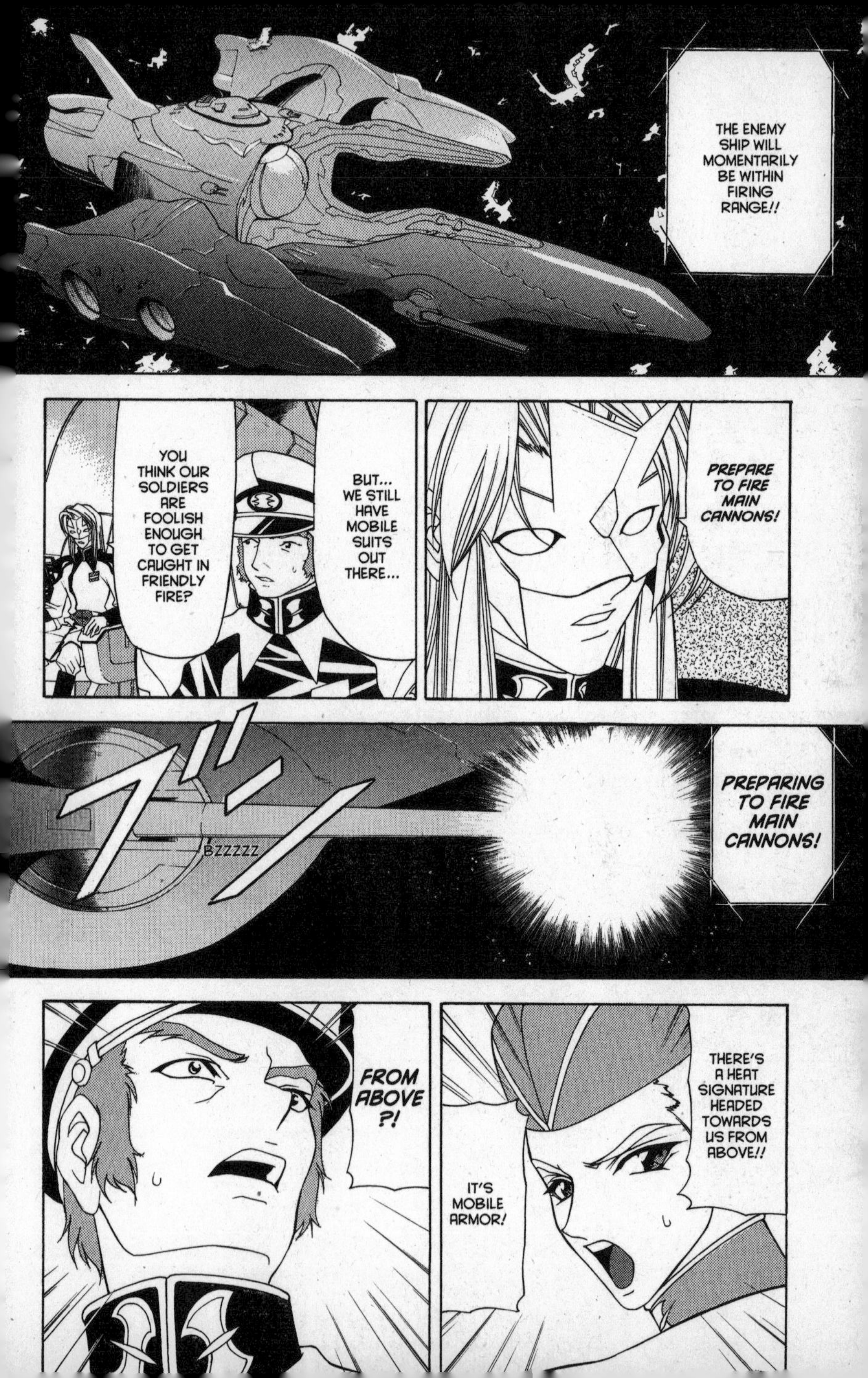
THE ENEMY SHIP WILL MOMENTARILY BE WITHIN FIRING RANGE!!
PREPARE TO FIRE MAIN CANNONS!
BUT... WE STILL HAVE MOBILE SUITS OUT THERE...
YOU THINK OUR SOLDIERS ARE FOOLISH ENOUGH TO GET CAUGHT IN FRIENDLY FIRE?
PREPARING TO FIRE MAIN CANNONS!
ブーン
BZZZZZ
THERE'S A HEAT SIGNATURE HEADED TOWARDS US FROM ABOVE!!
IT'S MOBILE ARMOR!
FROM ABOVE?!

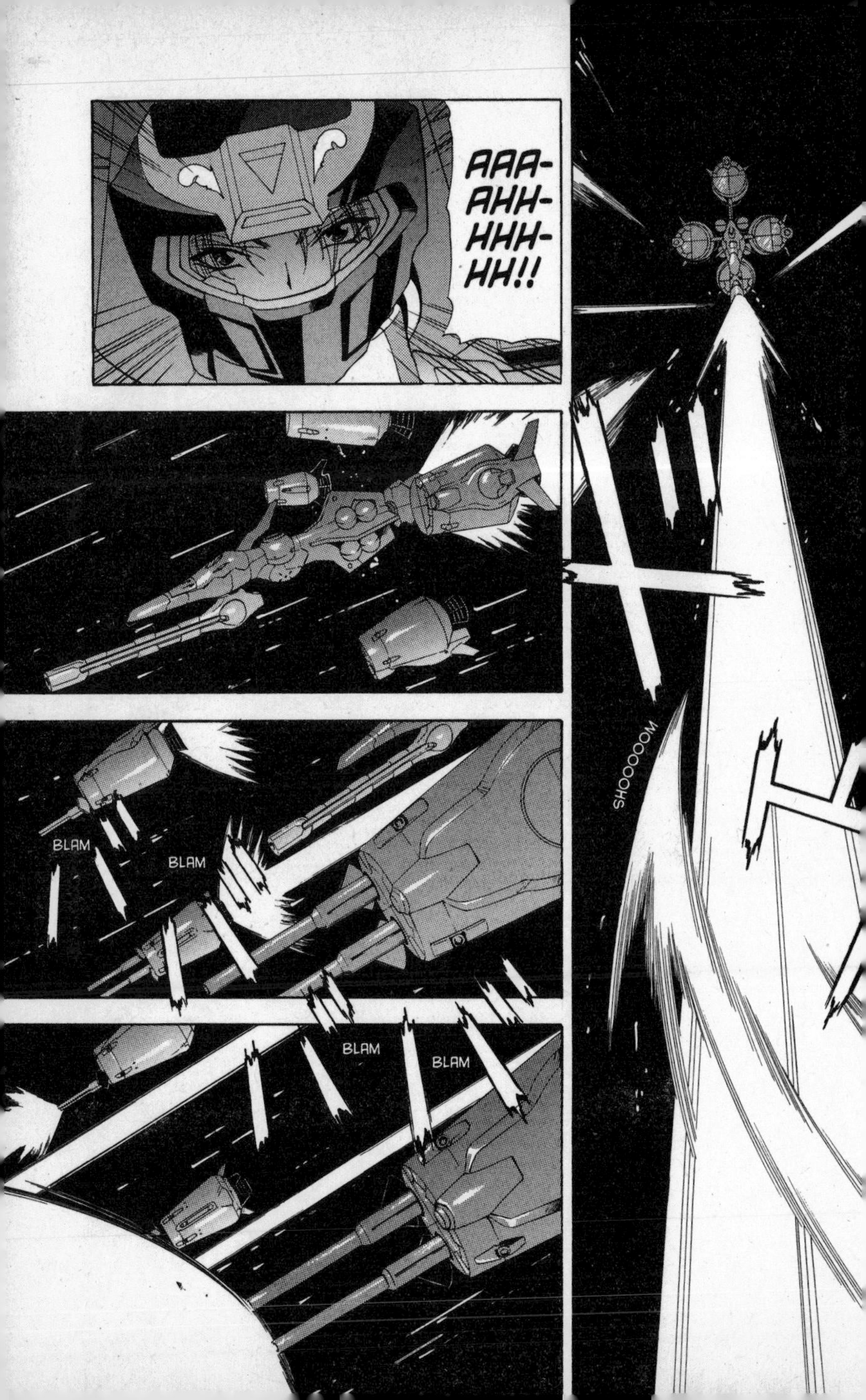
SHOOOOOM
AAA-AHH-HHH-HH!!
BLAM
BLAM
BLAM
BLAM

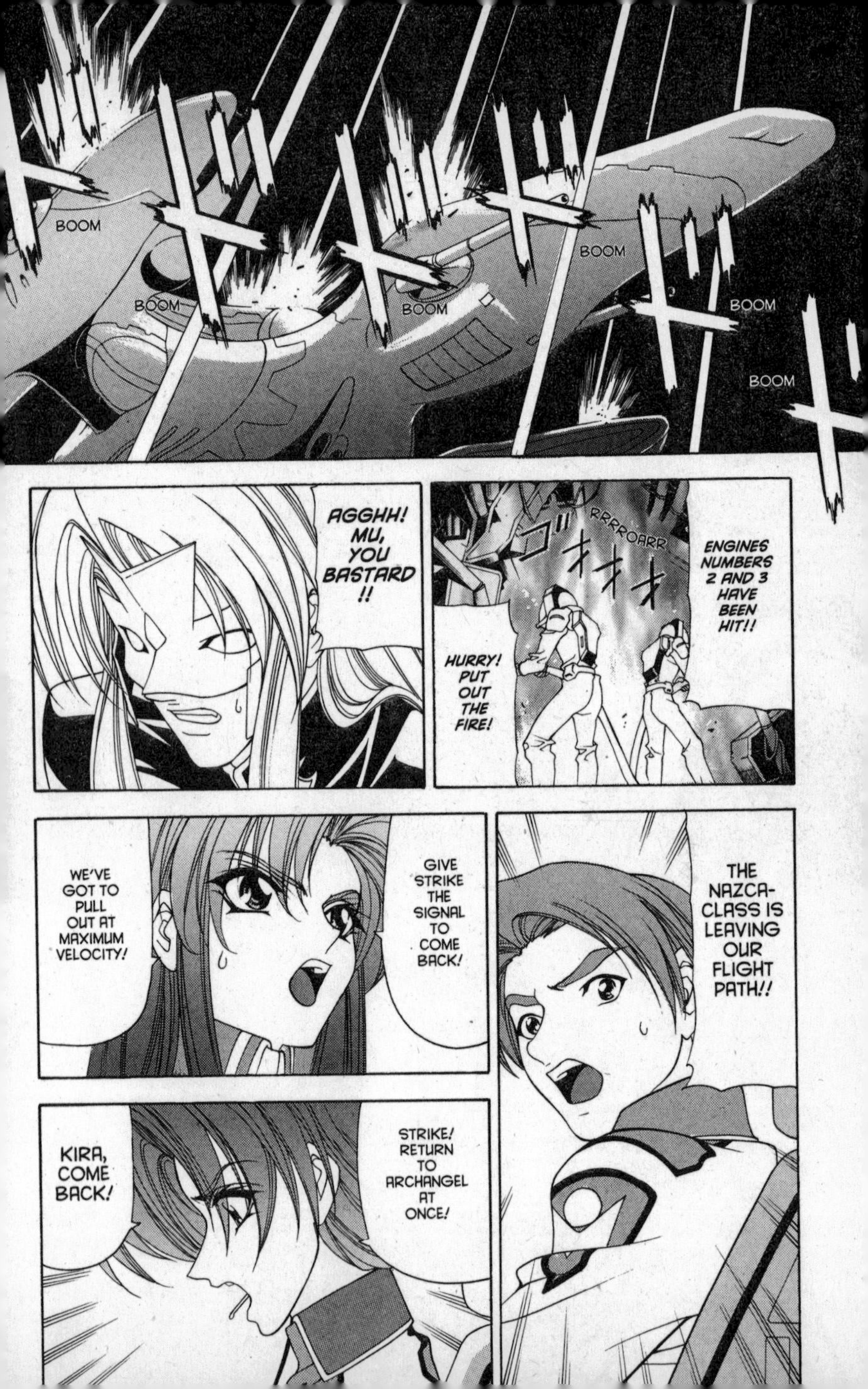
BOOM
BOOM
BOOM
BOOM
BOOM
BOOM
ENGINES NUMBERS 2 AND 3 HAVE BEEN HIT!!
RRRROARR
HURRY! PUT OUT THE FIRE!
AGGHH! MU, YOU BASTARD!!
THE NAZCA-CLASS IS LEAVING OUR FLIGHT PATH!!
GIVE STRIKE THE SIGNAL TO COME BACK!
WE'VE GOT TO PULL OUT AT MAXIMUM VELOCITY!
STRIKE! RETURN TO ARCHANGEL AT ONCE!
KIRA, COME BACK!

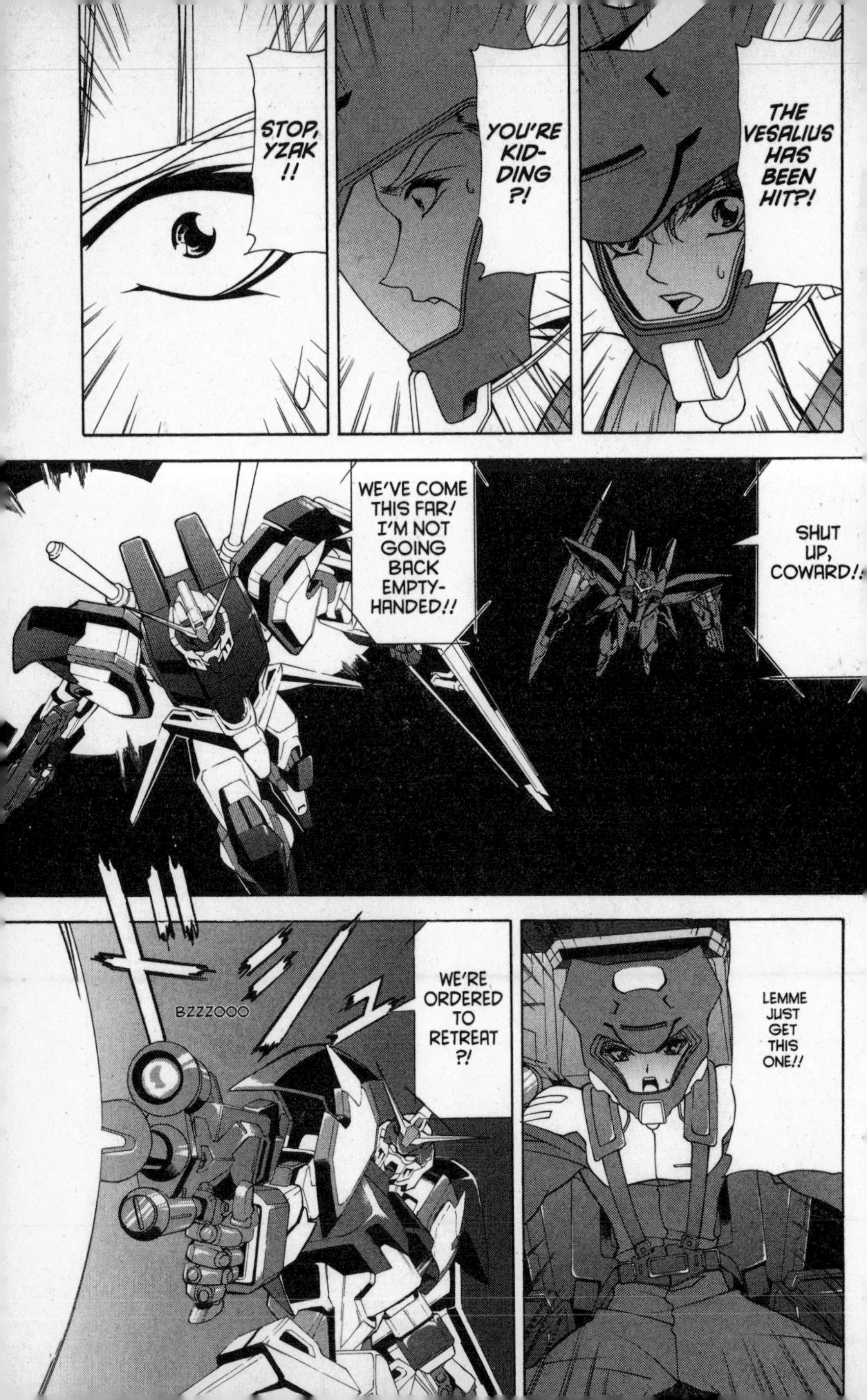
THE VESALIUS HAS BEEN HIT?!
YOU'RE KID-DING ?!
STOP, YZAK !!
SHUT UP, COWARD!!
WE'VE COME THIS FAR! I'M NOT GOING BACK EMPTY-HANDED!!
LEMME JUST GET THIS ONE!!
WE'RE ORDERED TO RETREAT ?!
BZZZOOO

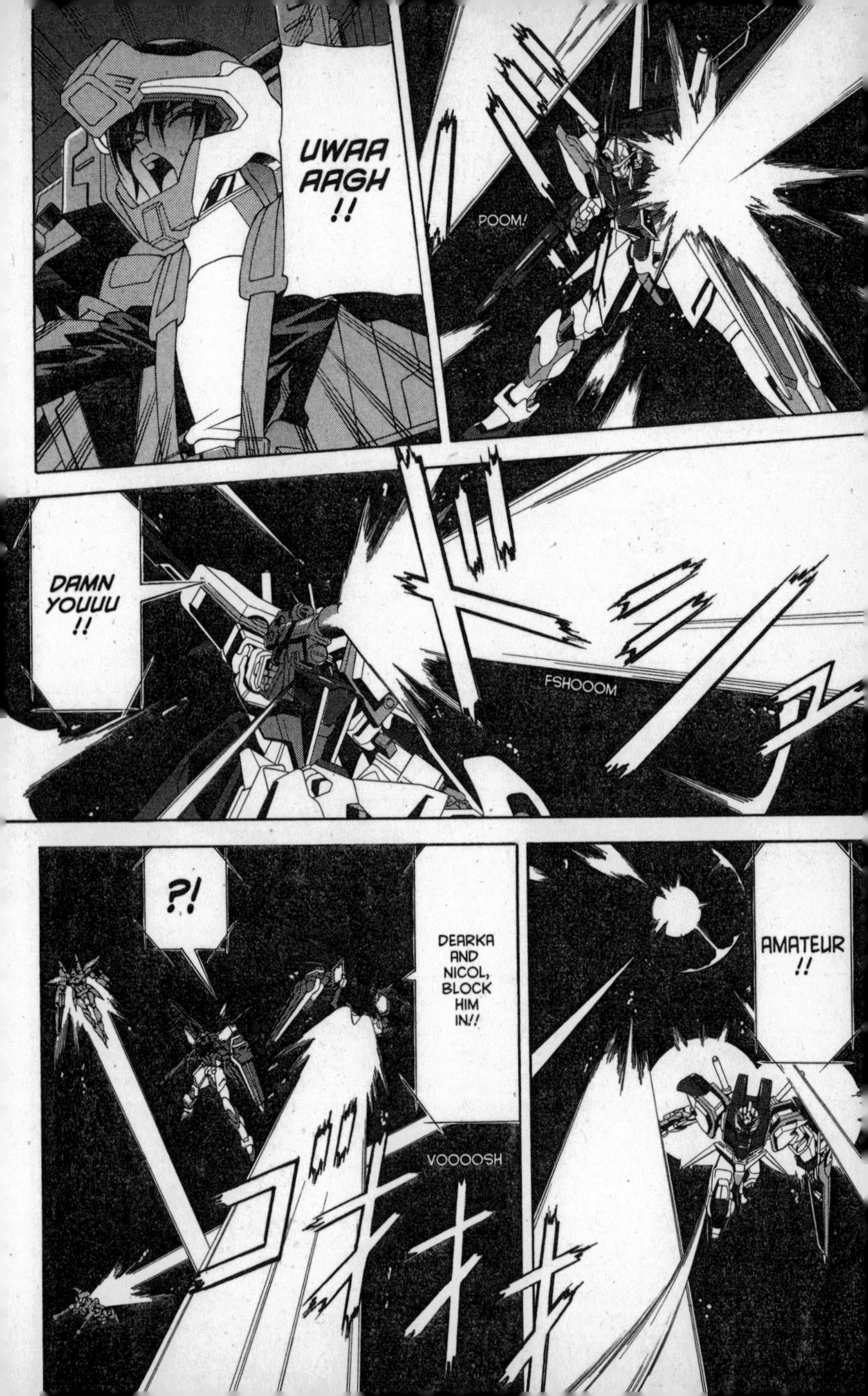
POOM!
UWAA AAGH!!
DAMN YOUUU!!
FSHOOOM
AMATEUR!!
DEARKA AND NICOL, BLOCK HIM IN!!
?!
VOOOOSH

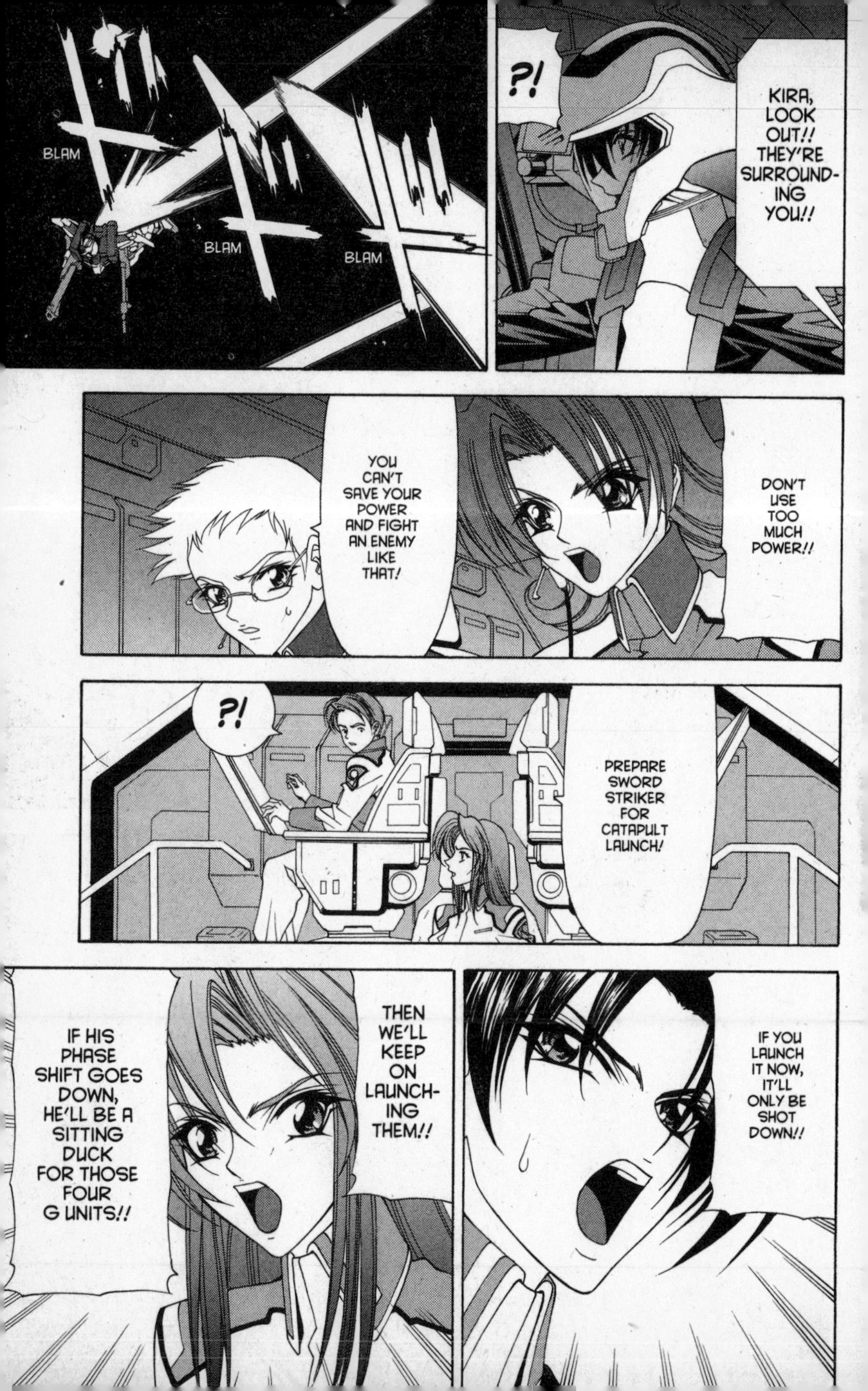
KIRA, LOOK OUT!! THEY'RE SURROUND-ING YOU!!
?!
BLAM
BLAM
BLAM
DON'T USE TOO MUCH POWER!!
YOU CAN'T SAVE YOUR POWER AND FIGHT AN ENEMY LIKE THAT!
PREPARE SWORD STRIKER FOR CATAPULT LAUNCH!
?!
IF YOU LAUNCH IT NOW, IT'LL ONLY BE SHOT DOWN!!
THEN WE'LL KEEP ON LAUNCH-ING THEM!!
IF HIS PHASE SHIFT GOES DOWN, HE'LL BE A SITTING DUCK FOR THOSE FOUR G UNITS!!

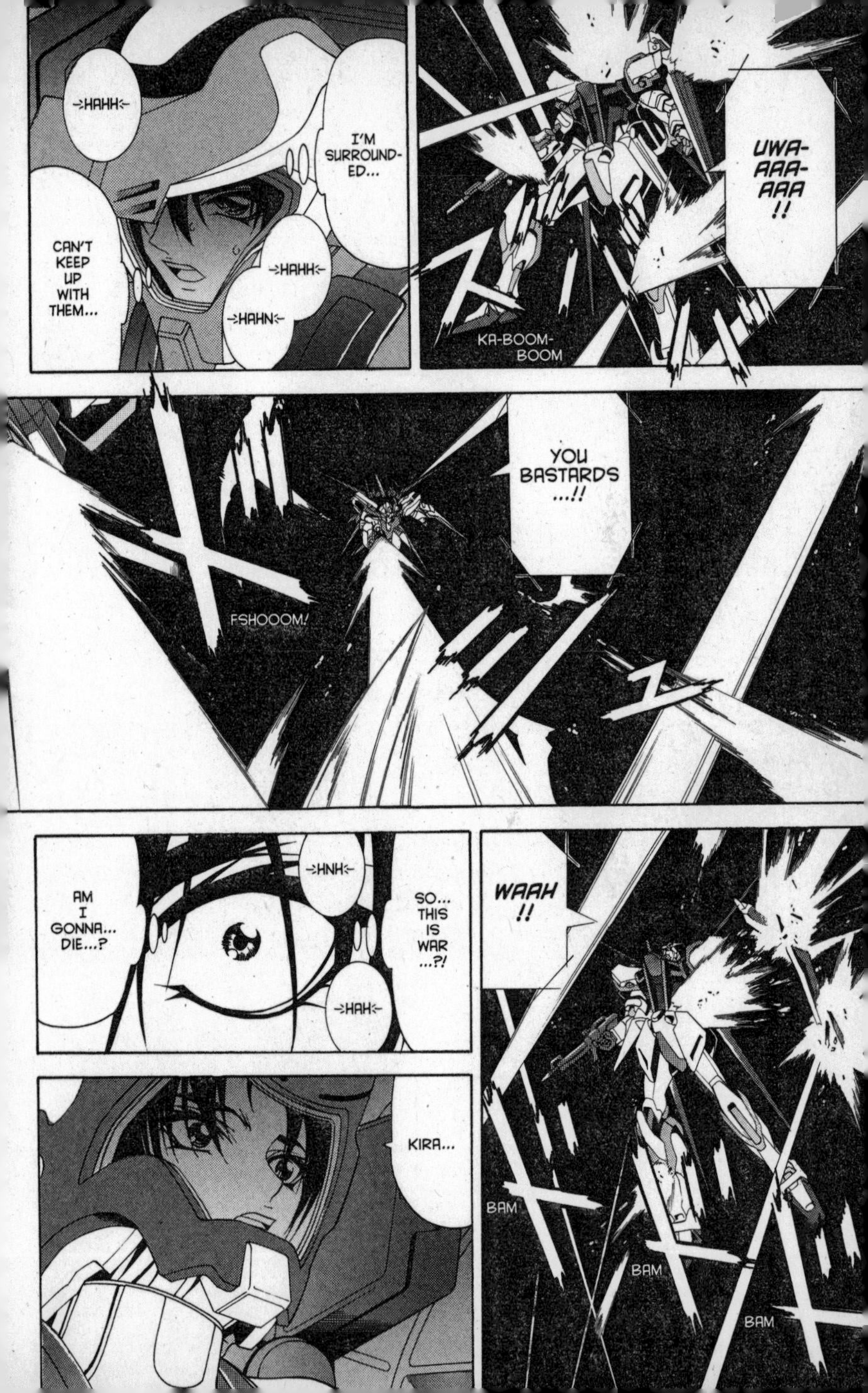
UWA-AAA-AAA!!
KA-BOOM-BOOM
I'M SURROUND-ED...
-HAHH-
-HAHH-
-HAHN-
CAN'T KEEP UP WITH THEM...
YOU BASTARDS...!!
FSHOOOM!
WAAH!!
BAM
BAM
BAM
SO... THIS IS WAR...?!
-HNH-
AM I GONNA... DIE...?
-HAH-
KIRA...

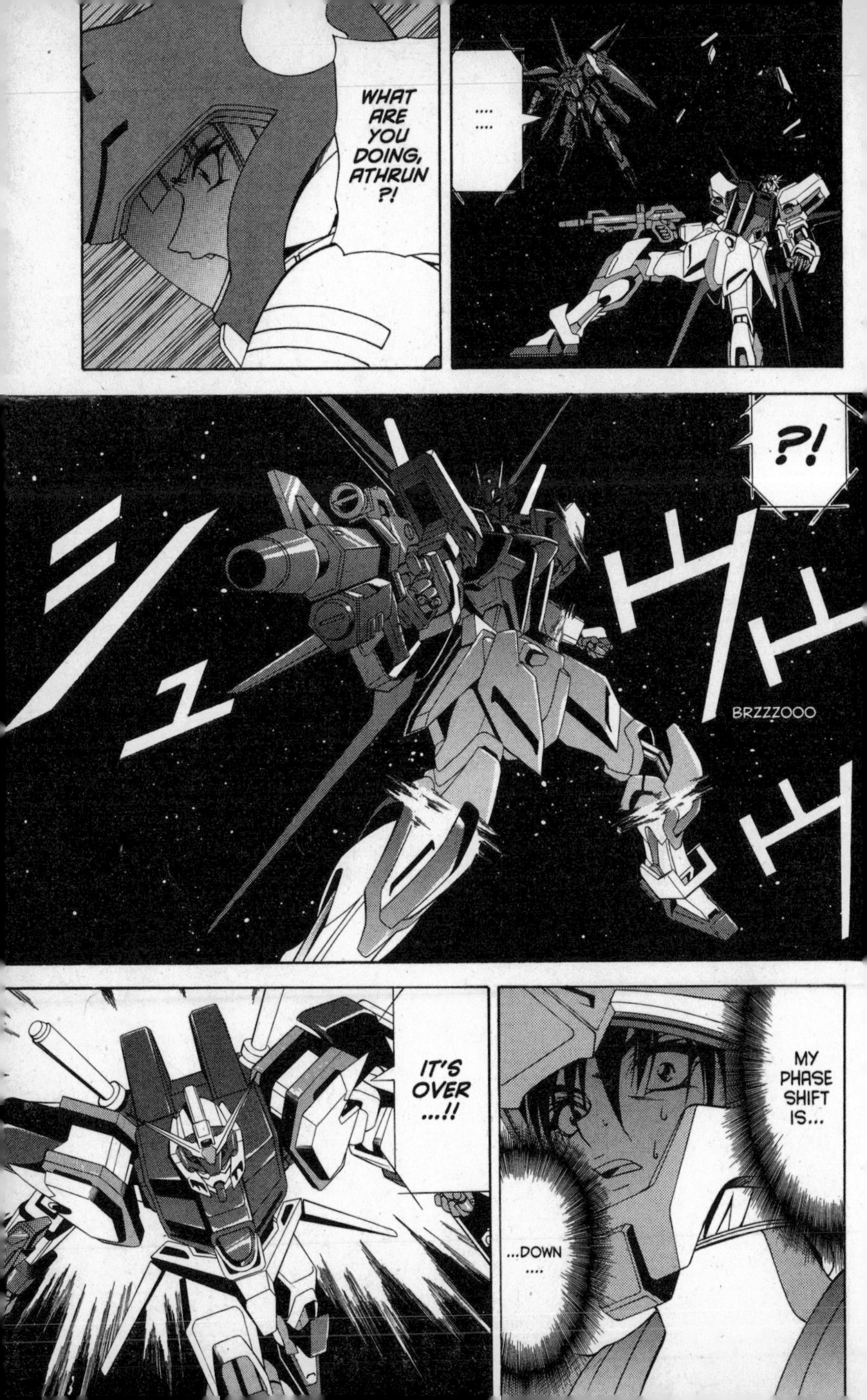
....
....
WHAT ARE YOU DOING, ATHRUN ?!
?!
BRZZZOOO
MY PHASE SHIFT IS...
...DOWN ....
IT'S OVER ...!!

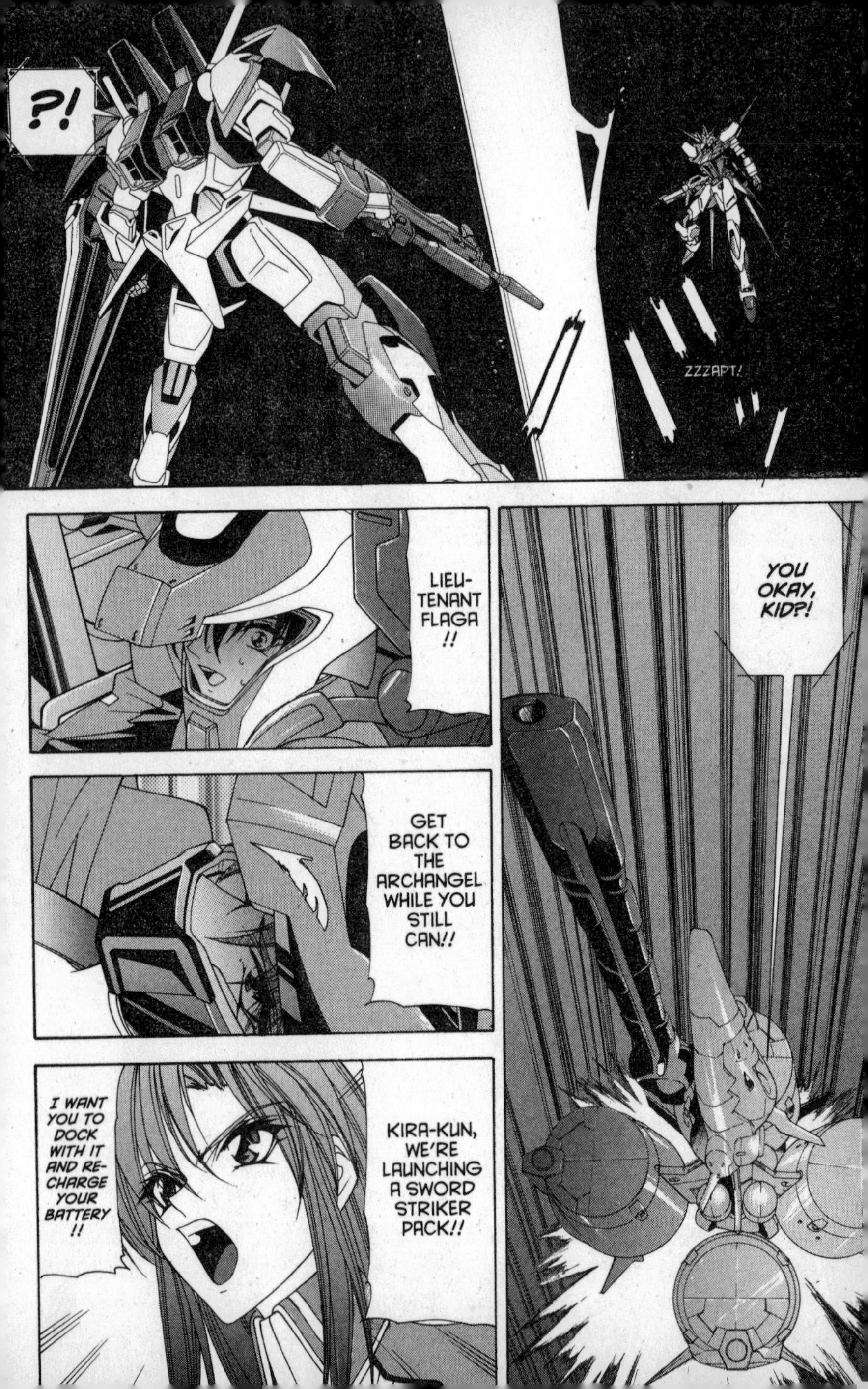
?!
ZZZAPT!
YOU OKAY, KID?!
LIEU-TENANT FLAGA!!
GET BACK TO THE ARCHANGEL WHILE YOU STILL CAN!!
KIRA-KUN, WE'RE LAUNCHING A SWORD STRIKER PACK!!
I WANT YOU TO DOCK WITH IT AND RE-CHARGE YOUR BATTERY!!

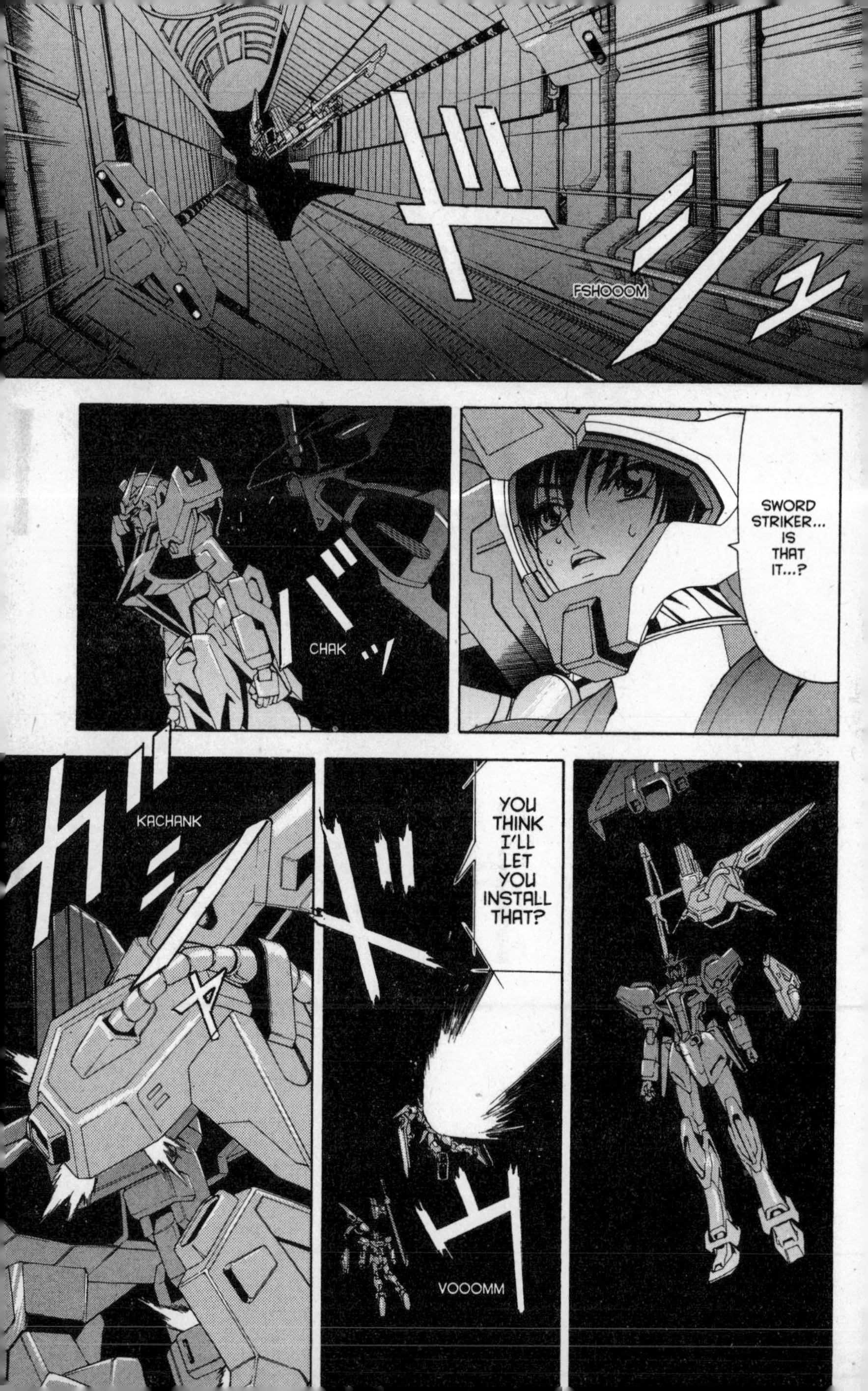
FSHOOOM
SWORD STRIKER... IS THAT IT...?
CHAK
YOU THINK I'LL LET YOU INSTALL THAT?
VOOOMM
KACHANK

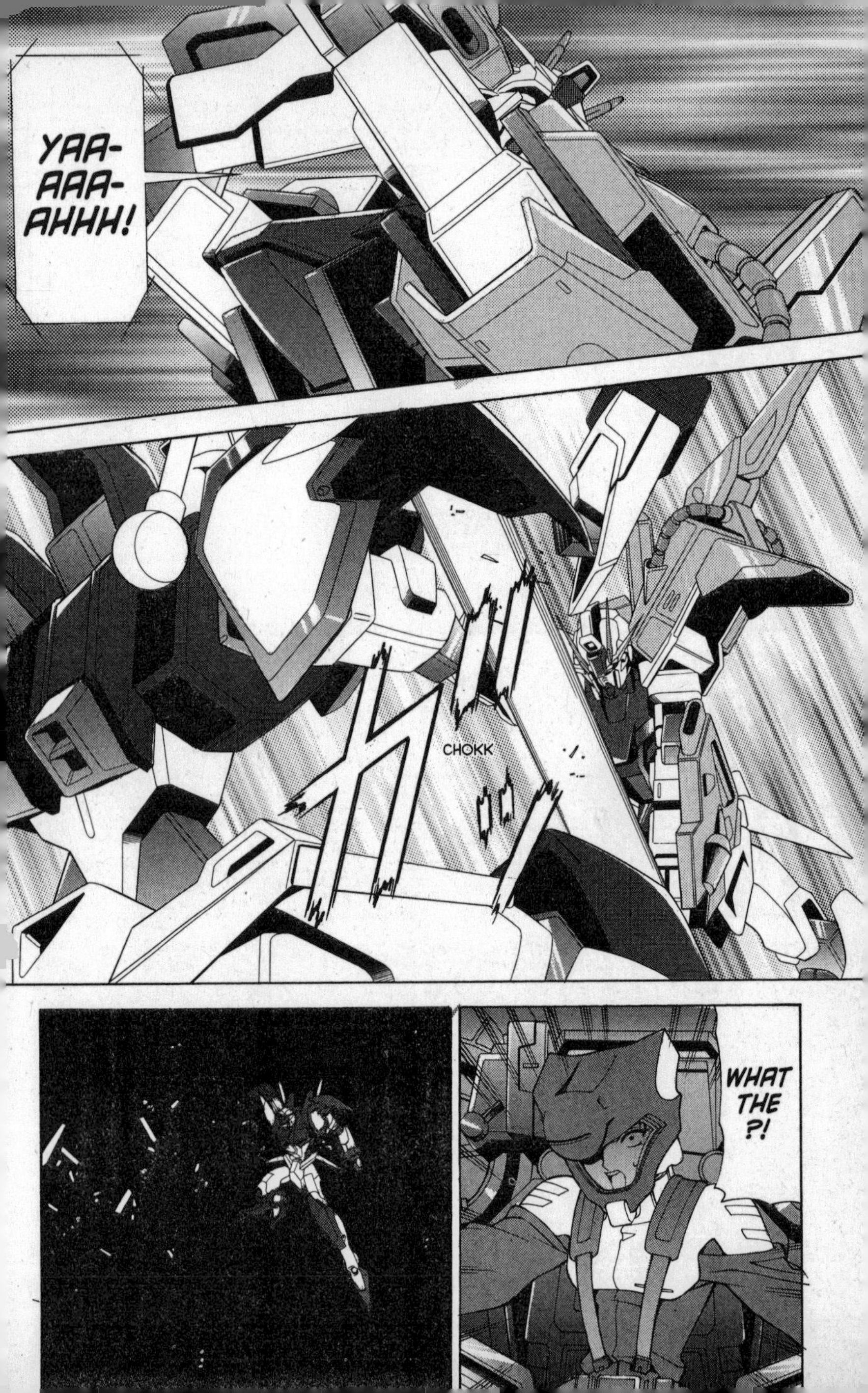
YAA-AAA-AHHH!
CHOKK
WHAT THE ?!

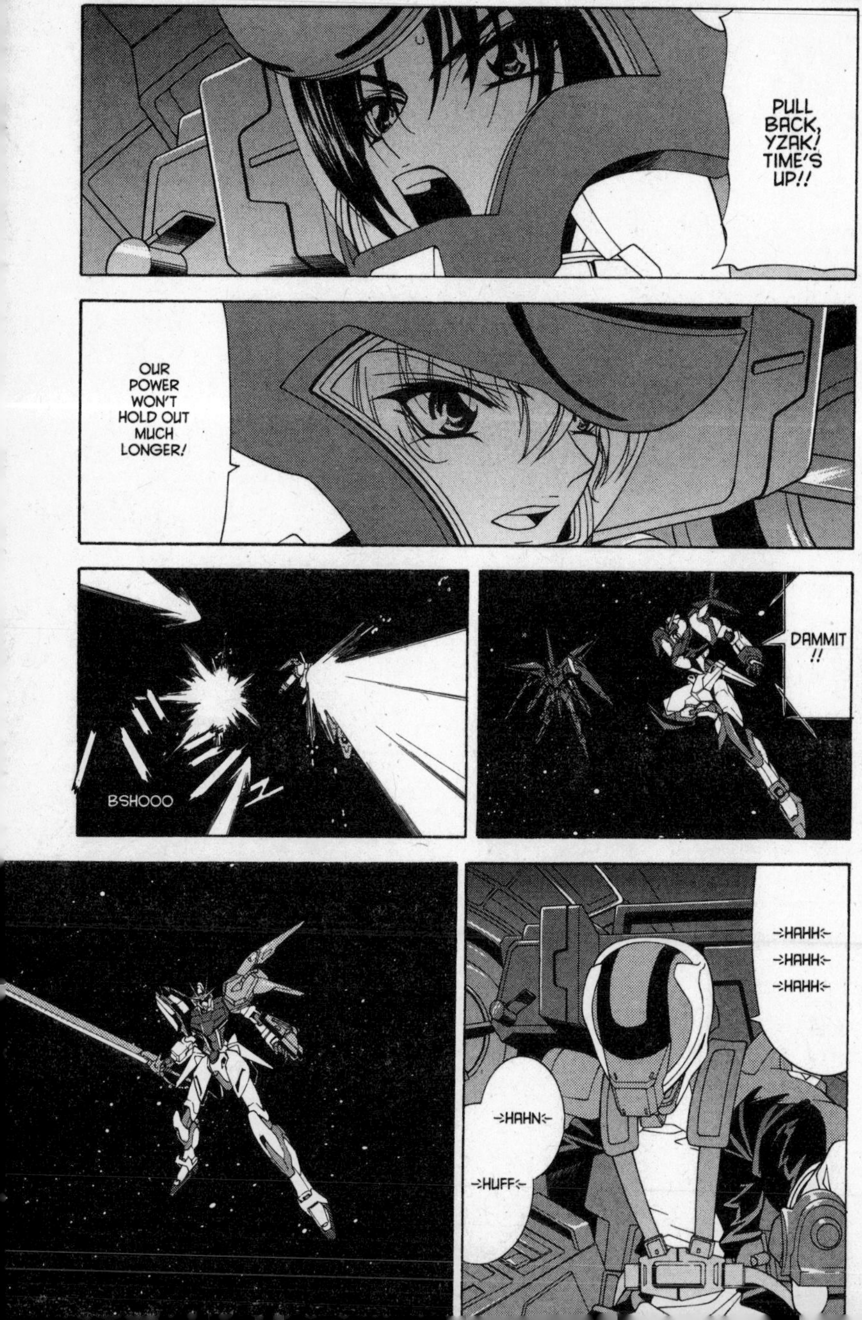
PULL BACK, YZAK! TIME'S UP!!
OUR POWER WON'T HOLD OUT MUCH LONGER!
DAMMIT!!
BSHOOO
HAHH
HAHH
HAHH
HAHN
HUFF

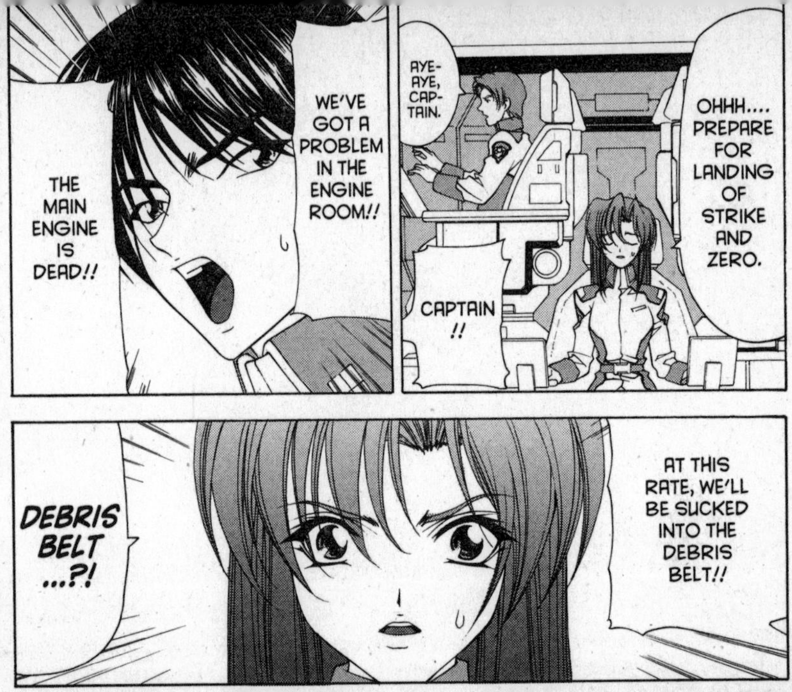
OHHH.... PREPARE FOR LANDING OF STRIKE AND ZERO.
AYE-AYE, CAPTAIN.
CAPTAIN!!
WE'VE GOT A PROBLEM IN THE ENGINE ROOM!!
THE MAIN ENGINE IS DEAD!!
AT THIS RATE, WE'LL BE SUCKED INTO THE DEBRIS BELT!!
DEBRIS BELT ...?!

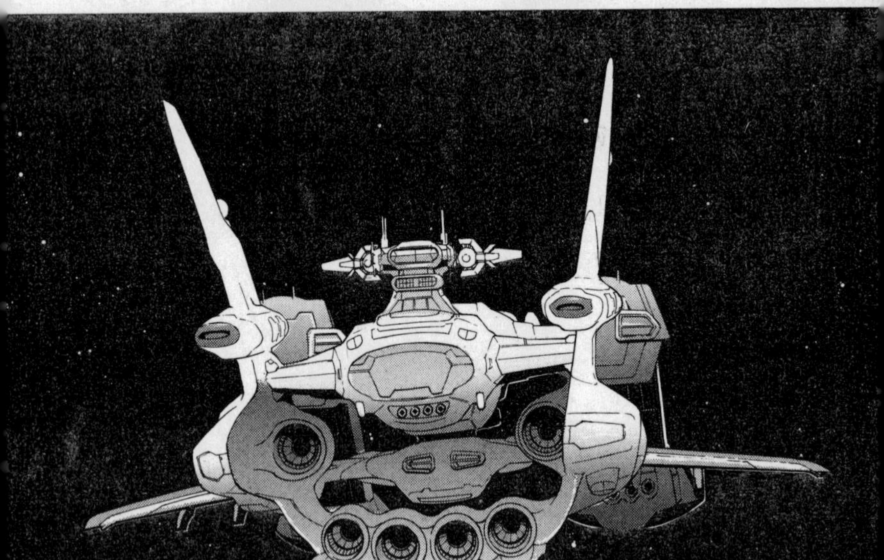

■ CONTINUED IN VOLUME 2 ■

MASATSUGU IWASE'S GUNDAM SEED DESIGN FILES

NOW, IWASE-SENSEI WILL EXPLAIN SOME OF HIS CHARACTER DESIGNS, WHICH HE INITIALLY DREW PRIOR TO SERIALIZING GUNDAM SEED.

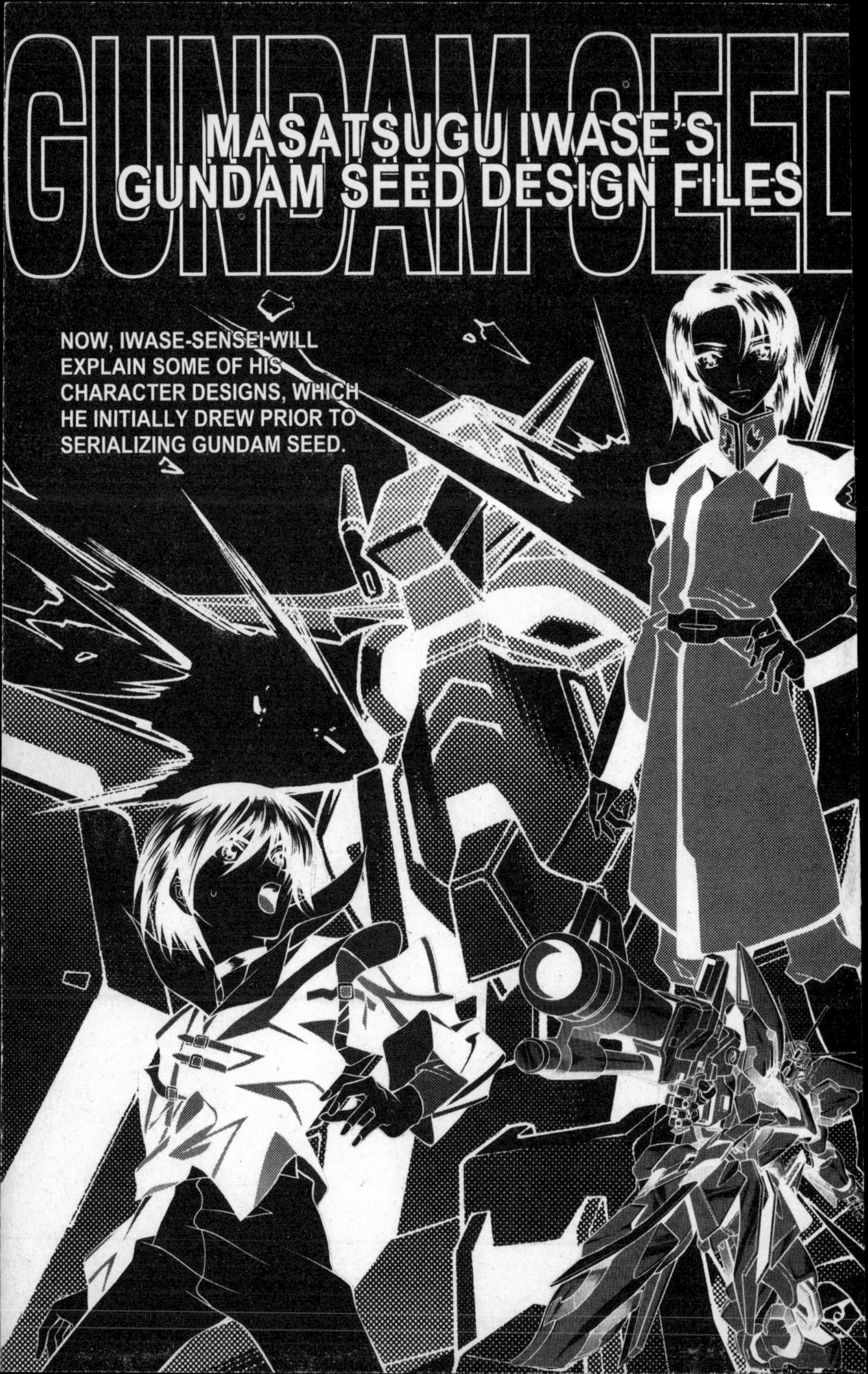

STRIKE GUNDAM

〈ストライクガンダム〉

BOTH SIDES OF THE HEAD ARE EQUIPPED WITH 75MM ANTI-AIR VULCAN GUNS (IGELSTELLUNG).

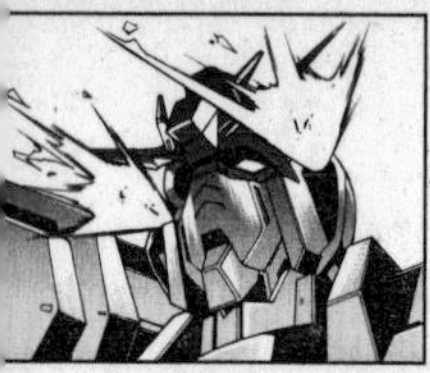

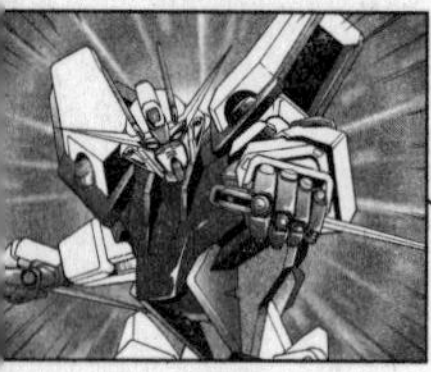

ARMED WITH TWO COMBAT KNIVES (ARMOR SCHNEIDER), ONE ON EACH HIP.

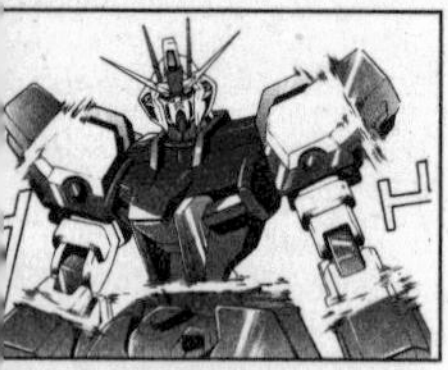
ゴ

WHEN PS (PHASE SHIFT) ARMOR IS ACTIVATED, ALL OTHER PHYSICAL ATTACKS BESIDES ENERGY BEAMS ARE RENDERED USELESS.

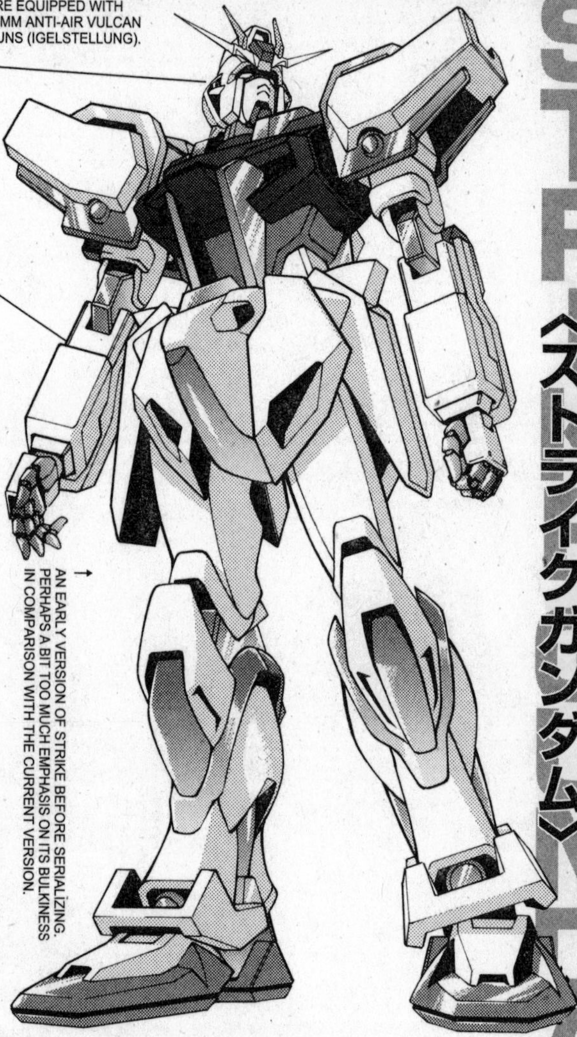

AN EARLY VERSION OF STRIKE BEFORE SERIALIZING. PERHAPS A BIT TOO MUCH EMPHASIS ON ITS BULKINESS IN COMPARISON WITH THE CURRENT VERSION.

DATA:

MODEL: GAT-X105
HEIGHT: 17.72 m
WEIGHT: 64.8 TONS

ABLE TO INSTALL 3 DIFFERENT TYPES OF STRIKER PACK: THE SWORD TYPE, FOR SHORT-RANGE IN-FIGHTING, THE AILE TYPE, A MEDIUM RANGE HIGH-MOBILITY MODE, AND THE LAUNCHER TYPE, USED FOR LONG RANGE ARTILLERY FIRE. THE LAUNCHER STRIKER PACK HAS NOT YET BEEN INTRODUCED IN THIS VOLUME.

A WORD FROM IWASE-SENSEI

FROM THE OUTSET, MY OVERALL IMAGE OF STRIKE WAS OF ITS LINEAR AND COMBATIVE NATURE. ITS MOST DISTINCTIVE FEATURE IS PROBABLY THAT IT USES KNIVES AS WEAPONS. THIS GIVES A SENSE OF COMBAT-READINESS. WHEN DRAWING STRIKE, I TRIED TO EMPHASIZE SPEED OVER BULK, AND A SMART AND STYLISH MECHA IMAGE, RATHER THAN PLACING TOO MUCH FOCUS ON ITS WEAPONRY.

KIRA YAMATO 〈キラ・ヤマト〉

A WORD FROM IWASE-SENSEI

MY FIRST IMPRESSION OF KIRA WAS THAT HE WAS A BIT SPINELESS FOR A HERO, BUT AFTER DIGGING FURTHER I REALIZED THAT, OUT OF ALL PAST GUNDAM SERIES, HE WAS PROBABLY THE STRONGEST PROTAGONIST...BESIDES, HE'S POPULAR WITH THE GIRLS! WHEN DRAWING KIRA, I ALWAYS FOCUS ON NOT MAKING HIM APPEAR TOO CHILDISH.

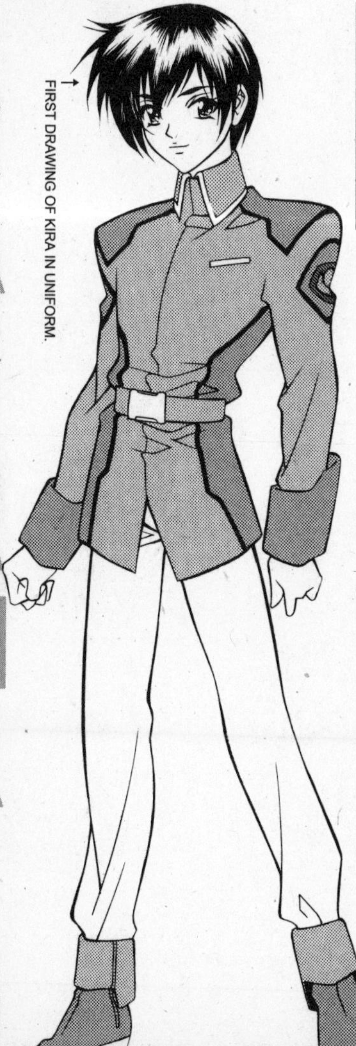

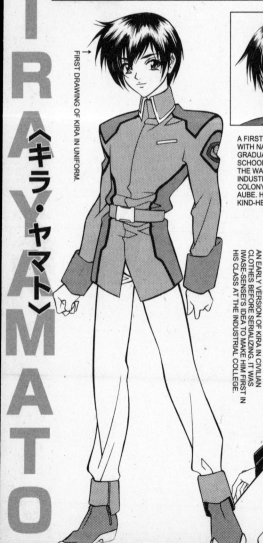

← FIRST DRAWING OF KIRA IN UNIFORM.

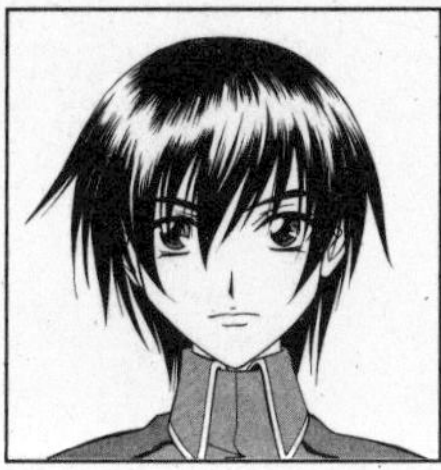

DATA:

HEIGHT: 165 cm
WEIGHT: 65 kg
DATE OF BIRTH:
MAY 18, 55 C.E.
(16 YEARS OLD)
BLOOD TYPE: A

A FIRST GENERATION COORDINATOR WITH NATURAL PARENTS. AFTER GRADUATING FROM PREPARATORY SCHOOL ON THE MOON, HE AVOIDED THE WAR AND ENROLLED IN AN INDUSTRIAL COLLEGE ON HELIOPOLIS, COLONY OF THE NEUTRAL NATION OF AUBE. HE IS A BIT OF A SHY, YET KIND-HEARTED YOUNG MAN.

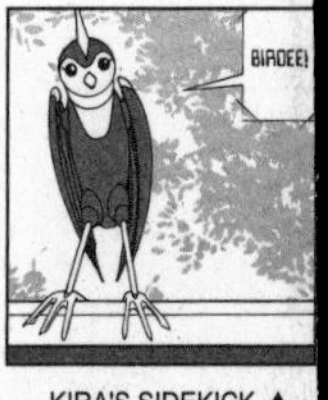
BIRDEE!

KIRA'S SIDEKICK, A ROBOTIC BIRD NAMED "BIRDEE," WAS MADE BY HIS BEST FRIEND ATHRUN. ↑

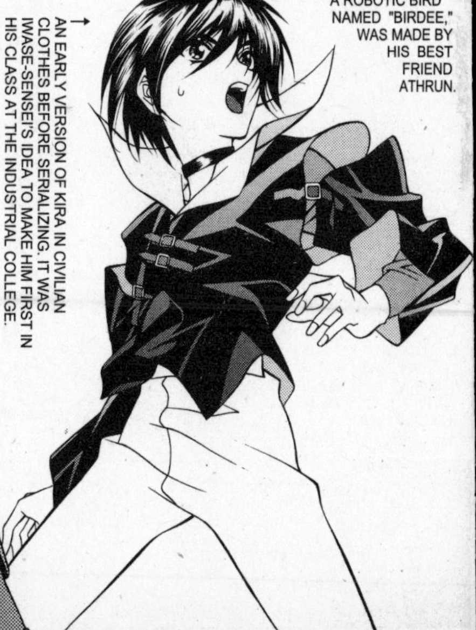

← AN EARLY VERSION OF KIRA IN CIVILIAN CLOTHES BEFORE SERIALIZING. IT WAS IWASE-SENSEI'S IDEA TO MAKE HIM FIRST IN HIS CLASS AT THE INDUSTRIAL COLLEGE.

AEGIS GUNDAM

〈イージスガンダム〉

A WORD FROM IWASE-SENSEI

INITIALLY, I WAS IMPRESSED BY THE INCREDIBLE TRANSFORMING ABILITY THAT THIS GUNDAM HAS. IT'S FUN FOR ME BECAUSE ITS DESIGN IS THE MOST UNCONVENTIONAL OF THE GUNDAMS. ESPECIALLY ITS MOBILE ARMOR...WHEN DRAWING THE AEGIS, I TRY TO MAKE SURE YOU CAN IDENTIFY IT BY ITS SILHOUETTE ALONE.

HE CREUSET UNIT

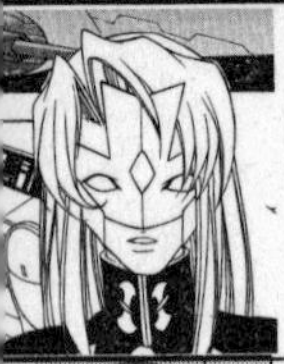

RAU LE CREUSET: COMMANDER OF THE CREUSET UNIT. MU LA FLAGA IS HIS RIVAL. HE PILOTS THE MS CGUE

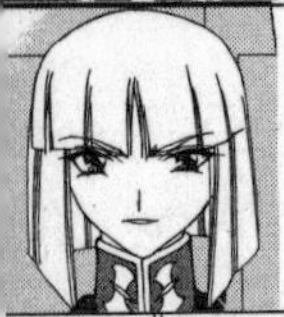

YZAK JOULE: PILOT OF THE DUEL GUNDAM. QUITE VINDICTIVE.

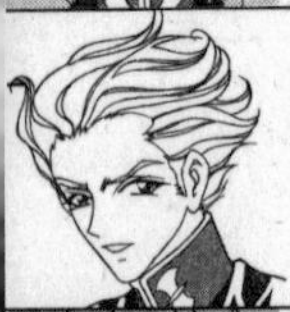

DEARKA ELSMAN: PILOT OF THE BUSTER GUNDAM. A NIHILISTIC YOUNG MAN.

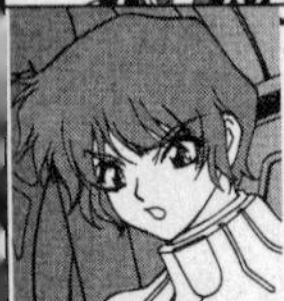

NICOL AMALFI: PILOT OF THE BLITZ GUNDAM. A GOOD FRIEND TO ATHRUN.

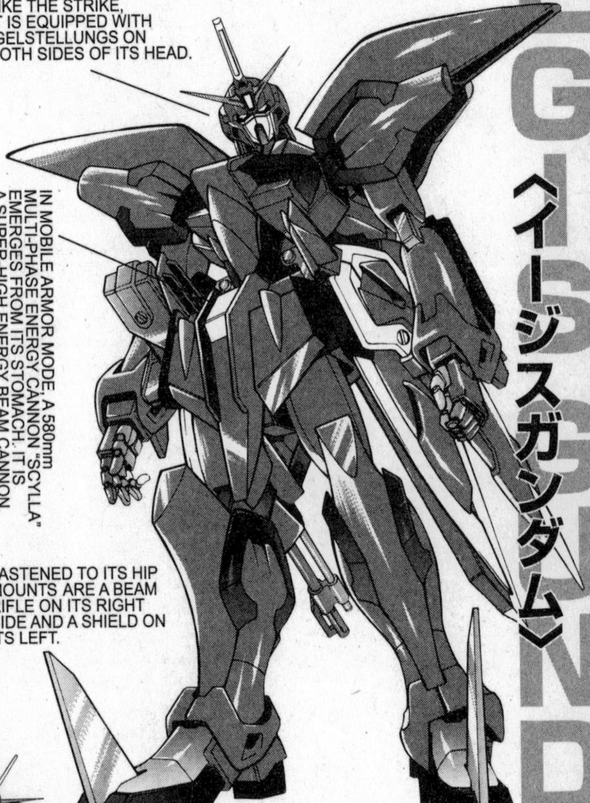

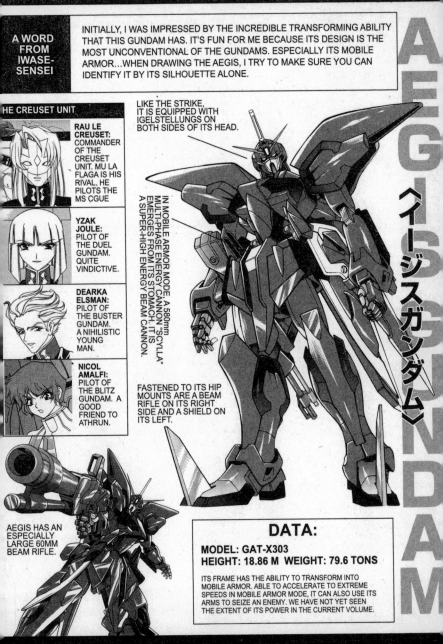

LIKE THE STRIKE, IT IS EQUIPPED WITH IGELSTELLUNGS ON BOTH SIDES OF ITS HEAD.

IN MOBILE ARMOR MODE, A 580mm MULTI-PHASE ENERGY CANNON "SCYLLA" EMERGES FROM ITS STOMACH. IT IS A SUPER-HIGH ENERGY BEAM CANNON.

FASTENED TO ITS HIP MOUNTS ARE A BEAM RIFLE ON ITS RIGHT SIDE AND A SHIELD ON ITS LEFT.

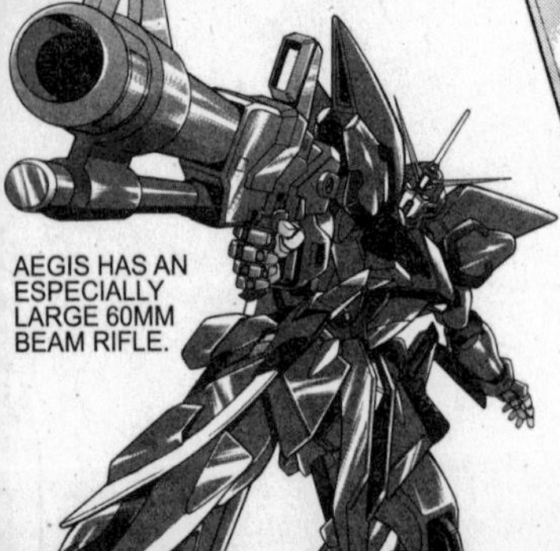

AEGIS HAS AN ESPECIALLY LARGE 60MM BEAM RIFLE.

DATA:

MODEL: GAT-X303
HEIGHT: 18.86 M WEIGHT: 79.6 TONS

ITS FRAME HAS THE ABILITY TO TRANSFORM INTO MOBILE ARMOR. ABLE TO ACCELERATE TO EXTREME SPEEDS IN MOBILE ARMOR MODE, IT CAN ALSO USE ITS ARMS TO SEIZE AN ENEMY. WE HAVE NOT YET SEEN THE EXTENT OF ITS POWER IN THE CURRENT VOLUME.

ATHRUN ZALA

〈アスラン・ザラ〉

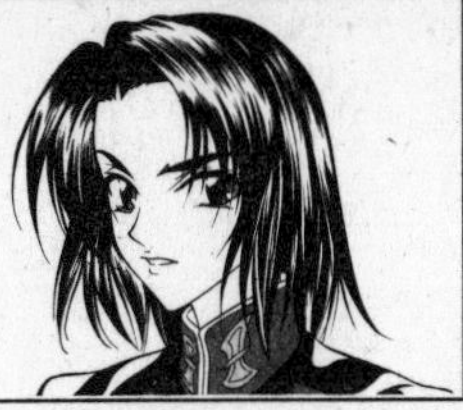

DATA:

HEIGHT: 170 CM
WEIGHT: 63 KG
DATE OF BIRTH: OCTOBER 29, 55 C.E. (16 YEARS OLD)
BLOOD TYPE: O

A COORDINATOR WHO WAS KIRA'S BEST FRIEND AT THE LUNAR PREP SCHOOL. HE LOST HIS PARENTS IN THE "BLOODY VALENTINE," AND AFTER THE WAR BEGAN, HE ENLISTED IN THE ZAFT ARMY AS A VOLUNTEER SOLDIER. HIS HOBBY IS FIDGETING WITH GADGETS AND THERE IS A DELICATE SIDE TO HIS PERSONALITY.

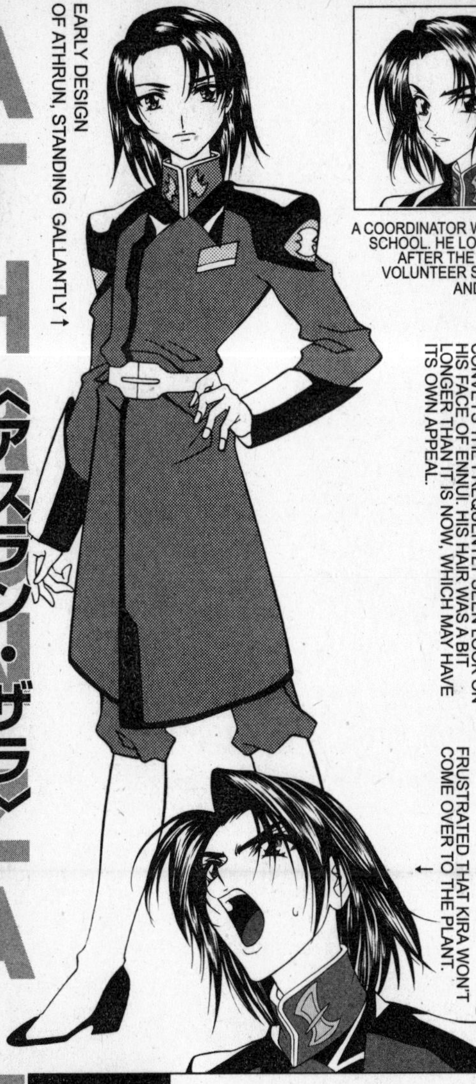

EARLY DESIGN OF ATHRUN, STANDING GALLANTLY ↑

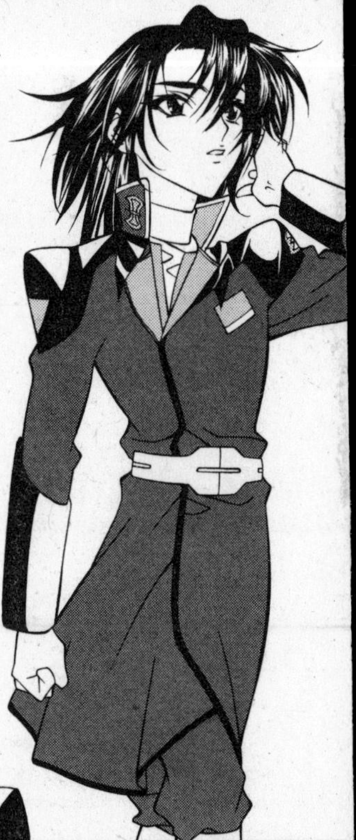

↑ AN EARLY DESIGN OF ATHRUN THAT CONVEYS THE FREQUENTLY SEEN LOOK ON HIS FACE OF ENNUI. HIS HAIR WAS A BIT LONGER THAN IT IS NOW, WHICH MAY HAVE ITS OWN APPEAL.

← FRUSTRATED THAT KIRA WON'T COME OVER TO THE PLANT.

A WORD FROM IWASE-SENSEI

ATHRUN SEEMS TO BE HEAVILY AFFECTED BY KIRA, AND OFTEN HAS A LOOK OF INNER TURMOIL ON HIS FACE. HE MAKES US WANT TO ROOT FOR HIM. WHEN DRAWING ATHRUN, I TRY NOT TO MAKE HIM TOO FEMININE, WHILE STILL MAINTAINING A SENSE OF GALLANTRY.

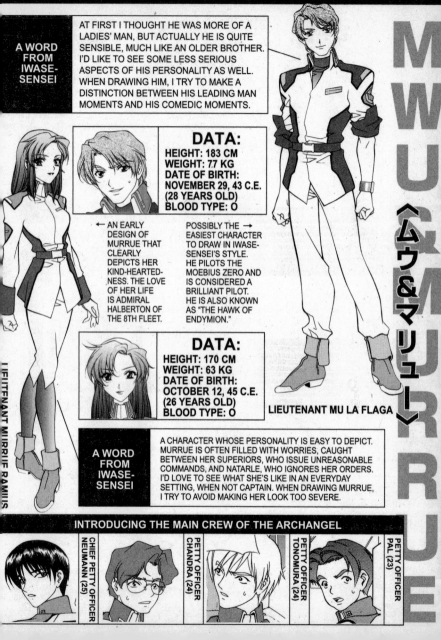

MWU & MURRUE

〈ムウ&マリュー〉

LIEUTENANT MU LA FLAGA

A WORD FROM IWASE-SENSEI

AT FIRST I THOUGHT HE WAS MORE OF A LADIES' MAN, BUT ACTUALLY HE IS QUITE SENSIBLE, MUCH LIKE AN OLDER BROTHER. I'D LIKE TO SEE SOME LESS SERIOUS ASPECTS OF HIS PERSONALITY AS WELL. WHEN DRAWING HIM, I TRY TO MAKE A DISTINCTION BETWEEN HIS LEADING MAN MOMENTS AND HIS COMEDIC MOMENTS.

DATA:
HEIGHT: 183 CM
WEIGHT: 77 KG
DATE OF BIRTH: NOVEMBER 29, 43 C.E. (28 YEARS OLD)
BLOOD TYPE: O

POSSIBLY THE EASIEST CHARACTER TO DRAW IN IWASE-SENSEI'S STYLE. HE PILOTS THE MOEBIUS ZERO AND IS CONSIDERED A BRILLIANT PILOT. HE IS ALSO KNOWN AS "THE HAWK OF ENDYMION." →

LIEUTENANT MURRUE RAMIUS

← AN EARLY DESIGN OF MURRUE THAT CLEARLY DEPICTS HER KIND-HEARTEDNESS. THE LOVE OF HER LIFE IS ADMIRAL HALBERTON OF THE 8TH FLEET.

DATA:
HEIGHT: 170 CM
WEIGHT: 63 KG
DATE OF BIRTH: OCTOBER 12, 45 C.E. (26 YEARS OLD)
BLOOD TYPE: O

A WORD FROM IWASE-SENSEI

A CHARACTER WHOSE PERSONALITY IS EASY TO DEPICT. MURRUE IS OFTEN FILLED WITH WORRIES, CAUGHT BETWEEN HER SUPERIORS, WHO ISSUE UNREASONABLE COMMANDS, AND NATARLE, WHO IGNORES HER ORDERS. I'D LOVE TO SEE WHAT SHE'S LIKE IN AN EVERYDAY SETTING, WHEN NOT CAPTAIN. WHEN DRAWING MURRUE, I TRY TO AVOID MAKING HER LOOK TOO SEVERE.

INTRODUCING THE MAIN CREW OF THE ARCHANGEL

PETTY OFFICER PAL (23)

PETTY OFFICER TONOMURA (24)

PETTY OFFICER CHANDRA (24)

CHIEF PETTY OFFICER NEUMANN (25)

ARCHANGEL CREW

FLAY & FRIENDS

〈フレイとキラの友人達〉

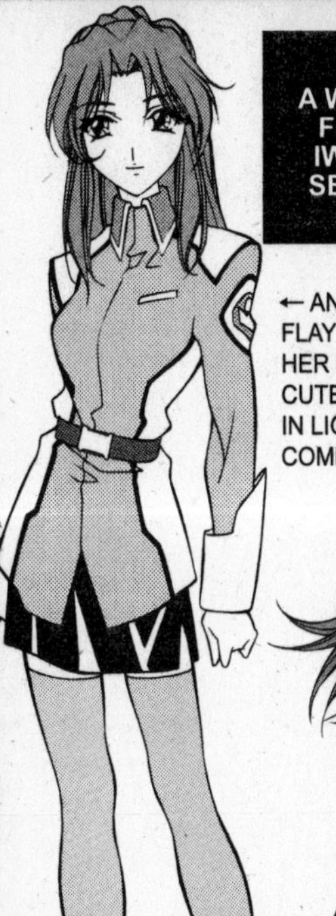

A WORD FROM IWASE-SENSEI

THE MOST SURPRISING OF THE CHARACTERS. AT FIRST, I THOUGHT SHE WAS LITTLE MORE THAN A MASCOT...BUT SHE'S ACTUALLY THE MOST HUMAN OF THE CHARACTERS. WHEN DRAWING FLAY, I PICTURE HER AS AN ACTRESS ON THE STAGE, IN A DRAMATIC PLAY.

← AN EARLY VERSION OF FLAY THAT EMPHASIZES HER MASCOT-LIKE CUTENESS. INTERESTING, IN LIGHT OF THE COMMENTS ABOVE.

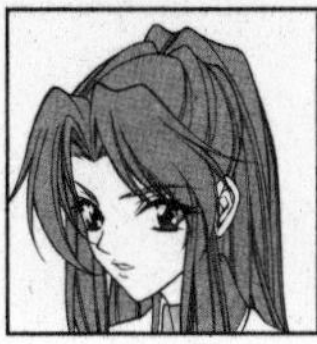

DATA:
HEIGHT: 162 CM
WEIGHT: 53 KG
DATE OF BIRTH: MARCH 15, 56 C.E. (15 YEARS OLD)
BLOOD TYPE: A

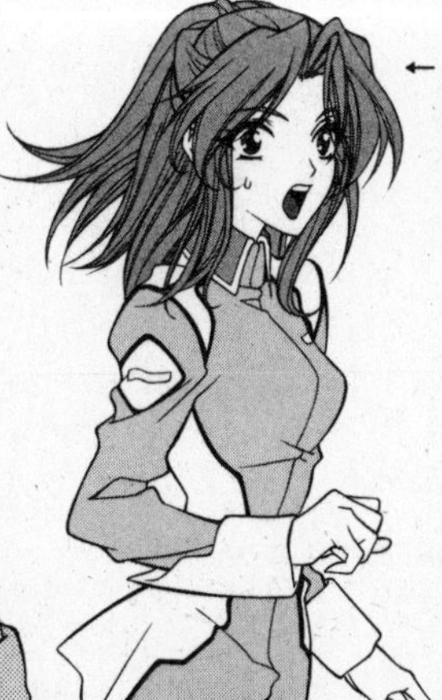

← FLAY WILL BECOME A KEY CHARACTER WITH REGARD TO KIRA, SO YOU CAN EXPECT TO SEE A LOT MORE OF HER IN UPCOMING VOLUMES

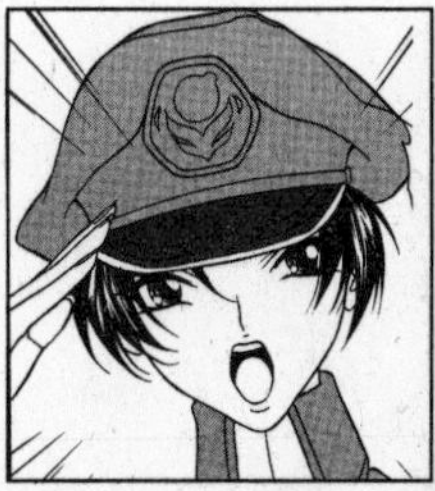

A SERIOUS-MINDED MILITARY TYPE. THE STUDENTS THINK OF HER AS A SCARY LADY!

NATARLE BADGIRUEL (25)

ENSIGN AND 1ST MATE OF THE ARCHANGEL, SHE IS THE TYPICAL HARD-NOSED MILITARY TYPE, WHO GOES BY THE BOOK AND REFUSES TO BEND THE RULES. SHE FREQUENTLY LOCKS HORNS WITH CAPTAIN MURRUE, WHO FINDS HER A BIT AGGRAVATING.

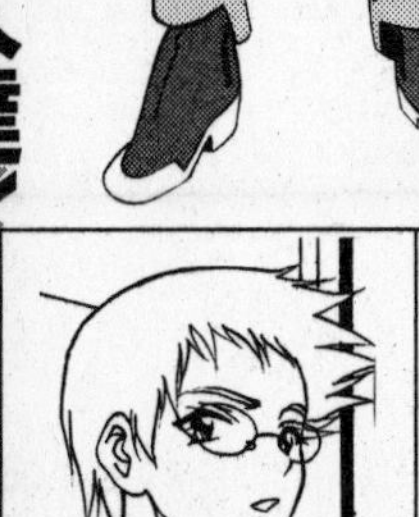

SAI ARGYLE:
A STUDENT IN THE SAME CLASS AS KIRA, HE APPARENTLY IS ENGAGED TO FLAY. HE GIVES THE IMPRESSION OF A COOL EXTERIOR.

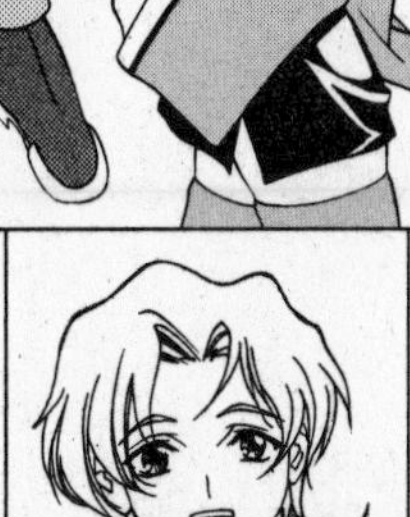

TOLLE KOENIG:
LIKE SAI, HE IS A CLASSMATE OF KIRA'S. HE HAS AN EASYGOING PERSONALITY, AND GETS ALONG WELL WITH MIRIALLIA.

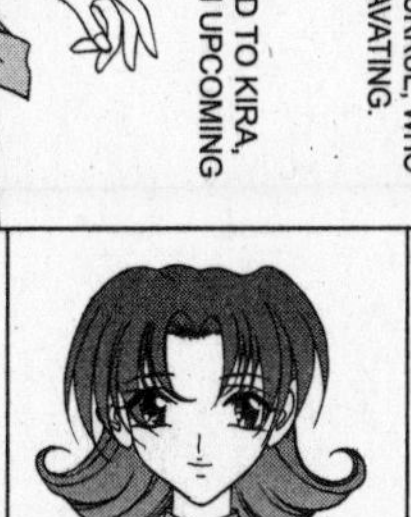

MIRIALLIA HAW:
CLASSMATE OF KIRA'S. SHE HAS A GIRLISH PERSONALITY, YET AT TIMES SHE CAN BE BOTH DECISIVE AND QUITE COMPETENT.

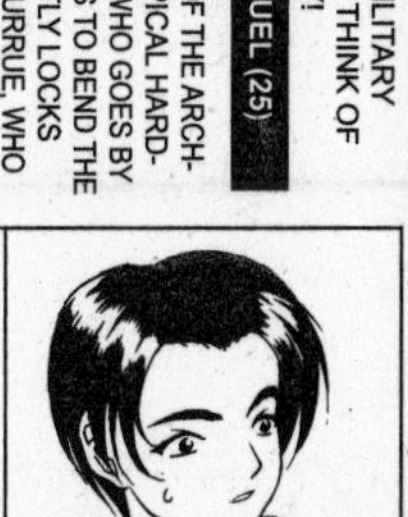

KUZZEY BUSKIRK:
CLASSMATE OF KIRA'S. HE EXPRESSES HIMSELF QUITE FRANKLY TO KIRA. PERHAPS HE HARBORS FEELINGS OF ENVY?!

Welcome. . .

. . .to the launch of the Del Rey Manga line! It all starts here, with four new series from Japan: *Negima!* by Ken Akamatsu; *Gundam SEED* by Masatsugu Iwase; and *Tsubasa: Reservoir Chronicle* and *xxxHOLiC*, both by CLAMP. Together, these four series represent some of the best and most popular manga series published in Japan.

We're dedicated to providing our readers with the most enjoyable, authentic manga experience possible. Our books are printed from right to left, in the Japanese printing format. We strive to keep the translations as true to the original as possible, while making sure the English versions retain the same sense of adventure and fun. We keep Japanese honorifics intact, translate all sound effects, and give you extras at the back of the books to help you understand the context of the stories and keep track of all the characters. It's the next best thing to being able to read Japanese!

For information on upcoming releases, visit www.delreymanga.com, and while you're there be sure to sign up for our newsletter. If you do, you'll be the first to hear all the scoop on Del Rey Manga, and you'll have the opportunity to talk directly to the editor (that would be me) and say what works for you in our books, and what doesn't. Manga wouldn't be the red-hot phenomenon it is without your support, and we want your feedback.

See you in Volume 2!

Dallas Middaugh

Dallas Middaugh
Director of Manga, Del Rey Books

A Brief History of Gundam
By Mark Simmons

Welcome to the World of Gundam

In the not-so-distant future, humanity's settlement of space leads to a bitter war between the people of Earth and rebel space colonists. The space-dwellers use giant humanoid fighting vehicles called "mobile suits" to even the odds against the Earth forces, and the war reaches a stalemate. Meanwhile, the Earth forces secretly begin developing their own mobile suits at a remote space colony, which suffers an enemy surprise attack just as these prototypes are completed. As his peaceful home becomes a battlefield, a gifted young man finds himself the accidental pilot of the Earth forces' newest weapon, the white mobile suit known as "Gundam". . .

Such is the starting point of *Mobile Suit Gundam SEED*. But it's also the basic premise of *Mobile Suit Gundam*, the Japanese television series that launched the Gundam saga back in 1979. For twenty-five years, this saga has continued to unfold in animated TV serials, theatrical movies, original video series, novels, games, and manga. Its latest chapter, *Gundam SEED*, is a stand-alone tale that reprises the themes of its famous ancestor for a new generation of viewers, with a new story line that takes the premise of the original series in a very different direction.

SEEDs of the Saga

When the original *Mobile Suit Gundam* series premiered back in 1979, it seemed at first like just another of the kiddie-friendly "super robot" serials that had populated Japanese television during the preceding decade. In these shows, heroic metal warriors and their bold young pilots battled against the clearly labeled forces of evil, preserving world peace and enriching the toy companies that sponsored them.

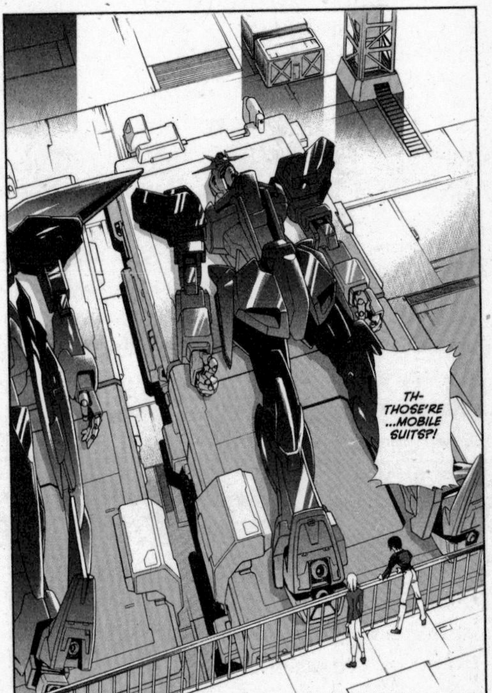
TH- THOSE'RE ...MOBILE SUITS?!

Gundam departed from this formula by presenting complex, morally ambiguous characters fighting on both sides of a realistic political conflict. Rather than invincible superheroes, the robots were depicted as military vehicles, operating according to consistent laws of science. Not surprisingly, *Mobile Suit Gundam* was initially considered a flop, only to turn into a cult phenomenon as it was embraced by older and more sophisticated viewers.

VREEEEEEEEE

Thanks to the loyalty of its fans and the success of its accompanying merchandise (including a wildly popular line of scale model kits), *Mobile Suit Gundam* was soon followed by a succession of sequels, turning this science fiction adventure into a bona fide franchise. With the story line growing ever more convoluted and the show's original fans now settling into adulthood, the Sunrise studio decided to take the saga in a new direction in order to make it accessible to new viewers. Starting with 1994's *Mobile Fighter G Gundam*, a succession of new creators began devising their own original Gundam worlds, unconnected to the Universal Century setting of previous stories. It was one of these new series, 1995's *Gundam Wing*, that went on to become a smash hit in the United States, drawing millions of newcomers into the ranks of Gundam fandom.

STAY BEHIND MY SEAT!

I SHOULD AT LEAST BE ABLE TO GET THIS THING MOVING...

The Newest Branch

By the middle of 2002, the Gundam saga had expanded to include eight TV series, four video series, ten movies, and a live-action TV special—roughly half of which have been released in English—as well as countless novels, video games, and manga stories. And in October of that year, another new Gundam world was born with the debut of the animated series *Gundam SEED* on Japanese television. *Gundam SEED*'s director, Mitsuo Fukuda, set out with an ambitious agenda: to reinvent the original *Mobile Suit Gundam* for the twenty-first century, revisiting its dramatic story line and challenging themes and reinterpreting them for this new era. In this manga adaptation by artist Masatsugu Iwase, we see the vision of *Gundam SEED* begin to unfold, in ways both classically traditional and strikingly modern. . .

Continued in Volume 2!

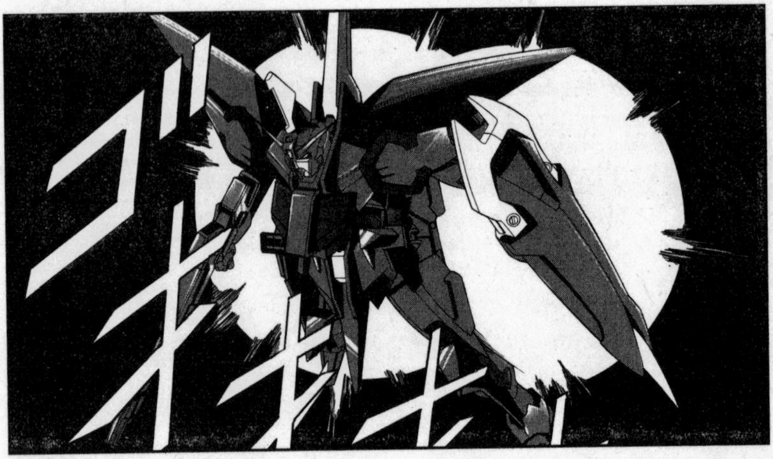
ゴオオオ

About the Creators

Masatsugu Iwase

Masatsugu Iwase writes and draws the manga adaptation of *Gundam SEED*. It is his first work published in the U.S. The manga creator is better known in Japan, however, for his work on *Calm Breaker*, a hilarious parody of anime, manga, and Japanese pop culture.

About the Creators

Yoshiyuki Tomino

Gundam was created by Yoshiyuki Tomino. Prior to Gundam, Tomino had worked the original *Astro Boy* anime, as well as *Princess Knight* and *Brave Raideen*, among others. In 1979 he created and directed *Mobile Suit Gundam*, the very first in a long line of Gundam series. The show was not immediately popular and was forced to cut its number of episodes before going off the air, but as with the American show *Star Trek*, the fans still had something to say on the matter. By 1981 the demand for Gundam was so high that Tomino oversaw the re-release of the animation as three theatrical movies (a practice still common in Japan but rarely, if ever, seen in the U.S.). It was now official: Gundam was a blockbuster.

Tomino would go on to direct many Gundam series, including *Gundam ZZ*, *Char's Counterattack*, *Gundam F91*, and *Victory Gundam*, all of which contributed to the rich history of the vast Gundam universe. In addition to Gundam, Tomino created *Xabungle*, *L.Gaim*, *Dunbine*, and *Garzey's Wing*. His most recent anime is *Brain Powered*, which was released by Geneon in the United States.

Translation Notes

Japanese is a tricky language for most Westerners, and translation is often more art than science. For your edification and reading pleasure, here are notes on some of the places where we could have gone in a different direction in our translation of the work, or where a Japanese cultural reference is used.

A Chirp by Any Other Name

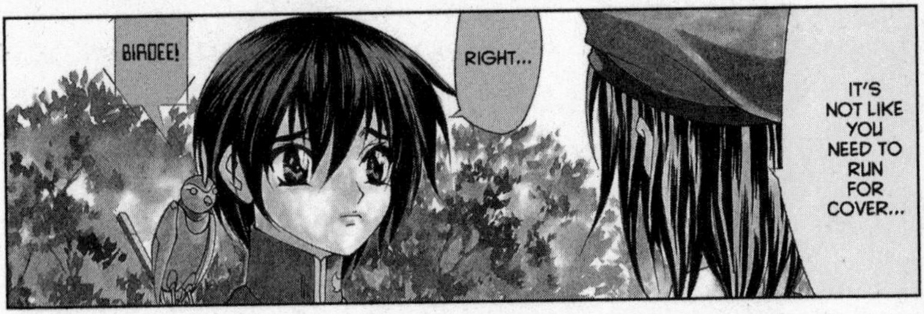
IT'S NOT LIKE YOU NEED TO RUN FOR COVER...
RIGHT...
BIRDEE!

The noise this robotic bird makes is *TORI!*, which means *bird* in Japanese. The sound of *tori* is entirely different from *bird*, so we opted to add an *ee* sound to the end, so it sounds slightly more like a noise a bird would make.

He Said, She Said

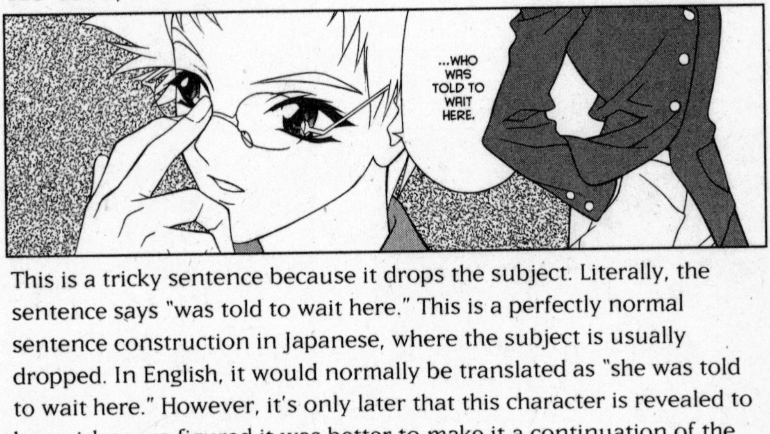
...WHO WAS TOLD TO WAIT HERE.

This is a tricky sentence because it drops the subject. Literally, the sentence says "was told to wait here." This is a perfectly normal sentence construction in Japanese, where the subject is usually dropped. In English, it would normally be translated as "she was told to wait here." However, it's only later that this character is revealed to be a girl, so we figured it was better to make it a continuation of the previous sentence.

13 and up!

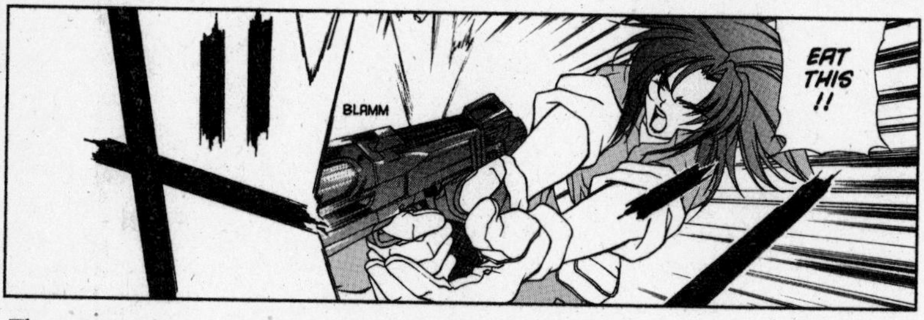
EAT THIS !!
BLAMM

The original Japanese is *kono!!*, which literally means *this!*. It may be an abbreviation of *kono yarou,* which can be translated as "you bastard," among other things. Basically, any profanity would work here, but we thought *eat this* was the most appropriate.

Preview of Volume 2

Because we're running about one year behind the release of the Japanese *Gundam SEED* manga, we have the opportunity to present to you a preview from Volume 2. This volume will be available in English in September 2004, but for now you'll have to make do with Japanese!

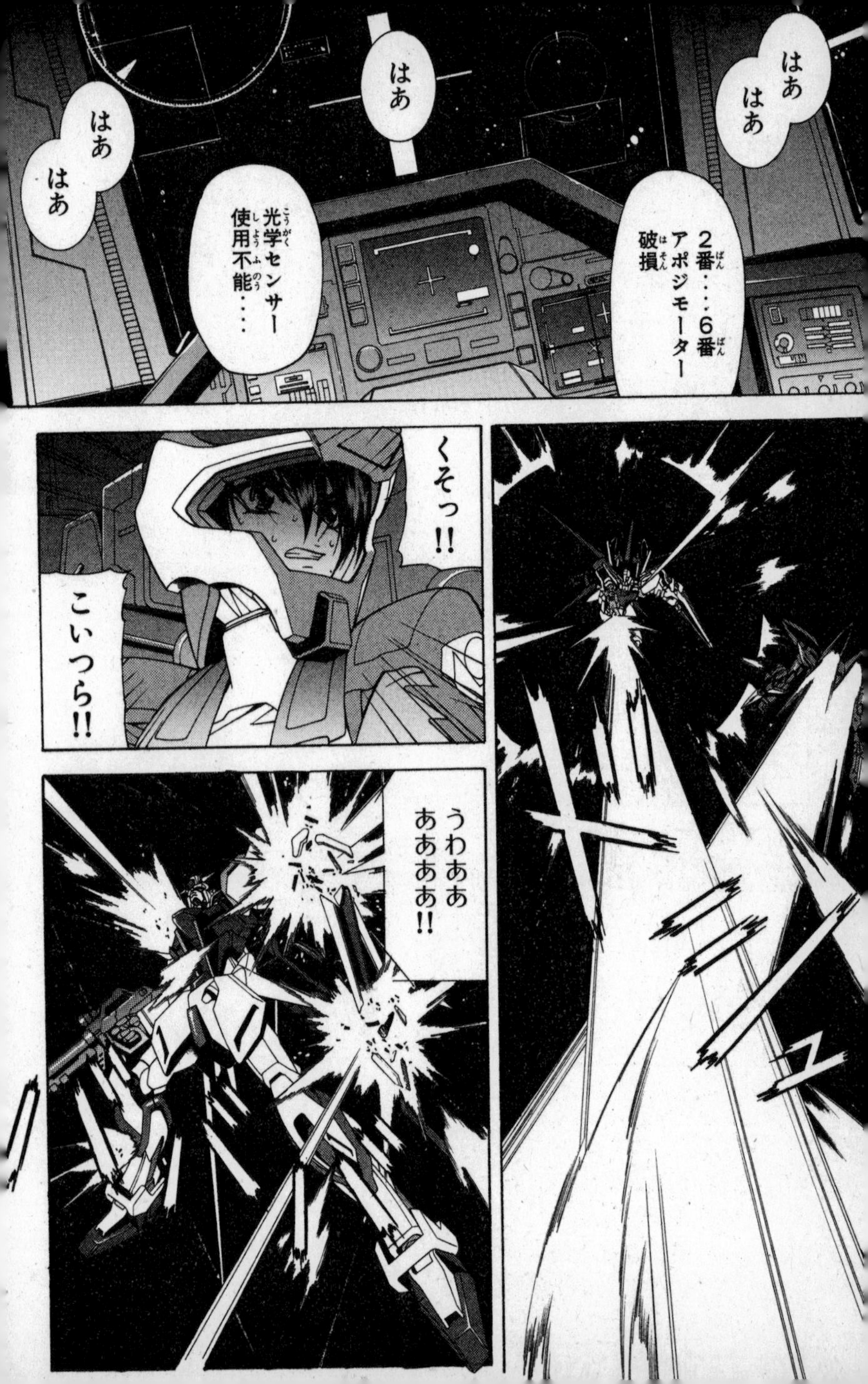

はあ はあ
2番・・・6番アポジモーター破損
はあ
光学センサー使用不能・・・・
はあ はあ
くそっ!!
こいつら!!
うわああ あああ!!

シュ

フェイズシフトが

・・・・
落ちた・・・
・・・・!!

うわああああ
あああ!!

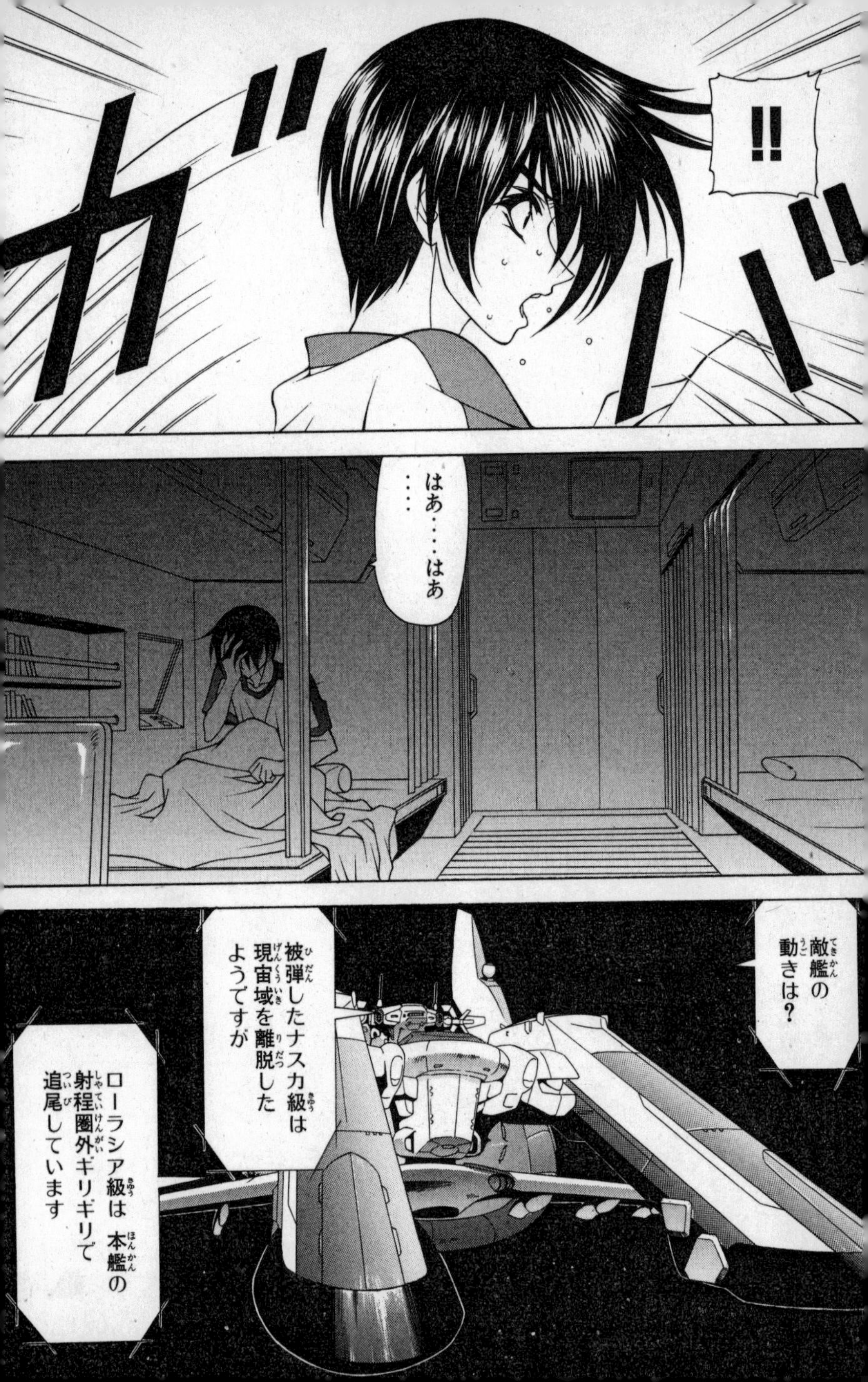
!!
ガバ
はあ……はあ……
敵艦の動きは？
被弾したナスカ級は現宙域を離脱したようですが
ローラシア級は 本艦の射程圏外ギリギリで追尾しています

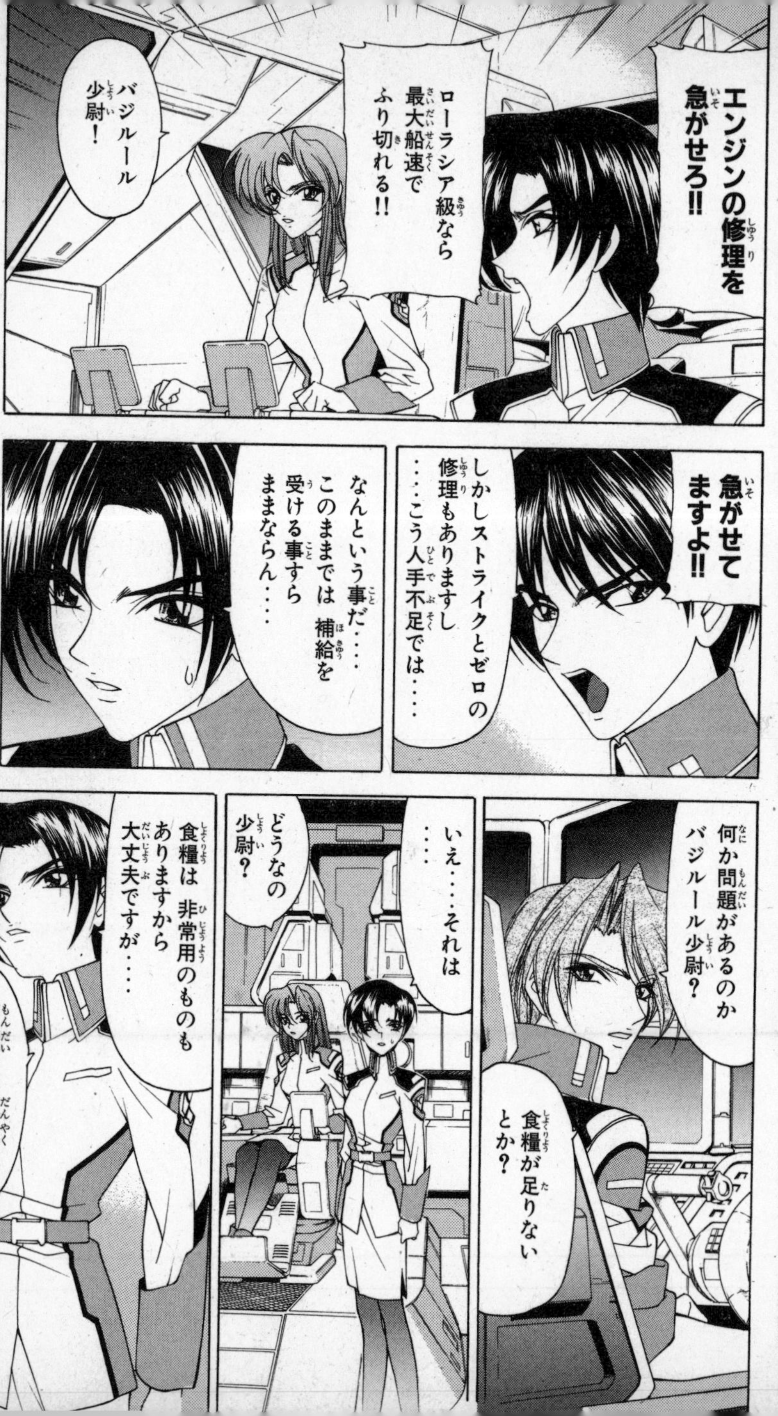
エンジンの修理を急がせろ!!
ローラシア級なら最大船速でふり切れる!!
バジルール少尉!
急がせてますよ!!
しかしストライクとゼロの修理もありますし……こう人手不足では……
なんという事だ…… このままでは 補給を受ける事すらままならん……
何か問題があるのかバジルール少尉?
食糧が足りないとか?
いえ……それは……
どうなの少尉?
食糧は 非常用のものもありますから大丈夫ですが……
問題は 弾薬と水です

COLLECT ALL FOUR SERIES FROM DEL REY!

▌First time in the U.S.!　　▌Printed in the authentic Japanese style!　　▌Bonus materials inside!

Tsubasa: RESERVoir CHRoNiCLE
by CLAMP

Negima!
by Ken Akamatsu

xxxHOLiC
by CLAMP

Gundam SEED
by Masatsugu Iwase, Hajime Yatate,
and Yoshiyuki Tomino

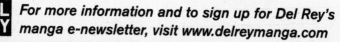

DEL REY　*For more information and to sign up for Del Rey's manga e-newsletter, visit www.delreymanga.com*

xxxHOLiC
by CLAMP
Creators of *Chobits!*

Watanuki Kimihiro is haunted by visions of ghosts and spirits. Seemingly by chance, he encounters a mysterious witch named Yuko, who claims she can help. In desperation, he accepts, but realizes that he's just been tricked into working for Yuko in order to pay off the cost of her services. Soon he's employed in her little shop—a job which turns out to be nothing like his previous work experience!

Most of Yuko's customers live in Japan, but Yuko and Watanuki are about to have some unusual visitors named Sakura and Syaoran from a land called Clow. . . .

Volume 1: On sale May 2004 • Volume 2: On sale July 2004
Volume 3: On sale November 2004

 For more information and to sign up for Del Rey's manga e-newsletter, visit www.delreymanga.com

Negima!
by Ken Akamatsu
Creator of *Love Hina!*

Ten-year-old prodigy Negi Springfield has just graduated from magic academy. He dreams of becoming a master wizard. Instead he's sent to Japan to teach English . . . at an all-girls high school! All the students are delighted with their cute new teacher—except for Asuna, who resents Negi for replacing the teacher she secretly has a crush on. Although he is forbidden to display his magical powers, sometimes Negi can't resist. And when Asuna discovers Negi's secret, she vows to make his life as difficult as possible. But no matter what, it's up to Negi to guide his class through the trials of high school life—and whatever other adventures may come their way.

Volume 1: On sale May 2004 • Volume 2: On sale August 2004
Volume 3: On sale November 2004

For more information and to sign up for Del Rey's manga e-newsletter, visit www.delreymanga.com

GUNDAM SEED...
New Weapons, New Armor,
New Ways to defeat the enemy!

Build and customize your own fully articulated SNAP-together, all-new GUNDAM SEED action figure model kits.

Visit our Gundam Web Site at:
gundamofficial.com and **bandai.com**

TOMARE!

[STOP!]

You're going the wrong way!

Manga is a completely different type of reading experience.

To start at the *beginning*, go to the *end*!

That's right! Authentic manga is read the traditional Japanese way—from right to left. Exactly the *opposite* of how American books are read. It's easy to follow: Just go to the other end of the book, and read each page—and each panel—from right side to left side, starting at the top right. Now you're experiencing manga as it was meant to be.